D.P. ROWELL

The Emerson Chronicles

Book One

First published in the USA in November 2018

Cover Illustration by Wisdrawin

ISBN:
9798555943019

To my mom, dad, and brother. I couldn't ask for a more supportive family. Through my pursuits in music, school, and writing, they have continually encouraged me, and I'm grateful beyond words for it.

To Ben Morgan, my favorite beta reader and best friend since third grade. I'm grateful for all my beta readers, but I have to give a special shout out to this guy. His feedback and encouragement through the process is what sparked my final decision to not just write this series but to also publish it.

BREEN
YUTARA
The Great Ocean
Gulf of Eden
Naraka
Gulf of Gorleg
The Dry Mountains
Hilrun
The Solomon Forest
Adamsville
the Flats
Lake David
Westclear
New Lathelyn
OOLA
EVELAND

CHAPTER ONE

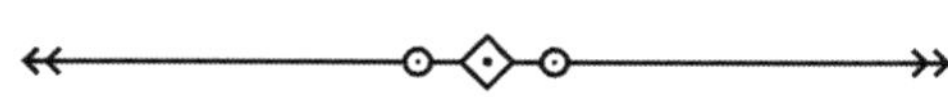

Grandpa's Secret

Ace Halder had one more night to take his chance. All it would take was a bit of courage and a little curiosity. He fidgeted with his sheets. He twitched, squirmed, and kicked his feet as his brain wrestled his gut. What if it wasn't worth it? What if it was? Grandpa's knack for mystery had him reeling with anger.

Is it a room full of ancient treasure? A key? A safe?

What if it was something stupid like work documents or bills? If they caught him sneaking around, Julie and Tamara Peppercorn would wake everyone on the ship and do so with glee. He'd have nothing to show for it either. But if Grandpa's secret was good—juicy—he could have the Peppercorns eating out of the palm of his hand.

"Just tell us what it is, Ace!" He smiled wickedly at the thought of it. *"C'mon. We'll do anything! Anything!"*

Oh, Ace thought. *Anything?*

Chores.

Allowance.

Ace's heart leaped a hundred feet in the air. What *did* the Peppercorns get for allowance? Had to be upwards of a hundred credits a week. Uncle Marcus was the best basketball player on the *Genesis Sabercats*, and he was more than generous to his daughters. *And* wife. He had them spoiled rotten. So, on top of being filthy rich, the Peppercorns were fortunate enough to still have a dad *and* mom. They could use a lesson in living like a Halder. Ace and his brother, Cameron, didn't have the power to give said lesson. But . . .

Grandpa's Secret.

Now persuaded that he must take his chance, he threw off his sheets and placed his feet on the damp surface of the floor. He listened to the ocean slap the side of the ship, watching his brother's hammock above him rock gently in kind. He glanced to his left to find Julie and Tamara sound asleep in their hammock bunks. He thanked New Realm's Age he had the bottom bunk. There would have been no way to sneak from the top one unnoticed. He stood and inched his way toward the door. The boy stepped on a loose wooden panel and it creaked. He gritted his teeth, squeezed his eyes shut, and lowered his head like a turtle retreating into its shell. One of his eyes crept open, the other followed. No one seemed to be disturbed. He sighed with relief.

The boy stuck his hand forward and inched the door open, squeezing himself through the crack and into the hall leading to the Officer's Meeting Room. From the open cannon deck behind him, the yellow moonlight lit splotches on the rippling windows in the door. Family pictures, ropes, and candles hung from the ratlines dangling on the hallway of dark wood. He squinted at the door to his left, where Grandpa and Grandma lay sound asleep. His heart pounded in his chest. He was all in now. No turning back.

He looked back at the Officer's Meeting Room and stepped quietly across the hall. The wood moaned, and the ship gently leaned one way, then the other. Each of his steps delivered a tiny thud and creak.

Maybe that's why Grandpa picked an ancient Earth ship. To keep people from sneaking.

It was a curious thing. With all the money Grandpa had from something he called "investing," he could've bought a ten-million-credit yacht. Why pick a rickety ship from some ancient world? Ace recalled the day Grandpa had bought the ship. Among the dozens of hover craft yachts with expensive accessories, Grandpa walked straight to the ship with stained sails and rotting wood.

"It's full of rich history, Ace!" Grandpa had said. *"What if it belonged to pirates before? That'd be exciting, wouldn't it?"*

Ace hadn't thought so. He preferred hologram TVs and luxury furniture. Instead, yearly vacations with Grandpa consisted of swabbing the deck and various carpentry tasks disguised as "arts and crafts." In all of which the Peppercorns consistently did better than him and his brother. Ace snapped back to the moment. This was the last day of vacation. The last chance to see if he could uncover Grandpa's secret. The last chance to have something over the Peppercorns.

He was only a few steps away when he fell to the ground as the stern leaned to conquer a small wave. It tilted just enough to catch him off guard and send him tumbling across the deck. His back smacked against the very door he sought to break into. The ship splashed back in the water and calmed once again. Ace sat wide-eyed, back against the door, facing the open cannon deck lit well by the full yellow moon. He anticipated Grandma Martha opening the hall to the Captain's Quarters ready to give him a whipping. It would be the end of him. But seconds later, the gentle sea was all he heard. He swallowed a lump in his throat and stood to his feet.

His knees wobbled as he regained his composure. When he turned around to face the door, he noticed something strange.

There's no lock.

Where had the lock gone? Had Grandpa removed his secret? Ace hadn't imagined one from before, had he? Of course not. He for sure saw it the first day they had set sail. As always, the grandchildren had rushed to see the ship the minute they arrived at Grandpa and Grandma's house. Ace had been the first one to head for the Officer's Meeting Room when he noticed the lock on the door.

"Oh, no, no, no," Grandpa Marty had said, his wrinkly hand fastened tightly around Ace's wrist.

"Why's there a lock, Grandpa?"

"I have a . . ." Grandpa swallowed and scratched his head. *"Secret . . . young man. Not for my grandchildren's eyes. I will have to take care of it when we return."*

His eyes threw Ace for a loop; they were the eyes of an old, worried soul. Too worried.

Ace turned the door handle and went inside. Had this all been for naught? Had Grandpa already gotten rid of whatever it was he didn't want Ace to see?

He nervously looked around the room. How could he be so dumb? The moonlight hardly shone through the rippling windows with not the slightest effect on the pitch darkness. He should've brought a flashlight. There had to be one around there somewhere. He stumbled around, nearly tripping, but caught himself.

A blinding white light blared in his eyes.

"Ahh!" He jumped back in a fright and fell to the deck. He knocked down a few chairs on the way in a ruckus; sounding his doom. An old man's laugh rumbled in the dark with a frightening familiarity. Grandpa Marty caught him red handed. Beads of sweat formed at his hairline and rolled down his face as he imagined his possible punishments. Would he be forced now to do all the chores while Julie and Tamara laughed at him?

"Looking for this?" Grandpa Marty said, wiggling the flashlight and trying to contain his laughter.

"Oh! Uh!" Ace covered his eyes from the blinding light. "Grandpa, I can explain. I was—uh—"

"Calm down, Ace of Spades." The old man's tone seemed strangely playful. "I knew you would sneak in here the minute I told you I had a secret."

Ace's insides exploded. "But, I wasn't—"

"Oh, spare me, son. I know you better than you know the back of your hand."

Grandpa clicked the flashlight off. Ace stared wordlessly

through the dark. No point trying to weasel his way out of this one. The old man had him pegged.

"I told you there was a secret," Grandpa said, "so you *would* sneak out here. And I have to say, I'm surprised it took you so long. Learning to control your impulses is a part of growing up, I guess. Too bad . . . those impulses will come in handy later."

"What? Why would you *want* me to sneak into your meeting room, Grandpa?"

"Because." Grandpa's peach fuzz head cast a round shadow from the timid moonlight outside the windows. The floor croaked as he stepped forward. "The secret is for you, Ace. Not for Cameron, and definitely not for the Peppercorns."

Ace rose to his feet with a wide smile. "What secret, Grandpa?"

The old man stepped forward again and slowly reached his arm around Ace's back. A beam of light followed the sound of a click. Grandpa shone the flashlight on an ancient Earth Safe Box made of wood, about the size of a large book. The light reflected off its golden edges running along the sides and over its arched roof. Ace had seen one of those safe boxes before. He heard Grandpa call it a treasure chest once. It was something ancient man used to lock away valuable items. It seemed like it gave off some kind of energy. It fascinated him. The world around him fell dark and silent as if only he and the chest were in the room.

"Only someone who would dare to sneak around Marty Halder's ship has the guts needed for this task," Grandpa said. Hearing his voice startled Ace back to reality.

"Wh—" Ace coughed and swallowed. "What task?"

Grandpa gently nudged him as they walked to the chest, then pulled his shirt sleeve back to reveal a matte black watch. "Now, Ace," he said, "what I'm about to show you is sacred. Rumors of its existence have flocked about Yutara since creation. You must swear to me, before I open this chest, not a word of this will escape your lips."

Ace's eyes widened. Grandpa's adventurous spirit didn't surprise him, but his eyes told of an uncertainty the boy had never seen before. Whatever lay in the chest had no part in legend or myth. Something authentic stirred the air, and the mystery of it persuaded Ace to ignore his reservations.

"I swear, Grandpa."

Grandpa smiled, twisted the top of his watch, and placed his thumb on the ticking surface. Two timid lights blinked from the chest, following a sound like a thunk, and the lock snapped free. Dust pockets formed, and dirt crumbled to the ground as he lifted the top of the chest open. Ace's pulse beat faster. Beams of red and violet shone dimly behind a gray cloth in the chest. Ace's jaw dropped, and he brought his hands to his cheeks. Grandpa reached in, picked up the cloth, and held it before his grandson's eyes.

"Is that . . . ? " Ace said.

"Behold," Grandpa pulled the cloth from his hand. Bright white lights swirled on the inside of the deep red gem in the old man's palm; its rays of rose and violet brightened every corner of the room with wonder. "The Emerson Stone," Grandpa said.

CHAPTER TWO

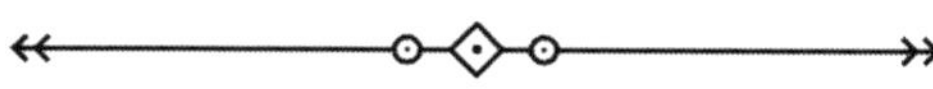

Stick Together

"Grandpa!" Ace forgot his need to breathe. "Wh—I mean—how—The Emerson Stone?"

"Shh! Quiet now!" Grandpa said. He threw the cloth back over the stone and darkness took the room again. He frantically put the stone in the chest and locked it. "You knowing I have it is already dangerous enough. You're about to wake up the entire crew!"

"Where did you get that stone? And why are you telling me this?" Ace asked.

"I—" Grandpa scratched his chin. "It was a gift. Let's just leave it there." His eyes squinted with a hint of suspicion. "And I'm telling you this because you've been chosen."

"Chosen for what?"

"To be the stone's keeper. To fight the power of the seventh realm with an even greater power."

Ace opened his mouth, then closed it. He repeated this a couple times until he decided which of questions flying through his brain he wanted to ask first. "What? But the seventh realm is a myth."

"That's what I thought too. But I have reason to believe otherwise."

"What reason?"

Grandpa leaned in to Ace's ear. "A map."

"A map? So, I'm going *to* the seventh realm?"

Grandpa rubbed his head. "That's a good question. I think it's a mixture of yes and no." He shook his head and wagged his hand. "No matter. The point is, you will be the stone's keeper soon, and the seventh realm will be woken to it."

Ace quarreled with his adventurous nature. It sounded like one of Grandpa's stories. The boy's mind split into three pieces. One believed Grandpa was telling a story and had taken his method acting to a new extreme, the other believed the old man had finally gone insane, and the final believed it to be true, but didn't trust his twelve-year-old self to perform the task.

"But . . . why me?"

"Haven't I told you? You're gutsy, determined, and you won't stop searching until you find the answer. What else would compel you to sneak into my Meeting Room?"

Ace stood baffled. The past few years on Grandpa's over sea trips had made him feel less qualified than how Grandpa described him. The Peppercorns finished their chores first. They beat him and Cameron in every family game. They were richer, more talented, better looking. Grandpa had made a mistake.

"I am? But—I mean—the Peppercorns—"

"The Peppercorns don't matter right now," Grandpa said, cutting down Ace's words like a razor. "*You've* been chosen for this. Forget everything else. Julie and Tamara will just have to deal with it."

Ace's heart couldn't decide whether to leap or fall. He only settled on trusting Grandpa.

"Okay, Grandpa. So, are you just going to give me the map and send me away? Or . . . how is this supposed to work?"

The old man laughed. Ace thought a lot of old people sounded like they had piles of phlegm and mucus gathered in their throat when they laughed. But not Grandpa. His laugh was smooth, lighthearted, and could bring joy to the most broken spirits.

"You have been chosen to *lead* your family. Not leave them. You are to protect them. But defeating the seventh realm is a task great and far. You will conquer many trials before reaching this place," Grandpa said.

"Do you mean that I am—" Ace paused, unsure whether this question was appropriate or not, "*in charge* of the rest of the family?"

Grandpa nodded. "You will be. But you must understand that leading your family is serving your family. Until you understand this, you will be in charge of nothing but your imagination."

"But, Grandpa. I don't even know how to get to school. Dad still drives me. And you want me to go to the seventh realm? Until just now, I thought it was a myth. And I've never even used a map before . . . How will I know how to read it?" Ace said.

"When it's time, you will find your way," Grandpa said. "I wish that I could tell you more than this, but the way the Emerson Stone chooses to operate is out of my control. But listen close. When the map is revealed to you, you may not even know it, but the stone will then become yours."

Ace didn't pretend to understand what Grandpa said. Had the old man lost his mind? Was Ace dreaming? He scratched his head as an orange glow crept through the rippling windows. The tip of the sun had just breached the horizon. Dawn had arrived.

"For now," Grandpa said, "go back to sleep with the rest of the grandchildren. You will find out more soon enough."

Ace nodded. Best to get back to the sleeping quarters before the others grew suspicious. He turned back down the hall, a fresh perspective in his mind as he crept his way back across the deck. He had expected to find some treasure, or ancient artifact, or maybe some Earth weapon. But the Emerson Stone? No way. The thought of it dizzied him. The Emerson Stone only existed in Yutarian myth. Some spoke of its magical power to grant wishes. Others said it to be a weapon, and any country possessing it would become Yutara's next world power. Ace most enjoyed the stories where the stone held the source of all light in Yutara and destroying it would bring eternal darkness to the seven realms. All differences aside, each rumor agreed on one thing. The witches of Yutara wanted the Emerson Stone and would do anything to get it.

Pffft. Witches? Actual witches?

Did Grandpa *actually* have the Emerson Stone? Maybe Grandpa tricked him. Tried to teach Ace a lesson or something, right? It wouldn't be unlike him.

He stumbled on the door leading to his bed. He pushed it ajar, squeezing his way through quickly as possible. He didn't want the morning sun waking the others. Especially with Julie and Tamara sleeping right by the door. To his misfortune, he wasn't sneaky enough.

"Hey," Julie said, wiping her eyes, "What are you doing, Ace?"

Her voice whined enough to wake everyone up. Cameron and Tamara moaned and groaned in their waking as they sat from their hammocks.

"I just—uh—had to go to the bathroom," said Ace.

Julie squinted and stood from her hammock. "No, you were sneaking around, weren't you? I can tell by the look on your face."

"What?" Ace chuckled nervously. "That's ridiculous."

"Grandpa told you not to go into the Meeting Room, Ace. But you just had to, didn't you? I knew you couldn't go the whole trip without peeking." Julie wagged her finger at him with the other hand on her waist. "That's why Grandpa and Grandma love us more. We actually listen to him."

Ace was already tempted to give away Grandpa's secret. *Actually, Grandpa put me in charge of all of you! He seems to think I'm a better leader. So, you and Tamara can spend the rest of the trip swabbing the decks! Get to work!*

Ace bit his tongue as the hope of earning Grandpa's trust tugged on his heart.

Cameron yawned and stretched as he mumbled some gibberish. He finished his stretch and spoke again, this time with more clarity. "What's going on?"

"Your stupid little brother is going to get us all in trouble," Tamara said as she stood from her bed.

"I'm not stupid!" said Ace.

The door flung open and Grandma Martha stepped inside, dressed in a night gown, her gray hair pulled into a ponytail.

"What's all the racket in here?" the old lady said.

"Grandma! Ace went sneaking around last night. I'll bet he went into the Meeting Room. The exact place Grandpa told him not to go," Julie said.

"Oh? Is that so?" Grandma stepped closer, leaning toward Julie.

"No," Cameron said, now stepping from his bed. "She doesn't know that. Ace just came back inside. He said he was using the bathroom and Julie is just throwing out accusations."

Ace smiled at Cameron. Having always looked up to Cameron, he felt uneasy about being put in charge.

"Well then, Ace. Were you using the bathroom?" Grandma asked. Before Ace could answer, Grandma gave him a subtle wink. Did she know about the stone too?

"Yes, Grandma," he said.

"Well, Julie. Maybe you had better learn a little bit more about a situation before you start drawing conclusions," Grandma said.

Julie folded her arms and pouted. She stomped outside the door.

Grandma sighed. "You three, get your stuff ready. We should be arriving shortly. I'll deal with Julie."

The old lady turned to the deck and shut the door behind her. Ace smirked, trying to contain the joy of seeing Julie not get her way for once.

"What were you doing, Ace, really?" Tamara said. She stood from her bed and walked to him. "Grandma never sides with the Halders. Something is up."

Ace glanced at her as she towered over him. She and Julie never had to try and look nice when they woke up. *He* still had bed hair, and could nearly feel the circles forming under his eyes from his sleepiness. As much as he hated to admit it, Tamara looked like the seventeen-year-old princess she thought she was the second she woke up. Her smooth brunette hair fell perfectly by her shoulders, not a single hair out of place, and her green eyes glimmered in the morning light creeping through the window, complimenting her light brown skin.

"Well, there's a first time for everything, I guess. Grandma obviously trusts Ace. So just deal with it." Cameron said. "C'mon, Ace, let's start getting our stuff ready."

Ace nodded at his older brother, then gave Tamara a smile loaded with sarcasm. She stomped down the hall, probably on her way to try and defend her sister to Grandma.

Once she left, Cameron stepped closer to him. The timid light revealed the details in Cameron's unkempt morning look. Crust gathered in the ducts of his brown eyes and broke into pieces around the gray circles. And his black hair, just longer than his ears, looked like a hurricane.

Cameron put his arm over his little brother. "Okay, but for real. What's going on?"

"I can't really tell you. It's a secret," Ace whispered.

"What? C'mon, little brother. We Halders have to stick together, right?" Cameron said.

Ace bit his tongue, desperately wanting to share Grandpa's secret with him. Halders were supposed to stick together. But Grandpa, he was a Halder too, and Ace couldn't let him down.

"I know, Cameron. But . . . I just can't. You're just gonna have to trust me."

Guilt welled inside him as Cameron's face grew long. "Fine. But you owe me," he said, gently punching Ace's arm.

CHAPTER THREE

The City of Waterfalls

Morning came and went, the sun climbed to its midday peak, and Ace leaned over the port side of the ship, overlooking the sea. The sun reflected on the purple waves like flickering stars, and his shirt flapped from the warm, humid wind as it gently brushed his skin. He loved the open sea. But, beautiful as it was, Yutara's oceans couldn't keep his mind still.

Why did Grandpa have the Emerson Stone? How was it connected to the seventh realm? What kind of map would Grandpa *reveal* to him? What did such a thing even mean? First chance he got, when they arrived home, he would grab the chest, and talk Grandpa's ear off with questions. They should be arriving by—

"Grandpa! Where are we? This isn't Eveland," Julie yelled from behind. Ace turned to see Grandpa and Grandma by the steering wheel, smiling with a youthful cheer. The Peppercorns sat beside them.

"Aye! It's not!" Grandpa said.

Cameron, who had been standing next to Ace enjoying the view, nudged him with his elbow. "Why does he always say 'aye' when he's steering the ship? I'm not even sure what that means."

Ace shrugged. "Beats me."

Damion, one of the crew members working for Grandpa, strolled by with rope hung over his shoulder. "It's an old Earth term. Captain Marty says pirates used to say it." He leaned close and drew circles in the air beside his ear. "If you ask me, it sounds a bit looney."

Ace and Cameron chuckled. "He just really likes getting into character, I guess," Cameron said.

Damion patted Cameron's shoulder and his loose clothing wiggled underneath his arm. "That he does, m'boy. That he does." Damion was Cameron and Ace's favorite crew member. His skin had tanned to a crisp from his work on Grandpa's ship, and he never had a full beard or a clean shave. His stubbly cheeks looked like sand on leather. The crewman smiled and walked away to continue his work.

Julie and Tamara stood from their seats and looked over the starboard side. "Well, where are we?" asked Tamara.

"New Eathelyn. The City of Waterfalls," Grandpa said.

Ace and Cameron looked at each other with big smiles, then ran to the bow of the ship. Mountains cast navy blue shadows over the distant horizon. Ace tried to contain his joy at the thought of visiting a new country. His entire life, he had not seen much outside Abes City, Eveland, other than the beach towns along the coast they visited during vacation. Now they were visiting New Eathelyn, Oola.

"Drake Country," Cameron said, his eyes lit with fascination. "Why is Grandpa taking us here?"

Ace kept his wide eyes on the land across the purple ocean, anxiously awaiting their arrival. "I don't know." Few drakes lived in Eveland, and those few only resided in the bigger cities. He had only met one before—G'raka, the janitor in Dad's office building. Her light, yellow skin shone as if it were laden with wax. She stood about five feet tall, and her beady snake eyes and razor-sharp teeth always frightened the kids. Except Ace. Her cheerful nature contradicted her appearance, and he would always smile and wave to her. He often sympathized with the kind drake for having to constantly deal with judgmental kids. He enjoyed their conversations and how she hissed when she talked. Every time a word had an "s" in it, her forked tongue would whip in and out of her mouth.

"What?" Julie yelled from behind. "But, Grandpa, we've been out on the sea for a week now, the trip is supposed to be over."

How could anyone be upset with an *extended* vacation? And one with Grandpa, in a brand-new country. What could be more exciting?

"Surprise, princess!" Grandpa said. He patted her on the back. "Turns out, we get to have a longer vacation this year."

"Uh, how much longer?" Tamara said. "I'm supposed to be going to Late Spring's Ball in a few days, and if I stand Ian up, we'll never end up going out."

Wow, Ace thought. *The guy's lucky and he doesn't even know it.*

"Some things," Grandpa said, "are more important than boys and fancy balls, Tamara. C'mon, not very many Evelanders get to see Oola. It'll be an adventure!"

Tamara folded her arms. "This sucks!" She and Julie marched down to the sleeping quarters.

Ace and Cameron spent the next hour talking of what they imagined Oola to be like, exchanging their excitement until the ship made way to the docks. The closer they got, the more beautiful the city became. Stone buildings towered over the forest just behind the beach of snow-white sand. Hills and mountains grew larger as the land rolled on behind the city, and waters rushed from atop the mountains, down to the ocean in mighty waterfalls. Rivers scattered among the foothills like spider webs.

Schools of water drakes swam by their ship, leaping to be level with the ship's deck and splashing back into the water. These drakes had silver skin cloaked in fish scales, webbed feet and hands, and human-like faces. Their eyes, like every drake's eyes, surrounded a diamond pupil in a glossy gold. The fins on their backs and necks were perhaps their most unique trait.

They entertained Ace and Cameron until Grandpa Marty pulled the ship to the marina and the grandchildren helped the crew tie off to the dock.

"Grab your things, youngins," Grandma Martha said. Everybody went to gather their bags and they stepped onto the dock. Ace bumped into a few drakes while walking, his eyes fixed on the city. Some looked like fish men, others like lizards and dragons. Some even looked like little dinosaurs.

"Orders, Captain?" Ace turned around to find Damion and Grandpa talking to one another. The old man leaned into Damion's ear. The crew member looked uncomfortable with whatever he was being told. Grandpa clapped Damion's shoulders and nodded. "As you wish," Damion said, returning to the ship.

"Damion, you're not coming with us?" Ace said.

He shook his head. "Looks like I'm not, m'boy. Don't worry, shouldn't be too long before we see each other again." He leaned close and held out his fist. Ace bumped it with his own. "Enjoy Oola. Looks like a cool place." He high-fived Cameron and rubbed Ace's head, then returned to the ship with a wide smile.

Lines clanked against the masts of the boats lining the marina. Hundreds of ships were tied to the docks. Most of them were modern and expensive, the kind Ace had wished his Grandpa had. But, oddly enough, the boy spotted a few ships like Grandpa's—Old and rickety. Drakes and Evelanders raced back and forth. The wind carried the sound of bartering voices and the commands of captains both bringing their ships ashore and setting sail. Seeing as some drakes spoke the same language as Evelanders, but hardly any Evelanders spoke drake language, the voices were an odd mix. Drakes spoke with the snapping and rattling of their tongues. The noises their language made proved too difficult for Evelanders, and when drakes spoke in the common tongue, they would click their t's and rattle their s's

"Oh my, my," a drake's voice said from the bustling busy bodies. The voice was even deeper and rustier than Grandpa's. He stood roughly six feet tall, lanky, but toned. Splotches of dark green covered his slimy, light-green skin. His beady yellow eyes protruded from their sockets which bulged from his wide mouth. He wore a ripped dark black vest and tattered shorts. "Are my eyes playing tricks on me? Or is that Marty Halder himself?"

Grandpa spread his arms out wide. "In the flesh!" He and the drake embraced each other with cheerful laughter. The grandchildren glanced at one another with confusion. "It's so great to see you!" Grandpa said.

"It has been far too long, my friend," the drake said. He turned his head to see past Grandpa. "So, are you going to introduce me?"

"Ah, yes!" Grandpa stepped to the side and extended his arm. "Family, this is Rio Atarion. He's been one of my best friends since we were lads. Go on, introduce yourselves."

"Well, since *I* was a lad." Rio smirked as he stepped forth. He held out his shiny green hand. Ace shook it first, more than happy to meet another drake in person.

"Ace Halder. Pleased to meet you, Mr. Rio." Ace took notice of the drake's smooth skin. It wasn't as slimy as he imagined, but more like stroking a surface of glass.

"Pleased to meet you too, kid. And you are?" said Rio. Cameron shook the drake's hand.

"Cameron Halder!"

Then came Julie, who gave her snotty look of disgust at the drake's hand.

"Julie!" Grandma pinched Julie's arm, and the little girl flinched. "Mind your manners."

Ace and Cameron chuckled, but Grandpa corrected them, and they straightened up.

"Oh, it's just fine ma'am. Probably just their first time meeting a drake is all," Rio said.

Julie and Tamara shook Rio's hand, wincing the entire time. Afterward, the drake stepped back to Grandpa, and they led the family from the docks, and further into the city.

"Stay close, youngins," said Grandma. "It's easy, to get lost in here."

CHAPTER FOUR

The Armory

Rubbery drake skin brushed against Ace's arm as they squeezed through the crowds in the marina. Rio led the family to the palm trees towering over the city ahead. At nearly two hundred feet tall, their leaves slumped over in a glossy yellow-green, covering the city in a blanket of shade and shadow. Speckles of light found a path through the leaves to the ground and glimmered along the narrow winding roads, where drakes traveled on varying giant beasts. Some feline, some canine, and some like bears. Giant buildings of smooth stone went on for miles through the foothills on either side of the streets. Hundreds of drakes poured into the streets, and the sound of their speech clicked and clacked through the air.

It seemed a bridge awaited them around every corner to help them navigate the hundreds of rivers scattered throughout the city. The sound of the crashing waterfalls in the distance was so powerful, it hummed audibly over the hustle of the city. Every now and then, a glimpse of rich purple and cloudy mists from the falls surrounding the city could be caught behind the stone buildings and trees. Every time Ace got a peek, he'd stretch his neck, hoping to see more. The waterfalls met the pools in clouds of white foam, suggesting a sense of serenity among the power the waters spoke of.

During their hike they passed by a large statue of Nahanmi Lock'Lara, the Drake Elder. The statue was carved from the same stone the buildings were, and it stood in the center of a cul de sac of buildings, bridges, and rivers, at roughly fifty feet tall. The sculptor had taken the time to carve the deep, lizard-like bags under his frightening eyes. Ace had only seen him on TV before, but the statue looked as creepy as the TV hologram projection he was used to.

"This city is amazing," Cameron said to Ace. They had fallen behind everyone else in the group, both observing every inch of New Eathelyn their eyes could feast on.

"I know," Ace said. "I don't think I ever want to go back to Eveland."

The Peppercorns turned around. "Will you two stop dorking out over this place? It smells here, and I want Grandpa to take us home as soon as possible," Tamara said.

"Aren't you enjoying this at all?" Cameron said. "I mean, it's not every day we get to visit an entirely new country."

"Oh, I have an idea." Julie's eyes lit up. "Let's just have Grandpa take us two back, Tamara. We can leave the Halders here where they belong. With the smelly lizards."

Ace, who had grown tired of Julie's attitude, lashed out without thinking. "Shut up, you witch," the boy said.

"Hey!" Grandpa called out from ahead of the group, and the family stopped abruptly. Fewer things set off Grandpa more than mentioning a witch outside a story, and Ace had been foolish enough to call one of his granddaughters one. Not the wisest choice of words. Grandpa turned around and walked toward the boys, his eyes red with fury. "I don't know which one of you said that." He pointed his old bony finger at Ace and Cameron. "But don't you ever use that word again. Are we clear?"

The two boys nodded. "Yes, sir," they said. Dozens of drakes walked by, staring and pointing at the Evelanders getting yelled at by the old man. Ace should have known better. He felt like crawling in a hole to avoid more embarrassment.

The Peppercorns laughed, and Julie stuck her tongue out at him. Grandpa turned around and led the group again.

"Hey," Cameron whispered, "you should know better than to use the 'w' word, lil bro."

"I know, I'm sorry, it just slipped out."

"Oh well, what's done is done."

Rio led the family to a large cabin further up the mountains in the outskirts of the city. Massive brown logs stacked on top of each other, making the walls of the cabin. The open windows had no panes of glass and showed only darkness inside. Palm tree leaves fell in an arch covering the roof of the cabin. Ace turned around once they reached the front porch. He stared, eyes wide at the radiant city from their distance. It sat in a valley embraced by mountains of spirited yellow-green. Rivers tangled and scattered throughout the hills until they collided and spilled in a vigorous rush over the top of the valley. The sun shone on the surface of the purple falls as it drifted below the horizon behind them.

"Ahh, I'm so glad to not be walking anymore," Julie said. Ace turned his attention back to the family.

"Tell me about it," Tamara said. She and Julie walked into the cabin and threw their bags on the ground. They went to the biggest room they could find, yelled "dibs," and plopped on the beds.

"Why don't you two go to the beach? It's a vacation after all," Grandma said. Tamara and Julie scoffed and whined on their beds.

"Vacations are supposed to be fun, though. It's muggy outside, I got bit by a million bugs, and the whole city smells like rotten fish," Julie said.

"Fine, sit in here and whine all you want," Grandma said. "But it's not going to change anything. You might as well learn to enjoy your time here." The old lady turned to Ace and Cameron, who had just sat down on the squeaky, dark leather couches by the fireplace. "What do you say? Want to take a trip to the beach?"

"Sure, Grandma," Cameron said.

"I'd love to," Ace said.

"Now, wait a second," Grandpa Marty said. He and Rio walked in from the porch. "Ace, I need you to come with me and Rio for now. You can visit the beach another time."

Cameron shrugged at Ace. Julie and Tamara snickered from their room. Julie stood and walked to the door, sassing him inaudibly. Apparently, she wasn't too tired to pass up the opportunity to mock her cousin.

Ace ignored her. The more Julie and Tamara mocked him, the less power he felt over his tongue. It was like a bad itch.

"Yes sir," Ace said.

"Sorry, man. We'll go tomorrow," Cameron said, patting his little brother on the back. Ace stood from the couch and followed Rio and Grandpa out the cabin door. Once they were further into the tropical forest and far enough away from the family, the drake started talking.

"So," Rio said, "you think this is the one, huh?"

"I'm sure of it," Grandpa said.

Ace tugged on Grandpa's shirt. "The one what?"

Rio chuckled. "You haven't told him yet?"

"I wanted it to be a surprise," Grandpa said. The way they were speaking, it didn't seem like Grandpa was talking about the Emerson Stone. But, what else could it be? Ace wasn't going to ask either. He wouldn't dare risk telling Rio that Grandpa had the stone if the drake didn't know. He did what he thought was the wisest and kept his mouth closed. Knowing Grandpa, he would have his answers soon enough.

A dirt path lay not much further from the cabin. Thick palm trees stood like giants on either side of the path, offering a bit of shade for their travel. The path led to a cave in the mountain wall.

Rio looked all around before entering, as if to make sure no one could see them. The drake moved some leaves on the ground and flipped a switch hidden under the leaves. Light bulbs hung from strings on the walls of the cave in a cozy invitation. The three stepped through the mouth of the cave and walked to what seemed to be a larger opening further in.

"You see, Ace," Grandpa said, "I'm not just an investor. I've owned my own. . . uh. . . business? . . . For some time now. But don't you go telling anybody about this."

"What business?" Ace asked.

The hall lead to a larger part of the cave. Ace's jaw dropped to the floor. Along the rock walls hung the biggest collection of weapons the boy had ever seen. Hand-blasters, shot-blasters, and more blasters he had no name for. Ancient chests sat on the sand under the racks of the chrome weapons, and in the middle of the floor lay a trap door.

"I'm kind of a witch hunter," Grandpa said.

"Not just any witch hunter." Rio slapped Grandpa on the shoulder. A smile stretched across his face, revealing his sharp, shark-like teeth. "Your grandfather is the best witch hunter that's ever lived."

"Oh, stop it now," Grandpa said.

Ace took a step back. The three pieces of his mind finally narrowed down and agreed on one. Grandpa was telling the truth, and this armory proved it. The reality of it sank in, and he caught his breath.

Dumbfounded, he spoke the first thought on his mind. "A witch hunter? But how?"

"What do you mean, 'how?' Look at this massive armory, kid!" Rio said. Grandpa laughed.

"Listen, son. I'm getting old, as you can tell. And I need someone to carry on my work when I'm gone," Grandpa said.

Ace stared at the hidden armory. "You mean, you want me to be a witch hunter? Like you?"

"Yes," Grandpa said.

What about the Emerson Stone and the seventh realm? he

thought.

"But, Grandpa." Ace paused. He turned to Rio and realized he couldn't mention anything of the stone. "Uh. . . aren't I too young?"

"You're never too young to begin training," Rio said.

"Ah," Ace said, scratching his neck, "training. And that's why we're here?"

Rio grabbed a thick, camouflage vest from the cave wall and threw it to Ace. It was heavier than the boy anticipated, and he almost fell when he caught it. "Suit up," the drake said.

CHAPTER FIVE

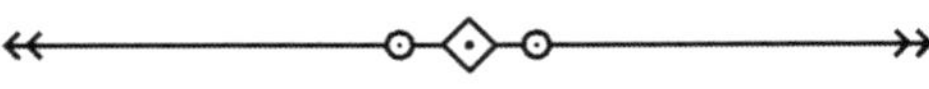

Training

After Grandpa left, the drake strapped a chrome blaster rifle to his back and took Ace further up the mountain, deep into the vacancy of the tropical rain forest. He told the boy about how the chrome rifles and hand blasters work. They were made to look like any other blasters, so as not to give away their identity as witch hunters, but they were hybrids. Each weapon had a switch on the handle within a thumb's reach, to switch the material they fired with.

While most blasters shot a plasma material capable of burning holes through metal, these blasters could switch between plasma and anti-magic. The hybrid rifles were called AMRs for anti-magic rifles, and anti-magic hand blasters, AMHBs.

"What's anti-magic made from?" Ace said as he reached out. The drake reached down, grabbed the boy's hand, and helped him over a rock ledge.

"Trees. They excrete a strange, orange substance."

Ace wrinkled his brow. "You mean tree sap?"

Rio chuckled. "No, not sap, although sap is mixed in with it. Don't really know what it is or much about it even. Your grandfather discovered it . . ." He placed his hand on his head. "What was I saying?"

Ace reminded him, and he continued to tell the boy about the key difference between plasma and anti-magic. Plasma shot to kill, but anti-magic did just what it sounded like. It neutralized magic. Because, Rio explained, hunters don't kill witches, they capture them.

"Speaking of them, tell me everything you know about witches," the drake said as he swatted a dangling branch in their path.

Ace slapped a bug on his neck. "Uh . . . basically nothing."

"Nothing? Surely you've heard the four signs of a witch before."

Ace paused a moment to think. "Well, I remember Grandpa told us stories a couple times. Sometimes, witches would leave trails of black dust behind. And there's the one famous story about Billy Mills and how he woke up thinking his house was on fire, but it turned out a witch was in the house and he was smelling her smoke. But those are just children's stories." His impatience crept into his tone. He wanted to ask Rio about different things. Like why was Grandpa keeping all these secrets from his family?

They reached a thin river flowing through a path of boulders staggering downhill. Rio stopped and turned sharply at the boy. He clacked his drake-tongue a couple times and said, "Just stories, huh?"

Ace nodded timidly.

"You'll commonly hear tale of four signs a witch is nearby. Black dust, the smell of smoke, the feeling you're being lied to, and the sound of whispers when there's no light. Other than the black dust and the lying part, you're right, those are mostly just stories. Even the stories with black dust and lying are only slightly true."

An unpleaseant tingling crawled on Ace's skin. He eyed Rio curiously and gulped. "So . . . how do you actually tell a witch is around?"

"Patience and training," the drake said abruptly. "Witches aren't so easy to tell apart as they are in the stories." The drake pulled two black discs from a pouch in Ace's vest as he spoke."Some stories even go as far as saying they have green faces, or warts on their noses. Ridiculous things like that. The truth is they hide in plain sight. Their disguises are indistinguishable from a regular person, but not impenetrable." Rio pocketed the black discs and handed Ace the blaster rifle from his back. He moved the boy's hands into position on the handle. "The black dust you hear about in stories is partly true. But it's not so easy to track. When a witch lies and gets away with it, their disguise becomes harder to detect. If a hunter is skilled enough to detect the lies, he can call them out with the truth. This is a dangerous game, kid." He bent close and stuck his slimy nose in Ace's face. His snarl came through every word. "If you try to catch a witch in her lie, and you fail, she becomes stronger, and you become weaker."

"How can I become weaker?"

"Witches are after power. Every witch lies to get it, and when she succeeds, she will use her power to take down anyone who tries to prevent her from keeping it. You know who falls into that category? Hunters. Now, if you do catch her in her lie, and it works, her disguise will start to break apart."

Ace backed away from Rio's breath. It smelled like rotten fish. "Is that where the black dust comes from? Her disguise breaking apart?"

Rio nodded and smirked. "You learn quick." He patted Ace on the shoulder.

"So, if we're just stopping them from lying, what's the rifle for?"

"What do you think happens when a witch's disguise starts to fall apart?"

Ace squinted at the drake, pooling his thoughts with no luck.

"Magic. They resort to magic. Guess how you stop their magic." He gently tapped the chrome rifle while giving the boy a facetious grin. He patted Ace's shoulders, turned around, and began leaping uphill like the frog man he was as he placed the black discs on the staggered rocks by the river, all the while shouting, "Try not to shoot any people. Only witches!"

The discs projected holograms of pixelated cities and villages throughout the rain forest. The boy looked at his rifle, then at the crowds. How was he supposed to tell who the witches were? He wiped the sweat from his forehead, praying he'd come into some natural ability for detecting magic he never knew he had.

For hours, it seemed, Ace took his best guesses, but couldn't nab one. Wondering why Grandpa had all these secrets kept him too distracted. And what exactly was the Emerson Stone? Do the witches know Grandpa has it? Were witches *actually* real? If so, how was Ace supposed to know what they looked like? Eventually the drake lost his patience.

"What was that?" Rio yelled from the hills. He shut off the hologram projectors and overlooked the hill down to Ace.

"What? That wasn't a witch?" Ace asked. "Looked like a liar to me!"

Rio hopped at great lengths down each hill and landed just in front of the boy. "What in Eathelyn Summers made you think that was a witch?"

"Uh—I don't know—she looked suspicious, I guess," Ace said.

"Oh, she just looked suspicious, huh? Children look suspicious when they steal candy, Ace. You can't just up and shoot someone with anti-magic because they looked suspicious!"

The frog man's tone affirmed the rumors of drakes being short-tempered, and it started to anger the boy as well. He was sweaty and exhausted. Not to mention, hunting witches wasn't exactly the future he had dreamed for himself.

He puffed his chest and poked Rio with his first finger. "Look, up until an hour or two ago, I had no idea that I was a witch hunter's grandson. Much less that I'd be responsible for taking over the family business! I'm new to this, so give me a break!"

Rio scoffed at him and hopped up a couple of hills ahead. Then he stopped and turned to face the boy. "Go back to your family for the night. We'll resume training again soon."

Ace threw his blaster rifle to the ground and stormed into the tropical forest. Rio mumbled under his breath in anger, but Ace heard every word of it.

"Of all the gifted kids that old man could pick, he chose that talentless little snot," Rio said. Ace clenched his fists and grit his teeth.

He violently whacked at the plants in his path. Without a blade, it was going to be a long trip. The training had taken place about a fifteen minute's hike away from the cave with the armory, which existed another half hour away from the cabin. The humidity crawled on his skin, bugs attacked him by the hundreds, and his fatigued legs and feet ached with every step. Maybe there were some negatives to this city after all. Only one thing urged him to carry on trudging his way back home—a long discussion with Grandpa. He was determined to get to the bottom of this.

After a grueling journey, Ace made it to the cabin. He burst open the front door and plopped down on the soft couch. Oddly, the whole place was empty, and his eyelids grew heavy. The sounds of the animals in the forest outside, and the faint rumble of waterfalls in the distance complimented the silence in the cabin. Slowly, his surroundings faded, and his consciousness drifted.

"Ah, done with training I see," Grandpa said. Ace shot up and tried to gather himself. The room spun and his head felt fuzzy. He saw Grandpa standing in the doorway of the cabin. It took a second, but the room stopped spinning, and Ace finally told dream from reality

"Grandpa," he said. "Where's everyone else?"

"They're at the beach," Grandpa said. "Your grandmother finally convinced the Peppercorns to get out of the cabin and enjoy themselves." Good. They were alone. Time to get to the bottom of things.

"What's going on? What's this business about you being a witch hunter?" Ace asked.

Grandpa stepped closer, looking around the cabin as if someone may be watching. When the old man saw the coast was clear, he sat down on the couch next to his grandson.

"I haven't had much chance to speak with you since we've arrived. We must be very careful, Ace. I don't know who may be listening."

Grandpa's curious behavior sobered Ace from his sleepiness.

"Rio doesn't know about the stone. He only knows that I'm leaving my business to you, and that he's to train you. In fact, no one knows about the stone. You must keep it that way."

Ace nodded, then stood from the couch and paced the floor. The past couple of days, a frantic unraveling of wild events, proved too much to handle. Brimming at the boy's lips, questions finally gushed forth like a New Eathelyn waterfall.

"Grandpa. What does the stone do? I mean, I thought it was just a legend until you showed it to me. Why do you want me to take over the business? Since when have witches been real? How long have you been a witch hunter? Is Marty Halder even your real name?" Ace panted and paced and soon grew frustrated to see Grandpa laughing at him. "This isn't funny! I'm sore all over from training, and I don't even know exactly what I'm training for. Tell me what's going on!"

"Alright, alright, calm down, son. Have a seat and take a deep breath," Grandpa said. He walked over to the kitchen and poured a glass of water from the sink, then handed it to the boy. "I know you have a lot of questions, that's to be expected. I will do my best to explain what I can, but much of what's happened recently is as much a mystery to me as it is to you."

Ace took a large gulp from the water, which turned to several gulps, which turned to an empty glass and a thirst still unquenched. Grandpa chuckled as he brought the empty glass back to the kitchen.

"Alright, Ace," Grandpa said as he turned on the sink to refill the glass. "Let's start with what I know." He walked back to his grandson and handed him the water. "The reason I've brought us to New Eathelyn is to introduce you to Rio. His training and guidance will help you better understand the task you've been chosen for." Grandpa leaned his head close and whispered, "Evil creatures are lurking everywhere, all over Yutara. And the closer you get to destroying the power of the seventh realm, the bigger a target you become."

Chills ran up Ace's spine. The dark cabin and the sound of the forest outside was a spooky combination with Grandpa's lore.

"Why, Grandpa?" Ace whispered back.

"Because they're looking for something," Grandpa said. His voice was quieter every time he spoke.

Ace's eyes widened. He stood quickly from the couch, his heart pounding through his chest. "The stone?"

Grandpa tipped his head with a yes and a sly smile.

"But, I don't have it. *You* do. And I thought I was the only one other than you who knew about it."

"As of late, that is true. But soon it will not be the case."

"I don't understand."

"Listen, son," Grandpa placed his hand on Ace's shoulder and brought him back to the couch. He lowered his head, revealing his intense eyes. "There's an evil greater than you can imagine lurking through Yutara. Those who belong to this evil know things beyond our understanding, and they will use it against you if they can. The worst part about them is that they hide in plain sight, just before your very eyes. You won't know it until it's too late. Trust *no one*.

"Now, listen close. Once the map is revealed to you, you may not even know it. But the stone will become yours at that time. Keep your eyes and ears peeled, son. When you begin to uncover the map, all the evil in Yutara will be awakened to your presence and possession of the stone. This will not happen until you are prepared to meet the challenges this journey will bring."

Ace felt chills again. He sank further into the couch. What had Grandpa gotten him into?

"Oh man!" Cameron yelled from behind. Ace and Grandpa shot

up and saw the older Halder brother standing in the doorway. They hadn't heard him walking up the porch steps. How much had Cameron heard? "Those stupid Peppercorns are gonna drive me insane!" he said as he walked further in the house. Cameron shook his head, and sand spilled to the wooden floor.

Ace and Grandpa looked at one another with relief. It seemed Cameron had just walked in and heard nothing of their conversation.

"What did they do?" Ace asked.

"Well, I was just making a sand castle, minding my own business. This girl walked by, and I stopped to wave at her. Then, out of nowhere, Julie and Tamara come from behind and shove me into the castle I made. And as if that wasn't enough, they dumped a bunch of sand all over my head. Apparently, they had been planning this, because they conveniently had a bucket filled to the brim with sand."

"What's their problem?" Ace said.

Grandpa leaned over the back of the couch, "Go ahead and wash up, I'll have a talk with the Peppercorns."

Cameron nodded and walked down the hall, mumbling in frustration.

"We'll have to continue our discussion later," Grandpa whispered to Ace.

Ace nodded. But before he could leave, Grandpa pulled him close and whispered even quieter, "I've put the stone in a trap door under your side of the bed and the watch that unlocks it is beside it. I changed the settings to match your fingerprints so only you can open the chest. When the time is right, take it with you. Until then, don't so much as look at it."

CHAPTER SIX

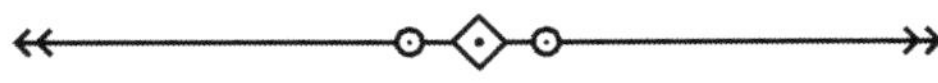

Grandpa's Story

Cool water streamed down Ace's back in the cabin shower as he enjoyed a moment spared from all the madness. It had been the first time he had a chance to clean himself since he arrived in New Eathelyn. Usually, he preferred hot showers. But the sticky air outside had been enough to persuade him otherwise. Once he was clean enough, he stepped out and grabbed his pajamas from the counter. Before he put them on, as usual, he stared at the skyscraper design printed on them. Something about the grandeur of the big city captured him. Plenty of Grandpa's stories involved big cities. Those stories were Ace's favorite. As his eyes followed the pattern of towering buildings sewn to his nighttime attire, he wondered how many grandpas lived in those big cities. Must be tons. So many stories Ace hadn't heard yet.

He wiped the fog from the mirror, smiled, and turned to open the bathroom door. Cameron sat on the bed, swiping the virtual screen on his computer with annoyance.

"I think you might be wasting your time, Cameron. I'm pretty sure there's no connection out here," Ace said.

"Yeah, I know," Cameron said. He sighed, closed the laptop, and put it on the stand next to the bed. "I was bored. Figured I'd just give it a shot I guess."

Ace shrugged and plopped down on the bed next to his brother's bed.

"Ace are you ever going to tell me what's going on with you and Grandpa?" Cameron asked.

Ace hung his head. Cameron really deserved to know. "I don't know, Cameron. Honest . . . I don't really know what's going on."

"At least tell me what you *do* know. Are we like, okay? I mean, the family and everything?" Cameron said.

Ace swallowed a lump in his throat as he remembered Grandpa's telling of lurking evil creatures. "I think so."

He hated lying to Cameron. But he couldn't say anything for fear of begging more questions. Keeping the secret had been hard enough already.

"Well, that's good at least. But it's been bothering me like crazy ever since we got here. The Peppercorns too, you know. They've been especially vicious," Cameron said.

"They've been vicious their whole lives, Cameron," Ace said.

"I know. But you haven't been around them as much as me lately. They've gone insane! You having some sort of secret with Grandpa is really starting to get to them." Cameron stood from the bed.

"I'm sorry, Cameron. But look at the positive side. We've finally one-upped the Peppercorns. Imagine how Dad will react when we tell him we have something *they* want!" Ace's smile widened.

Cameron crossed his arms and leaned against the wall. "No. *You* have something they want."

Ace stood on top of the bed, so he could be eye level with his brother. "No. *We* do," he said, gently nudging Cameron on the shoulder. "Even if you don't know the secret. Because Halders stick together."

Cameron smirked at Ace and replied under his breath, "The way Halders are supposed to."

The door to their bedroom swung open, and Grandma Martha stood in the doorway.

"Good evening, you two," she said, "Your grandfather has started a fire. He's got s'mores ready if you two would like to join us."

"Sure, Grandma," they said together.

They walked from their room, opening directly to the den. A crackling fire covered the somber room in flickering, tepid light, and a tame breeze carried a complementing mist through the windows from the distant waterfalls.

Julie and Tamara sat roasting their marshmallows with a dull look on their faces, and Grandpa walked in from the kitchen with a handful of graham crackers and chocolate. All the grandchildren loved s'mores. It was an unusual treat for Yutarian youths. But Grandpa, being so well learned in ancient Earth culture, made the delicious treats a frequent occurrence for his grandchildren. Even Julie and Tamara didn't complain about s'mores.

But, for Ace, this meant more than the whiff he caught of sugary dessert from the burning logs. Or the succulent mix of creamy chocolate, gooey white fluff, and a honey-dipped crunch he anticipated—as if those weren't good enough—but fire and s'mores always meant one thing better. Grandpa had a story to tell.

"Boys, come on in!" Grandpa said. The Peppercorns turned to see the Halders walking in, scoffed, and turned their attention back to their marshmallows on their metal hangers. Ace and Cameron grabbed their hangers just as their cousins finished.

The Halders stepped to the fire, and as Julie stood, she took Ace's marshmallow off the hanger and tossed it to the fire. All behind her back.

"Oops," she whispered. Ace nudged her with his shoulder and she fell to the couch.

"Hey, watch it, twerp!" Tamara said as she helped her sister up.

"Oops," Ace said with a smile. Cameron chuckled under his

breath.

"Enough!" Grandma snapped. Her tone sharp enough to cut lead.

"Now," Grandpa said as he stood between the two couches. "If you're quite finished being at war with each other, you might enjoy a tale I've prepared for you this evening."

Ace and Cameron turned to see Grandpa, and Julie and Tamara sit down on the left couch, opposite side of Grandma. Anyone who could get the Peppercorns to stop looking at their phones without force had talent. But maybe the s'mores they had their faces buried in had something to do with it too.

"This isn't another one of those super people things, is it?" Tamara asked.

"I hope so," Ace said as he reached in the bag for another marshmallow. "Superhero stories are my favorite."

"Of course, they are, dork," Julie said.

"Stop it, Julie," Grandpa said. "And no, Tamara. It isn't a story about a superhero."

Ace frowned.

"No, no." Grandpa waved his fingers. "Today, I have an extra special story for you all."

Ace's spirits lifted. He grabbed his s'more and sat on the couch next to Grandma, then scooted to the edge of his seat. Grandpa's stories never let him down before. This sounded like it had promise.

"This story happens at the end of Earth. It's about a prince." Grandpa turned and looked Ace directly in the eye, then gave him a familiar wink. "And a stone."

Ace's heart fell. What was Grandpa up to? Was he about to reveal his possession of the Emerson Stone to the whole family? He sank back on the couch. His stomach simmered with nerves, so he forgot the treat in his hand, now dripping melted chocolate on his city pajamas. Once he felt the burning sensation, he corrected himself and grabbed a napkin.

"A stone? What's so special about a stone?" Julie asked.

"Everything," Grandpa said. "This wasn't just any stone, Julie.

Nor was this just any prince." He crouched down and leaned in closer to his grandchildren, getting in character, the way he always did. "Long ago, on Earth, there lived a weak and frail young man named Oliver Halder."

Julie and Tamara's face scrunched with distaste. "*Halder?*" Julie said.

"Yes, Halder," Grandpa said. "Now, Oliver had many older brothers. No one really knows how many. Some say as few as five, some say as many as eleven. But what everyone agrees on, was that they were all much bigger, and much stronger." Grandpa puffed his chest and flexed his muscles. "Oliver's father had recently succeeded in taking over what was left of Earth. At this point, all the nations had crumbled, and for the past hundred years, there were only a few million people left. Oliver's great grandfather was the first to establish a new government. The last kingdom on Earth. And, as had been tradition, the throne went to the oldest son at the passing of the king."

"This sounds more like a history lesson than a story, Grandpa," Tamara said.

"He's just giving us the details," Cameron said to his older cousin. "It'll get better."

Tamara shrugged. "Whatever."

"Stop interrupting, guys, I wanna hear," Ace said.

"Now, now, calm down," Grandpa said. "Where was I now?" The old man scratched his chin, then lifted his index finger in the air. "Ah, yes. The throne. Well, one day, when Oliver was out journeying through Earth, as he did often, a strange thing happened."

Ace leaned further in, entirely dismissing his gooey treat.

"From a cave he saw a shiny red glow," Grandpa said.

The Emerson Stone, Ace thought.

"Oliver pondered what it may be. But he was a curious one, that Oliver." Grandpa winked over at Ace again. "And so, Oliver walked to the cave to find what it was."

"It was a dragon, wasn't it?" Julie butted in. "It's always dragons in the caves. And a red glow? That's got to be its fiery breath!"

"Dragon fire is orange, not red," Cameron said.

Ace jolted from his seat. He had had enough of everyone butting in. "Guys, let *him* tell the story for New Realm's sake!"

A sharp sting followed a correctional pinch from Grandma, and Ace sat down abruptly after wincing. Julie and Tamara giggled.

"It was no dragon," Grandpa began again. "It was the stone."

"What?" said Tamara.

"Lame," said Julie.

Grandpa chuckled. "Oh, it was far from lame, Julie. This stone changed everything for Oliver. He walked inside and saw the glowing red gem trapped in a boulder, jutting from the cave wall. Just above the stone was an inscription:

Whosoever frees the stone
Will venture not a realm alone
Seven of which will confess
Emery's chosen, Emery blessed

Come Emery, who knows Unknown
In search of no Haevyr
There is one, and one alone
Who is called a savior

Eldest, will the keeper be
'Till shadow clouds all truth
One is chosen, this day's Eve
One, all hear ye in youth

What's to come, some will believe
Despite some who deny
Stone in hand, one will deceive
And one will bear the lie

For there, in the Land of Faes
Once returned to its throne

By one, in this tamest place
The Light is set in stone

No race of faes
Nor jags, nor drakes
Nor shadow or tree
Says from Unknown
Should bear, the stone
For this fate of Eve's

Burdened will the chosen be
But should he seek his soul free
Stone and man shall trade their fate
Then, of him, come Emery

"And so, Oliver was intrigued to say the least. He reached out, ignoring the inscription, and took the stone free from the cave.

"Years passed, and Oliver kept the stone hidden away, but always close. It was nothing more than a precious gem to the little guy. But little did he know it was so much more. And he wouldn't find out until he was seventeen, when his father's kingdom was threatened."

"Who could have threatened the kingdom? I thought it was the last kingdom on Earth," Cameron said.

"That's right, but the kingdom that threatened it was *not* from Earth," Grandpa said.

"Witches!" Julie said. The little girl nearly jumped from her seat.

Grandpa nodded darkly at Julie. "Close, but no. It was a warlock!" he said.

The grandchildren gasped.

Grandpa continued. "When Oliver turned seventeen, his father asked to speak with him.

"'Son, I have someone I'd like you to meet,' the king said. And, standing next to his father, Oliver saw a tall man. This man had smoky gray skin. His eyes were white, and he was dressed in a black robe, the hood covering his face. The warlock had skulls and bones around his neck and covering his robe. Pointy shoulder pads carved from tusks, and a black staff tipped with a jag skull, and studded along its edges with teeth. Antlers tore through warlock's hood."

"A jag!" all the children said. Typical. Jags were always the villains in Yutarian folklore.

Grandpa continued his story. "But what seemed strange to Oliver was the king seemed not himself. It was almost as if the king were not even conscious, but being controlled by this new creature."

"Oh no," Ace said under his breath, unable to keep track of his rapid heartbeat.

"Oh no is right, son."

"'Oliver, this is Jakka,' the king said."

The fire in the cabin crackled louder, and Grandpa kneeled and moved his hands with the story, stirring up Ace's anxiousness all the more.

"Oliver didn't respond to his king, for as he looked closer, he saw the king's eyes were turning white, like Jakka's. Then Oliver looked around the room. The guards, the servants, the chefs. All their eyes were white, and it might as well have just been Oliver and Jakka in the room. But then he saw something else. All his brothers and his mother were rounded up together in the throne room. The entire palace was under this warlock's spell!

"'Hello, Oliver,' Jakka said." When Grandpa spoke for Jakka, his voice sounded shrill and wretched.

"Jakka stepped closer, and Oliver shook with fear.

"'What have you done with my family?' Oliver said.

"'I've made an improvement, if you ask me. Now they can't make their ridiculous decisions on their own,' the warlock said.

"'Fix them! Bring them back!' Oliver demanded.

"'I intend to, little one, although it's useless after all. This world is coming to an end, and your father's kingdom is about to crumble, then the world.'

"'What do you mean? What's happening?'

"'You'll find out soon enough, little one. Just do one thing for me, and I'll return your family. Bring me the red stone.'"

At this part in the story, everyone leaped from their seats.

"The Emerson Stone!" Cameron said. "That's what Oliver found, isn't it!"

"You mean it's from Earth, Grandpa?" Tamara asked.

Ace remained in silent shock, feeling pinned down by the rock in his gut.

"And so," Grandpa continued the story, ignoring the questions, "Oliver knew exactly what the warlock was talking about of course. The red stone he found in the cave. He agreed, and ran frantically looking for the little red gem, but when he found it, he stopped. What was this little stone? And why would Jakka need it? The creature seemed very dangerous. Was giving the stone away wise? So, he hid it on his person, and went back to the room where Jakka had his family held hostage.

"'Why do you need the stone? What's so special about it?' Oliver asked. That's when Jakka grew angry and stepped forward.

"'That's none of your concern,' the warlock said. 'Just hand it over, your family will be freed, and we will leave you to rot away with your world.'

"Oliver saw the look in this creature's eye. He wanted the stone, and he wanted it bad. But the creature was powerful! Why not just take it from him? After all, he had everyone in the room under a trance except for him. Oliver knew there was only one logical explanation—"

"The stone was keeping him safe!" Ace blurted. Grandpa smiled. Ace soon realized Grandpa had just revealed an important use of the stone. The reason why Grandpa wanted Ace to learn how to hunt witches. Having the stone made him immune to their magic!

"Exactly! So, Oliver began to negotiate with this warlock. He began to realize what power he may have at his disposal.

"'You free my family first! Then, I will give you the stone!' Oliver said."

Sweat trickled down Ace's forehead. This story had done

anything but disappoint. Everyone leaned in, and strange things ensued. The fire swelled and rose, and a stronger wind howled louder and louder through the windows as the story furthered in depth. New Eathelyn marched to the rhythm of Grandpa's story. The old man deepened in character. "'Listen to me, human, I am not one to test!' the warlock replied.

"'Really? Then why don't you just take the stone from me by force if you're so powerful? Why send me to get it? Why not just take it?' Oliver said. He was becoming sharp, and the warlock was becoming angrier by the minute."

Ace remembered Rio's training. Oliver was calling the warlock out on his lie!

"The palace began to shake and rumble, and the warlock yelled in fury. He was going to bring the entire place down.

"'If you will not give me the stone, then you and your family will die here and now with your pathetic world!' the warlock said. "You may think you're clever, but you're not. Wherever you run, wherever you hide. We will find you. We will never stop hunting you until the stone is found! Until the stone is ours!"

"Oliver was shaken with fright, and ready to take back what he said. The warlock was going to destroy them all. Oliver had no choice but to comply. So, he reached behind him, and grabbed the stone from his pocket." Grandpa held out his hand, mimicking what Oliver would be doing, and stopped speaking. The wind calmed, and the fire settled to its normal size.

"Then what happened, Grandpa?" Julie asked, now standing on her feet.

"What did Oliver do?" Cameron said.

"Yeah, like, seriously, Grandpa, you can't end it there!" Tamara said.

Ace said nothing, because he couldn't. His ability to speak had left him when he saw a tear roll down Grandpa's cheek. Grandpa looked at Ace and smiled the biggest smile the boy had ever seen. Grandma Martha stood from the couch and held on to her husband, smiling at all the grandchildren before them.

"Then," Grandpa said, "Oliver vanished."

The cabin shook and moaned. Pots and pans clanged together. The dark wood crackled. Winds like a hurricane rushed in and roared through the house like a dragon. They summoned the fire from the fireplace and surrounded Grandpa and Grandma in a fiery whirlwind, spiraling to the top of the cabin. With a flash of light, the fire drifted away, the wind stopped, and only the sound of chirping crickets in the rainforest crept through the pitch darkness it left behind. The cabin lay still, the air stagnant, spurring the urge to panic. But for a moment, none of them did panic. Ace stood next to his brother and cousins, staring and silently denying what lay in front of them. It was an emptiness. And it told a horrid truth none could bear to accept. Grandpa and Grandma had disappeared.

CHAPTER SEVEN

The Letter

Is everyone okay?" Cameron said. Ace hardly heard him over the ringing in his ears. The creeping darkness had him shivering. Where had Grandpa and Grandma gone? Were they dead? His body fell numb. He wasn't ready to lead his family. Where was he even supposed to lead them to? And why would they even listen to him? Grandpa never said he'd leave them alone!

"Yeah, I'm alright," said Tamara.

"Me too," Julie said.

"Ace?" Cameron said, placing his hand on his younger brother's back. "You good?"

Ace nodded as he trembled in his seat.

Julie stood and walked to where Grandpa and Grandma had been. "What just happened? Where are Grandpa and Grandma?" Her voice shuddered. Ace could tell she was fighting back tears.

"I don't know, Julie," Cameron said.

"Well, what are we gonna do?" Tamara said, pacing the floor. "We're stuck out in the suburbs of a big city in the middle of a country we've never been to before!"

"Everyone just calm down," Cameron said as he stood from the couch. Ace compared his shakiness with Cameron's statue-like demeanor. Cameron's leadership made Ace believe Grandpa had picked the wrong person for the job.

"What do you mean, 'calm down'?" Julie said, her voice climbing with fear. "Grandpa and Grandma were just eaten by a fire! And Tamara is right, we have no idea where we are!" She burst into tears and stomped on the ground. Tamara walked to her little sister and held her in an embrace, tears creeping down her cheeks as well.

"I know, I know. Look, we will just have to go to the city and ask someone for help. I'm sure they have a phone or computer where we can reach our moms and dads," Cameron said.

"That won't work," a familiar voice said. Everyone jumped back. Julie and Tamara yelped. They all backed away from the dark, shadowy figure in the doorway. Ace stood from the couch, realizing as the figure stepped forward that it was Rio. "There's no service out here. The drakes have made sure of it. They don't really care too much for other races, and keeping advanced technology away seems to keep others away as well," Rio said.

"What are you doing here?" Julie said.

Cameron stepped in front of Ace. "Step back!"

The sight of Rio settled Ace's jitters. Someone who could guide him had come along, making the task ahead seem more achievable. Maybe . . . maybe this was why Grandpa introduced him to Rio. Did Grandpa know he would vanish? The boy finally found the sense to speak. He stepped aside from his brother's protection.

"Guys, settle down, you all have met Rio before. We know he's a friend of Grandpa's," Ace said.

Tamara grabbed Julie as Rio stepped further inside the cabin. The Peppercorns backed themselves against the wall.

"How do we know he's not tricking us, Ace?" Tamara said.

"You're just being paranoid," Ace said.

"What would a Halder know about it? I'm not about to die because you're naïve!" Julie yelled.

"I'll tell you what a Halder would know about it!" Ace said, ready to tell her Grandpa had left him in charge. But before he continued giving Julie a piece of his mind, Rio placed his hand on the boy's shoulder. Ace turned, and Rio shook his head.

"The kid is right. Your grandfather and I were great friends," Rio said. "And unfortunately for you all, you really don't have much of a choice but to trust me."

"What are you doing here?" Cameron said.

"I came because your grandfather asked me to protect you all," the drake said.

"Protect us from what? We were perfectly okay when we were at home in Eveland. If Grandpa hadn't brought us out here, we wouldn't even need protection," Tamara said. She attempted to sound angry, but Ace heard the shakiness in her voice.

"There's an evil lurking in Yutara. The world is as unsafe as it's ever been. Your parents and grandparents knew that," Rio said. He stepped further in, Ace standing by his side. "It's hard to explain why right now, but your lives are in danger, and your family is trying to protect you."

"What do you mean? Are—are they o-kay? Our parents?" Cameron asked. It was the first time Ace saw Cameron shaken. Even slightly. And it didn't help his confidence. He too was heartbroken and terrified over the thought of his and the Peppercorns' parents in danger.

"I don't know," Rio said. All the grandchildren gasped. "The less you all know the better. It's safer that way. Right now, all of you need to gather what things you need for traveling. Only take what is necessary for survival. We will have to travel light."

"Where are we g-going?" Julie said.

"Gathara. It's the safest city in Yutara right now. Many allies and friends await us there," Rio said. His nose flared a little and his tongue clacked a couple times at the end of his sentence.

"Gathara?" Tamara said. "You're—you're joking, right?"

Ace found himself taken aback by the statement as well.

Gathara, like witches, was hardly spoken of in Eveland. Plenty of Evelanders believed the stories of the city were harmless children's stories. Fairy tales for entertainment. Others avoided speaking of it at all. The mention of the city made some uncomfortable, because the stories surrounding the city were so strange. Tales of an evil magic and . . . he caught his breath, eyes wide at the drake. *Witch hunters,* he thought. *Gathara is real!*

Rio stepped closer in, his eyes dark and telling. "Whatever you all think you know about Yutara, everything you thought was true, forget it. You just watched a fire swallow your grandfather whole, it should go without saying there's a lot you don't know about."

Julie whimpered timidly. Tamara squeezed her tighter.

"Wait a minute," Cameron said. "How did you know to show up here when Grandpa disappeared?"

Ace jerked his eyes to the drake. Cameron made a great point. Rio reached from behind his back and pulled out a piece of parchment. He opened it and read it out loud.

> *"Dear Rio Atarion,*
>
> *I regret to inform you that my time has come to an end. My generation, I should say. This may not make sense to you, but my family will not be protected from the evils of Yutara any longer. They will find me soon. After me, they will undoubtedly look for my children and grandchildren. Their lives will be in grave danger then, and I'm entrusting you and the Indies to protect them. Keep an eye out, because we will be arriving in New Eathelyn as soon as we can. Shortly after our arrival, I'm afraid they will find and take me. You must bring my children to Gathara, where they will be safe. I would bring them myself, but I'm afraid I wouldn't make it that far before evil found me and took me. I look forward to seeing you soon,*

one last time, my dearest friend.

Sincerely,
Marty Halder"

At this, the children became speechless. For a moment, the howling wind creeping through the windows alone disturbed the quiet.

"We can't wait any longer here," Rio said. "Gather your things. We must leave now." His firm tone told of his slipping patience.

The children scattered like mice, grabbing everything they could. But before Ace could head to his room and start packing, Rio pinched his shirt. Ace turned, and the drake handed the boy the letter, pointing to an area on the bottom of the paper.

"I didn't read the entire thing aloud," Rio whispered. Ace looked at his pointing finger.

P.S.

Keep my witch business hidden from the children. The less they know, the safer they are. However, I am entrusting one of my grandchildren to you for training. He has the heart of a warrior, and he will be a great leader in battles to come. When he is ready, he will take over your intermittent position as leader of the Indie Hunters. Thank you, Rio.

Ace looked to the drake, and a tear spilled out of the boy's eye. Rio winked at him and patted him on the back.

"Keep it between us," Rio whispered. "You will have more answers in Gathara."

He nodded, and Rio shooed him off to gather his belongings. The boy scurried to his room to find Cameron packing his things. He looked around, being sure to grab only the essentials. No one spoke. He and Cameron left their rooms once they had enough, but once they left the door of their room, Ace fell behind and out of sight. He let Cameron rush to the living room and snuck back into the bedroom unseen. Frantically, he scuffled to his bedside and pushed the bed just far enough to get to the trap door underneath. He moved the junk he and his brother kept under the bed until he saw the handle for the trapdoor Grandpa had told him about.

"Ace, c'mon, we're waiting for you!" Cameron yelled from the living room. Ace's heart beat quickly.

"On my way!" the boy said. He wiped his sweaty palms on his pajamas and pulled the handle to the trap door. There sat the chest of golden edges. Inside, a stone of secrets was now his to uncover. Ace remembered Grandpa's words. *"I've put the stone in a trap door under your side of the bed. When the time is right, take it with you. Until then, don't so much as touch it."* Hard to imagine a more appropriate time than this. He reached into the hole burrowed in the hardwood floor, placed the watch in his pocket, and pulled the chest free. His uncertain future. His last gift from Grandpa. A Grandpa who disappeared, leaving the weight of world to rest on the shoulders of a twelve-year-old boy.

CHAPTER EIGHT

Nothing Like This

The peak of the mountain teased Ace until they arrived. He'd been awaiting a break from the draping humidity. But the altitude offered no such comfort. The wind blew harder, but it still carried a miserable stickiness. The Yutarian moon, full and yellow as a lemon, sat high in the sky. Midnight was near.

Cameron pulled their wolf mount to a halt, and Ace glanced behind, taking in his last view of New Eathelyn. Hiding in the valley between him and the ocean, the muted rumble of the waterfalls rendered him still and quiet. This was the city he'd last see his grandparents. His stomach turned over.

"Goodbye, Grandpa and Grandma," Ace whispered to himself. "I'm gonna miss you."

Ace turned at the warm touch of his older brother's hand on his back.

"They loved us, Ace. They did what was best for us," Cameron said.

Ace nodded wordlessly.

"I think we've made it far enough tonight," Rio said.

"Aren't we still in New Eathelyn?" Tamara asked.

"We're almost out now, but yes. We're just on the edge of the city," Rio said. He hopped off his spotted bear mount and walked to the nearest tree to tie him off. Ace and Cameron climbed from their large wolf; the Peppercorns, from theirs. Rio had some animals prepared for travel outside the cabin after Grandpa had disappeared. Ace found himself envious of Rio's mount. Something about the bear with shiny teal fur and dark blue spots seemed to entrance him. He and Cameron's wolf was neat too. It was friendly, and its being five times their size conveyed its ability to protect him. But its thick, dark gray fur just wasn't as wondrous as the bear's. Nor did it blend in as well with the environment.

Rio hitched his mount to a tree, and the grandchildren did the same. The trees in the mountains grew taller and wider than the trees below. Interwoven vines scattered under the giant trees like spaghetti noodles.

The drake walked to one of the pouches hanging off his bear's saddle and threw a few sleeping bags to the kids. He pulled some fruit out and fed it to the animals. The children prepared their sleeping bags, spreading them out in a circle around each other.

Julie broke the silence. "All of this is your fault, Ace."

"What?" Ace said. "How is this *my* fault?"

"Julie, that's a terrible thing to say, this is nobody's fault," Cameron said.

Tamara chimed in, "How do you know that, Cameron? Grandpa has been treating Ace weirdly ever since we got here. How do we know what they were sneaking around about had nothing to do with this?"

Ace hawked in his throat. "So, what are you saying? You think I did something to make Grandpa and Grandma disappear and leave us stranded?"

"I don't know what you did. But it's just a little spooky that all this happened at once. That's all I'm sayin'," Tamara said.

Why didn't Grandpa tell them I was going to lead them before he left? The stupid Peppercorns will never believe me.

"You're being ridiculous, Tamara," Cameron said.

Julie stomped her foot and put her hands on her hips. "She's not! It's true, Cameron!" The little girl walked violently toward Ace, pointing her finger until she poked him in the chest. "You stupid Halders could never deal with the fact that the Peppercorns have always been better," she said with a continual jabbing of her finger. "Grandpa loved us more because we made him prouder! I'll bet you've been itching to get back at him! Make him disappear, even! That would make all your problems go away, wouldn't it?"

Ace grabbed his little cousin by the wrist. "You're nothing but a spoiled, evil witch!"

"Don't call her that!" Tamara said, now rushing to Ace.

"Ace, calm down. Julie, apologize," Cameron said. He ran to Ace and mistakenly tripped Tamara on her way to defend her little sister. She fell to the ground, face first into a pile of green leaves. "Oh, Tamara I'm sor—"

"Tamara!" Julie yelled. She slapped Ace's arm until it stung and he let go.

"It's what you are!" Ace yelled. "And your sister is too!" Tamara stood to her feet with rage and pushed Ace to the ground. Cameron bolted over to Tamara. Before he could reach her, Rio leaped in the middle of the fight with his frog legs.

"Enough!" the drake roared. His wide voice shook the air like thunder, scaring off a few birds, and the grandchildren ceased. "Let go of each other, now!" And they did. They all stepped aside, the Peppercorns beside each other and the Halders beside each other. "Now is not the time to be blaming people! We have a long journey ahead of us, and all the bickering and fighting is going to make it much longer, and much less bearable! Now, make up your beds, and help me gather wood for a fire!"

The grandchildren quietly remained as they were for a moment, unnerved at the thought of walking on drake-temper eggshells.

"Now!" Rio commanded. They hastily dispersed throughout the forest. Obviously, Cameron and Ace went on the opposite side of the forest as Tamara and Julie.

"And don't you dare go far. The forest in these mountains is hardly populated. All the wild animals live up here. And most of them are nocturnal," Rio shouted.

Ace and Cameron continued through the forest standing beside the road. Ace heard nothing but the varying chirpings of the wild forest insects borne of the groaning wind. Under the moonlight, the colors of the forest were vibrant enough to pop through the shadows of night. The richest green-yellow he'd ever seen before, with a hint of teal splotched throughout.

"What's with those stupid Peppercorns!" Ace said. Cameron gathered some branches he found on the ground.

Cameron sighed. "I don't know, little bro."

"I mean, what did we ever do to them? I can understand wanting to be ahead of us in competitions, or the chores we had on Grandpa's ship, but accusing me of hurting Grandpa and Grandma? Who does that little brat thinks she is?" Ace said.

His blood boiled. He clenched his fist. He paced back and forth. At this point, he'd stopped helping his older brother gather wood. He was just venting and flailing his arms in the air, occasionally swiping viciously at the vines. He wanted to go back to his backpack, pull out the chest, and show everyone the Emerson Stone.

Look what Grandpa gave me and trusted me with! He picked me above all of you. Especially you Peppercorns!

But he stopped himself, realizing the stupidity of the last thought. The Peppercorns wouldn't believe Grandpa gave the stone to him anyway. And Rio didn't even know about the stone yet. Then, another thought occurred.

The map. Am I the possessor of the stone now that Grandpa is gone? Where is the map? What is the map? Did I miss it?

"You have every right to be upset, bro. I'm not happy either. She took it too far," Cameron said. "I don't know what made her say that. Julie acts worse than Tamara sometimes. It's like ever since the day when she—"

"Please," Ace said. "I'd really rather not talk about that right now. Or ever again."

Cameron stared at Ace wordlessly with eyes hung low. When he spoke, it was somber and quiet. "Sorry, bro."

"It's okay. I know you didn't mean anything by it."

Cameron sighed and shrugged. "Well . . . guess we better get some wood and take it back to Rio."

Ace nodded and helped his brother.

After a brief silence, Cameron spoke. "Hey, Ace, what was on the letter?"

Ace jolted up from gathering branches. "What're you talking about?"

"I saw Rio pointing at something on the letter to you before I went to my room. What was he showing you that he didn't read to us?"

"Oh." Ace swallowed. "Uh—nothing."

"You know I would never side with the Peppercorns in a million years, bro, but it does seem a little strange. All these secrets between you and Grandpa, and then . . . *this.*"

"Hey, I know just as little about his disappearance as you do. That completely took me by surprise. In fact, because of the things he's told me, it was the last thing I expected to happen."

"What did he tell you?"

"I can't tell you, Cameron."

Cameron frowned and grunted. "Why not? Grandpa isn't even here anymore."

"That's not why I can't tell you. It . . . it . . . it's more important than that. It's bigger than that. It's for your own protection that you don't know, that's what Grandpa told me."

"My protection? What about yours? So, you can protect yourself, but I can't? You're younger than me!"

Cameron's comment made him speechless. Ace was hardly the ideal candidate for trusting with such information. He had no clever response, and no real answer. He didn't even have any answers for *his* questions.

"I don't know why Grandpa told me what he told me. But I trust him. And you should too," Ace said. Cameron scowled at him and returned to his chore. They spent the next few minutes collecting what they could find on the forest ground and brought it back to the shoulder of the road, where Rio had set up a camp. The Peppercorns had already arrived with, Ace noticed, more branches and twigs than he and Cameron, and Rio had set them up in a teepee shape circled by piles of stones. Their sleeping bags lay around the fire.

"Took you long enough," Julie said as the Halders approached. Cameron and Ace ignored her and tossed the branches next to the fireplace.

Rio started a fire and cooked some small animals he had killed and skinned while the children got the firewood. The night continued in silence, but not the tranquil kind. They ate in silence, stared into the fire in silence, cried in silence, and the fire crackled in a wild dance with the tension in the air. Ace remembered plenty of rough days—mostly involving the Peppercorns—this family had before, but nothing like this.

He observed the shared horror in everyone's eyes, all of them lamenting. Even though the Peppercorns fought their tears, they'd occasionally brush their shirt sleeves to their cheeks when their eyes brimmed. His mind wandered through all they'd just been through, and his insides caved under the weight of it. He had to find the map Grandpa warned him he might pass up. He had to find a way to convince the Peppercorns he had to lead and protect them. He had to take over Grandpa's business as a witch hunter. He had to fight the power of the seventh realm. Nothing made sense. Where was he even supposed to begin? His view of the fire was distorted through the welling of his eyes, which followed the immense grief of losing Grandpa and Grandma. His stomach rose to his throat, and his heart quivered. He wasn't prepared for this. Grandpa Marty picked the wrong grandchild.

CHAPTER NINE

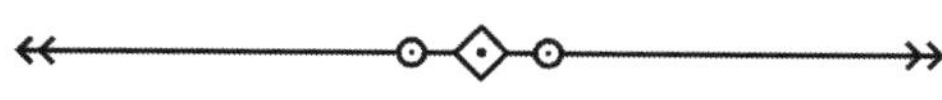

Rio's Grief

The sun had just barely crept above the horizon and peered through the trees. Ace hardly slept all night. A long day awaited him now. He sat straight with distaste at everyone else's peaceful slumber. It didn't make sense how Grandpa's passing left their sleep undisturbed. Maybe for the heartless witches he called cousins. But not for Cameron. Even Rio was . . .

Where was Rio? An empty sleeping bag sat on the ground in his place. Ace stood and looked around. No sign of him. He stepped quietly through the campsite and a faint sound of breathing came from the drake's bear. He tiptoed to the mount. Sniffling sounds became more audible with every step forward, and he peeked around the bear's side to find Rio sitting with his back turned, facing the rainforest.

The drake turned and invited Ace to sit. Rio's sad eyes didn't take from his confidence. The drake grieved shamelessly.

"How long had you known my Grandpa?" Ace asked as he sat next to Rio.

The drake's slimy green skin glistened all the more from his tears.

Rio sniffed twice, and his tongue clicked. "So long I can hardly remember, kid. He found me when I was just a boy."

"Found you? What do you mean?"

"I was an orphan." The drake wiped his nose. "Ever since I can remember I was living on the streets, eating scraps and doing whatever I could to survive."

"In New Eathelyn?"

Rio shook his head. "In Adamsville actually."

Ace looked up curiously. He had always wanted to visit Adamsville. It was the biggest city in Eveland. But Grandpa always warned him of the city's dangers. He never understood why either. In movies and TV shows Adamsville seemed a life-filled city of glamour and brilliance. Not to mention the irony of Grandpa's best stories taking place in big cities. Ace's stomach shriveled at the thought of Grandpa again, and he wanted to stop thinking about it.

"Adamsville! That's pretty cool. I've always wanted to go there. How did you end up there? I thought drakes were all from Oola."

Rio rattled his tongue in a chuckle and patted Ace on the back. "Well, originally, yes. But the different kinds have dispersed throughout Yutara a lot recently. There's plenty of drakes and jags in Adamsville. However, most of them don't travel to the smaller areas of Eveland. People in the suburbs aren't as welcoming to strangers as city folk. I was born in Adamsville, to answer your question. And trust me, it's not the same as how people rattle on about it."

Ace sighed. "Yeah, that's what Grandpa used to tell me." He remembered the drake in his dad's office. Everyone treated her like she was a monster, the poor lady. She was awfully nice. She used to tell him stories about the city. "G'raka, a drake lady who worked in my dad's office in Abes City, she told me a thing or two about Adamsville. She said there's people who live underground and steal food and cause earthquakes and sometimes suck people in. Mostly just stories."

Rio chuckled. "I've heard those rumors too. Just city lore though. When the Indies first were stationed in Eveland, they suspected those rumors may be witches, but we never found any sign of witches living underground. Turns out they really were just stories."

Ace smirked. The change of subject seemed to be easing the drake's grief, which made him feel guilty about asking his next question. Nevertheless, his curiosity persisted. "How did Grandpa find you?"

Rio scratched his head. He turned his eyes to the sleeping grandchildren, then back to Ace. "Let's just say I got mixed up with the wrong people, and your grandfather saved me."

Ace nodded.

"Your grandfather took me in like I was his own child. He taught me how to fight the very evil I was mixed up in. Marty Halder will be remembered as one of Yutara's greatest heroes."

"Rio," Ace whispered. "Why did Grandpa pick *me*?"

The drake stared into the forest wordlessly, and the wild animals howled in the distance. Seconds passed . . .

"It doesn't make any sense," Ace whispered. "He's never picked the Halders for anything. Especially me. Why trust me with such a huge burden? Why trust me at all? What in the world made him think I would be the best candidate for a witch hunter?"

Or trust me with The Emerson Stone? Or trust me to fight the seventh realm? But he couldn't say those things, of course.

"I'm sorry I was so cruel to you on your first day of training. Us drakes can be irritable at times," Rio replied. Ace was slightly taken by this response, and a little aggravated, as it answered none of his questions.

"It's okay, I guess."

"Your grandfather had some wild methods sometimes, Ace. I don't know why he chose you for this task. But let's just hope he didn't take his wild methods too far this time."

"I guess we'll find out once we start training again," Ace said as he shrugged.

"Guess so," the drake said. He looked around to make sure no one was listening again, then leaned in to Ace. "There's more than one reason I'm taking you to Gathara, you know. It's the capital of the Indies. The best witch hunters in the world are trained in Gathara. If there's anything you can learn about witch hunting, it'll be there."

Ace scratched his head. "I'm kinda confused, Rio. Most people, at least as far as I thought, don't even believe in witches. And Gathara is known as a fake place in Eveland. Up until yesterday, I thought witches were just a part of Grandpa's stories. Now you're telling me not only does Gathara exist, but it's a city dedicated to hunting down witches?"

Rio sighed. "There's a lot you don't know about. You've had it all thrown at you at once. Your grandfather had much more to him than meets the eye. Everything about him had some hidden message. I learned that pretty quickly about him. The stories he's been rattling about to you probably weren't just stories. The reason people don't believe in witches is because they are masters of deception. They live among us and cast spells right before our very eyes every day. They're hard to find, and only the most skilled hunters can pick them out in a crowd. They've even gotten so skilled as to convince an entire country, namely, Eveland, that a real city doesn't exist."

"Are you saying I could have met a witch before and didn't know it?" Ace asked.

"I'm sure you have plenty of times. And if you haven't met a witch, I'm sure you've met a parcel."

"A *what?"*

Rio sighed, and before he could respond, something rustled behind them. The grandchildren might have been awake then. Too dangerous to keep talking. The drake shushed Ace, anchored his weight on the bear as he stood, and looked toward New Eathelyn. The boy stood as well and set his gaze over the mountain. The sun had just climbed above the ocean, and a beam lit up Cameron, who had begun rolling his sleeping bag, in the early-morning orange.

"Rise and shine!" Rio said. Julie and Tamara rolled around and moaned before waking. "Come on now, let's get going. The sooner we leave the sooner we get to shore. We should arrive before nightfall if we leave now."

Cameron stretched his arms high in the sky and yawned a big yawn. "Something just came to mind," he said. "Why did we leave Grandpa's ship in New Eathelyn? Oola is an island, and we're going to need a ship to get from here to Heorg."

Julie and Tamara peered skeptically at the drake. Since they had already expressed their distrust, Ace imagined how this unnerved them. But it didn't set too well with him either. Damion! What about him? The boy remembered Grandpa whispering something to him before they left. Did the crewman know about Grandpa disappearing too?

"It's quicker this way," Rio said as he pulled the sleeping bags from under the Peppercorns. The drake kicked piles of dirt where the fire had been and covered the area in twigs and sand. "And your grandfather's ship is such a strange sight, it could be spotted miles away on the open sea. We'd be a perfect target. A sitting duck. We'll attract much less attention by taking a drake ship in Myrka."

"What's after us, Rio?" Julie said.

"Yeah." Tamara staggered to her feet. "You keep rushing us and talking about this 'evil' chasing after us. But I haven't seen anything. It's just a little sketch is all I'm sayin'."

"Oh." Rio placed his hand over his mouth. "I didn't realize I was rushing you. I'd just thought that seeing Grandpa Marty gobbled up by fire would be enough to concern you a little bit. I'm sorry."

Julie teared up, and Tamara pulled her little sister close to her side. "Way to be sensitive, frog boy," Tamara said.

"Your grandfather didn't ask me to be sensitive. He asked me to protect you. It'll be hard to do that if you don't listen to me." The drake packed the sleeping bags in the pouches of his bear and hopped on the saddle. He glared at all the grandchildren and began marching down the trail. Tamara sassed him silently behind his back.

"C'mon, we better go," Ace said as he untied his wolf. He hopped on the saddle, and Cameron hopped on behind him. Rio was getting ahead, nearly disappearing as he trailed down the mountain. "He's not stopping."

"Whatever," Tamara said. "I still don't even know if we should trust him."

"Me neither, Tamara," Cameron said. Ace scrunched his face in confusion and looked back to his older brother. How could Cameron not trust Rio? More importantly, how could he side with a Peppercorn? "But we don't really have much of a choice. If you and your sister want to stay back and starve or get eaten by some animal, then be my guest."

He kicked the wolf's ribs, and they leaped along the mountain trail. Good thing for the Halders, wolves were faster than bears. But Ace hardly paid attention to how fast they were catching up to Rio. For his eyes were glued to the rainforest of spirited teal the newly risen sun now commanded.

The trail twisted and turned down the mountain through the greens and yellows of the Oola Rainforest. The spaghetti vines, now resembling a threaded linen in the full light of day, allowed the sunlight not but the width of a needle's eye to pass through. Broad, oval leaves slumped over the sides of the winding trails with a glossy shine.

Luckily an irregular breeze swept by every so often to offer a break from the weight of the muggy air. It blew back Ace's hair and traveled through his shirt sleeves as the wolf huffed and puffed and kicked dirt from the path. Ace liked to watch the moist sand splatter on the glossy leaves and tumble back down to the ground. He looked behind, having to move his head a few times to see past Cameron, but eventually he caught a glimpse of the Peppercorns. They were a good bit further behind, and he was tempted to tell Cameron to lose them. But he wasn't cruel. Even though he thought the Peppercorns would do it to him in a heartbeat. They caught up quickly, an intimidating look in their eyes as they passed. It was the same way they looked when they did anything, really. Determined. Despite all the recent trauma, they maintained their competitive edge.

We're better than you, and we will always be better than you.

Apparently, competing with Cameron and him was still a priority in the midst of having to run for their lives. But what bothered him even more than their determination to be better than the Halders was, ironically, how much it bothered him at all. His heart played tug of war. One side told him being better than the Peppercorns wasn't important. It told him Grandpa loved all his grandchildren equally, no matter how good or bad they were at some sport or skill.

Yet he still couldn't shake the daunting shadow hanging over him every moment he spent with them. They really were better than him. At everything. But Grandpa chose him for some odd reason. This was his chance. He was going to prove the Peppercorns wrong once and for all. This was the true reason Grandpa chose him, and he was not about to let the old man die in vain.

CHAPTER TEN

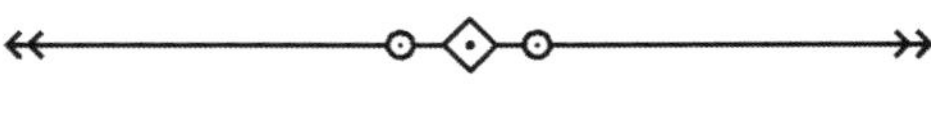

Secrets

An hour's worth of traveling brought them halfway down the mountain, where trees and shrubs grew more timidly. A sharp turn took them to a space visible between a split of the palms. There was an entrance to a short path ending in a ledge, overlooking a valley. Small stone structures poked their heads from the forest ceiling in the distance, and a hint of purple grazing the horizon's top layer suggested their journey's approaching end, where the beach city of Myrka awaited them.

The trail wound again and brought them back around to the meager valley. A waterfall spilled from the cliffs and into a spring. Ace may have been impressed with it if he hadn't just spent the past few days in New Eathelyn. This baby waterfall was a far cry from even the smallest New Eathelyn waterfall. Rio pulled off the road by the spring and hopped off the bear.

"We can rest and eat here for a moment," the drake said. The wolves and bear went straight to the spring and lapped the water.

The grandchildren weren't far behind. They all kneeled beside the spring and cupped the water to their mouths. Except Ace.

The unbearable sun had beaten down on him long enough. He leaped from his wolf and splashed in the pool with a perfect cannonball. The perfectly cooled water wrapped his body in a refreshing sensation. Once his head broke the surface, he swam to the waterfall, opened his mouth, and let the water slide down his tongue. One sip turned to a hundred gulps, and as the crystal pure water continued to slip down his throat, he closed his eyes and experienced bliss for a moment. He heard a few more splashes. His eyes opened to find the other grandchildren joining in the merriment.

"Man, this feels so good," Cameron said as he floated on his back.

Julie and Tamara giggled and splashed each other, and Cameron swam to the waterfall next to his little brother.

"Ace," Cameron said. Ace had just closed his eyes stuck out his tongue again.

"Whaa?"

"What did you mean when you said Grandpa picked you?"

Ace jolted his head up and looked at his brother eye to eye.

"What are you talking about?"

"Oh c'mon, don't play dumb anymore. I heard you talking to Rio up there."

Ace glanced at the drake, who swam on his back while the sun gleamed from his shiny drake skin. He looked back at Cameron.

"What did you hear, exactly?"

"All I heard was you ask Rio, 'Why did Grandpa pick *me?'* The rest was all mumbled and I couldn't make it out. I was kind of half asleep and I thought I was dreaming at first. When I woke up you guys had already stopped talking."

Ace felt a little relief. At least Cameron didn't hear everything. But why was it so dangerous to keep things from Cameron? Other than Grandpa telling him not to tell the other grandchildren, he really didn't understand why he couldn't tell Cameron what was going on.

"Cameron, I've already told you I can't tell you anything. Why do you keep pressing me about it? I hate having to hold this stuff in and you're not making it easy."

"Because, I'm just tryin' to find answers. I wanna know what happened to Grandpa, Ace!"

"So do I."

"Why do you trust that drake so much?"

"Because Grandpa trusted him."

"But don't you trust *me*?"

Ace sighed. It was no use trying to hide it anymore. He didn't have to tell Cameron about the stone. Just enough to make him satisfied.

"Alright, but don't tell anybody, Cameron," he said. Cameron smiled and wrapped his arm around him, rubbing his knuckles on the crown of his head. A classic nuggie.

"That's what I'm talkin' about, little bro!"

Ace laughed. "Stop it!" He shoved his brother away. "Okay. Grandpa has been running a secret business." He began to whisper. Which may have been pointless under the disguise of the rushing waterfall.

"What kind of business?"

"He kind of hunts witches."

Cameron's face drooped almost immediately. "You gotta be kidding me, Ace."

"What?"

"I thought you were going to tell me for real!"

"I *am* telling you, Cameron! It's true."

Cameron furrowed his brow. "You're getting too old to still believe his stories, Ace."

"His stories are true, Cameron! He took me to his armory even."

"Armory?"

"Yeah, in a little cave away from the cabin. It's full of all kinds of weapons and blasters. But not just regular blasters. They have a setting that can only capture magic. That's why he brought us to New Eathelyn. Rio's a witch hunter who worked for Grandpa, and he can protect us."

Cameron itched his head and squinted. Ace could tell his older brother wasn't sure whether to believe him.

"So, you're saying that witches are actually . . . *real*?" Cameron said.

"Apparently so. And they're after us."

"Why would they be after us?"

"Uh, I'm not exactly sure." Of course, he knew it probably had to do with the Emerson Stone.

"Okay, okay. But why did he decide to tell this to *you* and no one else? You said he *picked* you."

"Yeah," Ace said. He chuckled and rubbed the back of his neck. He wasn't sure how to break this to his older brother, someone he looked up to, and someone who was ten times more qualified for the job than him. "About that. Grandpa kinda turned the business over to me. He wants me to run it."

"What?" Cameron's face flushed. "But why you? You're the youngest!"

"Shh!" Ace covered Cameron's mouth. He looked over to Rio and the Peppercorns still swimming around in the pool, paying no attention to their conversation. A wave of relief came over him and he let go of his brother's mouth.

"Do you even know anything about witch hunting?" Cameron said.

Ace shook his head. "No. I trained with Rio one day for a couple of hours. That's it."

"This doesn't make any sense," Cameron said.

"I'm as shocked about it as you are. Look, I've told you something Grandpa asked me to keep a secret. You *have* to keep this between us. Grandpa told me that the more that you and the Peppercorns know, the more dangerous it is for all of us."

"Okay, but on one condition," Cameron said.

"What?"

"If we're running away from witches, then we need all the protection we can get. You should teach me whatever you learn about witch hunting. If we have to defend ourselves, then two is better than one."

Ace sighed at his brother's persistence. He closed his eyes and rubbed his hands over his face. It did make sense. Cameron was probably going to be better at it than him anyway. He just didn't know how he was going to be able to train Cameron in secret.

"C'mon. Halders stick together!" Cameron said. It didn't seem Ace had much of a choice.

He sighed again and looked his older brother in the eye. "Fine. Deal," he said. And they shook hands. Cameron pulled him into a tight, one-armed hug.

"Now we really *are* sticking together, little bro. Like Halders are supposed to. No more secrets between us, okay?"

Ace gave a weak smile and nodded. "Sure. No more secrets."

CHAPTER ELEVEN

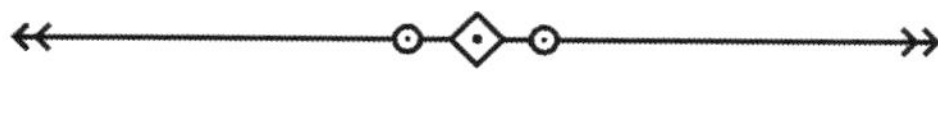

Myrka

As they made their final approach from the forest to the beach, Myrka became visible. It stretched along the coast. Most of the huts and tents and stone buildings sat on the sand, with a few here and there in the forest. Docks went on for miles over the ocean as numerous ships pulled ashore. It was like a stretched-out version of the New Eathelyn marina. Civilians passed by on similar canine and feline mounts as the drakes in New Eathelyn. Rio led the way as their mounts slowed to a steady walk, and the Halders were at the end of the line.

Drakes captained the trade ships, although there were a few jags and Evelanders here and there. Other than on television, it was the first time the grandchildren had seen jags. Frightening creatures, they were. It's the reason why they were typically cast as bad guys in movies and shows. Ironically, they were generally considered to be the most peaceful race within the four borders.

Many things made jags fearsome creatures. Their eyes of red, yellow, or white; their spotless skin, gray as a thunderstorm and smooth as a waterworn stone. While some jags had a dark, charcoal skin, other jags had varied in brighter shades of gray.

They soared in height. The average jag reached seven feet tall. The males' brute strength was terrifying. Especially the fat ones; though, most were cut like diamonds.

Two things made jags distinguishable from any Yutarian race. Their antlers and hooved feet. The antlers resembled those of a deer, but with variations. Jags' antlers grew specific to an individual jag at their coming of age. Some twisted from their temples and curled behind their ears. Others grew long and twisted by their shoulders. Some antlers grew from their foreheads and twisted up high.

The heavy wind of the beach carried the sounds of the city. Merchants either yelled from their huts (in their strange click-clack language) or bartered and haggled with the sailors and residents of Myrka. Crews of the larger ships unloaded their cargo while the captains collected payment. The overseas trading was booming. Rio took the grandchildren away from the path of merchants and brought them to the open beach, where ships were either anchored just offshore, or tied to a dock. Further down the beach, tens of drakes and humans formed a line under a tall wooden sign with drake language inscriptions. Pictographs clumped together to mean one thing. Below the pictographs was a translation:

Heorg Ferries

10 per ticket, 5 per mount

Once they all arrived at the line, the Peppercorns hopped off their wolf.

"Ugh, my butt's starting to feel numb," Tamara said.

Cameron nudged Ace and leaned into his ear. "It's probably trying to match her brain."

Ace laughed with his brother. Tamara scoffed at the Halders, then helped her little sister down and Ace and Cameron followed next. Ace stretched long and wide. He hadn't realized how much his back had been hurting from riding the wolf for so long until standing gave him relief. The long line crept along. No doubt they would be there a while. Rio eventually hopped off his bear and held the reins as they stood in line. He reached in the saddle pouches and grabbed a few canteens, then tossed them to the grandchildren.

"Drink however much you like. The ship tickets usually come with meals and beverages," the drake said.

"And hopefully a big, soft bed!" Julie said.

Rio rolled his eyes and turned around. Ace unscrewed his canteen and gulped the water left inside. It was the very same pure water they had at the spring a few hours back. He tilted his head, eyes fixed on the purple evening sky and the poufy scattered clouds, as he gulped every drop in a second.

"Haaa," Ace said in approval.

"So, little bro," Cameron said. He leaned closer into Ace's ear. "What do these witches look like, huh?"

"Cameron!" Ace said under his breath. He pushed his brother back a little. "Not here! Someone could hear us."

"Right. Sorry," Cameron said. "I'm just a little excited and curious. My mind's been thinkin' 'bout it nonstop since the spring."

"I'll tell you what I know whenever we get a chance to be alone," Ace said. Cameron nodded and winked. This dropped a rock in Ace's chest. His older brother's wink looked identical to Grandpa Marty's. Ace rubbed his eyes to keep anyone from seeing them water. He turned his attention away from his projections of Grandpa on his older brother.

Rio turned to face the grandchildren. "All of you get your things from your saddles."

Cameron and Ace looked at each other and shrugged but did as instructed. Ace didn't realize how fast the line had moved. They approached the sign much quicker than expected. A cramped wooden hut sat on the sand directly under the sign. A few drakes smiled from the ticket-collecting window. One of them was yellow as the moon with a head like a snake, another a water drake with shiny silver scales, and the last one looked like the snake one, only with red skin.

The yellow snake lady looked to Rio and spoke in the drake tongue. Rio responded. The lady looked at him with frustration and shook her head. Rio clicked his tongue again. She shook her head no again, now very annoyed.

"I think Rio doesn't have any money," Ace said.

"Oh! Say no more!" Julie said. She reached into her purse—which she apparently brought because it was a necessity for survival—and took a handful of credits out. Eveland credits. Parchments in different shades of blue. In the middle of each parchment was the face of an Eveland leader. On the one-hundred-credit parchment—the only ones Julie had—was the face of Angus Kar. Famous for winning The Heorg War. Not much was taught to Eveland students about The Heorg War. Other than the Evelanders helped free the jags from some dictatorship spreading through the country.

Well, Ace thought, *looks like I was right about her huge allowance.*

The little girl burst to the front of the line and slapped the credits down on the shelf.

"That oughta cover it!" Julie said. The drakes behind the window chuckled with each other.

The yellow drake clicked several times at Julie with a playful smile.

"She wants to know how old you are," Rio said to Julie.

Julie gave a curtsy and smiled from ear to ear. It was time to put on a show and do what she does best. Soak up all the attention.

"I'm twelve and a half," she said. The snake lady patted her head and handed her back the pile of credits.

"They don't accept Eveland currency, Julie. Credits are no good here, only owes . . ." Rio's eyebrows popped up, and he leaned close with a glint in his eye. "Unless your rich dad somehow had a collection of fae crystals he gave you?"

Julie pouted and slowly shook her head no. Rio sighed and gently nudged her aside.

Fae crystals, Ace thought. *That's something I'd like to see.*

The drake yanked the mounts with the reins in his hand and

handed them to the snake lady. Rio and the drakes behind the counter exchanged a few more click-clack words with one another. The snake lady seemed to get angrier by the minute, and Rio wasn't very persuasive. After a moment or two, Rio finally stopped trying to argue with her.

Rio looked around in frustration. "Fine." He walked to the open beach area followed by the grandchildren. What was happening? No tickets? How were they supposed to get to Heorg?

They all gathered in a circle to the side of the ferry line.

Julie pouted and crossed her arms. "That lady was extremely rude."

"What's going on, Rio?" Tamara said.

Rio looked intensely at the snake lady behind the counter. "Ace, come with me quickly," the drake said.

Julie put her hands on her hips as she scoffed at Rio. "What? Why do you need *him*?"

Ace waved at his little cousin and smirked as he walked to Rio. She stuck her tongue out.

"You all stay put. Don't go anywhere here," Rio said.

"Like, where would we even go?" Tamara sassed.

Rio grabbed Ace's arm and walked him far enough away from the circle of the grandchildren, so they couldn't hear.

"We're in danger," Rio whispered.

"What do you mean?"

"I mean that one day of training we had together better come in handy, because this town is crawling with witches."

CHAPTER TWELVE

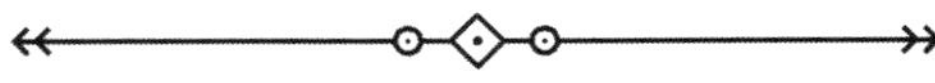

The Map

Rio looked around and pulled a small hand blaster from his pouch and slipped it to Ace unnoticed. The cool slick surface of the gun's metal caught him off guard. The AMHB's chrome body shimmered as it caught the light of the falling sun. Ace grabbed it and placed it in his back pocket, then threw the bottom of his shirt over it to hide it.

"I—is there one close by?" Ace said. He hadn't anticipated being this nervous. What if the witch cast a spell on him or something?

Rio eyed Ace keenly. "I have a sense about these things, Ace. I've been doing this a long time. They're everywhere in this city, and the longer we are here, the more likely they will come after us. Or, to be more specific, the more likely they will come after you and your family."

Ace swallowed a lump in his throat. "Shouldn't we give some blasters to the others? I mean, at least Cameron. The more arms we have the better, right?"

Rio grabbed Ace by the arm. His sharp fingernails pinched Ace's skin and the boy grimaced. "Do not tell them a *thing* about this. Your grandfather picked *you*. Not them, got it? Witches know it when they're being sensed, and they don't like people knowing they're around. They want to stay hidden. Being a hunter makes you a target. And you, being Marty Halder's relative, makes you an even greater target. You must be trained not to give it away when you feel one is near. I'm probably putting us in more danger by telling you about the witches here. If all of you are walking around sweating and shaking, scoping out every Myrkian you think might be a witch, they will pick up on it, know we have something to hide, and come after us."

Ace's heart pumped faster with every word the drake spoke. Rio's teeth showed through his snarl, and being this close revealed just how sharp they were. The boy nodded in silence, and the drake let go of his arm.

"What can I do to not give away that I'm looking for one?" Ace said.

"For starters, don't look for one. The last thing you want to do is snoop around. Just keep your eyes open. The witches are scoping out people themselves. And as many as there are in this city, one will eventually find us."

"Why are they after us?"

"I think they know who you are, and they're trying to stop you from getting to Heorg."

"Who I am? What are you talking about?"

The drake leaned close and whispered. "You're Marty's grandkid. They know him better than you think. Just keep your eyes peeled and lay low, okay?"

"How will I know it's a witch?" Ace whispered back.

"Trust me," Rio said as he placed his hand on Ace's shoulder, "if they find out who you are, you will know right away."

"Okay. But what makes you think there are witches here?"

"Drakes are natural barterers and hagglers. Our mounts are easily worth ten times the amount of money they were asking for those tickets. Mounts are priceless in Oola. None of the ticket collectors acted strange when that lady turned down the mounts. And what's even worse is that none of the drakes in the line did either. I think they're lying. Trying to delay us. They must have some sort of suspicions."

"Are you sure that means they're witches though? I mean, the lady could have just been having a bad day."

"I've been doing this a while. I know what I'm talking about."

Ace looked around suspiciously, then caught himself. No snooping. Dead giveaway. "Okay, Rio. So, what are we going to do?"

"I know some Indies stationed here. I'll bet somebody either has a ship or knows someone who does. But they won't accept visitors, even a young hunter like yourself. You all will have to set up camp outside the city and wait for me while I look for them," Rio said.

"Are you sure that's the best idea? I mean, if there's witches around, I would feel much safer if you were next to us," Ace said. "You saw how bad I was in training. What if—I mean—I can't do this Rio. This is insane."

"You will be fine," the drake said. "I will lead you to a safe place outside Myrka. If you stay off the roads and away from the shadows, you'll be okay. I will move as quickly as I can, and hopefully bring help back."

Ace stared wordlessly at the drake.

"Your grandfather picked you for a reason. Like it or not, protecting this family is your responsibility."

Ace tipped his head with an agreeable hesitance. Rio led him back to Cameron and the Peppercorns huddled together.

"We're going to set up camp outside the city for the night. I will have a ship ready for us in the morning," Rio said.

"But how?" Tamara asked.

"I have my ways, little girl."

"Why don't we just go back to New Eathelyn and get Grandpa's ship?" she said.

"Enough with that! I've already told you all that's not going to happen, and I don't want to hear another word about it!" Rio said with a growl.

After a few moments of bickering, the drake convinced the grandchildren to do as he said. He saddled the mounts again and took them further along the path they'd entered the city on. Deeper into the rain forest, the roads disappeared behind them. It frightened Ace, seeing as the only way they would find the road again is if Rio came back. He pulled some strange food from the saddle and handed it to the grandchildren. It was long and green like a cucumber, but slimy and wet. Ace broke his apart, and yellow ooze dripped from the middle. He made a face like he'd bitten into a rotten berry.

"You expect me to eat this goop?" Tamara said.

"Eat it or starve, your choice," Rio said. "It's all we've got." The drake stepped further from the circle of children, ready to venture off. But he stopped and turned to face them first. "I'll be back as soon as I can. Stay hidden and you'll be alright." Rio and Ace stared at each other, the drake nodded, Ace nodded back, and then Rio disappeared into the forest. Rays of white light beamed into the rainforest as the sun slowly fell into the horizon.

"Okay, that's it. I'm going," Julie said.

"What are you talking about?" Ace said.

"I'm not following that frog man anymore! He gives me the creeps!"

"Anything unfamiliar gives you the creeps, Julie," Cameron said.

Tamara stood up and put her hands on her hips. "Julie's right, Cameron. We still don't know if we can trust him or not. I say we go back to New Eathelyn and get someone to take us back to Eveland with Mom and Dad."

"You heard Rio. It's not safe," Ace said.

"What is it with you and the weird frog thing?" Tamara said.

"Yeah, Ace. I'll bet you're working together, aren't you? Rio made Grandpa disappear, and now you're helping him make us disappear!" Julie said, wagging her finger at him.

"Believe me, if I could make you disappear, you'd be long gone by now," Ace said. Cameron chuckled under his breath.

Tamara jumped in between Julie and Ace. "Okay, stop, you two," she said as she spread her arms between them. This shocked him. Tamara not taking Julie's side? A first if there ever was one. "Fighting isn't going to get us, like, anywhere right now."

"She's right," Cameron said as he stood. "I say we wait here 'til Rio gets back. He's protected us so far."

"No, he hasn't," Julie said. "He's only taken us to Myrka with no money to get us on a ship. He hasn't done anything to prove that he's protecting us."

"Julie's right, Cameron. We just met Rio a couple days ago, how do we know we can trust him?" Tamara said.

"But you've known me and Cameron your whole lives," Ace said. At this, there was a break in the argument, and an eerie silence filled the air for a moment. Ace finally broke it. "Trust *me*, at least. If you don't trust Rio."

Julie scoffed and crossed her arms. "Trusting my life to a Halder? That's about the dumbest thing we could do."

"Grandpa was a Halder, wasn't he?" Cameron said. "Like it or not, you two are Halders by blood. But we're not so much as an ounce of Peppercorn. We should stick together."

Tamara sighed and patted her little sister on the back. "I'm totally not comfortable trusting my sister's life to a weird drake we don't know. We've followed him long enough, and now we, like, finally have a chance to run."

"Tamara, don't do this. It's way more dangerous to travel the roads right now, I'm telling you," Ace said.

"What're you hiding?" Julie said.

Ace's heart fell to his gut. The little girl stepped closer to him, squinting as if she were trying to penetrate his secrets with her eyes.

"You and the frog man have been all buddy-buddy since Grandpa's disappearance. Well, I'm not buying it! You stupid Halders are gonna have to follow that stupid drake by your stupid selves." Julie grabbed her things, and Tamara hers. They untied their wolf and hopped on, moving further into the rainforest.

"Guys!" Cameron yelled. "Why would Rio leave us like this

with the perfect chance to escape if he was trying to kidnap us? You're being dumb!"

Ace flailed his arm at the Peppercorns. "Ah, let 'em go. They wanna be stupid and get attacked by a witch, that's their problem."

"Get *what*?" Cameron said. He grabbed Ace by his shirt and pulled him to his face. "Are you saying there's witches in New Eathelyn waiting for them?"

"Something like that, I guess. Rio just said that Myrka is crawling with witches, and if we don't want to get captured by one, to stay off the roads. We need to leave Oola as soon as possible," Ace said. He then yanked Cameron's hands off his shirt.

"Ace, we have to go after them if there's really danger like that. We can't just let them run away. What could the witches do to them?" Cameron said.

"They did it themselves. It's not my fault they're so stubborn. And honestly, I have no idea, Cameron, probably cast some spell on them and turn them into chickens or pigs." Ace began to laugh. "Now I *really* want to let them go."

Cameron grabbed his bag and threw it over his back. "Grandpa probably just told us that in his stories to make them more kid-friendly. They could be in serious danger, Ace. We have to go."

Ace sighed and grabbed his bag. "Fine, fine." He turned and untied their mount. "Rio's gonna wonder where we are, and we're probably gonna get lost in this jungle."

Cameron shrugged, and they climbed on their wolf. Anger welled in Ace. Going to risk themselves to help the Peppercorns? Probably the worst day he could have imagined. On the other hand, Cameron's point was valid. Who knows what witches were truly capable of doing? After all, like Rio said before, Grandpa's stories were not just stories.

Ace's mind paused, and his eyes grew wide.

Grandpa's stories aren't just stories, he thought. A light bulb went off in his brain. How had he not thought of this before? He should have kept it in his head, but his excitement overtook him, so he said aloud, "The map!"

CHAPTER THIRTEEN

The White Light

Cameron didn't hear Ace's epiphany, thank goodness. He was focused on following the Peppercorns. The brats weren't too far ahead yet, and the Halder brothers were getting close. Unfortunately, the large tree leaves covered what was left of the sun, and darkness had enveloped the forest. The only good thing about it was Julie using her phone as a flashlight. A bright white light made it easy to follow them in the pitch darkness.

Ace found himself aggravated when he thought the night might relieve them of the heat, but the humidity still crawled over his body, and countless sweat beads fell from his hairline as he and Cameron chased after their cousins.

"Julie, Tamara! Just stop for a minute!" Cameron shouted from behind. They didn't respond, but it seemed they were picking up speed. How far had they gone from the campsite? It was only a matter of time before they were completely lost. The Peppercorns stopped for a split second, then cut a corner behind a tree. The flashlight from Julie's phone flickered as they ran by the leaves and bushes.

"I think they found the road," Ace said.

"Jeez, how did they do that? I nearly thought we were lost for good," Cameron said.

"I dunno, Cameron. They've never been lost in the woods before. I guess they're just good at everything without even trying." Evident frustration hid behind his every word. He and his brother chased the light further into the rainforest, and just as he predicted, they were led to the Peppercorns riding their wolves along road. All they had to do was follow it to New Eathelyn now. The brothers needed to stop them. Fast.

The eerie, dark rainforest sent chills down Ace's spine. A strange sense of fear rose in him, and his gut twisted in a knot. Even if they made it to New Eathelyn, whatever waited for them there would not be pleasant.

"We really need to catch up to them, Cameron. I have a bad feeling about this place," Ace said.

"Yeah." Cameron paused and inspected the rainforest around the road. "I feel it too."

Ace looked ahead, and the light flickered wildly, beginning to fade.

Julie's battery must be dying, Ace thought.

Cameron sniffed. "Do you smell smoke?" he asked.

Wait. Julie's and Tamara's phones hadn't been charged for days. The Peppercorns hadn't even touched their phones the entire trip. Their phones had to have been dead already! They weren't following a flashlight. . . The Peppercorns weren't using the light to see. . . the light was using them. . . the light was. . .

"Hurry, Cameron!" Ace yelled.

"I'm trying. They have the faster wolf. Don't worry, they will stop when her phone dies."

"I don't think that's her phone," Ace said. *It's magic.*

Cameron kicked the wolf's ribs with all his might. The wolf howled and dug its paws deeper into the sand, but the Peppercorns sped away. Cameron kicked it again, and again. Ace wiped the sweat from his forehead and slushed it away.

"C'mon, wolf! Let's go! Let's go!"

The wind brushed Ace's skin. His pulse quickened. His sweaty palms slipped as he reached for his slick chrome gun. Rio was right. Once a witch came after them, he would know it was a witch. Hopefully his one day of training paid off. He tried slowing his breathing, but it was no use. His wrist shook violently at the grip on his AMHB. He wasn't cut out for this. They were finished now. The boy swallowed and prepared himself as he saw the Peppercorns slowing down. He heard their faint cry ahead.

"Help! Help!" Julie screamed. Cameron kicked again, and the wolf snarled and howled. Its paws dug deep into the moist dirt, kicking it up into Ace's jeans. The Peppercorns' wolf had now come to a halt, but the light wandered into the forest. Cameron stopped beside the Peppercorns' wolf, but only Tamara sat on the mount, her eyes wide with fear and confusion. With no time to talk, Ace hopped off the mount and bolted into the forest, the blaster now held in the palm of his hand.

The sound of Tamara's panicked crying echoed behind him. "Julie! Julie!" Ace heard Cameron's feet crunching the twigs and leaves behind him as he followed Ace into the woods.

"Ah! Let go! Let me go!" Julie screamed. The ball of white light blinded him from seeing his younger cousin. But he heard her being thrown against the trees and bushes in the forest as the light zipped around, dragging Julie behind. Ace dodged, hopped, and ducked every obstacle the forest had to offer. The light brightened. He was catching up.

"We're coming Julie! Just hang on!" he yelled. The light took a sharp turn into a large set of boulders in the middle of the rain forest, much like the stone buildings of the drakes. It was shaped in several domes, and the light dragged Julie inside the biggest one in the middle, with a dark, arched entry. Ace ran into the cave without hesitation. The light had completely faded, and there was only pitch black all around.

"Julie! Where are you?" Ace said. His voice echoed through the nothingness. His desperate voice bounced back to his ears and attacked his confidence.

"Help, hmf, hmf!" Julie's voice became muffled and hidden. Then came a laugh. A shrill laugh. A laugh Ace compared to a sharp knife scraping a metal surface. No mistaking it for anything other than what it was. A witch had Julie.

Waves of fear coursed through his veins. What to do? He gripped the handle of his blaster, tight as he could, ready to meet his end with a fight.

"Release her, now!" Ace said. His voice shook with fear, even though he tried to hide it. The witch laughed, and it echoed through the hollow cave. No way of telling where she was hidden in the darkness.

"I*ss* thi*ss* the Halder? Look at your arm*ss* and leg*ss*. They're hardly the *ss*ize of a twig," the witch said. She hissed horridly with her words. "You *ss*hould quit now, little one. Ju*ss*t quit and walk away, before anyone el*ss*e gets hurt."

Ace spun in circles, trying to find where the witch was. Darkness surrounded every corner. What did she mean quit? He couldn't give up! If he was going to die, he was going with a fight. He clenched his fist and thought hard. There had to be a way out. He took the blaster, aimed it high, and squeezed the trigger.

CHAPTER FOURTEEN

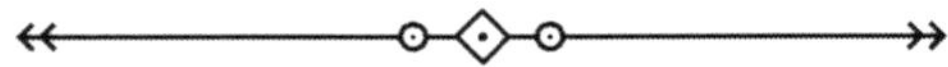

Death and Destruction

The witch screamed. The sound of the blaster thundered through the hollow cave. From the weapon, a large ball like a tiny sun shot into the cave ceiling, and waves of a bright orange light fell down the walls of the cave. It grazed over a shadowy figure in the corner, revealing her position. The witch screeched and bolted away. Ace caught a small glimpse of her. It was the snake lady with red skin from the ticket counter, and she held Julie close with her slimy hands over her mouth. The light from the orange ball in the ceiling faded, and darkness took the cave again.

"You almost got her," Cameron whispered.

"Do that again . . . and I'll cur*s*se thi*s*s little girl for the re*s*st of her mi*s*serable life," the witch said.

"What do you want?" Ace said.

"I thought I made that clear. Quit. Agree to walk away now, and I will relea*s*se your friend," the witch said.

Friend. She doesn't know Julie is my cousin.

"Walk away, and bring an end to the Indie*ss*," the witch continued. "It's usele*sss* to defy the will of the council. It will only bring death and de*ss*truction."

Council?

The urge to comply with the witch tempted him. It seemed a fair trade, given his desire to return home and pretend none of this had happened. But even worse than his fear was a pressing sensation on his heart, telling him negotiating with a witch was even more dangerous than resisting one. But one thought occurred to him. Just like Oliver in Grandpa's story, the Emerson Stone was his. He was immune to the witch's magic. He smirked.

"Quit what? I don't know what you're talking about," he said, attempting to stall while he looked for the witch again.

"Don't play dumb. That weapon in your hand wa*ss* made by the Indie*ss*. I know who you are, Halder," the witch said. "And the council would like to offer you the chance to retreat now. Thi*ss* path you will take in Marty's foot*ss*tep*ss* will only bring ruin to you and your loved one*ss*. *Sss*tarting with thi*ss* little girl."

Ace went to respond when something came over him. It spread in waves of tranquility through his body. It seemed as if a light turned on in the cave. It seemed as if he was looking through a pale film, revealing the witch and Julie in the corner. Did they see this light too? The witch and Julie weren't reacting to it. Something snapped inside him, and he knew just what to do. He drew his blaster like the blink of an eye and pulled the trigger. The tiny sun left the gun in a thunderous explosion and caught the witch in the chest. She screamed and dropped Julie. Beams of powerful light burst from the ball in the drake's chest as she fell to her knees. The cave lit up as the witch's magic lost its power. Julie rolled on the cave floor, and Cameron bolted to her and picked her up.

"C'mon, let's get outta here!" Cameron said, grabbing Ace's arm with Julie thrown over his other shoulder.

"Wait," Ace said.

"For what?"

The rays of orange light swarmed the drake witch and

wrapped her up. Her face grew pale, and she stopped fighting it as her power weakened. She rolled on the floor, wrapped in an anti-magic straight jacket, glowing with a radiant orange light.

"You've been warned, Halder!" the witch shrieked, rolling and struggling in a horrid display. "We will not stop coming for you! We will end you, the Indie*ss* will fall, and the coun*cc*il will have Yutara!" The witch laughed hideously until it turned to a cough.

"Just leave her!" Cameron said. Ace nodded. They turned and ran back into the forest.

Tamara yelled from the road to guide Cameron and Ace back. They rushed past the trees in the forest until they found themselves at the road. Tamara grabbed Julie hysterically from Cameron and sobbed. She held her little sister in a tight embrace.

"Oh, Julie! Are you okay? What happened?"

Julie nodded as her eyes welled with tears. She trembled in Tamara's arms and gripped her tightly, too frightened to say much else.

"We told you—" Cameron stopped to catch his breath. "We told you not to go running off."

"Is now, like, really the time for saying I told you so?" Tamara said.

"You knew about that lady?" Julie said, turning to Ace. "And you said nothing?"

"I said nothing to try and protect you. Which I can't do if you go running off into the forest by yourselves," Ace said.

"Protect us? A Halder? And you're the scrawniest little Halder there is! We can protect ourselves if you would just warn us next time!" Tamara said.

Cameron leaned in close to Tamara's face. "That scrawny little Halder just saved your sister's life! Which he wouldn't have had to do if you had listened to him in the first place!"

For a moment the sound of Julie's cries alone bothered the silence. She wiped her nose, sniffled, and said, "Thank you, Ace." Ace nodded. He might have said you're welcome if he were not so shocked. Did a Peppercorn just thank a Halder? "I hope I never see that lady again," Julie said as she buried her head in Tamara's shirt.

"What was that thing anyway?" Tamara said.

Ace and Cameron looked at each other. "I guess we have to tell her," Cameron said.

Ace shook his head in disagreement.

"Tell me what?" Tamara said.

"The less you know the better. If I told you, it would only make what just happened more likely to happen again," Ace said.

Tamara wasn't happy with this, which didn't surprise Ace. Even after saving Julie's life, the Peppercorns were too proud to trust him.

"I don't think we have to worry about that, Ace," Cameron said, placing his hand on Ace's shoulder.

"Why no—" Ace was interrupted as Cameron pointed into the forest. The very same ball of white light which had taken Julie before was returning, but with friends. Hundreds of them hovered in the distant forest shadows, and the grandchildren shot to their feet in a panic.

"Let's go! C'mon!" Ace said. They darted to their mounts, and the specks of light zipped faster.

"We have to find Rio!" Cameron said. Ace and Cameron climbed on their mounts, and the Peppercorns on theirs. Luckily Ace didn't need to worry about the Peppercorns' riding abilities. They took off past the Halders before Cameron could get his first kick in on the wolf's ribs. In seconds, they bolted down the path. Ace looked behind, quickly wishing he hadn't. The bright lights flooded the path behind them by the thousands, illuminating the rainforest, and they were catching up. Too bad they didn't have magic wolves. Ace pulled free his hand blaster, doing the only thing he could think of. He fired a few shots, and the magic lights scattered for a second, but returned to formation and zoomed even faster along the path.

"Can't this thing go any faster?" Ace said.

"I'm trying!" Cameron said as he kicked the wolf repeatedly.

Ace panted and fired at will. It was no use—the lights swarmed them. Two of them grabbed Cameron and yanked him from the wolf mount to the ground. It knocked Ace off and he tumbled along the path in a cloud of dirt. Pain jabbed at his body. He gathered himself and jumped to his feet, ignoring the aches he felt everywhere. The lights pinned his brother to a tree, and a witch came forth from the forest shadows. Then another. They manipulated the balls of light with their hands. The other lights surrounded Ace but didn't attack him. They went straight for the Peppercorns, who had stopped ahead to make sure Cameron was alright.

"Just go! I'll help Cameron!" Ace said. But the lights yanked Julie and Tamara from the wolf and dragged them violently along the road. The lights pulled them to their feet and pinned them against the tree next to Cameron. Their bodies were frozen under some magic spell.

Five or more witches emerged from the shadows. Moments ago no one had stood there, but the witches just appeared from nothing where the shadows were strongest. They stepped from the darkness and surrounded them in a circle. Ace smelled something burning as he watched black smoke wisp through the air. What was he to do now? One blaster wouldn't save them all. He looked around, but no ideas came to mind. There was no hope. They were surrounded. The witches were a mix of drakes, jags, and Evelanders, all seeping black smoke.

"Thi*ss*?" a witch said. Ace couldn't tell which one, because none of their mouths were moving. Only voices echoing in a slithery ambience.

"Thi*ss* is the one who captured our witch?" another said.

"No matter. Prodigy or not, he will learn his le*ss*on tonight. To defy the council, is to bring death and destruction," another said.

"His friends," another said. "Strike them down."

"No!" Ace said. He fired his AMHB at one of the witches. It caught one of them and wrapped it in the cocoon of orange light. But another thing happened he did not expect. More tiny suns rained from the sky and caught two or three more of the witches. The rest of the witches scattered about the rainforest, screeching and shrieking. The balls of white light holding Cameron and the Peppercorns disappeared, and they fell limp to the ground, choking and catching their breath. What was going on? Ace turned around.

"Rio!" He said as a smile stretched across his face. The drake ran after them, the chrome hunter's rifle in his hand. But he wasn't alone. There was a water drake to his left, and a jag to his right, both with hunter's rifles. An X-shape vest wrapped around their torsos with pouches holding weapons and orange ammo.

"Let's go, we don't have much time," Rio said. Ace nodded. The jag and water drake grabbed Tamara and Cameron, and Ace grabbed Julie. It was then he realized they had all been unconscious. No time to wake them, as Rio had already begun marching along the path, both hands holding his rifle forward. The other two hung their large rifles on their backs, holding an AMHB in the hand not being used to hold the children over their shoulders.

Since the hunters hadn't brought mounts, they left the childrens' mounts behind and trotted along the path. Not too fast. Not too slow. Rio told them running had no benefit, being impossible to outrun a witch's magic, even on a mount. Instead, a confident walk with their weapons forward let the witches know they meant business. Ace combed the forest with his eyes, twitching at every slight movement, expecting the worst.

"Don't look for them," Rio whispered. "Looking for them shows weakness and fear. And trust me, you will find exactly what you look for. Keep your eyes ahead and focus on getting to your destination."

Ace nodded, although he was painfully aware his confidence lacked. He found himself jerking his head back to the road constantly. Every time he heard a noise he would flinch and point his blaster. The water drake or jag would slap his arm.

Eyes ahead. Eyes ahead.

Flickers of white lights surrounded either side of the forest again, following them as they marched along. Ace's heartbeat quickened. Everyone else kept their eyes forward and didn't react, so he bit his frightened tongue and mimicked them. His palms shook at the itch to pull the trigger. But he couldn't give into fear. He couldn't panic.

Rio gave a hand signal behind his back, the jag and water drake nodded. Quietly, they pulled some orange ball from their pouches, and dropped them on each side of the forest. The white lights scattered away with the sound of several shrieks, and seconds later, the balls exploded into a bright orange powder.

Although shaking on the inside, Ace did as instructed, keeping his eyes ahead and ignoring the explosions and white lights following them. But the lights weren't following them anymore. From the corners of his eyes, Ace could see the forest showed only darkness.

The hike finished without another disturbance from a witch. Whatever Rio and the others did scared them off for good. Rio took them to a place on the beach where Myrka was long ended: a wide-open beach with nothing around but the sound of crashing waves. The moonlight glistened over a metal ship parked on the bare sand. The ship shone like it might under a spotlight as the clouds brushed under the moon.

Smooth glass arched over the cockpit, and the entire body of the ship looked more like a jet than anything else. Only it had a wider body and no wings. It was a standard hovercraft, meaning it hovered above the surface of the water. It didn't fly. The glass covering the cockpit opened. Rio and Ace set Cameron and the Peppercorns inside and buckled them in. He grew worried, for Julie, Tamara, and Cameron remained unconscious. How powerful was a witch's magic? And what had they done to his family?

"I can't thank you enough for this, Hurug. I will return your hovercraft as soon as I can," Rio said.

"Anything for a fellow Indie," the jag responded.

"Get that boy trained," the water drake said. "Tonight, he passed a great test. I'm certain he will prove to be a great leader, and a powerful hunter."

Rio nodded. "Thank you, Omnali. See you soon."

Ace climbed in and buckled himself in the co-pilot's seat, and

Rio climbed in the pilot's seat. The glass cover lowered till it sealed shut. The engine roared, its pitch climbing high and heavy. The surrounding ocean water seemed a blur as the hovercraft zipped away. The boy took a deep breath. He glanced behind at his family. Though they had not woken, their faces seemed peaceful. His heart finally began to slow down. They were safe now and making their way to Gathara, Heorg. Jag country.

CHAPTER FIFTEEN

The Council of Warlocks

Ace fixed his eyes on the endless ocean outside the hovercraft. Surrounded by nothing but the open sea again, he sighed. It reminded him of Grandpa and Grandma and their vacations. What would happen to Grandpa's beloved pirate ship now? What had Grandpa whispered in Damion's ear? Did the witches get him? He didn't want to think about it. He laid back in his seat and let his thoughts drift elsewhere.

The clouds cleared as he looked through the glass roof of the cockpit. Stars dotted the sky by the billions. They clustered together in an explosion of lime green, violet, blue, and yellow. Swirling, colliding, and illuminating the dark blanket over the sky.

"Nothing compares to the beauty of the open sea under a cloudless night," Rio said.

"I'll say," Ace whispered, head tilted and eyes fixed above. He glanced behind at his family again to find them still asleep.

"Don't worry," Rio said. "The witches just snatched their memory from them. They will wake by sunrise."

Ace's head jerked to Rio. "What? How much of their memory?"

"Just the past few hours. When we arrived and fired our weapons, the witches cast a spell on your family out of panic. Their magic was neutralized before the curse could have spread beyond memory loss. Sometimes when a witch casts a spell, they take your memory first, so they can keep their disguise around you. It might be the only thing working to our advantage right now. Keeping the witches a secret from your family is important to our survival. It's imperative we don't tell them what happened when they wake. Good thing for us witches want to be forgotten."

Ace tilted his head. "Why is that? I was—" Ace shivered as he finished his thought "—terrified when I had to face them. Don't they want that?"

The autopilot button glowed blue as Rio pushed it with his first finger. His seat rotated to face Ace. "Fear is only used after a witch has been caught and her disguise breaks free. Once they reveal themselves, they rely on fear and magic to control the situation."

"About that. What's with the weird little light balls that dragged Julie through the forest? In stories, witches turned kids to pigs and chickens and things like that."

"Those are stories, kid," the drake said with a hint of anger in his tone. He took a breath and calmed himself before he spoke again. "All witches don't have the same magic. I'm not exactly sure how all of it works, but some use their magic in different ways. There've been rumors of witches making water and trees and the wind obey their spells. I've never seen it though."

"Well, that sounds pretty intimidating. Why not use that? Seems like they could gain an awful lot of control with fear and magic."

Rio shook his head. "Deception."

Ace leaned in with a curious glance.

"A witch's most powerful tool isn't magic, it's deception," Rio continued. "Witches and parcels have manipulated their way into power in Yutara for the past few millennia. And they've been doing it right under our noses." The wind howled as it grazed the slick surface of the hovercraft.

"Right. Parcel . . . What's that?"

"Parcels are male witches."

"If parcels are male witches, what does that make a warlock?"

The drake's face turned cold and dark. "What do you know about warlocks?"

Ace shrugged. "Just stories."

"Warlocks are who witches and parcels report to. They started out as parcels and worked their way into becoming the most powerful sorcerers. They're so skilled with deception, one has never been seen before. We only know about them because witches speak of them often. They call them the council of warlocks." Rio leaned close and his voice darkened. "Witches say they have magic powerful enough to call fire, bring down buildings, and even cause earthquakes and storms. They say they can't be found or seen because they work in the shadows."

Ace's skin crawled. He shuddered and said, "So, you've never caught a warlock?"

The drake shook his head. "Never even seen one."

"What about a parcel?"

"*I* never have. Most hunters haven't, but it's happened only a few times before. Parcels are more difficult to catch than a witch. Most of the time it's just a witch controlling someone else's body, tricking a hunter into thinking they have the parcel, so the real parcel can get away."

Ace nodded timidly. He folded his arms and his brow wrinkled as a million thoughts buzzed in his head like a furious bee. "A witch captured Julie before you and your friends arrived. She told me I should give up and walk away, and if I '*defy* the council,' they will never stop hunting me. Is that what she was talking about? Are there warlocks after me?"

Rio's webbed ears pinned back. He rattled his tongue a few times and leaned close, elbow on his knee, chin in his hand. "I doubt a warlock is after you."

"Why's that?"

"Because, kid, they don't want to be seen. Parcels take witches as their slaves and have them do their dirty work. By the time they're warlocks, all witches and parcels work for them. They stay in the shadows and rule by the hands of their slaves."

Shadows. Hearing Rio speak of shadows reminded him of a line in Grandpa's story. The inscription above the Emerson Stone when Oliver found it.

Eldest will the keeper be
'Till shadow clouds all truth

Did the stone have something to do with finding this council? He couldn't remember the rest of it. How important was the story Grandpa told him before he disappeared? His brain racked his skull as he recalled bits and pieces of the story. He had to remember the poem. He had to remember the story somehow!

He faced Rio. "But don't the Indies want to destroy the council then? If so, then, eventually we will have to find these warlocks and destroy them, right?"

Rio nodded. "Well, that would be great. But it's impossible."

"Why?"

"Nobody knows where or how in Eathelyn Summers you find them, kid. It's hopeless. They're far too powerful. The Indies exist to protect the peoples of Yutara from the evils of the council. But destroying it will never happen," Rio said sharply. Ace sat back in his chair, not wanting to hear the drake any longer. Ace was dissatisfied with his response. Grandpa wouldn't have settled. If there were such a council, Grandpa would want it gone. It must have had something to do with the stone. Did destroying the seventh realm mean destroying the council? He needed time alone to sit down, consider the story, and look for the clues he needed to accomplish the task given to him by Grandpa Marty.

After the questions bothered him long enough, he couldn't resist the urge to speak again. "One more question." The drake nodded and rattled his tongue. "Why did the witches attack my family, but not me? Why didn't the witch just curse me and force me to give up? Instead she held Julie hostage and threatened me."

Of course, he knew the Emerson Stone kept him protected. He just wanted to make sure Rio *didn't* know.

The drake sighed. "Don't know. I was as shocked as you when I arrived, but the witches hadn't done anything to you. It does bring some things to light though."

"Like what?" Ace leaned closer in.

"Why your grandfather chose you. He had that same gift with witches."

"What do you mean?"

"Marty, your grandfather. Witches never tried to cast spells on him. He had the most unique ability to pick out a witch and capture them without the slightest chance of one resorting to magic. He faced countless of them, but they never so much as tried to curse or harm him."

Ace's eyes widened, his mouth agape. *Eldest will the keeper be . . .*

The stone protected him from the witches' power. But only the descendants of the keeper. The one who owned the stone. It all came together. When Grandpa gave the stone away, he gave away his protection. But not just his protection. All his children and grandchildren. Cameron, Julie, Tamara, and all their parents. Of all the Halders left in the world, to Ace belonged the only protection from the evil after them. This begged a deeper, more pressing question. One he feared he'd never find an answer for. Why did Grandpa choose *him?* Had he chosen his father, Colton Halder, all Grandpa's descendants would still be protected!

"I—I'm—" Ace stuttered. "I imagine this means the witches wanted my grandfather dead."

Rio nodded. "Yes. Your grandfather founded the Indies. His extraordinary abilities began to expose the deception of witches in countries across Yutara. Many civilians were persuaded by Grandpa, and eventually joined him. Overtaking witch after witch, your grandfather was a machine. He started a revolution. They became infuriated, not understanding why your grandfather was immune to their magic. They have wanted nothing more than to see him gone."

Ace's heart fell. The peaceful feeling of being safe fled once again. "And n—now that Grandpa *is* gone?"

Rio lifted his head, staring the boy directly in the eye. "I don't know. Honestly, when I first received the letter, I wasn't sure what to think. I still don't, actually." Rio scratched his head, sighed, and leaned back in his chair. "Many Yutarians thought your grandfather would discover this council the witches and parcels speak of. They thought he would bring an end to the evils that have taken hold of Yutara for so long. Now that he's gone, we realize that was a foolish dream. The council's hold is simply too strong in Yutara. Our only hope now is to fend off as many witches as we can and keep the Indies movement alive. But without Marty . . ." Rio paused and gave Ace a look of uncertainty. Ace returned the same look. Rio sighed, and he whispered hoarsely, "Let's just hope you have what it takes to be the next Marty Halder."

CHAPTER SIXTEEN

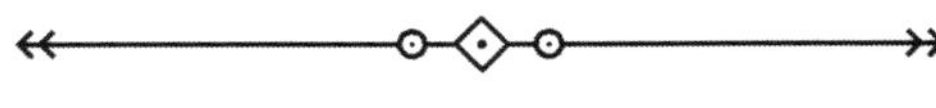

Marg

The tip of the sun breached the horizon, its light glimmering across the surface of the purple ocean. Ace had spent most of the night trying to remember the rest of the poem in the story with no luck, but eventually drifted into sleep. He woke to the sound of Rio's snoring bouncing off the metal walls of the ship. What about his brother and cousins? He looked back to them again. Still asleep. How much would they forget when they woke? Would Cameron still want to train as a witch hunter? A faint beep came from the cockpit interface. He sat straight. A square button flashed with a yellow light behind words reading, "Land."

Rio snarled as he woke. The sound of a male voice came robotically from a speaker on the dash of the cockpit.

Approaching Southeast Beach, Heorg. Approaching Southeast Beach, Heorg

The drake rubbed his eyes and pushed the button, turning the flashing light off. He grabbed the steering wheel and gained manual control of the ship. Ace leaned forward to get a better look at Heorg, but only saw a sandbar on the horizon.

The drake wiped his face with his hands. "Gonna be approaching soon."

Ace nodded. "Guess we'll have to prepare ourselves for witches again, huh?"

Rio shook his head. "No, no. Witches are few and far between in Heorg. Although, they do show up from time to time. But when they do, there's a hunter around every corner to take them down. Gathara and Heorg have a strange relationship. The city is still a part of Heorg, but kind of operates under its own law. So, hunters are in a lot of places in Heorg. It'll be the perfect place for your training."

Ace turned his head behind at the sound of a yawn. Cameron was waking up! Rio grabbed Ace's shoulder. The drake held a finger to his mouth. Ace read him loud and clear.

Quiet. They won't remember the witches.

Ace nodded. "Rise and shine," he said as he turned back to his older brother. Cameron rubbed his head and squinted.

"Oh man. I have a huge headache," he said. His brother looked out the cockpit glass cover to the ocean surrounding them, then around the ship. "How did we get here?"

"Uhh, we climbed in," Ace said with a chuckle. "You feelin' okay?"

"Yeah," Cameron said, rubbing his head. "I think so. Just needa wake up."

"We're getting close to Heorg. Maybe once we get some fresh air and start walking you'll get to feeling better."

Cameron nodded. Julie and Tamara's eyes slowly opened as they began to stretch.

"Ugh," Julie said, holding her stomach. "I think I'm sea sick."

Rio grabbed a bag and threw it behind him. "Please don't throw up in the hovercraft. It's not mine."

"I don't feel so great either," Tamara said.

"Well," Ace jumped in, "hope you all feel good enough to walk, because we're gonna be approaching Heorg soon."

"How long have we been on this thing?" Cameron said.

"Ten hours," Rio said.

"I—I don't even remember getting on," Tamara said, scratching her head.

"Me—" Julie covered her mouth as her cheeks puffed up. She removed her hand and relaxed. False alarm. "Me neither," she said.

"What are you talking about?" Ace said. "Don't you guys remember? After the ticket counter lady was so rude to us, Rio ran into an old buddy of his on the shore. He lent us the hovercraft. You guys must have been really tired because you fell asleep just as soon as we took off."

The other grandchildren looked around at each other, confused. Ace turned back to face the front of the craft. He and Rio winked at one another.

Small buildings rose from the horizon as the ship made its way ashore. Once land lay ahead, it became easier to see how fast the ship traveled. They soon made their approach to the docks. The wide buildings lay just past the beach. They weren't towering buildings, but they sat as long, block-like structures, built of white brick and stone.

They approached the land in between two of the docks. Only a few docks lined the beach, and off to the right and left was the civilian beach for recreational use. Jags surrounded the docked area as the ships arrived and departed. There were only a couple ships. It was much smaller than Myrka. Two jags dressed in reflective vests guided Rio's hovercraft ashore. The glass covering slowly lifted as they approached either side of the ship. The one approaching Ace's side was female. Yellow eyes, smooth, shiny skin, and a majestic way about her steps.

"State business in Heorg, drake," said the jag on the other side. Ace turned to face him. Male, lighter gray skin, a wide jaw, and pointy cheekbones. Anything but majestic.

"Rio Atarion, sir. I'm escorting my friend's family to Gathara."

The jag nodded. "How long will stay be?"

"Indefinitely," Rio said.

"What?" Julie said from behind. "What do you mean

indefinitely?"

"Are we, like, *moving* here? What about home? What about Eveland?" Tamara said, gasping in between each word. Ace turned and placed his finger over his mouth, shushing them without making a noise.

"Don't shush her, you stupid Halder," Julie said.

She's definitely feeling herself again, Ace thought. Julie didn't remember him saving her life. Any progress toward her accepting him as a leader had gone now. Back to being the stupid Halder.

The jag looked at Rio curiously. The drake shrugged. "If I had told them we were moving, they may not have come. Had to get them to safety, you know?"

The jag gave a suspicious look around the ship for a moment. He gave a hand signal to the female jag, and they both nodded.

"Good, sir. Ship inspection will only take moment," the jag said. They both walked away and signaled for other jags to come.

"Thank you," Rio said. The drake turned behind to face Julie, Cameron, and Tamara. "What's wrong with you? Are you crazy? These people are the good guys, why would you try and make them suspicious?"

Julie sassed Rio, using her fingers as quotations. "'Good guys,'" she said. "As far as I'm concerned, I still don't even know if *you're* a good guy."

"Would you shut up?" Cameron said. "The jags are coming to inspect the ship. Now is not the time."

Tamara punched Cameron on the arm. "Don't tell my little sister to shut up!"

"Enough!" Rio yelled. Everyone silenced. Jags jogged to the ship in navy blue jump suits, scanners in hand. The faint blue light from the scanners grazed over the surface of the ship in a gentle hum.

"All clear," said one of the jags. Rio nodded and climbed out of the ship. The rest of the family followed. The drake walked to the trunk and delivered each person their belongings. One of the jags hopped in the cockpit, but Rio stopped him.

"I don't have money to pay you for parking," Rio said. The jag looked at him.

"It's on house," the jag said. Rio tilted his head curiously, and the jag moved the hovercraft ashore, and out of sight, to, Ace assumed, the nearest parking facility.

Rio scratched his head. "Awfully nice of them. . ." He shrugged. "C'mon." The drake led them up the beach to a wooden walkway, leading from the beach to the city. Above was a metallic sign in blue neon lights.

Thraun Welcomes You!

Ace never understood why jags spoke in the common tongue. As he was taught in school, jag language had been a dead language for centuries. But they never taught him why. They walked to the end of the wooden path, leading to a paved road. The large brick buildings stood as high as a hundred feet on either side of the road. Hovercrafts of all different kinds sped through the streets at blazing speeds. They left only a timid hum as they zipped by just a touch above the ground. People bustled about on the sidewalks. The colossal jags made the few humans and drakes laughable in comparison. The buildings in the city were blocky, thick, and boring. They sat on either side of the road. Thraun was a city built in a barren wasteland of dirt with a few stout trees here and there.

"Okay," Cameron said as he made his way to Rio and Ace. "Where to now?"

"Well, we need to find some sort of transportation. It's a long, long walk from here to Gathara," Rio said.

"Ugh," Julie said, Tamara by her side as she walked the path to meet everyone else. "*This* problem again."

"Well, we solved this problem last time, didn't we?" Ace said.

"Out of luck," Tamara said. "And honestly, I don't even remember how it happened."

Julie crossed her arms. "Yeah, Ace. We can't just expect one of Rio's friends to just waltz on up every time we—"

"Rio?" said a voice. The group turned to face the voice. A male jag stood before them at least seven feet tall. His muscles burst through his thin t-shirt, and his voice was so thunderous, it made

Rio's voice seem friendly. His antlers shot straight up from his forehead, then bent directly backward and curled gently back up at the ends. He had blasters strapped to his sides on his belt. Ace squinted at them, guessing they were AMHBs.

"Marg!" Rio said. He bolted to the jag and they embraced one another in welcoming laughter. The gray giant's arms swallowed Rio. But once the jag noticed Rio's struggle to breathe, he released him.

"What brings you to Heorg? I thought you were deployed to Oola!" Marg said.

"It's a long story," Rio said, waving his hand. "Oh, I'm glad to see you. I'm protecting these children, and we need to get to Gathara. But we have no transportation."

The jag laughed and slapped Rio's back. Rio stumbled from the smack and rubbed his back where he took the hit. The thought of getting slapped by a hand of such a size made Ace wince. "Well this your lucky day, old friend. I headed there right now!" Marg said.

Ace and Cameron looked at Julie with a wide smile, trying to contain their laughter.

"Shut up," Julie said.

CHAPTER SEVENTEEN

Thraun

Marg led them down the sidewalk. The further in, the more people surrounded them. Not as many as New Eathelyn, but Ace enjoyed the ability to look around without having drake skin rub against him at every turn. Thraun's only downside was not having much to look at. The white brick buildings hardly varied in size or color. Not a whole lot of thought seemed to be put into the decoration of the city, but it sure was easy to get around in. Curiously, this jag town used at least twice as much technology as the Oolan cities, but somehow, seemed less lively. Dim neon lights lit the stores and their signs. Basic hovercrafts zoomed on the streets. And though they weren't on, the beams used for street lights reminded him of home.

Morning bled into afternoon, the sun climbing every hour. The dry, hot air rested on him, but didn't bear down on him like the muggy air in drake country. Rio and Marg conversed with one another, revisiting old times as they led the grandchildren along the sidewalk. Large window panes to their right revealed the stores and their merchandise. They passed restaurants—some fancy, some cheap. There were clothing outlets, grocery stores, phone stores, and pretty much any sort of store one could think of.

"So, you've been stationed in Thraun?" Rio asked Marg. Ace snuck his way forward and listened in as they continued. He and Cameron had been walking together, but his older brother was too focused on the city to hear Rio's conversation with the jag.

"For past two years," Marg said, his hand on Rio's shoulder. "I guessing you were pulled from deployment for recall, huh?"

Jag grammar confused Ace. He had trouble paying attention, as he'd still been dwelling on the first part of the jag's sentence by the time he'd stopped talking. Rio's webbed ears shot back. It was the first time Ace had seen something like that. Did it mean fear? Curiosity? Danger?

"Recall?" Rio said.

Curiosity, Ace thought.

Marg chuckled and slapped Rio's back again.

"You know," Rio said, "it stings when you do that."

Marg pulled his hand away. "Sorry. Too strong for my own good," he said.

Rio chuckled. "So, what's this recall thing about?"

"Oh. Seriously? I thought you kidding," Marg said. Rio's ears pulled back as he shook his head. "Elite recalled all hunters stationed in Heorg to Gathara. The deployed have stay where are. Some, like ones in Oola, have limited communication with Heorg, so they couldn't come anyway. I—I thought you knew. Honestly, I thought you one of ones in charge of recall."

"No. I had no idea," Rio said. "Why did I not have a say in this?"

Marg shook his head. "Dunno, ug."

Ace scratched his head, *ug? What's ug?*

"Have elite ever done this to you before?" Marg said.

Rio shook his head. "Never. I'm one of them. We make decisions together. Always."

"Hm. That strange," Marg said, scratching his head. "Maybe a'cause you in Oola, they couldn't communicate you."

"I hope so," Rio said.

"If you not back for recall, why traveling to Gathara?" Marg placed his hand gently on Rio's back and pointed his thumb behind them. "Anything to do with human children you brought?"

Rio chuckled and shoved Marg back. "Yes, actually."

Marg made a face at Rio which begged for more of an answer. He got none and gave up. The jag took them across a few more roads, and a few more turns. The sights didn't change much. The city lay in a basic grid. By the time they reached whatever destination they were headed to, Ace figured he'd know Thraun like the back of his hand.

Marg took them down one last street with hovercraft parking garages on either side. They flew up and down on the different levels and found their paths to the streets of Thraun.

"Hey," Julie whispered. Ace and Cameron turned their heads. "Aren't you two worried at all that Rio's friends have blasters strapped to their belts?"

"Not really," Ace said. "If someone comes after us, *they* will be the ones who are worried. It makes me feel safe."

"Yeah, what are you talking about? The jag is cool," Cameron said.

Tamara scoffed. "Can't wait to say we told you so when the drake and his buddies capture you, while Julie and I are safely running away."

Ace chuckled. "Whatever."

"You and that drake," Julie said. "Something is up between you two. And I'm gonna find out what it is."

Ace bit his tongue. *This again,* he thought. He fought the urge to remind the little brat he saved her life the night before. The thought of protecting the Peppercorns made him cringe. He remembered the only gratitude he'd ever received from Julie. Thanking him after he saved her from the witch. But her memory loss took it from her. It was a rarity anyway. So rare, he was sure it would never happen again, memory or no memory. What if he hadn't saved them? He chuckled. They probably deserved to be captured by a witch. Or . . . maybe that was a tad harsh. But not false. Especially after the time Julie . . .

"Hey, c'mon guys," Rio said. Ace and Cameron turned. Their conversation with the Peppercorns had them falling behind. Rio and Marg stood in front of a large building of brown brick. Blue neon lights lit a chrome surface over a set of double doors with glass.

Thraun Airport

Humans, jags and drakes rushed in and out of the doors, some fast, some slow, some at a regular pace.

"Oh man, I hate flying," Cameron said.

"C'mon, it'll be fun," Ace said, nudging him along to catch up with Rio and Marg.

"You only say that 'cause you've never flown before, bro," Cameron said.

Tamara and Julie giggled.

"Poor Camewon," Julie said.

"What are you? Three?" Cameron said.

The Peppercorns ignored Cameron's response as they all approached Rio and Marg. The two of them led the kids through the double doors.

"Hey, uh, we like, don't have money for a ticket," Tamara said. "We kinda ran into this problem back in Oola, remember?"

"Back in Oola, we didn't have Marg," Ace said.

Marg laughed. "I like this ug," he said, a finger pointing at Ace.

Julie stepped forward, hands on her hips. "We can't just ask a stranger to pay for our tickets."

"That right, little girl. I don't have money for that," Marg said. Julie smiled a snobby smile. "That why we not paying for tickets," the jag continued. Julie's smile faded.

"Your private jet is here?" Rio said.

"Well, I wouldn't call it private. It belongs to Ind—OW! What in world?" Marg said as Rio slapped him across the face.

Rio's eyes were wide and panicked. The grandchildren stared wordlessly in shock. Ace tried to contain his laughter. He knew why Rio slapped him. Marg was about to reveal the jet belonged to the witch hunters.

"That's, uh, for you slapping my back so many times," Rio said, nervously chuckling. "Gotcha, ug!"

Marg rubbed his cheek angrily. "Drakes are weird."

CHAPTER EIGHTEEN

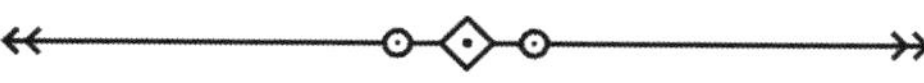

Hero

Hey Ace," Cameron said. Ace turned to face him. "What the heck is an ug?"

Ace shrugged. "Not sure." He had been wondering the same thing. "I guess it's some sort of friendly thing jags say."

They buckled themselves in their seats when the light came on. Cameron shook with the buckle in his hand. It took him a few tries to finally get it secure.

"Relax, Cameron. Flying can't be that bad," Ace said. Cameron smiled a weak smile at his brother.

Tamara, who had been sitting behind the Halders, next to her sister, leaned forward into Cameron's ear.

"Yeah," she spoke softly, "don't worry. I told Rio to bring plenty of extra diapers for you."

The Peppercorns giggled. Ace was about to respond, but the jet began backing up.

"Ow!" Ace said as Cameron clenched his leg.

"Sorry," Cameron said, releasing his hand.

Ace laughed and looked out the window. Excitement stirred in him as well as curiosity as to why Cameron hated flying so much. Lucky for Ace, his first time flying would take place in a luxury jet. The white seats were spacious and soft, cupholders were on the arm rests, and a hologram TV was in front of them, just behind the cockpit. White couches surrounding a finished wooden coffee table, and a bar were behind them. To the left, across the aisle, sat Rio and Marg, discussing things in a hushed tone.

Ace peeked out the window, watching airplanes take off and land, eager to see what Heorg looked like from the sky. The jet taxied to the runway. The engines fired and let forth a low hum climbing higher and louder every second. They were at the point of no return. Cameron closed his eyes and took slow, deep breaths. The jet sped across the runway, and the force pressed against Ace's chest and held him to his seat. The jet lifted, and moments later, they soared in the sky, everything now tranquil. The seatbelt light shut off and Ace unbuckled.

"C'mon, Cameron. Let's go sit on the couch," Ace said.

Cameron nodded nervously and unbuckled his seatbelt. The Peppercorns remained in their seats, watching the hologram TVs on the back of the headrests in front of them. Once they sat, Ace pulled a drawer from the coffee table. His eyes widened.

"What is it?" Cameron said. Ace pulled out a deck of playing cards, ripped and torn on the edges. Cameron sat up quickly. "I thought those were some ancient Earth game. Guess jags play cards too."

"Me too! I remember Grandpa used to call me Ace of Spades. He had a deck just like this on his ship." They both stared at the deck for a moment, reminiscing over the days spent with Grandpa on vacation, playing Go Fish, War, Blackjack, and all sorts of card games. Card games they often lost to the Peppercorns. He remembered the day Grandpa gave him the nickname . . .

They were outside the family hovercraft, headed to one of the Genesis Sabercats basketball games to watch Uncle Marcus play—as they frequently did—and as usual, the kids fought over who would sit in the back next to Grandpa.

"Ace," Grandpa said. All the grandchildren stopped their bickering. "It's just occurred to me I still haven't shown you my card trick. Whadaya say you hop in the back with me and I'll show you on the way, son?"

Ace's six-year-old-face lit with wonder. "Sure, Grandpa!"

The Peppercorns made sure everyone knew how displeased they were with this. But Cameron just smiled at Ace. Once they were on the way, Grandpa pulled three cards from his pocket and revealed them one by one to Ace.

"King of Hearts, Jack of Diamonds, and another Jack of Diamonds," Grandpa said.

"How'd you get two Jack of Diamonds, Grandpa?" Ace said.

"It's a secret," Grandpa said with a wink. Ace chuckled. Grandpa sorted through the trick, using his skilled sleight of hand to make the different cards appear at times and places no one would expect them. Each time Grandpa did so, it was followed by a wide-eyed Ace saying, "Whoa!" The other grandchildren silently peeked behind their seats to see Grandpa's trick as well.

"But really," Grandpa said as he readied for the trick's finale, "I've been a little dishonest the whole time. What I really have . . ." Grandpa said as he laid his cards on the seat by Ace one-by-one, "is a King of Hearts, Jack of Diamonds, and an Ace of Spades."

Ace gasped. "Wow! How—but—but—" Grandpa chuckled his usual heartwarming chuckle and wrapped his arm over Ace. "You made the Ace of Spades appear out of nowhere!" Ace said.

"Actually . . ." Grandpa leaned into Ace's ear. "The Ace of Spades was there the whole time. I just had you focused on the other two. I disrupted your expectations. When it came down to the end, I pulled out the secret weapon I'd been hiding the whole time. Now you're not even thinking about the two Jacks. Just the Ace of Spades."

Ace gave a wide smile at Grandpa.

"Kinda like you, Ace," Grandpa said. Then he chuckled. "I never realized the irony there."

"What do you mean, Grandpa?" Ace said.

Grandpa smiled and leaned close to his grandson. "Right now, you probably feel not a lot of people are paying attention to what you have to offer. But when the time comes, you're gonna be the secret weapon that makes everything worthwhile. Then, everyone will be looking at you." Ace smiled big at Grandpa as the old man laughed and pulled him close. "That's you, kid. You're my Ace of Spades."

Ace suppressed the prompt to mourn for fear of embarrassing himself. But his grief collided with a sense of peace as well. At six years old, he hadn't quite understood what Grandpa meant. But now it seemed unmistakable. How long had Grandpa known he was going to give him the Emerson Stone?

"Ahh," said Marg, who had made his way to the couches. "So, you know what those are, huh?"

The kids nodded. "My grandfather had a deck just like this," Ace said.

Marg raised one eyebrow. He glanced back at Rio, who was walking down the aisle from the bathroom. The jag turned his attention back to the children. "Grandfather, huh? Interesting."

Cameron and Ace nodded.

"Up for some Bslackjack, then?" Marg said.

"Sure!" they said together.

Rio stepped forward and interjected. "Ace, I need to speak with you first." Ace stood to follow the drake, and he saw Julie shoot an unnerved glance from her chair. Hearing the drake ask to speak with him privately must have triggered her already blatant suspicions. Rio took him to the back of the jet just past the bar, into a narrow hallway next to the bathroom.

"What's going on?" Ace said.

"Just wanted to warn you of some things I wasn't expecting

when we land. Apparently, there's been some sort of recall," Rio said, leaning his head down to meet Ace at eye level.

"Yeah, I actually wanted to ask you . . . what are the elite?" Ace said.

Rio tilted his head. "Where did you hear that?"

"You and Marg were talking on the way here."

"You heard us talking?"

"Well, yeah. I was kinda listening in."

"Did anyone else hear?"

Ace shook his head. "No. I was making sure of it. But I also was really interested in what you were talking about."

Rio sighed. "Your grandfather warned me of your incurable curiosity."

Ace shrugged with a crooked smile.

"The elite," Rio continued, "are a select few hunters. The best of the Indies. Your grandfather took them under his wing and trained them personally. They all share second-in-command under Marty only."

"And you're one of them, right?"

"Yes. Actually, that's what I needed to talk to you about. When Marty sent me that letter, I sent word to Gathara that Marty Halder passed, and I would be returning from Oola. But I didn't tell them I'd be bringing his grandchildren."

"Why not?"

Rio poked his head up as if he heard something. He tilted his head and looked down the hallway, then back at Ace. "For one, I didn't want anyone but you to know about your grandfather's business. Had Gathara been expecting Marty Halder's grandchildren, rumor might have spread, and rumors are liable to find the ear of a witch. But there is another, more important, reason. Until now, who your grandfather would have selected to take his place was all up in the air. It was fairly understood it would be one of the elite. All of us wanted the position. When we arrive, don't expect a warm welcome."

Ace's face scrunched. "What exactly do you mean?"

Rio placed his hand on the boy's shoulder and leaned closer in.

"I mean first I will have to convince the elite that you are the grandchild of Marty Halder. His family life was a complete mystery to us. No one even knew he had children. Second, I will have to convince them that he chose you, a twelve-year-old boy, to lead them. These elite have trained for years under his direct leadership, conquered many milestones in the name of the Indies, and even established the Indie-governed Gathara. They will not take lightly to this news."

Ace chuckled nervously. "Guess that's not so bad. I'm sure we can find a way to convince them."

"Exactly my thoughts before I heard about the recall," Rio said.

"What does the recall mean?"

"A recall can only occur under a direct order of the Halder."

"*The* Halder?"

"It's the name we chose for the elite leader. Since your grandfather established it, we chose his name for the job title. I think it rolls off the tongue actually." Rio shook his head. "I think you're missing the bigger picture, kid. If the order can only come from the Halder, that can mean only one thing. The Indies have already selected a new leader," Rio said, leaning against the bathroom door.

Ace rolled his eyes and sighed. Another group of people who didn't believe he was a leader. The further along the journey, the clearer it became. The only one who truly believed in him was Grandpa. Everyone else was against him. He glanced at Rio. The drake scratched his head as he thought about the situation.

"I'm starting to believe Grandpa made some kinda mistake," Ace said. "Nobody else thinks I'm supposed to be this leader or whatever. I have no idea how I'm going to convince a group full of highly trained hunters that I'm supposed to be their boss after one day of training. Cameron is usually more skilled than me. And the Peppercorns definitely are. It doesn't make any sense why he chose me."

The drake offered a grin and leaned in close again. "Your grandfather did a lot of things that didn't make sense at first. But they always had some purpose in the end."

"Not this time," Ace said.

"Look," Rio said, placing one hand on Ace's shoulder, "I thought it was crazy too, that first day of training. Honestly, you didn't show much promise."

"Good to know."

"But listen, kid. The way you protected your family from those witches in Myrka was impressive. They called you a prodigy themselves. When time came to see what you were really made of, you didn't disappoint. Your grandfather knew what he was doing, I trust that."

Ace half-smiled.

"C'mon," Rio said, waving his hand. "Let's get back to your family."

"Hey, Rio," Ace said. The drake stopped and looked at him. "When we were in the Thraun airport, I saw flights booked to Gathara. How can so many people think Gathara is a fairy tale if public airports are offering flights?"

"The nations of Yutara are in a very strange place. There isn't much communication between them. Gathara isn't really considered a fairy tale in Heorg, only in Eveland, really."

Ace nodded, and they walked the aisle to find Cameron and Marg playing cards together. The Peppercorns remained in their seats, watching TV. The jag had a joyful countenance. It seemed to light up the room.

"Gugra!" Marg said. "Kid so good at this game."

"It's a game of chance, really. Hard to be good at it," Cameron said with a twisted smile.

Ace smiled too, knowing Grandpa had taught him and Cameron how to count cards to win at Blackjack. Something no other Yutarian knew how to do. Marg's Grandpa-like banter seemed to ease Cameron's nerves of flying. Ace also felt a sense of peace around the jag. He thought back to Rio's words of advice when it came to witches. They never looked like witches, and their greatest talent was deception. As the boy observed the jag and his older brother joke and play cards, a thought popped into his head. Maybe, just as a witch never seemed a witch, sometimes a friend doesn't seem a friend.

And sometimes a hero doesn't seem a hero.

CHAPTER NINETEEN

A Fish on a Hook

Ace and Cameron found themselves next to each other once again, the seatbelt light on, and Cameron gripping at the armrests.

"I thought you weren't scared anymore," Ace said. Cameron's nerves had calmed since he and the jag's card playing.

"The most dangerous parts of flying are the takeoff and landing," Cameron said.

"You know, I think this is the first time I've ever been less scared than my older brother," Ace said.

"Whatever, bro. I don't even care right now, I'm just trying not to die."

Ace chuckled and turned to look out the window. The ground showed splotches of red and brown clay and dirt. The stubby trees surrounding the roads and rivers were surprisingly green. Roads scattered on the desert ground like a wiggly grid, coming together at a few mildly populated towns. Hovercrafts along the roads looked like ants on a hill, and the town buildings resembled the stone and white brick like those of Thraun.

The terrain grew wilder as they approached the foothills of the desert mountains. Roads, hovercrafts, and people steadily grew in number. The plane tilted on Ace's side to make its turn, giving him a clear view of the big city all the roads and small towns surrounded. The snow-capped desert mountains embraced Gathara in a crescent shape. Buildings rose and fell in waves of foothills, as if they were built on the surface of the raging ocean during a storm. Some looked unlike the type of structures he knew from Eveland. Grandpa had described them in his stories.

"Castles!" he said as the memory struck him.

Cameron let go of the armrests and leaned over to catch a glimpse. The biggest one sat in the center of the city. It was built of the same white brick, surrounded by towers. Towers surrounded the castle wall, and one large tower stood in the middle of the wall further back in the castle, bordered by a cluster of towers of varying size. The other buildings encircled the castle were staggered in such a way, it looked as if the city planner just threw the buildings down any place his heart desired. Shingles of dark red, brown, and black slid down either side of their roofs. Some buildings were towers like mini castles. Some varied in color, and others were made of wood, and some a mixture of wood and brick. Even a few stone buildings could be found here and there. Bridges, winding roads of cobblestone and brick, and people were everywhere. This was a far cry from his original bland view of Heorg. It was like Grandpa's stories come to life!

"I've never seen a city like this before," Ace said.

The Peppercorns had remained silent behind them since they had been flying over the city.

"Yeah, it's incredible," Cameron said. He turned to Marg and Rio.

"How come we've never seen this place before? Like not even in pictures at school or anything," Cameron said.

Rio shrugged. "Maybe when you return, *you* can teach your school something."

Ace knew the true answer to Cameron's question. This city was designed by and belonged to the Indies. If the witches had as strong a grasp on the rest of Yutara as Rio said, they would do everything in their power to keep knowledge of the Indies away from people. He looked at his older brother, wondering if he still remembered their agreement for him to learn witch hunting. Although Ace desired to keep his word to Grandpa, he secretly had been looking forward to having his older brother by his side on this journey. Cameron would make a great hunter, and Ace could have used the help.

A voice came over the intercom. "*We advise you to stay seated and buckled as we make our final descent.*"

"Those animals are beautiful," Julie said. "I want one!"

"They're called horses," Marg said from behind.

"I know what they're called," Julie snapped. The kids kept their eyes glued to the window of the train. The jet had to land at the top of the mountain at the only airport around. For, as Marg and Rio explained, the city was tight, and the roads and walls narrow. Too much for a hovercraft even. Planes landed in the mountains and trains carried passengers into the city. Their train hovered over the rails and smoothly glided down the winding tracks alongside the mountain slope. Humans, jags, and drakes ran through the mountains on their horses. Some were hunters, ready to catch their family's next meal, and others were tending their farms. They passed by barns and humble homes laid throughout the slope of the mountain.

"It's incredible," Cameron, who had been standing next to Ace, said. "It's like Grandpa's stories."

"Look!" Tamara said, pointing a finger.

Ace grinned. "Faes," he whispered. Some flew by on bird-like creatures called taebans. Their silver and golden feathers glimmered from the sunlight. They had beaks like birds, but four paws like a land beast, and purple eyes. Beautiful as the creatures were, Ace found his eyes had stuck to the faes on land. They walked down a mountain path in large numbers. Mostly sharing the appearance of an Evelander, their pale skin glowed like diamonds under a spotlight, and their silver and golden hair shimmered as if polished. Or at least for those who had hair. All male faes, save for those with golden hair, kept their heads shaved. Males with such hair chose not to shave their heads, as the gold was considered a rare sign of blessing and nobility among fae culture. Grayish blue streaks covered every fae's skin in elegant patterns and shapes. They were like tattoos, only they weren't ink; rather, they grew in naturally as a fae came of age.

The faes catching the grandchildren's eyes walked a path just next to the train. As they passed by, Ace got a better look. They were dressed in silver and golden robes, depending on the color of the fae's hair. Two of them had golden hair. A male and female led their two daughters into the city. The older of the two children stole Ace's attention. The young fae turned to face him as the train passed. The wind blew her polished silver hair gently across her radiant skin. Her eyes, a deep purple, caught him like a fish on a hook. A cluster of freckles lightly dotted her nose and the skin under her eyes. Her lips had a touch of pink, and her tattoos were a faded blue. They lined her forehead, curled under her eyes, then wound back and flowed down her neck as if placed there by the hand of a brilliant artist.

Ace felt a hand on his shoulder. He leaned his head further out the window, but they had passed the faes and were out of sight. The boy turned to find Rio standing behind him. The drake shook his head.

"I don't want you children speaking to the faes here," Rio said.

"Why not?" Tamara said.

"Faes in this city have a bad reputation. They may seem like wonderful creatures, but they're not to be trusted," Rio said.

Tamara and Julie scoffed. Julie folded her arms.

"Man," Cameron said, "I'd really like to meet one."

"Yeah, why are faes so bad, Rio?" Ace said.

Rio stomped his foot. "Enough! Stay away from them, okay?

End of discussion." Rio scowled at him.

The train pulled to the bottom of the valley in the surrounding mountains to a station outside the city wall, soaring nearly a hundred feet into the sky. Everyone grabbed their things, and Rio and Marg led the kids to the main road through the city entrance. The open gate welcomed people traveling freely to and from. Guards with AMRs stood at the opening of the walls. Two humans, two jags. They smiled and welcomed the entering guests.

Even the guards with large blasters make Gathara feel like home, thought Ace.

Inside, the roads were even more narrow than they seemed from the plane. They were made of bricks in different shades of red and brown, with hardly any space between the buildings. Everything was clustered together. The streets flooded with jags. Evelanders and drakes were seen often but not as frequently, and every now and then a fae appeared in the crowd. Ace fought his urge to stare at the intriguing creatures. He hardly thought it possible he would see a city bigger than New Eathelyn, but it stood right there before his eyes. Mighty, vibrant, and every bit as joyful as Grandpa. A bittersweet thing. Ace missed Grandpa every time the thought of him crossed his mind, but the city made him feel like Grandpa was somehow still alive.

The air filled with the clip-clop of horse hooves and bartering merchants, and it seemed every corner they turned someone laughed merrily. The further along they traveled, the steeper the hills became. It kept reminding him of ocean waves, which brought him back to the thought of the young fae and her ocean-purple eyes. He held his tongue on the train, but he wished to fight Rio on speaking to faes. Although it was a longshot that he'd ever see her again, he desperately wanted to meet her. Something about the way they caught eyes struck him magically. Maybe Rio could be convinced that faes were harmless. Just meeting one couldn't hurt, right?

CHAPTER TWENTY

All the Fun

How much further?" Julie said. "It smells like horse butt here," Tamara said.

Rio and Marg took them through a few more turns until they came to a road less narrow. In the middle of this road a tree sprung forth. The bricks cracked and broke as if the tree had burst from the ground. Its branches covered the neighborhood in a welcoming shade, and its leaves were a rich green, clumped together to resemble the fluffiness of a cloud or balls of cotton. Houses stood on either side of the courtyard, and Rio and Marg led them to one on the right, up the wooden steps, and into the front door.

"Lights on," Marg said. Bright, cool light turned on from the ceiling. "Home sweet home." Everyone walked inside and laid their luggage on the ground. The front door led straight to a living room.

"This is where you live?" Cameron said.

"Yes. It's my home in Gathara," Marg said.

"Dibbs on the couch!" Julie said as she and Tamara ran and plopped themselves on the dark sofa.

"What do you mean in Gathara? You live in other places?" Cameron asked.

"Sorta," Marg said. "It, uh, complicated." The jag scratched his neck as Rio walked in beside him. "Hey, uh, make yourselves home, alright? There two rooms upstairs, you pick who shares."

"We have to share rooms?" Tamara said with a face like she'd just smelled a sewer.

"Get used to listening to Marg," Rio said, stepping in. "This is gonna be your home for some time."

"What?" Julie and Tamara said as they jumped from the couch.

"What do you mean our *home?* Like, we're gonna live here?" Tamara said.

"Yeah," Rio said. "That's what home means. Go put your things up." He pointed his finger to the hall upstairs.

"I thought we were just hanging here for safety until we could find our parents or whatever," Tamara said.

"Yeah! I can't live in Gathara! What about all my friends back home?" Julie said, her arms crossed.

"Your parents may be gone," Rio said. The room went still and all the children mildly hung their heads. "I'm sorry, but that's all we know. Gathara is the safest place for you right now. I promised your grandfather I would protect you and that's what I'm doing."

Tamara and Julie huffed and puffed as they stomped their way to the second floor.

"Uh, are they always like that?" Marg asked. Rio, Ace, and Cameron turned to the jag and nodded. "Great."

"You two go put your stuff in your room and try to get settled in," Rio said. "Get some rest."

Ace and Cameron turned to walk the stairs. As Cameron started up, Rio grabbed Ace's arm and whispered in his ear.

"You especially need rest. Tomorrow I will introduce you to the elite, and hopefully begin your true training," the drake said. Ace nodded as Rio let go of his arm.

He walked up the stairs behind Cameron, and they turned left because the Peppercorns had already claimed the room on the right. They entered a small bedroom. A bunk bed sat in the middle of an otherwise vacant room. It felt like boot camp.

Cameron walked beside the bed and threw his bags down. "Okay," he whispered, "when are you gonna start teaching me some witch hunting?"

Ace jerked his head back his brother. "Well, we're gonna need to be alone," Ace said. "I dunno how easy that'll be."

Cameron shrugged. "We're alone now."

"True. But we don't have enough space."

"You need space?"

"Well yeah. I mean, you use blasters and stuff."

"Blasters?" Cameron's eyes shot up as he stepped closer to Ace. "That's awesome!"

"Yeah." Ace smiled.

"But isn't there something you can tell me? I mean, there's stuff I can learn without having to practice, right?"

Ace looked around, then grinned back at his brother. "Okay," he whispered. "Well, uh, I guess the first thing is to teach you about witches and how you can tell they're nearby."

"Right," Cameron said. "Black dust, whispers in the dark . . . . uh . . ." He squinted and looked up as he thought. "The smell of . . . . of . . ."

"No, Cameron. Those were just stories. They're only partly true. Witches hide in plain sight and it's hard to tell who they are. They speak almost all lies. Hardly anything they say is truth. The black dust comes from their disguise. When they get caught in a lie, their disguise breaks down and it releases black dust. That's also where the smell of smoke comes from in the stories."

Cameron leaned close and squinted. "I'm sorry, Ace. This is really hard for me to believe."

"You know all those rifles the guards have around here?"

Cameron nodded.

"Those are hybrid rifles. They shoot anti-magic *and* plasma. This entire city was built for an army that fights witches."

"Does it really take blasters to take them down?"

Ace nodded. "Listen, Cameron, be careful with this information. Rio told me the reason Grandpa doesn't want you and the Peppercorns knowing about this is because hunting witches is dangerous. When they feel they're being caught in their lie, or someone is snooping around looking for them, knowing they're nearby, they'll resort to magic. They can take your memory, twist your limbs . . . all kinds of weird things. Unless you're trained to fight one, it's not good to know how to find one."

Cameron chuckled. "But Grandpa somehow thinks *you're* safe with that information, right?"

Ace paused a moment knowing the true reason he was trusted with this information. The Emerson Stone protected him from magic, but it didn't protect the other grandkids. Should he tell Cameron? "I . . ." he began to say, then remembered his promise to Grandpa. "Yes. For a reason I can't explain, he told me.

Cameron shook his head. "I don't get it."

"Neither do I, Cameron." He leaned close and placed a hand on his brother's shoulder. "Look. I really need you to trust me, alright?"

Cameron's face played with a few different expressions. Anger, frustration, then acceptance. He sighed, and a half-smile appeared at the corner of his mouth. He clapped Ace's shoulder. "Of course, I trust you, bro. Halders stick together." Ace smiled at him. "Let's get some sleep. You better teach me how to shoot one of those rifles, though. Can't let you have all the fun, right?"

CHAPTER TWENTY-ONE

Rio's Detour

Time inched by like a snail, and Ace found himself in a daze. He looked around and wiped his eyes, but everything kept its feathered edges. Where was he? It wasn't Heorg. The walls of bookshelves reached twenty feet high, surrounding smaller bookshelves in the middle, and they were laid out as if he were in a maze. The carpet was immaculately clean, and the air carried the smell of leather. He had been here before. He found himself in the "Tales of Earth" section, hoping to find a manuscript of one of Grandpa's fun stories with no luck. The haziness drifted as his head cleared. It was Eveland! At the Peppercorns' house. But why was he there? Footsteps pounded behind him and the sound echoed in his brain. Every thump delivered a more heightened sense of deja vu. Despair awaited him shortly. He turned to find a younger Cameron with longer dark hair rushing from the stairs.

"Ace." His voice echoed like the footsteps. "Come quickly, it's Mom!"

Ace ran with all his might, but it felt as if he hardly moved. Instead, the room around him drifted into darkness, and ahead lay his mother, Dad weeping by her side. He brushed his wife's hair by her face. A tear rolled along his cream skin and fell off his round jawbone, splashing against her still face. Her thick brunette hair lay sprawled on the tile floor like a mop.

"Who did this?" Father said, choking on his tears. Aunt Kaitlyn appeared behind him, placing a hand on his back. Her looks reminded Ace once again of how the Peppercorns outdid them in every way. She stood as tall as his dad, long, silky blond hair, crystal blue eyes, and a graceful gaze even with tears in her eyes.

"No one, Colton," Aunt Kaitlyn said. "It was just an accident."

"Get away from us," Dad said, shooing his sister with his hand.

"Dad?" Ace said, stepping forward.

"I swear!" Julie yelled from the distance. Her voice rang loud, carried by the vast and hallow darkness. He couldn't see her, but the shrill voice he recognized anywhere. "I didn't mean to," she choked and coughed on her tears. "I would never do anything like that! Please believe me!"

Ace stared at his mom, her eyes shut, Dad weeping over her. Ace's heartbeat grew heavier. His stomach rose to his throat. His breath went too fast for his lungs and he collapsed to his knees.

"Mom?" he screamed. "Mom get up! You're okay!"

"Ace!" a voice called. Ace searched in all directions, but there was no one around. Only darkness. "Ace! Wake up!"

He jerked his head again and opened his eyes to waking life.

"Hey, calm down, calm down," Rio said, hovering over the boy. Ace felt the drake's hands on his shoulders as his breathing slowed. A pool of sweat under his back had soaked into the mattress.

"Sorry." Ace breathed deep. "Was I yelling?"

Rio shook his head. "Just squirming and panting. It was just a dream, though. C'mon, get dressed."

Rio left the room. Cameron lay asleep on the top bunk, and Ace prepared himself for the day. As he looked around his room, Cameron still asleep, he realized it was the first time in a while he had been alone. He reached for his backpack and pulled out the chest and watch. The stone remained safe so far. But leaving it there wasn't the safest thing to do. What if Cameron went snooping or something? He threw on his backpack and put the watch in his pocket. Rio stood at the front door as Ace made his way down the stairs.

"What do you need your backpack for?" Rio said.

"Just in case I need some extra clothes or whatever. You never know," Ace said with a weak smile. Rio shrugged, then turned his attention to the sofa. "Thank you for looking after the family today, Marg."

"No worries, ug," the jag replied. "Just question though."

"What's that?"

"What we gonna do tomorrow? I can't sit here for recall. And we can't leave family here by selves."

"Well, we definitely can't take them to Headquarters," Rio said.

"Exactly point."

Rio shrugged, a firm look on his green face. "I plan on discussing some things with the elite today. Perhaps I can work out some sort of arrangement."

The jag nodded, but his face showed question of Rio's plan. The drake led Ace through the front door, to the courtyard with the tree, and back into the city.

"Mind your eyes," Rio said. For a fae had walked by, catching the boy's attention.

"What's so bad about faes?" Ace said.

Rio looked at the boy fiercely. The drake hardly seemed to know another expression. "Faes are magic creatures, Ace. They're born with the abilities of a witch. The only difference between a fae and a witch is that you can spot them anywhere. Witches hide in front of your nose."

Ace furrowed his brow and tilted his head. "I thought Gathara was governed by the Indies."

Rio nodded.

"So, if faes are magic, why are they not prevented from coming in?" Ace said.

"Some are, actually. Not long after the city was built, many faes migrated from Breen to the suburbs of Gathara. Hundreds, maybe thousands, live in the surrounding mountains now. At first, we freely let them in, wanting Gathara to be a safe place for all Yutarians wanting to escape the clutches of the council."

"Even though they had magical abilities?"

"Well, we didn't know then. You see, any form of magic is outlawed here. Hunters guard this city day and night, trained to detect it. If such magic is detected, the witch is taken captive and interrogated. We've never had a breech in security."

"So, as long as the faes don't practice their magic, they're allowed to stay?"

Rio nodded. "Yes. The elite chose this. I, for one, voted against this law. Seeing as any creature with magical abilities should be a direct threat to what we stand for. But the others thought it unfair to banish a race of creatures simply because they were born with abilities. We compromised. All faes, if they are to be allowed in Gathara, must swear allegiance to the Indies and give up their magic. Some have even gone as far as to remove their tattoos to demonstrate their allegiance to us. Which, I'll admit, is impressive. Those faes are okay for you to speak with. In fact, some of them have become hunters, but still be cautious. Something about them makes me uneasy."

Ace nodded. Something seemed strange when Rio told him this. A gut feeling maybe. He pictured the eyes of the fae from his train ride. She seemed so harmless. So innocent and lovely. But he caught himself, remembering Rio's advice. A witch's strongest power was deception. The faes must have mastered this art if Rio was correct. But he still couldn't shake the persistent idea of Rio being wrong, the idea the faes had more to offer, and the drake just hadn't seen it yet. Maybe a fae without tattoos could offer an explanation. He'd find one and ask them the second he got the chance.

A thin, faint yellow line brightened on the eastern walls of the city as dawn approached. Streetlights lined the sidewalks, and sconce lights hung outside the buildings. Hovercrafts zoomed by over the city, but they were few and far between. The hovercrafts able to reach such heights were only of the most expensive kind, and the roads proved too narrow to fit normal crafts inside the walls. They trotted along through the winding paths of brick and stone until they approached an entryway of gray cobblestone, leading to a bridge over a large river circling the castle. It had walls nearly as large as the city walls.

"Remember the roads we took to get here. This is where you will train," the drake said.

Ace nodded. "*If* we can convince the elite I'm the new Halder."

"Yes. That's precisely why I'm not taking you to them first. A little detour if you will," Rio said.

"Detour? Where are we going?"

Rio turned to Ace, a sly look in his eye. "The witch cellar."

CHAPTER TWENTY-TWO

A Gathering Arranged

Two human guards stood past the pridge, one on either side of an arched double doorway of dark wood, the familiar X shaped vest wrapped over their torsos. They kept both their hands on their AMRs, a fierce look on their faces.

"Atarion. Elite," Rio said. The guards nodded, their eyes focused ahead. One turned and placed his hand on a chrome plate beside the doors. The doors squealed in a deep roar as they opened inward. The guards tilted their heads in a salute.

The drake led Ace through the gate of the outer wall into a great courtyard of manicured grass and perfectly trimmed hedges. One drake dressed in torn cloth drove a mower across its surface, and a few others—drakes, jags, and humans alike—trimmed the hedges against the castle walls.

The cobblestone path led them to another set of double doors, this one unguarded. The drake placed his hand on another chrome surface, and the double doors flung open. A vast hall of stone and brick awaited them past the entrance. Pillars of polished stone glimmered from the sun glaring through the windows. Each of the pillars connected in an arch. The charcoal-colored floor was so beautifully finished, Ace felt guilty for walking on it. Ahead, complementing the elegance of the vast hall in such a way the boy's heart skipped a beat, was a mural: a portrait of an old man. An old man who looked young, had a wide smile, leathery skin like Damion, stubby-white five o'clock shadow, and thick white hair slicked perfectly back. Underneath, the person's name was written.

Marty Halder: Founder of the Indies.

Ace had to swallow before he spoke. "Did this castle belong to —"

"Yep," Rio said. "Your grandfather helped design this whole city, you know."

The boy's jaw hung to the floor as he turned to Rio. "How did he keep all this from his family?"

"He didn't have to try very hard, really," The drake said as they turned to a narrower hall. "Witches and parcels have such a strong hold on Yutara, knowledge of The Indies and what we stand for has been purposely labeled as myth and legend among the younger generations. You should know this better than anyone because most people in Eveland believe Gathara is a myth."

"Do witches even need magic? They seem to have done just fine without it."

Rio nodded. "Yes, they have. But they still need magic. Although some have mastered the art of deception, there are those few that still see through their lies." He jabbed a thumb at himself, then pointed a finger at Ace. "That's when it's time to take someone's memory. If that doesn't work . . . things can get ugly."

Two hunters stopped them in the hall—one water drake female, another male human.

"Rio?" the water drake said. Scales of silver, purple, and blue layered themselves on her skin in a glittery shine. Webbed fins grew out of her elbows and spine, and closed gills wrapped the curve of her neck.

"Ihana," Rio said. "George." All three shared the same salute as the guards had earlier.

"W—what are you doing here?" Ihana said.

"We thought you were stationed in Oola," George said. The man had dark brown skin, a bald head, square jaw, large muscles, and a deep voice like Rio's. He spoke like someone from Northeeves, Eveland. Those in the north didn't pronounce their r's, sometimes their o's sounded more like a's, and their e's were almost always short.

"I was. But I've returned."

"We, uh, well . . ." Ihana rubbed the fin on the back of her neck and clacked her tongue a few times. "We weren't expecting you," she said, a weak smile on her face.

"I know," Rio said with no emotion in his eyes.

A moment of silence took the room, and the tension left an awkward presence.

"Who's the pigeon?" the man said, finally disturbing the quiet. Ace smirked. He was definitely from the Northeeves area. Pigeon was a term they used in the north to describe someone who's lingering, unknown by others in any given group.

Rio nudged Ace along gently and began to walk further down the hall. "His name is Ace. Don't want to be rude, but we need to go. I will return shortly. Might I request a gathering?"

"When?" George said.

Rio backed up, Ace behind him, the drake still facing the other two. "Thirty minutes. The Great Hall."

Ihana and George looked at one another, then back at Rio. They nodded, Rio nodded back. Another salute. Rio turned and brought Ace to the end of the narrow hall. A familiar set of double doors stood at the end, but an open path awaited them to the right of the large doors. They walked through it and candles lit the walls of rough, sharp stone in a flickering light.

"Who were those people?" Ace said.

"Two of the elite. I was hoping not to run into them while we were here. But we did," Rio said.

"How many are you?"

"The elite?"

Ace nodded.

"Five. Two drakes, three humans."

The hallway of rough stone surrounded a winding staircase, and the further down they traveled, the more rancid the air became. Ace held his nose, and a sense of dread arose. The last time he'd seen a witch was far from pleasant. He imagined this to be no different.

"Why are you bringing me here?" Ace said. "And why do you keep witches down here?"

Rio stopped and faced him. The sound of a witch's screech echoed from below and sent chills down Ace's spine.

"There's something you need to know about witches, Ace," the drake said.

"What's that?" he replied. His eyes jerked back and forth between the witch cries below and the drake in front of him.

"There's a reason we don't kill them, you know. Some of them don't choose this path. If someone in a witch's family is a parcel, they could be under a generational curse. If they are, they will be forced to work for the council without choice. They don't quite know what they're doing. Most witches have freely given themselves to the council, but we have no way of knowing which of the witches have freely chosen this life, and which have been cursed."

Hearing this made the boy nauseous and weary. What a dreadful thing.

"Your grandfather discovered this," Rio said. "There are rumors that some have found a way to escape their generational curse. His whole life was bent toward finding the cure. That's why he gave the order that all hunters should capture and never kill a witch. He's kept them here, trying various ways to cure them."

"So, witches are just slaves of parcels?" Ace said.

"In a way, yes."

"What do you mean, in a way?"

Louder screeches in greater numbers echoed from below. The boy jumped back.

"Parcels are also slaves of the council. However, they work a little differently. We have reason to believe they are somehow chosen by the council and given some sort of offer."

"What kind of offer?"

"Riches. Power. Fame. And slaves."

Ace leaned in. "Witches?"

"Yes. Many times, a parcel who accepts this offer will be cursed. His daughters, and daughters' daughters, will become slaves of the council at the age of eighteen. They will lose themselves and be taken by witchcraft."

"How can we find the cure?" Ace said.

Rio lowered his head as it shook. "We don't know." The drake lifted his head and faced the boy eye to eye. "As far as we know, the only way is to defeat the council."

Ace stepped back. "And you think that's impossible?"

Rio frowned and nodded slowly. "Yes. But we don't have to stop there. We can still prevent the council from finding parcels. We can defeat what parcels exist now and prevent the further spread of evil in Yutara. The council only has power if the people are persuaded by their deception."

Ace stared blankly, unsatisfied with the drake's optimism. It wasn't enough. It couldn't be. He felt a stirring inside he knew stirred Grandpa before. The council had to be defeated. They had to be stopped. And though he didn't know how yet, he knew somehow the Emerson Stone could help him do it.

"You still haven't answered the other question," Ace said. Rio tilted his head with curiosity. "Why are you bringing me here to see this?"

"We need to prove who you are to the elite, don't we?" Rio said.

Ace nodded.

"Well, bringing you around these witches may confirm my suspicions. And if it does, we will have all the proof we need."

"I'm not sure I understand what you're getting at."

"The witches," Rio said, "they can't curse you."

CHAPTER TWENTY-THREE

The Witch Cellar

Ace froze with fear as the shrill screams scraped his eardrums. Had Rio lost his mind? The witches circled him, staring him down with their beady, black eyes. Drakes, humans, and jags. Hundreds of them, maybe thousands. Some of them disappeared into a black smoke and floated through the great cellar. The gate had been locked, and Ace left inside.

How long is Rio going to leave me here?

Whispers traveled through the air. He hardly told the difference between his thoughts, or the thoughts of the witches.

Halder. Halder, he heard in his head. *You can't ssave them. It's uselesss. Turn around. Walk away. Your grandfather couldn't, and neither can you.*

Ace ignored the voices, simply facing ahead where the cage to the cell had been shut. The floor was damp, and a foul odor crept into his nostrils. Faint whispers of names caused him to shiver. They were barely audible at first, but as his pulse quickened, the whispers grew louder.

Julie. Tamara. Julie. Tamara. Julie. Tamara.

How did they know his cousins? His eyes shot open and the witches screeched and swirled around him like aggravated bees wickedly pleased at his worry.

He thinkss we don't know. He doessn't know.

"Know what?" Ace said.

"Ignore them!" Rio shouted from outside the cellar. "Do not speak to them or entice them. They will put lies in your head."

The drake is the liar. The drake is the liar. The drake is the liar.

Ace closed his eyes again, clenched his sweaty palms, and fought his quivering nerves. The witches were the liars, he reassured himself.

"Ok—k—kay, Rio. This obviously works! C—c—can I come out now?" Ace said. He covered his ears and knelt, for the witches erupted with sharp laughter. It echoed through the cellar and rang painfully in his head.

Rio held his AMR forward. The witches backed away from the door hissing and screeching.

Julie. Tamara. You can't ssave them, Halder. You can't ssave them.

Ace kept his hands over his ears. He felt the drake's grip on his wrist and they ran outside the cellar. The door slammed shut and Rio pressed his hand on the chrome plate in the stone wall. The bars of the gate became beams of orange light, as well as the walls surrounding the cellar. The witches backed away and clustered together, moaning at the orange light.

Rio patted Ace's back as the boy slowed his breathing. "Good job, kid."

"You—" Ace breathed. "You're insane."

Rio shrugged. "Desperate times." The drake nudged Ace up the winding staircase. "Let's go meet the elite."

Ace caught his breath and nodded.

What did they mean, Julie and Tamara? How did they know them? What did they mean I couldn't save them? Ace thought.

Rio brought him to the Great Hall again, where the elite stood in the middle, awaiting the drake's arrival.

"Rio!" the female human said. She had long blonde hair pulled into a ponytail and a fragile voice to compliment her toothpick figure.

"Keele, Sebastian, good to see you both, I suppose," Rio said. They all shared their same salute. He and Ace approached them and joined in a circle.

"Come, let's sit," said the pale human. Ace assumed this must have been Sebastian. He had tan skin, a thick jaw, and a neatly trimmed, blonde beard. His short blond hair swirled at the top like cotton candy. The man led the elite, and Ace, through the Great Hall, and turned to open a door just before Grandpa's portrait. It opened to a room with a long table of dark, finished wood, surrounded by hoverchairs. The male gestured with his hand, offering a seat to them all.

"Who's the tyke you've brought with you?" Sebastian said.

"My name is—" Ace was cut off.

"He's with me," Rio said. "That's all you need to know for now." The drake winked at him, and the boy followed his lead.

"Good and well," Sebastian said, "so long as you trust him with the information we will discuss here."

"I do," Rio replied.

"Why've you come back from ya assignment in Oola?" George said.

"My assignment was a direct order from the Halder," Rio said. Everyone looked at Sebastian. The pale man shrugged his shoulders as if he didn't know what Rio was talking about. "The *real* Halder," the drake stated.

"But you sent us a letter saying he'd passed away," the water drake said.

"And didn't Marty send you *ta* Oola?" George said.

"Yea, yea. But it was for a specific reason, and a short period of time. I realize that now," the drake replied. "What I wanna know is why you went on to select a new Halder without my knowledge. We all have a say in Gathara's government. Marty chose us all, not just you four."

The other elite looked at one another, baffled and confused. "Rio," Keele said, "you said that's what Marty wanted."

Rio furrowed his brow and tilted his head, "What are you talking about?"

"The letter you wrote," Sebastian jumped in, "you said Marty Halder had passed, and a new leader will be selected for Gathara."

"Yes, a new leader *has* been selected! You misread," the drake said, his voice growing fiercer.

The four of them went on back and forth. Unfortunately, no one had the original letter in writing, which made Rio angrier. Sebastian had been selected as the new Halder, and sworn in, regardless of what the letter said. But Rio persisted.

"Look, Rio. It's well and good you and Marty were close, but he never had a chance to choose you," Sebastian said. "I'm sorry . . . it's just the way things have panned out."

Rio slammed his hand on the table and stood to his feet, "I'm not talking about *me!* Marty Halder has chosen a new leader, and as the law commands, the one he has chosen must take the position!"

"Who are you talking about then?" Ihana said.

Rio pulled something from a pouch in his X vest. It was the letter Grandpa had sent him—the one he read to the grandchildren in the cabin. The drake slid it across the smooth surface of the table until it reached Sebastian. The pale elite unfolded it, looked at Rio, then showed the rest of the elite.

"So, he *has* selected you as the Halder," Ihana said.

"Only temporarily," Rio said.

George interjected, the letter in his hand, having reached him as it had been passed around. "This letter hardly makes sense. Marty kept his personal life hidden from Gathara and the Indies. Even us, his elite."

"Have you done what Marty instructed?" Sebastian asked. "Have you brought his family here safely?"

Rio nodded. "I have."

"Then where is this grandch—?" Keele had begun to ask but was interrupted by an apparent epiphany. All eyes went to Ace.

Rio nodded at the boy.

"I am," Ace said as he stood. "My name is Ace Halder."

The elite's eyes widened, and they leaned back in their hover chairs.

"*You?*" Sebastian said, his face scrunched.

"Rio, you can't be serious," George said.

"You read the letter yourselves. Why would I lie about this?" Rio said.

The elite stood from their table, throwing out every reason why this wouldn't work.

Sebastian said, "That's tosh! There must be some mistake." The others shouted so close to one another, Ace could barely make out the following words.

"He's just a boy!"

"He could be snapped like a twig, he's so small."

"Marty must have meant a different grandchild."

Ace didn't fight the accusations. He stood calmly. These were things he had been used to hearing his entire life. Mainly from the Peppercorns. Rotten as those brats were, perhaps their persistent bullying over the years had been good for something after all. Not letting insults get the best of him.

The Peppercorns . . .

As the elite continued ranting and complaining, his mind drifted elsewhere. Their voices became muffled, and the world around him, fuzzy. He was taken back to his nightmare. Since this morning he had a lot to distract him. But now, as he stood there, the nightmare caught up with him once again and shook him. It took him back to the day his mother died. One of the worst days of his life. He was only seven then, and they were visiting the Peppercorns. He remembered Julie's piercing yell echoing through his brain. The family never found out exactly what had happened. Only the blame was pinned on Julie.

Another one of Julie's pranks, Ace thought, *gone wrong.* It was a wretched day for Ace. One he dreaded to revisit in his sleep. He never wanted to talk about it or think about it. This needed to stop. His stomach churned, and his blood boiled.

"Enough!" shouted Rio, loud enough to jolt the boy back into reality.

The elite stood in silence, mulling over the situation.

"I know how unusual this looks. But to be fair, Marty was known for his unusual methods," Rio said. The elite silenced. "This boy has a gift. I've seen it with my own eyes."

"What kind of gift?" Keele asked.

"The very same his grandfather had," Rio said.

There was a moment of silence, the elite looked at one another, then back to the drake. Sebastian chimed in, "Even so, the tyke is far too young to lead the Indies."

"That's not your call!" Rio said.

Ihana snapped her tongue sharply and said, "Yes, it is, Rio. Like it or not, Sebastian has already been sworn in. We're sorry, there's not much to do about it now."

"Grandpa wouldn't have done it like this, would he?" Ace said. He swallowed a lump afterward, wishing he could take the words back. It didn't seem his place to interject in such a meeting. But if Grandpa truly thought he was the next leader, then maybe it was his place. Nevertheless, it didn't settle his anxiousness.

"Done it like what?" Sebastian said.

Ace swallowed again. "I mean, he would have at least left it up to some sort of vote, right? Not just whatever he says goes," said Ace. Rio crossed his arms, a wide smile on his face as he chuckled.

The elite looked at Sebastian, who was snarling with anger.

"Fine. All in favor of Ace Halder leading the Indies, raise your hand," Sebastian said. Three hands shot up. Ace, Rio, and surprisingly, Keele.

"Keele?" Sebastian said.

Keele looked at Sebastian and shrugged. "I have a feeling about the boy, what can I say?"

Sebastian scoffed, then turned back to Ace. "Either way, the vote still works against you."

"But it's three against three!" Rio said.

"You're not seriously counting the kid's vote, are you?" Ihana said.

"Why wouldn't I?"

"Doesn't that beg the question, Rio?" George said. "We're voting on his validity as an elite."

"As a *leader,"* Rio corrected. "Leader or not. He's still an elite."

Ace glanced at Rio, surprised to hear him say such a thing. Did the drake really consider him good enough to be on this team of warriors?

"There must be a compromise," Keele said. Silence filled the room for a moment once again, until it was broken by Keele. "Let's at least see what he can do."

"Yes! Allow him to train, at least. If he proves himself worthy, he can take the Halder position," Rio said.

Sebastian scratched his chin. "And what of the interim leader? Will you challenge my authority 'till then, drake?"

Wrinkles spread like spider webs over Rio's face. He snapped his tongue and clacked a few times. Ace wasn't sure if he was making angry noises or saying things in his native tongue. The glare in Sebastian's eye made Ace feel uneasy, the glare of a man hungry for power.

Rio's mouth remained closed, his teeth clenched together as he said, "No."

Sebastian nodded, a sly grin on his face. "I don't know. I still feel uneasy about this."

Rio nodded angrily. "I think I can help your decision-making process," he said. "There's something you all should see in the witch cellar."

CHAPTER TWENTY-FOUR

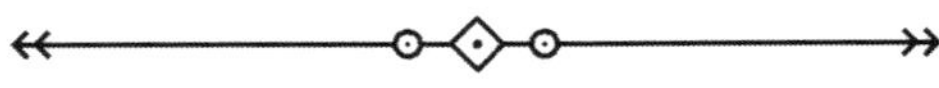

Curse

That *is* impressive," Ihana said. "There's no doubt he's got the Halder's blood in him," Keele said.

Ace stood rock solid, listening to the elite's comments outside the cellar as the witches swarmed him. This time in the witch cellar he felt more confident. He knew he had to impress the elite to prove his worth.

Sebastian chimed in from outside the closed gate. "I'll admit, it's promising. But just because the tyke's immune to a witch's magic doesn't mean he's immune to deception. We still have no way of knowing if he's worthy of being a leader."

"What will be enough for you, Sebastian?" Rio said. "Tell me."

Their bickering continued, but the witches whispered a name to snatch Ace's focus.

Peppercorn, Peppercorn, Peppercorn.

He tried to fight it, to convince himself the witches were lying.

You can't ssave them, you can't ssave them.

The elite's debate outside the cellar went mute in his head, so he only heard the witches surrounding him. So, he whispered back, "What do you mean, save them?" The witches shrieked and laughed, apparently only in his head, for the elite had not seemed to notice it.

The Peppercornsss, they belong to usss.

"How do you know them?"

He doesn't want to sssave them. He doesn't want to sssave them.

The air grew cold, and a whistling breeze wrapped around him in a blanket of fear. He hardly had the strength to respond. Could they tell what he was feeling? When he heard the witches whisper the Peppercorns belonged to them, he felt no sympathy. How did they know this? He'd tried convincing himself the witches were lying to excuse his lack of care. But the more he thought about it, the more he seemed . . . *happy* when the witches said the Peppercorns were in danger. So what if they were? They were terrible children.

"How do you know the Peppercorns?" he whispered. He fought the chills crawling on his skin when the witches shrieked again. Even though he was immune to their magic, they still creeped him out.

"Ace?" Rio said. Ace looked at the elite, now staring at him from the cellar. A nervous sweat trickled along the standing hairs on the back of his neck. He couldn't be caught whispering to the witches. What if the elite thought he was conspiring? Or being deceived? They'd never give him a chance.

"Everything okay?" Rio said.

Ace gathered himself and nodded.

How do we know the Peppercornsss? Come back, come back, come back. We will ssshow you.

Ace stepped forward and addressed the elite. "You've seen enough, right?"

"He wasn't ready for this," Sebastian said.

Rio scoffed at Sebastian.

"Well, if he wasn't ready, I'd love to see what he can do when he *is* ready," Keele said. Rio smiled as the elite nodded in agreement with her.

"Come on out of there," Rio said, turning to Ace.

The boy made his way to the cellar door. Outside, all the elite pulled their weapons, and the witches backed further into the dungeon. They turned off the orange glow from the bars and freed him as he caught his breath.

"Afraid?" Sebastian said. "I thought you were immune."

"Well, I didn't know I was immune until recently, Mr. Sebastian," Ace said trying to calm himself.

"Quit trying to downplay what you just saw Sebastian. He's got a gift, one that could be of great value to us," Rio said.

"Rio's right," Keele said. "We at least need to train him."

Sebastian looked around at all the elite. They were against him on this one. "Get some rest, kid," Sebastian said. "You're suiting up tomorrow."

Ace sat on a dark wood bench in the Great Hall as Rio spoke his parting words to the elite. He placed his hands on his head and tried to understand what he had just heard the witches say to him.

Come back and we'll show you, he thought. Was it something important? What if it had to do with the stone and the map? He still hadn't taken the time to sift through Grandpa's story and find clues to the map. When could he? His training would fill his schedule. Gathering the skills to lead the elite was his only shot at convincing the Peppercorns he was put in charge of the family too.

The Peppercorns. He remembered the witches' whispers. The longer he thought about it, the more it bothered him. It warbled in his insides. What the witches had to say could be vital to the overall mission. He argued with himself. Were they just deceiving him? He thought not. Perhaps the warbling was just his natural curiosity, which was a good thing. After all, his curious nature brought him along this journey in the first place. Had he not worked up the guts to sneak into Grandpa's room on the boat, he may never have been given the Emerson Stone.

This persuaded him. He had to find out. But when? How could he get back there? Guards covered all the gates to the castle. How would he sneak from Marg's home to the castle unnoticed? He wouldn't have a good enough explanation for why he was out at night. Especially for so long. He looked at Rio, still talking to the elite. Now was the time to move.

"Rio," Ace called. His voice carryied in a deep reverb through the Great Hall. The elite stopped talking and the drake looked at him. "I—uh—I have to go to the bathroom."

The hunters chuckled together. Except for Sebastian, who maintained his usual unhappy glare.

"Down the hall, past the double doors, and to your right," Rio said. Ace gave the drake a thumbs-up and smiled. He pulled his thumb away.

Stupid, stupid!

He never gave a thumbs-up. And his smile felt quirky and unusual. He was about to give away his motives and he hadn't even pursued them yet. Luckily, Rio turned back and spoke to the elite, brushing it aside. Ace walked the hall in front of him. The double doors were straight ahead, and the entry to the cellar to the right.

He peered around him to make sure nobody saw, then sprinted down the winding staircase. Halfway down the stairs, the witch whispers came to him again.

He'sss coming back. He'sss coming back.

They had been expecting him. They could sense his presence. He knew this because he felt theirs in a darkness like impending doom. He walked to the cellar door coated in anti-magic orange.

"I'm back," he whispered. "Now tell me." His whispers seemed to be only in his mind, but not escape his lips.

One witch screeched so high, he covered his ears and his back hit the wall. He slid to the ground. The whispers grew louder. Yelling. They yelled in his brain.

You came back for usss! You came back for usss! You came back for usss!

"Yes!" Ace said, his teeth gritting, and face scrunched. "Now tell me, witches! How do you know the Peppercorns? You gave me your word!"

Their laughter turned to a deep roar.

We are no witch. We are no witch.

He tilted his head. He looked through the glowing orange bars of the cellar door. The witches stepped aside, leaving a pathway in the middle of the cellar. Four shadowy figures stood in a line together, their heads bowed. They held staffs of skull and bone, and necklaces of skulls hung around their necks. Tipped shoulder pads rested over their shiny black robes, and hoods covered their faces. They wore plate armor around their torsos and gauntlets on their wrists. Ace kept moving closer to get a better look from outside the bars. He saw nothing else of their faces. Were they Evelanders? Jags?

"Who are you?" Ace said.

"We are the gods of Yutara," they said in unison. Their voices filled Ace's chest with a deep bass. "The gods of the seven realms."

"I don't understand."

"We rule from the shadows. No one sees us. No one knows us. But all of Yutara will bow to us."

His heart plummeted. He stepped back, tripped over the stairs, and fell on his back.

The council, he thought. *These are the Warlocks.* He sat straight.

"You call us the council," the warlocks said. Apparently, they could hear his thoughts. "We call us the divine guide."

He swallowed a lump, wanting to run, but he still hadn't discovered what he came here for.

"What do you want with the Peppercorns? How do you know them?"

"What we want with them we already have. The question is what *you* want with them."

"I don't understand this nonsense. Just tell me what you want."

"Don't you know? The Peppercorns belong to us now."

He stuttered a moment, then his mouth dropped. How could he have not guessed this before? No wonder the Peppercorns were so terrible! No wonder Grandpa wanted to find a cure so badly! He was trying to save the Peppercorns! They were witches! But neither of them were eighteen yet. The curse must not have taken effect. Only one thing seemed to make sense. It was something he could hardly bear to discover. If the Peppercorns belonged to the council, but they were not yet eighteen, there must be a curse on their family. A curse under the name Peppercorn. Marcus Peppercorn, their father, was a parcel. The more he thought about it, the more it made sense. He was a point guard for one of the best basketball teams in Yutara. Quite possibly the most talented. One of the richest men in the world, and most famous. Riches, fame, glory. The council granted this to him. But at what price?

"You're a smart one," the council said perceiving the boy's thoughts again.

Ace stepped back at the force of fear driving him away.

"You're not prepared for this journey," the council said.

What journey? Ace thought. Did they know about the—

"The Emerson Stone?" At the council's mention of the stone a thunderous roar of shrieks and cries echoed through the vast of the castle. Or so it seemed to Ace. "Don't you know why you were put on this journey?"

Ace's eyes began to well. "Why?"

"Once a witch belongs to us, they are indebted to us. We own them. There's only one way to reverse this: a soul for a soul. The only way to save a witch is to die for one. Marty found the cure, he just didn't tell anyone. Because he knew you'd take on the task, knowing full well that the seventh realm cannot be destroyed. Once you find it, we will be waiting for you. You will not stand a chance against us. You will die in Marcus's place, pay his debt to us, and the Peppercorns will be set free."

"You're lying!" Ace yelled. "Grandpa would never do that to me!"

The halls erupted with their laughter and screeching.

"All will bow to the council! We cannot be defeated!" They roared. Ace turned and ran back up the winding staircase, and the warlocks continued to yell from below. "To defy the council brings death and destruction! Our will be done! Our will be done!"

The voices stopped once he reached the hall again. He held his head, hands over ears, and fell to the ground as he lost the strength in his body. He lay still and bundled, save for the heaving from tears he couldn't hold back.

Grandpa wouldn't do it! Grandpa wouldn't do it! he thought.

"Ace! Are you okay?" Rio said, rushing toward him. Ace hyperventilated and sweat poured from his body. No one else was around other than Rio. The drake picked him up, looked all around, and carried him away. Perhaps the weight of what he'd just heard proved too painful to bear, or perhaps the nonstop travel had left him exhausted and his body couldn't take it anymore. Whatever the reason, Ace's consciousness slipped into darkness.

CHAPTER TWENTY-FIVE

Cameron's Tricks

Ace woke in his room in Marg's house. He hopped from his bed and looked at the top bunk. Cameron wasn't there. He took a few deep breaths. It was all a bad dream, wasn't it? The council? The sacrifice? He fell to his knees as his eyes welled again. The last thing he remembered was Rio carrying him away. It wasn't a dream, it really happened. But why would Grandpa do such a thing? He really *did* care more about the Peppercorns than him and Cameron. He was willing to sacrifice his youngest grandson to save his granddaughters. No wonder he couldn't tell the others what was going on. He opened his eyes, the hardwood floor a blur through his teardrops. A few of them fell and splashed on the ground, and his vision cleared for a moment.

He looked up at the muffled sound of feet thudding up the stairs. He wiped his face and nose as Cameron opened the room door.

"Ace, you're awake!" Cameron fell and wrapped his brother in an embrace. "Are you okay?"

"Oh—uh—" Ace reached around Cameron's neck and wiped his own nose again. "I just had a bad dream is all. It seemed so real."

They held each other a moment and Ace wrestled with his insecurity. Why keep secrets from his brother anymore? No reason to listen to Grandpa after what he'd learned.

"Cameron."

"What is it, bro?" Cameron said, pulling away from the embrace.

"There's something I need to tell you," Ace said. "I—"

"You're awake!" Rio said, from down the stairs. He leaped up the stairs, his webbed feet clapping the wood on the way. "I was getting a little worried."

Ace shot a strange look at the drake. "What happened, Rio?" he said, rubbing his head.

"Not sure," the drake said. "We went for an early morning jog together, and halfway through you just passed out."

Drakes really suck at lying, Ace thought. The boy nodded in agreement anyway.

"How are you feeling?" Rio said.

"Better."

"Good! Supper will be ready shortly. You need to eat and keep up your strength."

Ace smiled and nodded as the drake left the room and the door wide open. Cameron kept his eyes on the drake the whole way down, then jerked his head back to Ace.

"You weren't really jogging, were you?" Cameron whispered.

Ace shook his head.

"Did it have something to do with the witch hunting?"

Ace nodded. Cameron glanced around.

"I found a way to sneak out of here," Cameron whispered. "How about tonight after dinner we head out and you can start showing me some stuff."

Ace wiped his eyes and nose. "Sounds good."

At the first bite of dinner, Ace realized how hungry he'd been. Marg really knew how to cook roast conies with mash and beans. He knew how to tell jokes too. Every few minutes he had a new one, leaving the table spitting up their food. Save for Rio, who only cracked a timid smile every now and then. Ace laughed, but barely. His eyes were glued on the Peppercorns all evening. They complained about how the mash was too squishy, and the conies too dry. Their attitudes would bother anyone, but he saw it in a new light. He despised them. Being family, he just learned to put up with them all these years. Not anymore. How could Grandpa pick him for this? Sacrificing him to save those bratty girls. Forget it! By the time Tamara turned eighteen, he would have enough experience as a hunter. He could capture them and keep them in the cellar under his castle. And if he had the Emerson Stone, he was immune to anything they'd try to throw at him. They deserved it. No one should be allowed to take a parent from a Halder without suffering the consequences.

After dinner, when Rio wasn't looking, Ace snuck by the drake's belongings and grabbed some training discs. After everyone had gone to bed and the lights went out, Cameron jumped down from the top bunk.

"C'mon," his older brother whispered. Ace threw off his sheets and tiptoed with Cameron, being sure to grab his backpack first. The one with The Emerson Stone. They opened the bedroom door. The lights were off in the entire house. In the hall between his room and the Peppercorns was a bathroom, and inside sat a small window in the tile wall.

"Shut the door," Cameron whispered.

Ace shut the door quietly.

"I thought it was permanently shut at first," Cameron said. He opened a door underneath the sink and reached for something. The window grew bright, and the glass disappeared.

"How did you do that?" Ace said.

"I have a few tricks up my sleeve, little bro." Cameron poked him on his chest. "Don't forget it either."

Cameron climbed out the window first; a tree branch led straight to the back of the house, thick enough for them to walk across. He helped Ace next. They climbed down the tree and landed in an alley of grass. The backs of houses faced them on either side.

Cameron led him further down the alley to a pile of shrubs. The street lights shone from the courtyard in front of the houses, casting shadows as they trotted along. The shrubs ahead had glossy leaves, reflecting the streetlight beams in a fuzzy glow. His older brother brought him inside the bushes. They ducked and jumped over obstacles for a minute, getting scratched by the sharp branches every now and then, until the shrubs led to a hollow opening inside. Speckles of light covered the ground as the streetlights found their way through the spaces in the leaves.

"How did you find this place?" Ace said.

"It's like I told ya," Cameron said, his arms spread wide. "Tricks up my sleeve."

CHAPTER TWENTY-SIX

Ace Spills the Beans

A knot twisted in Ace's stomach so tightly he could barely stand. He sat on the soft grass as the weight of the world brought him down. He didn't feel like training. But he wasn't going through this alone anymore. Cameron was the only one he could truly trust.

"You okay, bro?" Cameron said.

Ace placed his face in the palms of his hands and shook his head. "I have so much to tell you, Cameron."

Cameron sat crisscross in front of his younger brother and placed a hand on his shoulder. "You can tell me anything. Halders stick together."

Ace half smiled. Where to begin? How could he even go about explaining what was happening? What would his older brother think? Cameron broke the silence before Ace could find the right words.

"So, when do I get to fight a witch, huh?" he said playfully.

Ace chuckled. "Well actually, you already met one."

"Huh?"

"You promise you'll keep this between us, right?"

Cameron nodded and crossed his heart. "Promise."

"We were ambushed by a group of them in Oola. They attacked us, but Rio came with his hunter friends and saved us. They took your memory in a spell just before Rio got there. That's why you can't remember."

Cameron rubbed his head, a confused look on his face. "But why would they take my memory?"

"They don't want to be found. Rio told me that whenever a witch casts a spell, memory is the first to go."

Cameron scratched his head, eyes wide. "They really are everywhere, aren't they?"

Ace nodded. "Except here."

Cameron tilted his head with curiosity.

"Grandpa had so many secrets from us," Ace said, lowering his head in sadness. "To protect us. Well, *you* anyway." He lifted his head to look back at his older brother. "This city is governed by a group of people called the Indies. Witchcraft is outlawed here in any shape or form. The guards are all hunters who have been trained to detect witchcraft and capture anyone who practices it. It's the last safe place in Yutara. And the craziest thing is that Grandpa founded this movement. Our Grandpa, Cameron. He even helped design Gathara."

Cameron scooted closer. "That's why Grandpa wanted us here?"

Ace nodded. "The witches are after us. They despise Grandpa and what he's done to the council. They wanted him dead, so they took him from us. And now they're after his family. More specifically, me."

"Council?" Cameron said.

Ace took a deep breath as he looked at his older brother. This was it. Time to spill the beans. Everything he and Rio had been trying so hard to keep secret was coming out now. After what he found out about Grandpa, there was no reason to keep his promise any longer. It wasn't like he was going to the seventh realm anymore. Not to die just to save the Peppercorns. What a waste. He was tired of all the secrets. He thought back to the day at the waterfall when he and Cameron agreed there would be no secrets anymore. It was time to hold up his end of the bargain. Forget his promise to Grandpa.

"Listen carefully, and repeat nothing," said Ace. "Though we're safe here, the witches will want information from us. I found this out today. Witches kept whispering to me in my head and tempting me to speak with them. All I had to do was feel the wrong thing, and suddenly they knew who I was, and who I was related to."

"I thought you said there weren't witches here."

"Well, not in the streets. The Indies keep them in a dungeon."

Ace went on to tell Cameron everything, start to finish. He told Cameron about the Emerson Stone and how once Grandpa gave Ace the stone, he gave away his protection, as well as the protection of everyone older than Ace. How Grandpa's story possibly revealed the secret map to the seventh realm. How Grandpa had set him up to die for the Peppercorns. How the council had taken hold of Yutara. Everything. Cameron sat silently while Ace went on, hardly able to fathom the news. Once he had finished explaining everything, his brother took a deep breath and sat quietly for a moment.

"The Emerson Stone," Cameron said, finally breaking the silence. "It—it's real?"

Ace grabbed his backpack, unzipped the largest pouch and pulled the chest from his backpack. He pulled the watch from his pocket and opened the chest. Cameron stretched his neck to look in the chest. The stone's red glow beamed across the curves of his of his wide-eyed, mouth-agape expression.

"Wow," he said quietly.

Ace shut the chest and put it back in his bag. The red glow could have attracted unwanted attention.

"Okay, okay," Cameron said, his hands forward as if he were pushing something. "So, let me get this straight. Grandpa told you that having the stone means you will have to fight the seventh realm, right?"

"Yes."

"But the witches told you—"

"The council," Ace corrected.

"Right," Cameron said. "Council. Anyway, they told you this was a set up? A way to save Julie and Tamara?"

Ace nodded.

Cameron stood, his hand on his forehead. "I—I can't believe it."

"Me neither."

"When will Julie and Tamara be handed over to this council?"

"When they turn eighteen."

"Okay, so, we have less than a year to find this realm then."

Ace stood, confused at what his brother just said. Was he deaf? Did he not just hear Ace had to die to save the Peppercorns? Certainly his only sibling wouldn't choose the rotten Peppercorns over him! Would he?

"What are you talking about? I'm not going to find the seventh realm!" Ace said.

"We can't just let the Peppercorns be turned to slaves, Ace," Cameron said.

"So, you're okay with *me* dying then?"

"No, no, no. Of course not. There—there has to be some other way."

"What then? Tell me! I'd love to hear it!"

"Just calm down, Ace. Think for a second. Why would you believe everything the council said?"

He stepped back. "Well—I mean—I don't believe *everything* they said," Ace replied.

"Okay, so what *do* you believe?"

Ace sat again and folded his arms. "I'm not sure. Something tells me the curse is real. The Peppercorns kinda already act like witches anyway. And Uncle Marcus. He's had so much success and fame. That's usually a sign of a parcel, at least from what Rio told me. It's also exactly the kind of person Aunt Kaitlyn would go for. Another way to stay ahead of Dad. And, if the council really wanted to get at Grandpa, having his daughter marry a parcel is a genius move. It makes perfect sense really."

Cameron nodded in agreement as he sat next to his brother again. "Right. I'm with you there. But do you really think the only way to save them is for you to die?"

Ace wiped his nose, sniffed, then looked at Cameron. "I don't know. Grandpa dedicated his life to finding this cure apparently. I guess it would make sense that he gave me the stone and sent me away to accomplish it once he found out how to save them."

"C'mon, Ace. The warlocks said the only way to save her was for someone to die. If Grandpa discovered that, he would have sacrificed himself, and you know that. He basically sacrificed himself when he gave you the stone. Why would he do that if he could have saved the Peppercorns by dying himself?"

Ace remained silent and slightly annoyed. He wasn't sure why, but somehow this news seemed to bother him more than the original news.

He shrugged. "We don't know that. Maybe there's some reason he couldn't have done it. Maybe he needed a kid or something. He's always loved the Peppercorns more than us anyway. It makes sense when you think about it, honestly."

Cameron smacked his teeth and tilted his head. "C'mon, Ace. You know that's not true. Grandpa loved us all the same. The Peppercorns may not know that, but you and I do."

He stood to his feet. "No, I don't know that. For all I know he'd rather I had never been born." His face grew hot.

"Okay, Ace. What's really bothering you?" Cameron said.

"That *is* what's really bothering me!" he said. How could Cameron tell he was lying? Every time Cameron called him out, the knot twisted harder in his stomach. "I just don't want to die," Ace said. "I think that's pretty reasonable, don't you?"

"You know the council was lying to you, bro. You know Grandpa would never do that to you," Cameron said as he stood, contesting his brother and winning with his height. He was right, of course. Sending him off to his death seemed too far out of character for Grandpa. And his point about Grandpa sacrificing himself by giving the stone away made sense as well. Ace was backed into a corner. Nowhere to go. No excuses anymore.

The knot in his stomach pulled so tight it burst. It traveled up his throat and spewed out of his mouth. "I don't *want* to save them!" he yelled.

Silence took over as Cameron faced his younger brother, eyes wide. Ace turned his back and sat back down as tears brimmed in his eyes. Saying it out loud made him realize what had been bothering him. If Grandpa had betrayed him, if Grandpa truly loved the Peppercorns more than him, then he had an excuse not to embark on the journey to save the Peppercorns. He could pin their misfortune on Grandpa's selfishness, rather than his own. He could finally be better than the Peppercorns and make Dad and Grandpa proud. Even though he didn't want to admit it out loud, his heart leaped at those thoughts. But the Peppercorns deserved it! They were rotten girls. His heart pumped waves of anger through his veins. Cameron sat by his side.

"You know," his brother said softly, "you can blame whoever you want for what happened to Mom, but it won't bring her back."

He looked at Cameron as he wiped the tears from his cheeks. "This has nothing to do with Mom."

"I know you better than you think, little bro," Cameron said.

He did. Which made Ace angry. He didn't want to talk about this. It felt gross.

"The Peppercorns are basically little witches already. They're evil . . . and spoiled . . ." Ace said. "Why should I help them?"

Cameron gently placed his hand on his brother's back. His body relaxed at the warm touch. "I'm not saying it's fair . . . I'm saying it's right."

"Why are you defending them?"

"Because, like it or not, they're still family."

Ace jerked his head to Cameron with a scrunched face. "How can you say that? After everything they've done to us over the years! After what Julie did to M—" Ace stopped himself. Cameron shot him an eager look, waiting to hear more. Ace looked ahead and wiped his nose again. This subject had been discussed long enough, so he changed the topic to avoid his unsettling stomach. "Rio knows about the hunting obviously. He's a hunter himself. But he doesn't know about the stone. Other than you, me, and Grandpa, no one does. We need to make sure it stays that way."

Cameron let out a sigh of frustration.

"Well," Ace said as he stood, "even if we *do* go to the seventh realm, we're gonna need to learn how to defend ourselves. Let's not forget what we snuck out here for in the first place."

Cameron smirked, standing with his brother. Ace pulled the chrome AMHB Rio had given him from his back pants pocket and handed it to Cameron. The older Halder took it without hesitation.

Cameron chuckled. "Sweet."

Ace reached in his backpack and pulled his target discs. He placed a few on the other end of the shrub, then stepped back.

"Targets on," he said.

CHAPTER TWENTY-SEVEN

Dreams

Hologram people shot up in beams of blue light from the discs. They walked through a city landscape of blue pixels. Hovercrafts stacked in lanes as tall as the skyscrapers. Flashing lights covered the city. It couldn't be mistaken for a city anywhere other than Eveland.

Ace moved a small lever on the side of the blaster in Cameron's hand. The word *Practice* was inscribed on the chrome surface under the lever. "Which one is the witch?" Ace whispered. Cameron looked at his younger brother, then back at the hologram people.

"How am I supposed to know?" Cameron said.

"Pay attention," Ace said. His older brother squinted as the hologram city people walked along in their daily lives. His eyes moved back and forth, combing every part of the city. Ace stepped back and observed his brother in silence, nearly certain Cameron would prove himself a better hunter than he.

"By the seventh!" cried a voice. It crackled and popped as if the voice were made of the same pixels as the virtual city. *"They have no right. We ought to go in there and give 'em a nice beat down."*

Cameron walked closer, holding the blaster by his side. He walked into an alley occupied by two men and a woman, and Ace followed close behind to observe. The virtual people spoke under a tavern sign just outside the door. The lady draped herself over one of the man's arms. *"Oh, Johnny, you would do that for me?"*

The man puffed his chest. *"'Course I would. They'll think better of kicking us out next time. Now first, we need to get him alone, let's plan on . . ."*

"Blaster! He has a blaster!" a voice shouted nearby. Cameron jerked his head to find a lady in the streets pointing at his AMHB and shrieking.

"Lady calm down, it's—" Cameron began to say, but police sirens sounded in the distance. He looked down the alley, and the three people had started running the other way. He took off after them, and when he got close enough, he pulled the trigger. The blue hologram version of an anti-magic bullet zipped through the sky and hit the lady in the back, sending her to the ground.

"Got her!" Cameron said. The simulation froze, the blue pixels turned red, and letters popped in front of him reading *Mission Failed.* "What? How?"

"Remember," Ace said, "a witch's most powerful tool is deception. Look closely." Cameron turned and squinted. His face dropped as he realized what had happened. The lady who saw his blaster and shouted for the cops. She was the wit—

A bright light cut on blaring from outside the bushes. Cameron and Ace jumped back.

"What's going on out here?" said a voice. A familiar voice.

"We were just getting some fresh air, Rio," Ace said, his hand covering his eyes from the blaring light.

"Yeah right!" Rio said as he jumped into the bushes and grabbed Ace's arm.

"Hey! Let go of me!" Ace said.

Marg stepped inside the bushes as well. "You two shouldn't be out here training," the jag said. "It not safe."

"Ace and I just needed some time to talk. Bro to bro," Cameron said.

"Sure, right," Rio said, his voice climbing in anger. The drake held his flashlight down and he and Marg's faces became more visible. Rio stared at Cameron, an angry glare in the frog man's eyes. It looked spooky even from Ace's angle. "What did he tell you?"

Cameron looked at Ace, Rio's grip grew firmer. Weird how strong a grip the drake had for such a slimy hand. Every time Ace thought he could slip out, the drake somehow held him in place.

"What are you talking about?" Cameron said. Marg stepped forth, placing his beefy hand on Cameron's shoulder.

"Please, ug," Marg said. "Let us know what told you. You two don't know what dealing with, and we trying to help."

Ace finally pulled free from Rio's grip and yanked his arm away. "I told him everything!"

"Do you have any idea how stupid that was?" Rio yelled. "First you go running off back to the cellar by yourself, whispering to the witches, nearly getting yourself killed, and now *this.* If the elite hear that you've been whispering with witches and telling your brother their secrets, you will *never* be allowed to lead Gathara!"

"Maybe I don't want to!" Ace yelled back.

Rio clicked and rattled his tongue in such a way Ace was sure he was saying bad words. "It's just as well, then! I knew your grandfather made a mistake picking you! You were showing promise for a while, but you just couldn't help running your mouth, could you?" Rio said.

"Hey everybody, calm down," Marg said.

"Look, Rio," Cameron said, "I'm sorry, okay? I convinced Ace to bring me out here. I kept pestering him about it. It's my fault, not his."

"No, no. It was *all* my fault!" Ace said, waving his hand around. The words poured out of his mouth like hot lava. "I told Cameron everything, Rio! You know why? Because we're brothers! We stick together. We tell each other things, you know? Unlike you!"

"What are you rattling on about?" Rio said.

"When were you planning on telling me about the Peppercorns, huh? When were you planning on telling me that my uncle is a parcel?" Ace said.

Rio's eyes widened as he stepped back. He sighed. "The witches told you. Didn't they?"

Ace nodded, his head pulsing with rage.

"You weren't supposed to know about that yet," Rio said. "Had you not been so stupid as to run off by yourself—"

"But I did!" Ace interjected. "And you know what else I'm doing? Quitting!" Ace stormed out of the bushes.

"Wait," Cameron said, rushing after him.

"Ah, good riddance!" Rio yelled from behind.

Ace stomped away until he felt Cameron's hand on his shoulder.

"Ace don't do this," Cameron said, turning him around to face him. "Grandpa asked you to take his place for some reason. You can't turn your back on him."

"You heard Rio. Grandpa made a mistake," Ace said as he folded his arms.

"No, he didn't," Cameron said.

"He did, Cameron. He did. I'm the youngest, and least talented. It's always been that way. The only reason he wanted me along was so he could save his precious granddaughters."

"If Grandpa thought you were the least talented, he would've never chosen you, bro," Cameron said.

Ace pouted, his arms crossed again. Why was Cameron so good at arguing?

"You had another dream, didn't you?" Cameron said. Ace's head jerked toward his older brother. Why did he persist on this subject? He knew how much he hated it. He knew how terrible it made him feel!

"Stop bringing this back to Mom. This has nothing to do with her!" Ace stomped his foot, clenching his fists next to his side. "You're not listening to me, Cameron."

"Actually, right now, I'm the only one who is," Cameron said. "I have dreams too, Ace. I miss her too. But we can't bring her back. You have to for—"

"Shut up!" Ace said, storming away. He ran to the house, up the stairs, slammed his door shut, locked it, and fell to his bed. He grabbed his pillow and threw it against the wall. He wanted to grab other things but there wasn't much to grab. Instead he fell to the floor and squeezed his pillow with all his might, letting the rage escape him little by little.

Moments later, he heard the muted tone of the front door opening and footsteps coming inside the house.

"See! I told you!" Julie said, her voice muffled from outside the room door, "I told you they were sneaking out!"

"Quiet, Julie," Marg said. "Go back bed."

"Aw, Julie," Tamara said, laughing with her sister. "You made the poor baby cry."

Ace threw his pillow at his bedroom door. "Shut up, you witches!" The insult had a fresh, more powerful meaning this time.

"Back to bed!" Rio yelled. "Now!"

The Peppercorns laughed as they walked to their room and shut the door. The sound of footsteps coming up the stairs was interrupted by Rio's voice.

"Cameron, let him be alone for a little while," the drake said. "The sofa turns into a bed. You should stay down here for the night."

Cameron didn't respond. Ace only heard the footsteps retreating downstairs. He clenched his fists and grit his teeth. He stood and paced the floor.

I hate them! I hate the Peppercorns! Grandpa loved them more. He never loved me. They deserve to rot! Let them rot! I won't save them! I won't!

The knot in his stomach loosened as he spoke these things to himself, and he plummeted back to the bed and lay on his pillow. But as he lay staring at the plain wall ahead, Cameron's voice kept popping into his head, and he could find no strength to fight it.

I have dreams too, Ace. The knot tightened again. *I miss her too.* It tightened more. *But we can't bright her back, you have to for*

—

The knot popped and burst once again. He wept until his eyes were empty of every drop. Ace knew what Cameron was about to say, and he wouldn't have it. Never, in a million years, would he forgive the Peppercorns for what happened.

CHAPTER TWENTY-EIGHT

Compromise

Ace woke to the sound of a knock on his door. Being too groggy to tell if he was dreaming or not, he rolled his feet off the side of his bed and stared at his bedroom door, listening to see if it would happen again. The door cracked open, and Rio poked his head inside.

"Good, you're awake," the drake said. He stepped in further, shut the door, and turned the light on. "I didn't want to have to wake you up myself."

Ace rubbed his eyes. "What do you want?"

"Your training begins today, kid, remember?"

Ace scoffed at Rio. "I told you, I'm quitting."

"Yeah? What are you gonna do then? Hide here with your family until the witches find you and Gathara turns to chaos?"

Ace didn't respond. He only shook his head and looked away. Rio's footsteps thumped against the hardwood as he stepped closer.

"Look, kid, I want to apologize for last night. I shouldn't have spoken that way toward you," Rio said.

Ace turned to face him slowly. Still, he said nothing.

"I have to admit, I've been a little shaky about you. Not knowing whether Marty made the right decision by picking you for such a task. But the more I get to know you, the more I see what your grandfather saw in you. There's a little more to it though. Every single one of us—the elite I mean—we all thought Marty would pick us when he retired or something. But I didn't think he'd pick me," the drake said, now sitting on the bed beside Ace. "I *knew* he'd pick me. Marty and I were the closest. He taught me everything I know about hunting. We stood together side by side every day. He and I chose the elite together. Even the elite—though they hoped otherwise—thought I would end up taking Marty's place someday. But I didn't. *You* did." Rio's eyes glossed over like they were covered with smooth glass. "We've been working years for this. Fought so many battles next to Marty. He kept his family in the dark about all of it because he wanted to protect you all. We never thought this would happen. *And* of all his descendants, he chose you. The youngest, and least experienced. I don't mean to be rude, it's just simply the truth." Ace nodded in agreement. "But," Rio continued, "I've seen something in you that I haven't seen in anyone else. Not even your brother. And *especially* not your cousins." Ace smiled, and his anger slowly melted. "I see Marty in you. You learn quick. I'm not saying it doesn't upset me that Marty didn't choose me. Because it does. But there's no doubt in my mind that he made the right decision. We need you, Ace. If what the Indies stand for is going to last for any amount of time, or make any difference in the world, it's not going to happen without you."

Ace's mouth slanted in a half smile, but he still felt the need to contest the drake's conclusion. "What makes you so sure, Rio? I've only captured one witch."

"Capturing witches isn't the only thing a hunter does, kid. The way you put Sebastian in his place in the meeting. Or the way you fearlessly entered the cellar without question. Not to mention how you went by yourself just to learn more about them," Rio said. "No one your age has ever done any of those things without consequence."

Not to mention, the council showed up to see me, Ace thought. He hadn't truly considered what such a thing meant. Rio said warlocks were never seen, and no one knew the members of the council. They appeared to him in physical form and threatened him. They even knew about the Emerson Stone. It had to mean something. But he couldn't tell Rio about the stone. He had better keep the information about the council appearing to himself.

"So, you really think I'm that special, huh?" Ace said, a smirk on his face.

Rio chuckled. "Don't get cocky, now."

"I'll come and train with you on one condition," Ace said. "Cameron trains as a hunter and helps protect the family."

Rio clacked his tongue and his next words cut through the air. "Absolutely not. I've arranged with the elite to have hunters guard the house when Marg and I are at the recall today. They will be plenty protected."

"Then forget it," Ace said, falling back into his bed. He thought about his connection with his brother the previous night. Even though he didn't appreciate Cameron constantly bringing up Mom, his brother was who he trusted most. He was tired of being alone in this journey. He already told Cameron everything, and the older brother would make a great hunter.

"Ace, I can't risk the safety of your family anymore. Cameron may not have the immunity to witchcraft like you do. Your grandfather picked you for a reason. He didn't want to risk the lives of his family," Rio said.

"I'd say their lives are already in danger as it is. You have hunters protect us every day."

"Being a hunter and knowing about witches makes you a target. I won't do that to your brother."

"Then the hunters you sent to protect us are targets too," Ace said.

Rio sighed. "It's different, Ace."

"How?" Ace said, sitting back up and staring eye to eye with

Rio. "Cameron knows the risks. He's talented and smart and could be a great help! It should be *his* choice, not Grandpa's."

Rio shook his head softly. "Your cousins are cursed. You're taking over leadership of the Indies. How am I supposed to sleep knowing I let Marty's last safe grandchild join the hunters?"

"*Safe?* You're living in a fairy tale, Rio. None of us are safe. It's only an illusion. False security. You know what I think safe is? Having the necessary training to defend yourself." Rio stared at Ace silently for a moment. Ace sighed and spoke softly, "It's more than that though . . . I *need* him. We're Halders you know, and we—"

"Stick together," Rio said under his breath. "You say that a lot, kid. It gets annoying sometimes."

Ace smirked. "Deal with it."

The drake stood from the bed, hands on his hips, facing the wall as he pondered the situation. After a moment of quiet, he turned to Ace.

"Let me tell you something," Rio said, pointing his finger. "If I let Cameron train, and anything happens to him, you will know then it could have been avoided had we not had this conversation."

Ace raised an eyebrow. "And if you *don't* let him train and something bad happens to him, same goes for you."

Rio chuckled. "You're a stubborn little thing."

Ace snickered and crossed his arms.

"Just like your grandfather," Rio said under his breath. "Go wake your brother. Tell him he's coming with us."

CHAPTER TWENTY-NINE

The Simulation Room

Ace compared the training room to his hologram discs on a much larger scale. The inside walls wrapped around in the shape of a cylinder and were lined with a muddy-colored brass. Thick glass covered blaring lights on the roof and ceiling. So clear, when he glanced at his feet, it looked like he was hovering above the lights. Ihana followed Ace in the room.

"Stop there," she said. He turned around. She walked to him with a blaster rifle in her hand. It was nearly half his size. She handed it to him and pointed to the areas of the blaster as she named them.

"Barrel. Generator. Trigger (*obviously*). Pistol grip. Front grip. Rear sight. Front sight. Buttstock." She stopped and looked at him. "There's more, but that's all for now, got it?"

Ace nodded. "What's the generator for?"

"It holds the anti-magic and needs to be replaced when it runs out of juice."

Ace inspected the weapon with interest.

"Know how to shoot?"

Ace nodded. "Grandpa taught me when I was seven actually."

"Know how to shoot a *hunter's* rifle?"

"Uh—is there a difference?"

"No. Just wanted to remind you that having a famous Grandpa doesn't make you an expert on witch hunting, got it?"

Ace swallowed and nodded.

Keele's muffled voice came over an intercom. "Why are you giving him the rifle?"

"Aren't we running target practice? Simulation Twelve?" Ihana replied to the ceiling.

"Nope. Twenty-seven," she replied. A sly smile came over the water drake and she snatched the rifle from Ace's hand.

"Your mission is to find the witch, capture her, and bring her to the cellar. If you can find the parcel, that's a plus. Any questions?" the water drake said. She placed a chip on the right side of his head.

"Without a rifle?" Ace said.

"Start the program!" Ihana yelled as she walked away. "Good luck, kid. Although you shouldn't need it. Being immune and all," she said with a smirk. The door slammed shut behind her, and the lights dimmed until pitch darkness swallowed the room.

Pixels popped into existence by the millions. Large white columns surrounded him one-by-one. They stretched to a coffered ceiling of gold and dark blue. The hardwood floor reflected the warm lights surrounding the room everywhere the dark blue rug hadn't covered. Stairs with waxed and polished railing wound on either side of him, leading to a balcony looking over the grand hall. Beam lights hung on the walls, under and above the balcony. Recessed lights sank into the ceiling. Chairs surrounded large round tables draped in white tablecloths scattered across the rug, and a small stage sat in the middle of the room with a chrome podium. Above the stage hung a banner which read:

Congratulations, President Kar

Ace was in the Capitol building. In Adamsville! At the night Angus Kar won the Eveland presidential election. Years before he was even born. His eyes fixed on the banner as people popped into existence around him. Almost exclusively humans other than a drake here, and a jag there. All of them were frozen in place. The last person who appeared was President Kar, dressed in a suit of shining silver, a navy blue collared shirt underneath, and a white tie. His brown hair was slicked perfectly back, and he wore his smile famous for melting hearts.

Once the room was filled with people, something like a deep click echoed in the hall, and he jumped at the sound of thunderous applause coming into virtual existence. Angus Kar waved his hand slowly to settle the crowd. Ace looked at himself in shorts and a t-shirt, completely underdressed for the occasion. He stuck out like a sore thumb. Not to mention, he was only twelve years old. This was probably part of the elite's attempt to set him up for failure. He thought back to the advice Rio gave him before Ihana took him to the simulation room. The drake had pulled him aside in the Great Hall when no one else was around.

"Listen to me," the drake had whispered, checking around him to make sure no one was listening, *"the elite are going to start you off in a difficult simulation. They don't want you to prove what you're made of. This won't be like the training we had in New Eathelyn. Luckily, you've already had some field experience. But keep in mind, there might be thugs and gangs. We're not policemen. We're hunters. Often, the witches will be hiding in less likely places."*

"What should I look for?" Ace had asked.

"Power and influence. Anyone who has these things is a suspect. Most likely traveling in some kind of group with a leader. Dressed as good guys, because they're harder to find that way."

"Like policemen?"

"Ironically, yes."

"But how will I know for sure whether someone is a witch or a real good guy?"

"Call out anything that looks suspicious or out of place. But casually, as if you're just curious. If something feels off, chances are it

probably is. Talk about it out loud. The group will get defensive, but the more you challenge their beliefs, the angrier the witch will get. Her disguise will begin to fade, and she will resort to magic.

"There are two types of truths a witch will lie about. Ultimate truth, and immediate truth. Ultimate truth is part of the council's overall plan—the type every witch tries to hide. For instance, every witch wants people in Yutara to believe that witches are just fairy tales. Immediate truths are the things she's lying about in the moment to support their lies about ultimate truth. Like, let's say a witch is friends with the daughter of a governor. She may lie about being broken hearted over family issues while she's venting to her friend. The immediate truth is that she's not actually broken hearted. The ultimate truth is that she's trying to befriend someone with power, so she can deceive them and eventually take that power for herself. As hunters, we're always searching for the ultimate truth because it's our job to defend it. However, it's much easier to convince others of the immediate first and work your way up. Don't try to catch a witch lying about witches being real. All Yutara believes witches are fairy tales, and this will be a far more difficult route to take. Start small. What is she lying about then and there? Get the immediate first."

After Rio said those things, Ihana came and took Ace to the simulation. Which was unfortunate, because it confused Ace. He didn't fully comprehend the difference between the two truths.

"Hey, what you doing?" said a soft voice. Ace turned to his left. A female jag sat at a round table next to him. "Sit down," she said. He realized a seat was behind him, and everyone at the table glared strangely at him. The boy took a seat, a little confused as to why no one pointed out him being a twelve-year-old boy in shorts and a t-shirt. He saw a name tag on the table in front of him.

Reserved: Senator Starland

"He hasn't even said anything yet, Senator," said a deep voice. Ace turned his head to find a human male with dreadlocks pulled into a ponytail speaking to him. "I hardly think it's time for a standing ovation."

The rest of the table laughed along with the dark man. Ace

chuckled back, nervously adjusting to the simulation. He looked around his table. Other than the female jag and the man with dreadlocks, he saw a red lady drake just ahead, and two more humans, a male and female to his right and left.

"Today," Angus Kar spoke from the podium, "the people of Eveland have spoken!"

The room erupted with cheer.

"No longer will the people be subject to the paranoid policies of the Indies!" Kar said.

First suspect, Ace thought. Had this really happened in history? Maybe it was just part of the simulation. He had no knowledge of these policies Kar stood for when he ran. He didn't even have knowledge of the Indies at all until Rio came into his life. The council must have had parcels and witches everywhere, keeping knowledge of the Indies hidden even from children. This sent an unpleasant grumbling in Ace's stomach. If Kar was the parcel in this simulation, how would he even get to him?

"Too long have the Indies bullied us with fear. Attempting to outlaw our very way of life. No longer will the people of Eveland tolerate their ridiculous notions of witchcraft and magic!" The crowd cheered back, booing in agreement with Kar's disgust with the Indies. "It's time we get behind Sam Radar and see the Neutrals as our ally. During my administration, we will join the Neutrals in bringing a new era of peace to Yutara . . ."

His words became muffled as Ace's thoughts drifted. He didn't remember anything about Angus Kar supporting Sam Radar. This may have been his biggest clue, but he couldn't tell. It all depended on the theories around Sam Radar. If the man was truly bent on bringing all nations together under his rule, like the rumors said, then Ace had found his parcel. But, how did he know they weren't just rumors? Rio was right; this was heavy, high end stuff. None of it seemed like immediate truth. All of it seemed to circle around the ultimate. The speech didn't last long; he talked about tax policies and foreign policies—mostly stuff Ace felt too young to care about.

No thugs or criminals, Ace thought, *but Kar definitely has both power and influence.* After his speech, Angus Kar instructed the crowd to enjoy the celebration and stepped off the stage. At this point it seemed nearly impossible to reach Kar, as he was escorted to the balcony and surrounded by agents. Next to him sat a young, familiar looking Evelander. He couldn't put a finger on it, but he knew he'd seen him somewhere before.

One thought swept over him, turning his attention elsewhere. Agents guarded the entire building. Two by each door. All of them with the same silver suits as Kar, only with visors over their eyes and wireless earpieces in their right ears. The visors allowed them to see behind them and on either side of them at once.

"Well, I didn't expect he would win it, but he did," said the male with dreadlocks, turning to face the rest of the table. Ace listened, but kept his eyes about the entire room, looking for any suspicious behavior. Something out of place. After seeing nothing, he worried his snooping might be an issue and sabotage his cover. Another thought passed through his head. If any of them at the table were lying, it would be immediate truth. He decided to ignore his concerns about Sam Radar and Angus Kar and take it slow his first round, focusing on the conversation at the table.

"How could you not expect it?" said the red drake. "Eveland is sick of the Indies. Kar ran a genius campaign." The small fins on the side of her head wagged as she spoke, and she clicked a few incomprehensible things.

"Yes, but many of the humans have become swayed by their arguments," said the jag. "I was surprised he won too."

"Well, no matter," said the male to Ace's right, "he won it. That's all that matters."

"I'll drink to that," the lady jag said. Everyone raised their glasses, and Ace quickly joined in with his. He fought not to wince when he drank the liquid. It tasted like medicine.

"Senator Starland," said the jag. There was an eerie moment of silence. "Uh, Senator Starland? Hello?" Ace jerked his head toward the jag. He had forgotten his name in this simulation.

"Sorry, Miss—uh—" Ace glanced to the name tag on the table before the jag, "Mrs. Ruhgi. I was distracted."

The jag dismissed Ace's apology and said, "What are your

thoughts on Kar's win? We haven't heard you say much."

He wasn't sure how to respond. He still had no idea who the witch was. Would anything he said sound legitimate?

"Well—uh—I—" Ace said. Everyone stared at him with anticipation and confusion. He swallowed and spoke the first thing on his mind. "I think Kar must've had some help winning." The table stirred anxiously.

"What do you mean?" the jag said.

"I mean, I think he must have a powerful influence in Eveland. Having such a strong stance against the Indies and still winning," Ace said. He wished he was more well learned in Eveland history. He worried only pieces of what he said made sense.

The man with dreadlocks chimed in. "Well, he does. He's been Mayor of Cains for fourteen years now, and never lost an election. Obviously, the people liked him."

"A little strange, don't you think?" Ace said. The table chuckled facetiously. The jag, however, seemed particularly upset with this. He looked at her; their eye contact confirmed it.

Jackpot.

"What's strange? That Kar knows how to win elections?" the jag said.

Ace smiled, feeling the simulation was a little easier than he'd expected. "*That* many elections?"

"Yes," the jag said firmly. "That many."

Everyone at the table went silent a moment. The debate continued, and everybody leaned in to hear it. Ace thought up every challenge he could to their beliefs. They went back and forth, the argument increasingly getting more heated. But, unfortunately, the jag never seemed to resort to witchcraft. Either this witch was far more skilled than Ace had anticipated, or he was at the wrong table. Eventually the debate subsided, and servers came by with trays of food. Ace hung his head in disappointment. What could he do now? Something caught the corner of his eye. He looked to his right in time to see a man dressed like a civilian moving between the tables. A drake, in fact.

Well, there's something out of place, Ace thought. He looked closer. A green drake, very young. That was all he could make out from his distance.

Talk about it out loud, Ace remembered Rio's words.

"Who's that?" Ace said. The table looked at where Ace looked.

"Who's who?" The jag said.

Ace pointed. "That young drake." He saw something he didn't expect. His heart dropped as the green drake reached behind his back and pulled something from his shorts. He was heading for Kar. He had a blaster. Ace shot up from the table.

"Senator? What are you doing?" the man with dreadlocks yelled. Ace didn't respond, he took off, weaving through the round tables, bumping into dozens of people, eyes still fixed on the drake. He was bringing too much attention to himself, and the agents had begun to take notice. The drake started his way up the winding steps leading to the balcony, hand on his blaster. Ace finally got to the bottom stair. The drake only needed a few more steps to reach Kar. Ace bolted, sweat seeping from his skin. The drake slowly pulled the blaster from his back and pointed it straight at Kar.

"Blaster! He's got a blaster!" Ace shouted just as he made it to the top of the stairs. He tackled the drake to the ground, but not before the sound of plasma fire echoed through the hall. Screams flooded the air, and agents sprinted to the newly elected president. Ace and the drake rolled around, fighting each other, until something caused him to stop. He and the drake caught eyes. It seemed as if time slowed, and Ace grew cold with fear. The beady eyes, and the frog-like face couldn't be mistaken for anyone else.

"Rio?" Ace said.

CHAPTER THIRTY

The Caged Witch

The simulation stopped, and Ace stood, staring at the frozen chaos about the room. Everything morphed into pixels and drifted into darkness. The lights turned on in the ceiling and floor and the brass walls became visible.

Was the simulation a real historical event? Did Rio really try to shoot Angus Kar?

Ace thought back to the day Rio told him of how he and Grandpa met.

"Let's just say I got mixed up with the wrong people, and your grandfather saved me," the drake had said. The wrong people? Had Rio tried to kill a president? The door to the simulation room flung open and Ihana came stomping in.

"What was that, Halder?" Ihana said. "We're not policemen, we're hunters!"

She grabbed his shirt and pulled him to the door leading to the watch room. Inside, George and Keele sat in hover chairs by a widescreen television. On the TV was a frozen picture of Ace and the simulation.

"Hey, let go of me," Ace said. The water drake did. "I can walk by myself, you don't need to pull me."

"Can you explain what you were thinking?" she said.

Ace shrugged. "So, if I'm in a room and a president's life is in danger, I'm just supposed to let him die?"

"We're not—"

"We're not policeman, I get it!" Ace said.

"Apparently you don't! Your mission was to find the witch, not save President Kar!" Ihana said, throwing her fist down. Her veins came through her shiny blue skin. Short-tempered drakes were starting to annoy him. He took notice of Keele remaining silent, leaning back in her chair with her arms crossed.

"It's not like I had time to do anything about it. Or a hunter's rifle for that matter," Ace said. "If I had waited for Kar to be shot, the whole room would have gone to chaos."

"And then you would've had a perfect distraction," George said.

Ace looked daggers at George. "And a president would also be dead!"

"No, he wouldn't be," the hunter replied. "You really think someone could've snuck into that room with a blaster unnoticed with all those security officers around?"

The boy stared at him wordlessly. He hadn't thought of it, but George had a point. "He was allowed in?"

"Look who's finally catching on," Ihana said.

"But . . . why?"

"There was an anarchist group arising in Eveland during that time, and police were trying to track down who it was. He had a dummy blaster, dropped off by one of Eveland's undercover policemen. When we learned this setup was happening, we knew we had the perfect distraction we needed to find a witch. She wouldn't turn to magic in front of all those people, and she probably had ties with Eveland's government. Could've been a great success for us, but you screwed it up."

Gang? Rio was part of a gang? "But I heard plasma fire," Ace said, dismissing his thoughts. "It wasn't a dummy weapon."

"The blaster you heard wasn't *his*," Ihana replied sharply. "It wasn't plasma either. The police wanted to catch him, not kill him." She sighed and placed her hand on her face. "Had you at least identified the witch?"

Ace looked at the water drake, his face scrunched with frustration. "The jag at my table was my suspect. Kar was my suspect for a parcel."

"And you tried to save him?" Ihana yelled. "What's wrong with you?"

"I didn't know for sure," he said. "I can't just leave someone's life to chance like that."

"No one was asking you to leave his life to chance. What we're saying is that you need to be more observant."

"Okay, fine. I messed up. I'm still learning," Ace said.

"When you're in the field, you can't afford to mess up," Ihana said. "Let's try another one."

Ace nodded. "Before we start again, tell me something . . . Was I right?"

"About what?" Ihana said.

"Kar and the jag. They were the witch and parcel." For a moment the elite quietly traded eyes.

"The jag, yes," Keele said, finally chiming in. "But Kar was not a parcel."

Ace felt a sense of dread in his heart. *Then why was Rio trying to shoot him?* he thought as the water drake led him back to the simulation room.

How am I supposed to catch a witch without a blaster?

The thought came and went as quick as the next simulation began. Like the snap of a finger, motion stirred around him. He found himself in a small jag town wedged between two mountain ranges. An arched sign hung over the town reading, "Traverser's

Valley: West Side." One or two hovercrafts came and went every so often. They crept along the town's roads and zipped away once they passed through.

Inside the town, jags merrily went about their days on giyas: long necked reptile-like mounts with thick, fat feet and slimy skin. When they held their necks high, they could reach heights of fifteen feet, but when they ran, they kept their necks parallel with the ground, making themselves like a razor cutting through wind resistance.

Other than the few huts, and a structure here and there carved from the mountain stones, the bland, white brick like Thraun made up the other buildings. This part of Heorg had a bit more trees and green than Gathara. Most of them looked like needles with leaves. Ace moseyed through the town, wondering why they placed him here and where he was supposed to go, when something caught his ear.

" . . .by New Realm's Age, Oglen! Have you lost sense about you?"

Ace peered into a tavern carved from the stone at the bottom of the mountain. Two large male jags stood facing each other, and a small crowd encircled them. He crept inside unnoticed.

"Enough with that! Listen here, Jegri, I not put up with this anymore. It high time this ends."

The crowds bustled a bit and Ace caught a better glimpse of the two jags. He realized the one called Oglen had a knife in his hand and gripped it so tight the veins in his forearm nearly burst through his gray skin.

A female jag came rushing through the crowd and draped herself over him. "Oglen, please stop. He didn't mean anything by it!" He brushed her aside like she was made of paper and ignored her with fury in his eyes. She fell into a crowd of girl jags beside them and they caught her.

"You come my tavern," Oglen said, "you speak way I ask you speak."

Jegri held up his hands as if to offer a truce. "Oglen, there no need take this too far. We friends."

"Ever since girl get in your head, you go crazy!" Oglen said, pointing at the crowd of female jags.

"Naneg right, Oglen! You fall victim here. Traverser's Valley fall victim 'less we do something about it!"

Ace's ears perked forward. He sat in the tavern, listening carefully, scoping the crowd, looking and listening for anything able to offer clues; this had caught his attention. Fall victim to what? He glanced at the girl named Naneg. She cowered next to the other girl jag who'd tried to stop Oglen at first. What had Jegri said? What could've caused Oglen to become so angry as to want to stab him?

Oglen pointed the knife at Jegri, turned his head to the crowd, and announced, "Jegri here seems think law not matter! For past few months, he spoke ill of Valley and wished ill of Mayor!" The crowd gasped. After the jag said this, Ace noticed the portrait behind the bar of a large male jag in a white suit with a name plate under it reading *Mayor Yegeg.*

"Not true, Oglen!" Jegri shouted. "Spoke ill of him? Yes. Never wished ill. He tries tear us apart!"

The crowd murmured. Oglen hung and shook his head. "Sorry, Jegri, law is law." Two jag officers, dressed in black vests, jeans, and visors like those in Kar's simulation burst through the doors. They came in and arrested Jegri.

"Speaking ill of Mayor does not break law!" Jegri said. No one responded. The officers carried him away from the tavern as he shouted, "Oglen, open eyes! You must see!"

Naneg had her hand over her mouth and tears running down her cheeks. The other girl jag comforted her with an arm over her shoulder.

"Nothing more to see," Oglen said. "Everyone back to your drinks." The crowd slowly dispersed and settled back to their seats. The girl jags sat at a round table beside them, and Oglen walked to them and said, "Naneg, let this be lesson for you. Keep mouth closed before you end up like your boyfriend."

He turned and walked the other way, taking his girl jag with him. She shrugged at Naneg and offered a remorseful glance before Oglen took her away. Ace walked to the table slowly. He sat at the table across from it, back turned to her, listening to her quiet sobs. Knowing New Realm's Age was something only mentioned in lore, and her boyfriend mentioned it, Ace sought to befriend the crying jag. Since he knew the council pushed the idea of witches being fake, Oglen became his first suspect. Maybe there was some connection between the two? There was only one way to find out.

"The New Realm is coming," Ace said softly, back still turned to her. He heard her cries come to a sudden halt. She sniffed a couple times but said nothing. "I need to know something, Naneg. How close is Oglen to Mayor Yegeg?"

He heard her hands brush against the wooden table a couple times as she situated herself. For a moment, she didn't respond, probably trying to decide whether to trust a strange Evelander. "Wh—who you?"

"I'm a friend," Ace said without hesitation. Simulated or not, the thought of asking creepy questions in search of a witch made him feel uneasy. He spoke sure of himself in spite being unable to stop his hands from shaking against the table.

"Friend of who?"

"Jegri. That's all you need to know."

"How I know you want help us?"

"You don't. But if you want Jegri freed, you're out of options." He caught his breath. Why did he say such a thing? He just said the first thing that popped into his head. His chest caved at the thought of it. He didn't know how he could back up such a statement.

"Y—y—" She sniffed and whined a moment to keep from crying more. "You're right."

Ace sighed with relief. He coughed and stuck his chest up to reassure himself of his confidence. "So, what's the nature of Oglen's relationship with the Mayor?"

"They good friends. Best, some say. Mayor comes by often and Oglen gives free drinks."

Ace grinned wide. He settled cozily into the simulation, awaiting the look on the elite's face when he nailed it. "Listen," Ace said softly. "I can free Jegri—" he was still winging it "—Dusk is approaching. Meet me in the woods behind this tavern, okay? The alley will lead you there."

"I . . . I don't kn—"

"You want him freed or not?"

She paused a moment in silence, but finally said, "Yes."

Ace waited in the dark. The greener part at the edge of the Heorg desert carried a chill into the night, unlike Gathara. He hadn't prepared himself for the cold. Simulated or not, his brain still thought it was real. He rubbed the chip Ihana placed on his head, annoyed it was working. The light from the crescent moon shone timidly on the edges of the trees, like a thin line of yellow in an otherwise shadowed wood. He wondered if time passed the same in the simulation as it did real life. Had the elite been in the watch room for hours while he waited in the woods? What a boring job.

Branches cracked, and Ace jerked his head up. His eyes followed the sound of feet crunching the ground until he caught the shadow of Naneg creeping through the woods. He ran to catch her and grabbed her wrist.

She jolted in a fright. "Oh!"

"Shh," Ace said, and whispered, "Come with me."

He guided her through the woods to a space he'd prepared for their meeting.

"Enough!" she said, yanking free from his grip. "Why bring me out here to woods like this?"

"Because you don't know who's listening," he whispered, getting close.

"I don't understand."

"Have you ever heard of the council? "Ace said.

She smirked at him, a goofy smile played around the highlights on her skin from the yellow moon. "You kidding."

"Think about it, Naneg. They want power. Oglen is friends with the Mayor, you said it yourself. That's why they threw Jegri in prison, because he was calling out the Mayor's wrongdoings, and the Mayor has the town's minds poisoned to never question him."

Ace's heart drummed in his chest. All of this was his best guess at what was happening, and if he was wrong, he would look like a fool in front of the elite. But . . . if he was right. He leaned close. "I think Oglen is influencing the mind of the Mayor." He knew this was a long shot, going straight for the ultimate truth. And the risk had him riding a nerve-wracking, electric tsunami in his brain. "Don't you think this is true?"

Naneg laughed a little. She shook her head, placed a hand on her forehead, and breathed deep. "Of course not! You're crazy. I'm leaving." She turned to leave, but Ace grabbed her by the wrist. She stopped and turned to him, fear and uncertainty in her eyes.

"Am I?" Ace said. He bent down, hand still gripping her wrist, and swiped his finger against the ground. Just under her feet, a pool of black dust had fallen to the ground. Ace stood, rubbing the black dust between his thumb and first finger, looking at her with victory in his eyes. "Because usually parcels have witches working for them. And you just confirmed both for me."

Her face scrunched like a rotten fruit, and black smoke began emitting from her skin. Her disguise was breaking down. But before she had a chance to react, Ace yanked her with all his might and threw her into a hole he'd burrowed out earlier, while he'd been awaiting her arrival. Her body hit the lever he'd fastened in the hole with rope he carved from tree bark (something Grandpa had taught him to do on hunting trips). The cage of tree branches closed in on top of her like a jaw clenching its dinner. She squirmed and moaned and whined, but he made sure the tree branches were soaked in enough anti-magic substance, so she couldn't do anything to get free.

"What i*ss* thi*ss*? What have you done?"

"I caught you," Ace said, a wide grin on his face. After moments of her squirming and twitching, the simulation froze, faded to blackness, and the lights turned back on, so he found himself standing in the simulation room once again.

Ace stood in the simulation room silently for a moment. He anxiously tapped his fingers against his jeans, wondering when the next simulation might start. He found himself growing a little frustrated that he didn't have the chance to find the parcel and take him down. Why'd they stop the simulation so soon? The metal door groaned and echoed through the room.

Ihana stepped inside and said, "Good job, kid. That's it for today." She turned around and walked away. Ace tilted his head.

Uh . . . okay?

He hesitantly made his way to the watch room. The whole place was empty, save for Keele, who was shutting everything down.

"Hey, Keele," Ace said. The woman turned from the chair to look him over. "Where are the others?"

She chuckled. "They're butthurt."

Ace scratched his head. "Butt what?"

"Angry. Jealous. Envious," she said as she swiveled on her hover chair to finish shutting down the screens and computers. "You showed them up and they don't know how to deal with it."

Ace took a couple steps forward. "What're you talking about?"

She sighed, stood, and placed a hand on his shoulder. "I got a little secret for you. That whole *catch a witch without a rifle* thing is supposed to be a prank for newbies. No one has ever successfully caught a witch without an anti-magic weapon before. It's impossible. Or, at least we thought it was." She laughed. "Not only did you catch the witch, but you identified the parcel. That was impressive, kid. How did you know about the trees and the trap and all that stuff?"

Strange feelings circled his insides. Pride? Anger? Joy? He smirked at Keele and shrugged. "Well—uh—Grandpa used to take us on hunting trips all the time. Taught us how to make ropes from certain types of trees. As far as the anti-magic thing, Rio told me that anti-magic was made from trees."

She half smiled and nudged him, so they started walking to the door. "Good for Rio. I love that drake. Smart move, kid. How'd you know she was the witch?"

"Well, the biggest thing that caught me off guard was the fact that she was supposed to be in love with the jag who said the thing about New Realm's Age. But, whenever the police came and took him, she didn't try to stop them. And, unlike Oglen's girl, she didn't jump in the fight and try to stop them. Made me think she was lying about loving him. That was the immediate truth."

Keele stopped and gave him a strange look. "You know the difference between immediate and ultimate truth?"

Ace nodded. "Rio taught me."

"And what was the ultimate, then?"

"Oglen and Naneg were working together to get Oglen to take over the Mayor's position. They were fighting for power and influence."

Keele smirked and shook her head. "Good job, kid. Good job."

She opened the door to find a large group of trainees standing in the hall. They were staring at him and watching the replay of the simulation on screens over the doorway. When he entered the trainee hall, everyone went still and quiet. The sound of a pen would've echoed like thunder, had one fallen to the floor.

"I think everyone else knows who the new Halder is, kid. Now we just have to convince the elite," Keele said softly.

CHAPTER THIRTY-ONE

The Interim Halder

"Alright, everyone," Keele shouted to the trainees. "Show's over. Get to the Great Hall. The recall is about to begin." The crowds dispersed like ants on a hill and their voices grew loud enough to fill the halls. Keele nudged him along and they followed the crowds to the recall.

While Ace enjoyed his new fame, a different question had been pressing him since the first simulation. He looked at Keele, finally ready to get his answers. "Keele. These simulations. Are they —you know—*real?"* Ace said.

She chuckled. "Well they wouldn't be called simulations if they were, kid."

"You know what I mean," Ace said.

Keele sighed. "Yes. Some of these things really happened. But we fiddled with them and put witches into the simulations for training."

"And Rio?"

Keele didn't say anything, she just looked ahead nodded gently.

"But, why?" Ace said.

"Listen to me," Keele said. She stopped walking and turned him to face her. "After the recall, I want you to head home and wait for me there. Tell Rio to expect me. I need to speak with him."

"Is everything okay?"

"Just do as I say," she said firmly.

He nodded, his eyes still playing with uncertainty. "Keele," he said. "I'm not sure I can do this."

"Do what?" Keele said.

"This hunter thing. I mean, if I'm put in a position of defending someone's life or chasing a witch, I'd feel too compelled to do something about the person."

Keele paused for a moment before responding, "You shouldn't have seen that simulation. You weren't ready yet."

"But I did," Ace said. "Is it really right? I mean I thought we were supposed to help people."

"You weren't taught properly. Ihana and George threw you into an advanced simulation with no training or context."

"You didn't answer me."

Keele glanced at him, grunted, and stopped. "You need to understand who the real enemy is. Especially in the case of Kar's election. Rio trying to shoot him is only one piece of the larger picture. There's a greater evil that hunters have chosen to fight. We already have policemen. The world needs hunters."

"That's not good enough," Ace said. "We're sacrificing innocent people at the end of the day."

"We're sacrificing ourselves too, Ace." She buried her head in her hand. "You need to trust the police to do their job, and you need to focus on yours."

"But it's my responsibility to help!" Ace said, clenching his fist by his side.

"No, it's not!" Keele demanded. Her voice bounced off the trainee hall walls and half the hunters stopped and stared a moment. "People like Kar are placed in those simulations to prepare you. Your mission is much larger than saving them. Witches hurt people all the time. Parcels send their slaves after anyone in the way of their road to power. Witches are placed all over the world, distorting the minds of millions into believing that wrong is right, and right is wrong. People who fall victim to a witch's deception may end up defending the assassin or thug or criminal. And one parcel may have hundreds of witch slaves." Ace stood silently as Keele ranted. The woman exhaled deeply and calmed herself. "If you were closing in on a witch, they would love for you to be distracted. To stop chasing them to save an old man, or help a lost child find his parents. Sacrifice one innocent, save hundreds more. That's the way I see it."

Ace grit his teeth. "I know my grandfather." He stepped close and placed his nose in her face. "He would never trade an innocent life for another. Ever."

Keele furrowed her brow. "You're missing the point." She sliced the air with her hand. "Never mind. We'll have to talk about this later." She led him down the trainee hall again. He let what Keele said resonate with him. It wickedly boiled his blood. He couldn't agree with it no matter how hard he tried. Neither could he remove the image of Rio trying to shoot a president from his head

"Ace!" yelled a voice. Ace turned to find his older brother coming out of a set of doors in Trainee Hall.

"Hey, Cameron," Ace said. "How did your first day go?"

Cameron shrugged. "Well, I didn't do much shooting. Just a lot of learning and stuff."

Keele nudged Ace. "That's where you should've started as well."

Ace ignored Keele. "Learning about what?"

"How witches operate, what witchcraft looks like, the two kinds of truths, things like that."

Ace smiled. Having Cameron next to him knowing all these things made him feel less alone. And even though he disagreed with Keele, he still trusted her. Cameron and Ace conversed about witch hunting as Keele led them to the Great Hall. Hundreds of chairs had been laid out in front of a stage. Hunters spilled into the room and took their seats.

"You two find your seats," Keele said.

Ace and Cameron nodded, but just before they began walking toward the chairs, she grabbed Ace's arm and leaned into his ear. "Remember," she whispered, "expect me to arrive at your house, and tell Rio; no one else."

Ace nodded and turned to enter the Great Hall. He and Cameron found empty seats a few rows back from the stage. Keele made her way to the stage and sat with the rest of the elite, including Rio. The elite sat behind raised desks, a name tag placed in front of each of them. In the middle was an empty chair behind a desk raised taller than the others. The name tag read *Marty Halder: Founder*. Another name tag read *Sebastian Yvonne*. Also empty. Ace read the other name tags. George Slider, Keele Adams, Ihana Tryackolo, and of course, Rio Atarion.

The elite waited patiently for the room to fill with guards and trainees. Ace looked around and caught a glimpse of Marg coming through the doors of the Great Hall. He turned back to his seat and had just begun to speak with Cameron when a male fae sat next to him. The fae looked to be Cameron's age, had a buzzed head of silver studs, and no tattoos. Instead, scars hugged his bone structure where the tattoos used to be.

The fae glanced back at him. "Problem?"

Ace shook his head. "No. Sorry." He hadn't realized he was staring. He turned his head to face the front again, but his questions kept bothering him. Rio had said scarred faes were okay to talk to. Now was his chance to learn more. His curiosity took over once again, and he looked back at the fae. "Hey. I'm sorry—I mean—I don't mean to be rude or anything. It's just, you're a fae. Right?"

The fae looked at Ace with a smile loaded with sarcasm. "Nothin' gets by you, does it?"

"I'm sorry," Cameron chimed in, leaning his head over Ace. "Don't mind my brother." He grabbed Ace's arm.

"I don't mean to be too forward," Ace said as he yanked his arm from Cameron's grip, "but didn't you have to leave all fae culture behind to join the Indies?"

"Gee, why would you think that?" the fae said, then gave him the cold shoulder.

Ace scratched his head and wrinkles formed at his brow. He was just curious about the culture, and the fae's sensitivity to the matter was starting to anger him. "Uh . . . your tattoos are gone?"

The fae turned toward him, his face hot with anger. "Look man, you tryna fight on your first day or somethin'? Who even are you?"

"Ace Ha—" Ace had begun to say but stopped when Cameron's elbow jabbed him in the ribs. "Ow!"

"Harrington!" Cameron said. Then he reached his arm over Ace to shake the fae's hand. "I'm Cameron Harrington. We're brothers."

The fae ignored Cameron's offer to shake hands. "Well keep your distance from me, Harringtons."

Ace turned to Cameron and whispered, "Why'd you tell him that?"

"Grandpa, like, owned this place, bro. If people find out who we are every hunter here will be looking to outdo us. Either that or they'll think we're only getting where we are because of who we know," Cameron said.

"So? Who cares what they think?" Ace said.

"Attention, all trainees, hunters, and returning fieldsmen," said a voice over the speakers. The dull roars of the hunters and trainees talking in the Great Hall came to a silence. Sebastian stood in front of the raised desks, a wireless mic over his mouth. "Thank you for attending the recall today. And let's give an especially warm welcome to all the fieldsmen returning from duty!" Sebastian said. The crowd applauded.

"Something feels strange about this," Ace whispered to Cameron. Cameron shushed him as the ceremony continued.

"Recalls are not something we do often," Sebastian continued. "And I wish with all my heart this one were under better circumstances. However, it is under grave circumstances indeed we elite have gathered you all here today."

The crowd murmured and stirred in their seats.

"Messengers were sent this morning to those deployed to areas they cannot return from. And many of the deployed are tuning in live, now. After this announcement, all of the Indies will be informed of what has taken place." There was a dull silence before Sebastian continued. He gathered himself, as if what he was about to say was more than he could bear. "It has been brought to our attention, that Marty Halder has passed away," Sebastian said. The whispers climbed to gasps of panic in an instant. "Marty was an incredible leader," Sebastian continued, but even with his mic he was in competition of being heard above the anxious crowd, "and will continue to live on in our hearts. But even more, he will continue to live on in all of you, the Indies. The movement he began will not have begun in vain. Until a more permanent decision can be made, I will be serving as the Interim Halder. I will not let Dodger take us down!"

Dodger? Ace thought. *Dodger Girdleg?* What did the Prime Minister of Heorg have anything to do with the Indies?

"We will stand and grow stronger, I promise you," Sebastian said. "We've asked that all available hands help establish the changes that will be taking place in Marty's absence. Nothing will change as far as hunter protocol or the order and structure of leadership. We know many of you may have questions and concerns. Your commanders and officers are well informed and would be happy to answer any of these. Thank you for attending. You are all dismissed." The crowds stood from their chairs rapidly. Yelling and demanding answers.

"Who killed him?"

"Did Marty choose you as interim?"

"What's going to happen to the Indies?"

All the elite, one by one, left the stage to the right. Rio caught Ace's eye in the crowd. It was an awkward exchange between the two of them. Ace found it hard to look at Rio the same way, knowing he had possibly been an assassin in his past. But he also noticed something peculiar in the drake's eyes. It was too rare a look to mistake it as anything else. He saw straight through the mask he wore for the audience. The drake was afraid.

CHAPTER THIRTY-TWO

Keele's Urgent Matter

Ace, Cameron, Rio, and Marg went home after the recall. Ace found time to tell Rio of Keele coming by the house, and Marg told three jokes on the way. One was about a jag and a drake walking into a tavern . . . but Ace couldn't remember the rest. He had more important matters on his mind. They opened the door to the house to find Julie and Tamara watching TV on the couch. Rio dismissed the guards of their duty, protecting the Peppercorns while everyone else was away.

"We're not babies you know," Tamara said.

"Yeah, we're perfectly fine on our own," Julie said.

"Something tells me you two would run away the first chance you got," Rio said.

Julie crossed her arms and pouted as she sank into the couch. "Can't we at least go somewhere?"

"Yeah," Tamara said, "being cooped up in here is like a prison. Ace and Cameron got to go with you somewhere!"

"Ace gets to go all the time," Julie said under her breath.

Rio grunted. "Fine." The drake turned to Marg. "Would you mind?"

Marg gave Rio a look of disgust. "You do it!"

"I can't. Please, Marg?" Rio asked.

Marg shook his head. "I not babysitter, ug."

"And we're not babies!" Julie demanded.

"Yeah," Tamara said, standing from the couch. "Just let us go wandering around Gathara ourselves. We'll come back. Promise."

Rio scoffed at the Peppercorns, then he and Marg traded eyes a moment.

"Ugh, fine," Marg said. "Come on, little girls."

"Uh . . . I'm seventeen, actually," Tamara said.

"What your point?" Marg said. Ace liked Marg. "Let's go."

Julie and Tamara gave a sigh of frustration and walked over to Marg as he led them out the door.

"Ever been horseback riding?" Marg said to the girls as he shut the door.

Cameron looked at Rio. "You sure the Peppercorns won't find some way to run away?"

"If there's anyone I trust, it's Marg. He's a nice jag, but that's one ug you don't want to make angry," Rio said.

Someone knocked on the door.

"Can I trust you two alone here?" Rio said.

"It's not like I have any more secrets to tell," Ace said. Rio smirked and opened the door to find Keele. The drake walked outside and closed the door behind him.

"What's going on?" Cameron said.

Ace shrugged. "Not sure. Keele told me she needed to come by and speak with Rio. I don't know what for."

Cameron shrugged and plopped down on the couch and breathed a deep breath. "So, how did your training go?"

"It was hard at first, but I think I'm starting to get the hang of it," Ace said as he fidgeted with his fingers and hung his head.

"What's wrong?" Cameron said.

"What are you talking about?"

"The way you said that. It wasn't you. Something's up."

Ace sat on the couch next to his brother. He sighed. "It's Rio."

"What about him?"

"In one of the simulations, I was put in Angus Kar's election day celebration."

"Wasn't that the day he was almost shot?"

Ace nodded and leaned closer to his brother. "And guess who the shooter was."

Cameron sat straight from the couch. "Rio? No way! That. . . that's crazy! How could it be?"

"I don't know," Ace said. "Rio told me he was mixed up with the wrong people when Grandpa found him, but . . . I mean . . . a president? That's serious stuff."

"No kidding."

"What should I think of this, Cameron?"

Cameron shrugged and rubbed the back of his head. "I don't know, bro. I'm not sure what *I* think of this. Well, was Kar working with a witch or something?"

"No, I thought he might've been. But this took place before Rio even knew about witches anyway. The elite told me he was part of some anarchist gang who was trying to bring down the government."

"Well, he's probably not the same person anymore," Cameron said.

"I'd hope so! But still, this isn't something I can just pretend isn't a big deal."

"Yeah, I'm with you. Maybe it's . . ."

Ace and Cameron went silent and jerked their heads at the sound of the front door opening. Rio stepped inside.

"Ace, we need to speak with you," the drake said.

"Me too?" Cameron said.

"Just Ace."

"Why are you still trying to keep things from me?" Cameron said.

"Don't push your luck, kid," Rio said. "I've already risked a lot by letting you train."

There was silence for a moment. Ace stood from the couch, shrugged at his older brother as if to apologize, and walked outside. Rio shut the door, and Keele stood next to him.

"Ace, we have a situation," Rio said.

"What?" Ace said. Rio looked at Keele, and Keele looked at Ace with the same fearful eyes Rio had at the recall ceremony.

"You sure he's ready to know about this?" Keele said. "I told him I needed to speak with you because I wanted only you to know."

Rio nodded. "He *has* to know about this."

Ace looked back and forth between them. "Know about what?"

Keele sighed. She glanced over her shoulders, making sure no one was watching as she leaned in. "The Indies have been compromised. There's a sorcerer somewhere in Headquarters," she whispered.

CHAPTER THIRTY-THREE

The New Halder

Ace's mouth moved without any words for a moment. His eyes of disbelief fixed on Keele as his jaw hung. He swallowed and finally forced the words from his mouth. "A—are you sure?"

Keele nodded. "I am."

"How do you know?"

"I was becoming suspicious in our first meeting together. When Sebastian was so hesitant to let you lead. Then, when Ihana and George ran your simulations, and set you up to fail so many times . . ." Keele said, her face overcome with disbelief. "I'm not saying for sure one of the elite is a sorcerer. Could be, but it might be that they're just being influenced by a witch or parcel in Headquarters."

Rio clacked his tongue a few times and said, "Well to be fair, I knew they were going to do that. Trusting the Indie's leadership to a twelve-year-old is risky. Marty's grandson or not, I can understand their concern."

"That's what I thought too, but in the watch room . . ." Keele said.

"What is it?" Rio said.

"They ran him through advanced simulations. No training, no context," Keele said. "They're trying to push him out. The boy himself even told me he was thinking about quitting after the simulations."

Rio looked at Ace with disappointment, then back to Keele. "I agree," the drake said, "they should have given him context first. But it's like I said, they're scared of a twelve-year-old running the Indies. I was too at first; I hardly think that's enough to think there're parcels and witches influencing them. It's especially not enough to believe one of *them* is a sorcerer."

"It gets worse, Rio," Keele said. "They started him off in Simulation Twenty-Seven. Also, with no context. I think they're trying to turn him against you."

Rio stepped back, and his hands fell to his side. Then he looked at Ace.

"Ace, I—" the drake placed his hand on Ace's shoulder. "I'm sorry you had to see that."

Ace didn't respond for a lack of knowing what to say.

"I was a different person; I nev—"

"A president?" Ace snatched the drake's words from him. "You actually tried to shoot a president?"

"You two need to discuss this later," Keele said.

Rio turned his sad eyes to Keele. "Right."

"Why would they be trying to turn me against Rio?" Ace said. His tone was bitter, like the churning of his stomach after picturing Rio shooting President Kar.

"Because," Keele said, "you and Rio are both working for the same thing: you becoming the next Halder."

"Keele," Rio said, his head lowered, "all the elite wanted to be the next Halder. Including me. It really shouldn't surprise us that the elite are unhappy with this."

"You don't understand, Rio," Keele said, her eyes now dark and cold, "you weren't in the watch room with me." Keele pointed at Ace, "That kid captured and identified a witch in his second simulation! But Ihana and George wouldn't accept it. They kept finding things wrong with him. He's a natural, just like his grandfather. He has the gift and he's done more than enough to prove it." Rio and Ace stood silently for a moment. Their faces processed the information. The woman made good points, and Ace had never really thought about it. The council really was everywhere, weren't they? Nowhere was safe. "Oh, and I should mention they pulled the whole *try to catch one with no weapon* thing on him," Keele said, using fingers as quotes.

Rio chuckled, and it sounded like a rattling percussion instrument. "That old trick? They really don't have any creativity, do they?"

"Um, hello?" Keele said, snapping at the drake's face. "Bigger picture here. Ace caught the witch with no weapon!"

"Don't snap at me, woman," the drake barked. He rubbed his chin and glanced at Ace. "But that *is* impressive . . . how did you do it?"

Ace half smiled. "I lured her into a trap I made from tree branches."

Rio laughed and smacked the kid's back. "By Eathelyn's Summer, that's genius!" He turned to Keele with a wide smile, but her face remained stale and unimpressed. He coughed and snapped his tongue. "Okay, let's say you're right. We're gonna need more evidence before we just start capturing hunters. Do you have any leads as to who it is?"

Ace chimed in next. "How do we know not *all* the elite are involved?"

Keele shook her head. "Impossible. Parcels and witches never group together like that."

Rio nodded. "She's right. The council's goal is to deceive Yutara. Witches and parcels can gain more traction by spreading out. Parcels only call their witch slaves when they're needed."

Keele scratched her chin. "Sebastian is a possible suspect. Although George seemed persistently against Ace in the Watch Room. So did Ihana though. But it just seems to me that a witch would have a hard time sneaking into the elite group of hunters. It would be much more like a parcel to do such a thing. Any number of the trainees, guards, or hunters could be one. There's really no way to tell yet because we haven't started investigating."

"Sebastian has named himself Interim," Ace said. "Doesn't his power make him a suspect?"

"Yes and no," said Rio. "It's true that parcels want power. But often they will stand alongside someone in positions of power. If someone who has power trusts them, a witch or parcel can use their magic to sway them, making themselves harder to detect for not being in the public eye, but still have as much influence in Yutara as if they were in power themselves."

Keele butted in. "Although it is entirely possible that Sebastian has been given the position of Interim Halder by the council as a reward for joining."

"Okay. So . . . we have no idea then," Ace said.

"Right," Keele said. "For now, just keep an eye out. But don't push anyone, Ace. Don't go around asking questions or trying to bring the witches free of their disguise."

"Keele's right. If there's a witch or parcel who's deceived their way into Gathara, or especially an elite position, they must have unimaginable magic," Rio said.

"But I'm immune, remember?" Ace said, a smirk on his face.

Keele furrowed her brow at the boy. "Watch it, kid. You were good today, but don't let that get to your head."

Rio said, "You're immune to a witch's power, yes. Possibly even most parcels'. But if one of them has found their way into the elite. . ."

"The point is, we don't know what we're dealing with," Keele finished.

Ace exchanged a blank stare with Keele and Rio.

"Be careful with this knowledge," Rio said, leaning closer to Ace. "Remember: witches and parcels know when you're looking for them. No snooping."

Ace nodded. "I'm guessing that means we can't tell Cameron."

Keele's expression went wide and long, "I wouldn't even

imagine such a thing! Tell no one! Absolutely no one. This must stay between us three. If we hone in on who the mole is, then we can come up with a plan together. The more people we have snooping around Headquarters looking for them, the more danger we risk for ourselves."

Rio nodded. "Agreed. This stays between us."

Ace squinted at the drake. "Rio . . ." he paused. He leaned his ear toward the boy. "Why did you bring me into this? Why are you telling *me?*"

Rio's mouth played at a smile but settled on no expression. "Because you've definitely Marty's blood in you. If the Indies stand a chance in this war against the Council, we're gonna need you. And we're not just going to need you as a hunter. Marty wanted you on top for a reason; I can see why now. Keele and I are with you. You are the new Halder. Even if the others don't like it."

Ace half-smiled at him. He didn't want to show Keele his soft side by smiling from ear to ear. Which, despite their circumstances, was exactly what he did on the inside.

CHAPTER THIRTY-FOUR

A Grain of Sand

Ace fell in love with Marg's cooking. At dinner, he served loaded hash with spiced krarlock, and myrberries with cream for dessert. Everyone sat together with nothing to disturb the quiet but the clanking of silverware and soft chewing. Even the Peppercorns had nothing to complain about. Come to think of it, the Peppercorns had been especially quiet since they had returned from their trip with Marg.

"So—" Ace had begun to say before he realized his mouth was full of loaded hash. He swallowed the creamy orange mush and returned to his question. "Where did you guys go?" He crunched down on the krarlock, and the spice exploded on his tongue in a sharp but pleasant way. It wasn't the type of stinging spice from hard peppers, but it spread over his taste buds in a welcoming warmth. It had a hard shell, and a gooey red center. His taste buds asked for more before he swallowed his first bite.

"Where did *who* go?" Marg said.

"You and the Peppercorns," Ace said. "When you traveled through Gathara today."

"Well," Marg began, a strangely delighted look on his face, "we went walking in Garden Park first."

"There were bugs everywhere," Julie added.

"Oh, quiet," Marg said. "It was wonderful garden and you know it."

Julie shrugged and went back to her plate.

"Then I took them Charles Street. Dozens of antique stores to see. Fun place," Marg said.

"It was kinda like Grandpa's heaven," Tamara said.

Rio dropped his fork and pointed at Tamara. "Don't you talk bad about your grandfather now."

Tamara's face showed remorse, but Ace had a hard time accepting the validity in it. "I wasn't," she said. "I'm just saying, I wish Grandpa could've come with us here. He would have loved all of the ancient things in the city."

Ace, Rio, and Cameron glanced at each other. Cameron and Ace fought back a smile, obviously delighted they knew all those things about Grandpa the Peppercorns didn't.

"Your grandfather saw this city many times before," Marg said. Rio looked at Marg with frustration. Marg let Rio's gaze pass over.

"You knew Grandpa Marty?" Julie said, her brow tightened with curiosity.

"Yes. Rio and your father were close work buddies," Marg said. "I met him once or twice. Great man. I sorry to hear of his passing."

Rio looked as if he were about to slap Marg. Ace tensed as well. Why was the jag telling this to the Peppercorns?

"You were all investors?" Tamara said.

Marg swallowed a bite of hash the size of a basketball. "Yes, we were. Well, Rio and your grandfather were. I was just an assistant."

Rio's face calmed. Ace relaxed. Marg may have been better off not saying anything; at least he answered some of the Peppercorns' questions without giving away anything important though.

After dinner, Cameron and Ace went to their rooms. It had

been a long day, but just as they had settled and got ready for bed, the door opened, and the Peppercorns stepped inside. For a moment they simply stood in an awkward silence.

"What?" Cameron finally said.

Tamara stepped closer, speaking soft but firm. "Something is up with you two, Rio, and that weird jag."

Julie stepped closer as well. "Yeah! You expect us to believe that massive gray thing with loads of shiny weapons was an investor? Gimme a break."

Cameron shrugged. "I don't know what you're talking about." He wore a smug look on his face. Ace leaned against the wall with an evil grin, loving every minute of it. The Peppercorns were stuck in the house all day for protection, being babysat, while he and Cameron were off training to be hunters. He couldn't remember a time he felt so satisfied. The only thing diminishing the joy of the moment was the thought of his quest to save them. As the Peppercorns each stood inside the bedroom door, their usually bratty mannerisms about them, his desire to see them as witches grew more intense.

"Look, Halders, we're not idiots," Tamara said, wagging her finger at Cameron's nose, "and we're gonna find out what it is all of you are hiding."

"Yeah," Julie chimed in, her hands on her hips, "but not before we find a way out of this stupid city to reach Mom and Dad."

The Halder brothers glanced at each other. Cameron turned to face Julie. "You don't want to do that," he said.

"You'd like that, wouldn't you?" Julie said. "Having us trapped in this place like a couple of prisoners while you and Ace go running around with your new, weird friends."

Ace chuckled. "Actually, that *is* pretty nice, yeah."

"Julie," Cameron said, "it's not like that. We're trying to protect you."

Tamara and Julie burst into laughter. "Like we need *your* protection," Tamara said, wiping a fake tear from her eye.

"Aw, look," Julie said with a puckered lip, "they're serious. It's kinda cute, actually."

"You don't understand. Our family is in very serious danger," Cameron said.

"I'll say. We've been kidnapped by a drake and are being held hostage in some weird city!" Tamara said.

"Rio's trying to protect you!" Cameron said.

They're practically witches already, Ace thought. His fury must've shown on his face, for Julie took notice. Their eyes met, and she stepped toward him with an evil smile. The smile of a witch.

"What's the matter, baby Ace?" Julie said.

"Don't call me that," he said under his breath.

"Why not?" Julie stepped closer, pouting her face in mockery of him. "It's your name, isn't it?"

He bit his tongue, keeping his boiling blood hidden behind his silence.

"Julie, come on, leave him alone," Cameron said.

Julie dismissed her oldest cousin as she stepped closer to Ace. "What do you think you're doing, baby Ace? All this running around secretly with that smelly drake. Do you think you're better than us now? Because you're not."

He kept his eyes on the floor, clenching his fists, and gritting his teeth as he fought back the words he wished to say.

"Oh, oh, I know!" Julie said, a wide giddy smile on her face. "Baby Ace is twying to make Mommy pwoud, but. . ." she gasped and put her hand over her mouth. "Mommy's not here, is she?"

The silence following Julie's remark was so still, a grain of sand could be heard, had one fallen on the bedroom floor. Even Tamara seemed shocked at what her sister said. For a moment, Ace hadn't quite taken in what Julie said. Perhaps his subconscious tried to block it away. Pretend her words hadn't felt like somebody stabbing through his chest and ripping him apart. If so, it didn't work; his rage soon stole the show. He lunged at Julie and pushed her with all his might; she fell back into Tamara. The Peppercorns collided with one another, smacked against the door, then slumped to the floor in a deep thunk.

"I hate you stupid Peppercorns! You're a complete disgrace to Grandpa Marty! That's why you don't know what's going on. That's why he's keeping you a prisoner under Rio's control!" Ace leaned close to them, his veins popped through his neck. "Before he died, Grandpa chose me to lead the family! To lead his business! He told me you two were becoming witches, and you deserve to rot forever in a cold cellar! Because being witches is all you two will ever be good for!"

Julie and Tamara laid on the ground before him, eyes wide and mouths open. Julie's bottom lip quivered, and Ace felt a soft touch on his arm. He turned to find Cameron gently pulling him away.

"Ace, just calm down," Cameron said. Ace yanked his arm free of Cameron's grip and burst out the bedroom door. He bolted down the stairs and out the front door, ignoring the warnings of Rio and Marg not to leave the house. It didn't come as a surprise to hear Rio's steps just behind him in the courtyard once he got outside. He turned to face the drake.

"Leave me alone!" he shouted, not a care at all of what the neighbors might hear. Rio continued to run after him.

"Ace, come back! Where are you going?" the drake said.

"Anywhere but here. Stop following me! I don't want to see you, murderer!" Pressure in Ace's chest set itself free in great waves with every sharp word. Rio stopped in his tracks, his eyes watery. The boy's remark must have caught the drake off guard. Soon, Cameron ran out of the house and grabbed Rio by the arm. Ace saw them look at one another, Cameron shook his head, and they stopped pursuing him. Instead they turned back to the house. Ace took the opportunity to run to the bushes he and Cameron had practiced in the other night.

He fell to the ground. He locked his fingers over the back of his neck and buried his head in his knees, rocking back and forth. He thought he was going to explode.

I hate them! I hate them!

Tears fell from his eyes and the droplets moistened the dirt beneath him. Memories and dreams he had buried deep reared their ugly heads. He shut his eyes tightly and tensed every muscle, but he couldn't fight them back.

He saw his father, Colton, leaning over his mother in Marcus

Peppercorn's library, her face the palest the boy had ever seen. Dad held Mom close, rocking back and forth, saying the same thing over and over.

"Who did this? Who did this?" Father said. Ace had walked to his dad, Cameron next, and all three of them wept over their mother.

"What's wrong with Mom, Dad?" Ace said. Ace turned to see Julie being dragged away by her father—tall as a jag, light brown skin, and five o'clock shadow that must have been trimmed by an artist it was so symmetrical.

"I didn't do it, Daddy! I swear! It was an accident!" Julie said, her feet dragging on the soft carpet as her father pulled her by her arms, her face a bright red, soaking wet from her tears.

It was a set up. Julie did mean to do it! Ace thought. *Her father told her to! He's a parcel! It's what he wanted!*

Ace let out a scream from the pain. Had something ruptured inside of him? He slammed his fist on the ground. Pockets of dust rose in the dry air. A terrible thought crossed his mind. Now, since he had the Emerson Stone, his father was no longer protected by Grandpa. Marcus! Was he going after Colton Halder now? Surely Grandpa would have prepared some way for Dad to be safe, the same way he set it up so the Peppercorns would be protected.

Either way, Marcus had killed his mother. Ace was sure of it.

I'm going to find him. The second I get a field assignment, I'm going to find Uncle Marcus and make him pay.

CHAPTER THIRTY-FIVE

The Elyr

Ace sat in the dirt for what seemed to be hours, mulling everything over. The sun had begun to fall and shone like a ripe orange behind the staggered bush leaves. He had cried, screamed, and tensed himself to exhaustion. At some point he would have to return to the house. Where else was he going to go? He knew he wasn't skilled enough to track Marcus down yet. He needed to train. But no longer was he training to abolish the seventh realm. He had a new mission. Everything else was far less important.

He stood and walked from the shrubbery. The dry air carried the rich tang of the courtyard tree, and the collision of violet, orange, and blue in the sky spoke of the approaching nightfall. Ace breathed slowly to calm himself before he had to face the Peppercorns again in the house.

Something caught his eye—something he'd hoped to see again, but never thought possible. From the road heading north of the courtyard, a shining silver speck shone in his peripherals. He turned, and his heart melted. The fae he had seen from the train! The very same one traveled along the road. She moved swiftly, like a breeze. Where was she running? She stopped at a house at the end of the courtyard, then glanced behind her and all around. Was she running from someone? Ace's eyes met with hers. He stood like a deer in headlights, unable to speak, unable to move at the sight of the fae girl staring at him.

She went along the road again and disappeared behind the buildings. Was she up to no good? Practicing magic? Ace looked at Marg's house, just a few steps ahead. The sorcerer! What if she was the sorcerer? But Rio and Keel told him not to go after them . . . and just as had been since he could remember, his curiosity took him over. He ran after the fae, landing on his toes to lessen the sound of his feet hitting the brick road. He peeked his head around the last building of the courtyard. A jag drove a carriage of two horses underneath a beam street light, and a thin mist hovered above the road. Ace squinted, combing the street before him. There she was! A silver dot rushed between two buildings down an alley. She moved like a piece of paper caught by the wind. Soundless and majestic. He ran after her.

The dry air cooled to a gentle chill, and the wind brought him a sense of tranquility. He felt around his waist and pants. No AMHB. Good thing he'd practiced how to capture a witch without a weapon in the simulation. He looked around for a tree. There had to be one somewhere. Was he really chasing her because he suspected her? She seemed too young to be a witch, but she was certainly up to something. She kept speeding up as he followed her and glancing around her like she was worried. How more obvious could it be? Maybe he was just captivated by her and looked for any excuse he could to follow her. He shook his head. No, Rio had warned him of faes. They were all suspects, and this one was up to no good. He had to find out why she was running around the city.

He caught up to the alley she had run into, but he only saw darkness. The air grew even cooler. He looked all about the alley. Where had she gone to? The alley led to a dead end and the only thing Ace heard was the clip clop of the jag's carriage against the cobblestone, now fading in the distance.

Ace sighed with disappointment and nearly gave up. But just before he turned to leave the alley, the fae leaped from above, seemingly straight from the darkness, and fell in a swift, silent motion. Ace tensed and raised his hands in defense, ready to face a witch one on one. His heart pounded, and he wiped the sweat on his palms.

She was dressed in a cloth robe of silver with streaks of purple winding about, mimicking her elegant tattoos. Ace dropped his fists, and all his fear left him at once. He stared blankly into the pools of purple surrounding her pupil. Then she spoke. . . and the strangest thing occurred to Ace. The fae did not speak in the common tongue, but in fae language. But he understood her.

"*Hum li rolldi frun*?" the fae said, which Ace understood as "Why are you following me?"

To which Ace responded, "*Hum ez'schdi frun andoom?*" which Ace knew to mean, "Why are you sneaking around?"

And for what seemed an eternity, silence and shock filled the air. The fae stepped back, eyes wide, as did Ace. What just happened? How did he understand her? How did he know how to respond to her? It was just as if she spoke to him in the common tongue!

"You speak fae!" she said, stepping back.

"I—uh—I," Ace stammered, not understanding what had just happened.

"Who taught you to speak fae?" she said.

"I—uh—I."

"I've never heard an Evelander speak fae before. . . Are you part fae?"

"I—uh—I."

There was only silence for a moment. The fae gave Ace a moment to gather himself, until she finally broke the silence.

"Who says I was sneaking around?" she said, changing back to their original topic. "Even if I was, it's really none of your business. Just because you think you're the next Halder doesn't mean you have any authority here."

Ace stepped back, eyes wide. "What are you talking about?"

The fae stepped forward gracefully, her calm eyes penetrating. "Please, you can't fool me, Ace Halder. I don't care what rumors are spreading around the city. I know exactly why you've come. And you're wasting your time."

Ace tensed again and stepped back. "You're using witchcraft right now. It won't work against me you know," he lifted his hands, ready for a fight. "I've become a decent hunter. I have no problem getting some early field practice in."

The fae smiled. "You Indies are so paranoid. Faes have dedicated their lives to destroying witchcraft, just like the Indies. How is it you know our language but are so ignorant of our culture?"

He kept his stance, unsure of what to believe. Was she deceiving him? Did she cast a spell on him to make him speak fae? But she couldn't have. He was immune to witchcraft. And something about her drew him in a way he couldn't explain. Her eyes were honest. She deserved a chance at least, didn't she? He remembered Rio's advice. Call out anything suspicious. Talk about it out loud.

"You can't fool me. Faes have a natural talent with witchcraft."

"I'd sooner die than learn the dark arts, human. We faes know the art of the elyr, and nothing else. But that doesn't matter to you, does it? You Indies have let the council put fear in you. So much so, you've outlawed the only true weapon the council itself fears."

Ace let his stance down. "What's the elyr?"

Her face remained emotionless. She tilted her head, then raised it again. "What? How can you speak the language and not know its art?"

Ace stared wordlessly.

The fae tilted her head. "How about I show you what it is instead of telling you?"

His palms grew sweaty again, and his body trembled. Was she tricking him? Was he falling victim to a witch's deceptive power? But he lost himself in her eyes, her glowing skin, and her voice which somehow sounded like a melodic tune.

"How do I know you're not tricking me?" Ace said.

"You're a hunter, right? Do you perceive me a sorceress?" She stood arms wide, displaying herself before him.

Ace stared blankly. His immediate response was *no.* But he was a new hunter and, as such, more liable to fail. "I don't know," he said, rubbing his chin. "You know practicing your magic is forbidden here. You also know I'm a hunter. And one who may become the next Halder. Why would you offer to show this power to me? Don't you know how much trouble you could get in?"

The fae half smiled. "I can sense something in you. I'm not sure what; but it's there. You're not like the other Indies."

"What? Yes, I am," Ace said.

The fae shook her head. "Never has an Indie spoken fae language before. Besides, any other Indie would have captured me by now simply by the words I've spoken. But you are different. You seem . . . curious. You have a desire to learn, to seek truth."

Ace had no words. The fae saw straight through him; her eyes truly did penetrate.

"I'll tell you something," she said. "If I show you my power, and you still suspect me, I'll walk to the cellar myself."

She smiled again, and Ace forgot his concern (and quite possibly his sense). For if she were a witch, he no longer had the strength to resist.

"Okay," he said. "Show me."

CHAPTER THIRTY-SIX

Kareena Flare

The fae led Ace through a maze of back roads in Gathara, weaving through alleyways, conifer, and stout pine trees.

"Will you know the way back? I'm afraid I might get lost trying to find my home," Ace said.

"Yes, yes," the fae said.

By now, night had swept over in a blanket of deep purple, and the only light they had for their path was a dim yellow from a half moon. The buildings surrounding them were swallowed in a grove ahead. The moonlight loomed on the edges of the pine's shy branches and needles.

She led him through the trees, entering a woodland part of the city, and leaving the residencies. He found himself surrounded by stubby desert shrubs, thin pine trees, and white fir. She took him by the hand and stepped through another couple of trees to a glimmering pond sunk into the ground surrounded by the wall of pine and white fir they came from. Unlit torches stood on staffs around the pool. The breeze came to a halt, and Ace could hear not even the sound of a chirping cricket. It was as if he and the fae were the only two people in Yutara.

"What is this place?" Ace said.

The fae circled around the pond, her eyes fixed on the water. "We call this place Throon High." Ace translated it as Shywater.

"We?"

"The faes of Gathara."

"It feels strange. It feels . . ."

"Alone?"

Ace nodded, expressionless. "Yes."

"This oasis can only be found by an elyrian. We call it shy, because it often refuses to be found. Even elyrians search long and hard to find it now and then," the fae said.

Ace smiled at her, not sure how else to respond to her gibberish. Maybe she wasn't a witch. Just crazy. "So, is this your power then? Finding strange pools of water?" he said with a chuckle.

The fae gave him a cold stare. She then closed her eyes, placed her hands together under her chin, and took three deep breaths. At the exhale of her third breath, something like a pale fire appeared on the tips of her fingers. A pure white. She waved her arms and legs in a fluid dance. The fire grew to her hands and trailed along her arms, and with the point of a finger, bits of the fire left her hands and began to light the torches. She did this until all were lit, then she stopped in the same manner she began, and at the third inhale, the white fire evaporated.

Ace stood speechless at the torches flickering against the surface of the crystal pool. The oasis was now purely lit, the tree colors popping in explosions of green and yellow. The fae walked over to Ace, grabbed his wrist, and pulled him to one of the torches.

"Touch the flame," said the fae.

Ace winced.

"It's okay, trust me," she said. Her face brightened, and Ace's heart turned over. What was the harm? He reached out slowly but felt no warmth. He let his hand into the fire, and still felt nothing.

The flames wrapped over his hand. He lost himself. Everything brightened around him. He breathed what seemed to be the purest air, and a surge of power flowed from the tips of his fingers to the bottom of his heart.

"This is incredible," Ace said, his words breathy and soft. The fae smiled at him from ear to ear. It was the first expression of emotion he'd seen from her.

"The light of the elyr doesn't burn the flesh of the innocent," she said. Ace smiled back and let the energy flow through his body. Was he dreaming?

What occurred to Ace as a strange phenomenon was the familiarity this brought to him. He had felt this peace once before but . . . where? His eyes opened as he remembered. The day in Myrka! When he saved Julie from the witch! The pale light came like a screen over his vision and he saw the witch hiding in the dark.

"So," the fae said, pulling his hand away from the fire. At once the world around Ace seemed dull and gray. "Are you convinced?"

"Convinced of what?" Ace said as he tried to gather himself from the wake of his high.

"That the elyr is safe," the fae said. "That I'm no witch."

Ace chuckled, stepped forward, and looked at the flickering light dancing on the still pond. "Of course I'm convinced!" He turned to the fae. "I've dealt with witchcraft before. Whatever this magic is, it's not witchcraft,"

"It's not magic either. It's the elyr," she said. "I dare not address the Light as magic."

"What's the difference?"

The fae stepped toward him as their eyes fixed on the oasis before them. "Everything is different. Magic spends souls, the elyr heals them."

Ace turned to her. "I don't understand."

"Don't you hunters know how the council fuels their magic?"

Ace shook his head, then shrugged. "I guess I haven't learned that far in training yet."

The fae went to respond to him but stopped when a voice

called from the distance.

"Ace!" said the voice. "Where are you, kid?" It was Rio. Ace and the fae looked all about them, but there were only trees.

"I thought you said this place could only be found by elyrians," Ace said.

"That's true. Don't worry, the drake can't find you here. But we must part ways now. The longer we stay here the more suspicious he will become. I cannot risk being caught practicing the elyr. And if the elite find out what has happened between us here tonight, you might even be in more trouble than me."

Ace nodded, still hearing Rio's voice calling for him in the distance. The fae was right, and though he longed to stay with her, there was no time to argue.

"How do I get back?" he said.

She pointed where the trees split to a path ahead. "Just follow the path, and you will end up where you need to be."

He didn't understand, but he nodded and headed there regardless. He stopped before he got too close and turned to face her again.

"Wait," he said. "Will I see you again? There's more I want to learn from you."

The fae nodded with a grin. "When time permits."

Ace smiled back. "One more thing. . ." he said, "what's your name?"

She smiled. "Kareena . . .Kareena Flare." Then, in a swift motion, she waved her hand as if to snatch something from the air, and all the torches went out at once. Before Ace could tell what had happened, she was nowhere to be found.

Kareena. He thought it was a nice name. His heart fluttered.

"Ace! Come back!" yelled another voice, this time it was Cameron. Ace snapped back into the moment. He turned along the path, a wall of the stout pines and white fir on either side again. The needles prickled his arms as he made his way through, until he saw a faint light at the end of the path. As he reached the light, the voices of Cameron and Rio calling him grew louder. He peered from the end of the tree walls, surprised to find the courtyard, with the large tree in the middle, hiding behind a screen of staggered leaves. The path had taken him where he needed to be, like Kareena said.

Wow, thought Ace, *Shywater is incredible.* He already missed the fae and wanted to go back to the magical—or—elyrian place rather. He stepped free from the pines, but when he turned around, the path to Shywater had disappeared, and he found himself in the large shrub, where he had run to previously. Rio and Cameron stood in the courtyard, walking about with their hands cupped over their mouths shouting for him.

Ace stepped forward from the shrub. "I'm here, guys!"

They each turned quickly and ran to him.

"Where did you go? We were getting worried!" Cameron said as they ran to meet him.

"Don't do that anymore, kid! I don't care how upset you are!" Rio said, wagging his finger. "It could be dangerous."

"I'm fine, Rio, calm down," Ace said. "I was in the bush. I just needed time alone."

Cameron gave a strange look to Ace. "But we checked, and you weren't there."

Ace's eyes shot up. "Well, I—uh—I went for a walk too," he said, rubbing his neck. "I just got back when I heard you guys talking."

Rio's eyes peered at the boy. "Where did you walk to?"

"Just—you know—" Ace pointed down the courtyard. "Around the corner, down the street a ways."

Rio's eyes squinted. "Well, don't do that anymore. It may not be safe. If you want to see more of the city, have me or Marg go with you. Understand?"

Ace scoffed at the drake. "I'm not the Peppercorns, you know. I'm not gonna try and and escape."

Rio grabbed Ace by the arm. "C'mon, kid. I'm not putting up with your attitude."

Ace yanked his arm free. "I can walk myself." He walked to the house and opened the front door. Marg and the Peppercorns watched TV in the living room.

Julie shot from the couch as she saw him. "Ace!" She bolted to him and then did something he never would have expected. She wrapped him tightly in an embrace. Ace's disgust with her told him he should push her away, pry himself free from her grasp, but he couldn't due to his shock. He could feel her crying as she held him tightly.

"I'm—I'm sorry," Julie said through her sniffling. Ace's mouth fell. Did she just apologize to him? Was such a thing even possible? He stood rigid and felt her warm embrace but didn't return the favor. "I shouldn't have said what I said," Julie sniffed again, pulling her head back to face him. "I took it too far."

Ace didn't understand what he felt, and it seemed as though something took over his body and acted for him. As if on auto-pilot, he pried her arms away, and looked at her rosy red face, stained with tears.

"Yeah," he said, "you did." His face was emotionless, much like Kareena's. Julie's face scrunched as she sniffled and fought back more tears. Ace turned and walked up the stairs to his room, then closed the door behind him.

CHAPTER THIRTY-SEVEN

Rio and Keele's Plan

At dawn the next day, Rio, Ace, and Cameron traveled nearly the whole trip in silence to Indie Castle. The entire walk, Ace's mind circled through the previous night's encounter with Kareena. Over and over again. He ached when he thought of the fae and Shywater. The way she spoke, how he understood fae language, her purple eyes like the ocean, her graceful skill with the elyr, her hair, silver like treasure, the school of freckles on her nose, which may as well have been the stars of a cloudless night. He felt a stirring inside he couldn't put to words. Had she put a spell on him? No. Couldn't be. The elyr was a good practice and it only worked on sorcerers. Then what was it? Why did he trust her so much?

"Why are you smiling?" Cameron said. Ace shook his head and looked at his brother walking next to him.

"What? I wasn't smiling," Ace said.

Cameron snickered. "Uh, yeah you were. You were flashing your teeth for all Yutara to see."

Ace turned his cheek. "I don't know what you're talking about."

Cameron laughed. "Sometimes you're weird, little bro."

Rio led them through the castle to the hall of trainees. Young hunters traveled to their appropriate training rooms, and rumors spread through the castle. Groups of young and mature hunters alike gathered at the walls, whispering of what may happen next.

Who made Sebastian Interim Halder?

Who killed Marty? He was the best! If the witches can get him, we have no hope.

Sebastian's not fit for this role.

What's going to happen to the Indies?

Rio stopped at Trainee Hall to send them off. "The elite have requested a meeting; this is where we part ways," he said.

"How come you never train us, Rio?" Cameron asked

"I'm no trainer, kid. Ihana and George are the only elite whos train," Rio said. Cameron shrugged as he and Ace turned to head down the hall.

"Ace," Rio said. Ace turned. "You're coming with me."

"What? Why?"

"You'll find out soon enough."

Ace shrugged. Cameron patted him on the back. "Good luck. . . or whatever, I guess."

Ace and Rio walked the other way.

"Is everything okay?"

Rio nodded, his eyes still ahead. "I think so. But I'm not sure. They just told me to bring you."

Ace faced forward as they walked along the halls of the Indie castle, sensing the paranoia stirring within the castle. During which, a familiar face walked by in the opposite direction. The fae he sat next to at the recall. The one whose tattoos had been replaced by scars.

Having just met Kareena, his perception of the tattoo-less fae took a new direction. The fae had left behind the wonderful gift of the elyr. Who would do such a thing? Ace wished to know the secrets of the elyr even if it were considered dangerous by the

Indies. And as he glanced around the Great Hall his heart played tug-of-war. Were the Indies actually on the right side of this war? What if they were wrong? If a sorcerer had taken hold of Headquarters, and especially if one were in the elite, how good could they be? What if the faes, the ones who still practiced the elyr, were the only real defense against the council?

"You Indies have let the council put fear in you. So much so, you've outlawed the only true weapon the council itself fears."

Rio led Ace through the hall with the double doors next to the witch cellar entrance. They opened to another courtyard with a path leading to a cluster of towers behind another wall. While in the courtyard, one set of double doors swung open to their left and a young, female jag hunter came out, pushing a barrel filled with yellow liquid on hover plates. The room behind her was a small factory of about ten hunters, manufacturing chrome rifles.

"Rio, what's going on in there?" Ace said.

"Smiths," the drake replied quietly. "That's where the AMRs and their ammo are made." As he listened to Rio's explanation, Ace watched the jag go to the courtyard and gather sap from one of the trees. She dumped it into the bucket and returned the other way. She was no longer in view when they reached one of the towers.

They entered through a small arched mouth, and climbed a winding staircase. After about the twentieth stair, Ace's legs were weighed heavy and throbbed. How high was this place? The staircase wound to a small room of brick with a bed, a table, and a few chairs. Keele sat in one of the chairs.

"Welcome to my quarters, Ace," Keele said with a smile.

"You're sure we're secure up here?" Rio said.

Keele nodded. "Quite. And I looped the security cameras, so no one will have any video evidence of you two being here."

Rio nudged Ace to sit in one of the chairs and they sat at the table. "Well, let's be quick then. We don't have much time," the drake said.

"What's going on?" Ace said.

Keele folded her hands and placed them on the table. "I've received word of a possible parcel in Hillrun, beyond the mountains."

"And you're sure of this, Keele?" Rio said.

Keele nodded. "The deployed hunter was assigned to my leadership. I trust his discernment. If he says there's one there, there's one there. I've instructed him to not capture any more witches and ordered him back to Gathara. I told him I will be sending special undercover hunters to take care of the parcel."

"Okay, so what?" Ace said. "There's parcels all over Yutara right? Why doesn't your hunter just take him down?"

"Ordinarily, I would agree with you, Ace," Keele said, "but this is a special occasion."

Rio leaned forward. "Parcels haven't reached within one hundred miles of Gathara since the city was established. If there's one in Hillrun, that can only mean one thing."

Ace's eyes widened. "It confirms your suspicions. There's a sorcerer here, and they're trying to close in on Gathara."

Keele grinned and nodded. "Bright fellow."

"Gathara is the last stand against the council left in Yutara," Rio said. "If they're closing in, this has to become a priority."

"However," Keele butted in, "we don't want the other elite to know about this."

Ace said, "Because if they're one of the parcels, then they're going to do something to compromise the mission." Keele nodded. "Okay," Ace said, "so have your hunter go and take care of the thing . . . problem solved."

Rio and Keele chuckled. "I like this kid," Keele said. She leaned over, elbows resting on her knees. "Again, I would normally agree with you. However, we have something a little different in mind."

Rio said, "We don't just want to get rid of the parcel in the suburbs. We want to find the mole in Gathara. Just getting rid of the Hillrun parcel would really be a band-aid solution."

"What are you suggesting?" Ace said.

Keele and Rio looked at one another, then back at Ace with uncertain eyes. "The Indies have tried to capture parcels, but all attempts have failed. Their magic is typically powerful enough to break the anti-magic. They've cast horrible spells on hunters before. That's why all hunters are instructed to kill parcels, and preferably with backup if they can. But we don't want to kill this one, we want him to lead us to the mole. We need someone who can withstand his magic; someone who is—"

"Immune," Ace said.

Rio nodded.

"Whatever happened to no snooping?" Ace said. "You specifically told me *not* to go looking for the sorcerer in the elite, now you want us to chase down a parcel in Hillrun?"

Rio stepped forward. "This is different. For one, the other elite won't know about this, so whoever the mole is won't get suspicious. Also, you and I are going together, and we won't be snooping. It's no different than any other field mission, and now's a great time for you to get some practice. The only difference is *after* we catch the parcel." Ace crossed his arms and turned away from them, pondering what decision to make. Something uneasy moved back and forth in his stomach. "Understand, Ace, we would never ask you to do this without knowing the risks. We have to consider what's at stake here."

"If Gathara falls to the council, all of Yutara falls with it," Keele said.

"What makes you think I won't fall for his deception?" Ace said. "What if he tricks me? You guys are more trained than I am."

"Not necessarily," Keele said.

"Why not?"

"Because," Rio said as he clapped Ace's shoulder and rattled his tongue, "you're Marty's blood. And we've seen what you can do. Imagine returning to Gathara and helping us take down the sorcerer in Gathara. There will be no question of your ability to lead the Indies. This is your mission. This is your chance to prove to the rest of the elite that you belong here."

Ace stood, exchanging looks with Rio and Keele. Would Grandpa have done it? Had he known there was a parcel in the Indies, would Grandpa have risked it? There was no way to tell for sure; but if there truly was a mole in Gathara, and this was an opportunity to discover who it was, it seemed wrong to turn from it. What choice did the kid have?

"Alright," Ace said. "I'll do it."

CHAPTER THIRTY-EIGHT

The Tree Goblin

Ace packed his things in his room—only what he needed. Who knew how long they would be in Hillrun looking for this parcel?

"I don't understand," Cameron said, sitting on the bed behind Ace, "how are you already being sent on a field mission?"

Ace shrugged, keeping his eyes focused on the backpack he stuffed with his clothes. "I don't know, Cameron. I'm just doing what I'm told. Be sure you keep your promise to me and don't tell the elite about this."

Cameron stood and walked to him. "You're doing it again."

"Doing what?"

"Keeping secrets from me."

Ace stopped and looked in his brother's eyes. He felt awful leaving Cameron out. It didn't seem like the Halders were sticking together anymore. Just Ace and Rio. But what choice did he have? This was the life Grandpa chose for him. He might have been the only one who could help save Gathara. He had to go, but telling Cameron put them both at risk.

"I didn't ask for this," he said. "If it were up to me, Grandpa would still be here, and we'd be sailing across the Great Ocean back to Eveland. If it were up to me, Grandpa would have chosen you and I to do this together. But he didn't, and I don't know why."

Cameron frowned. "I guess I understand."

"But there's still something only you and I share," Ace said. He pulled the chest from his backpack and displayed it for his brother. "The stone and the map." Cameron half smiled. "And when the time is right, you and I can crack the code to Grandpa's message together."

"So, you're still okay with trying to fight the seventh realm? Even if it means saving the Peppercorns?" Cameron said.

Ace's smile went away. He finished packing and zipped his bag, then threw his arms through the shoulder straps. "First, we'll have to see how we can uncover Grandpa's message. I've tried hard to remember the poem in Grandpa's story . . . but I just can't. Once we do that, then we can talk about finding the seventh realm."

There was silence for a moment. Cameron nodded and stepped forward. "Be careful, Ace," he said. "Something feels strange about you wandering off with Rio to this weird town."

Ace nodded. "I feel it too. But I have to do this."

"Well, be safe."

"I will." Ace turned out his bedroom door. He continued down the hall and steps. Julie and Tamara sat on the sofa watching TV with Marg.

"How long will you be gone?" Tamara said.

Ace shrugged. "Don't know for sure."

"Isn't that just great," Tamara said, looking at Marg, "We're trapped here like prisoners, and Ace gets to go on another vacation."

"You don't know what you talking about," Marg said. "And if you two didn't try escape every chance, we might trust you little more to go wandering around city. It like trying take care of pet."

Ace chuckled. Julie sat quietly, a somber look on her face,

staring at the TV. She turned her head slightly and her glossy eyes caught his for a moment. He turned away from her gaze abruptly and opened the front door.

Ace walked from the courtyard into the city, knowing Rio awaited him at Indie Castle. It was a beautiful day in Gathara. The gentle breeze, at a perfect temperature, complimented the smiling faces of families walking their children or heading to a park for a picnic. The businessmen even seemed happy. Businesspeople in Eveland always seemed to have a serious look. Like you'd better not get in their way, but not in Gathara.

The way the roads wove through the foothills mesmerized him. And as he looked ahead, the castle watched over the city in the distance, appearing just above the maze of buildings in the city it surrounded.

Ace sorted through everything in his head during his walk. Was he making the right decision by going to Hillrun? His recent encounter with the fae and the elyr had him questioning everything. What did he have to do to see her again? When would time permit? Her knowledge of this power might be the only true help for Yutara. And now he was leaving Gathara, not knowing when he'd come back. What if the Indies were dead wrong? Even Rio? The elyr could be the answer, but it had been outlawed by the only group of people in Yutara who opposed the council . . .

The parcel! The parcel in Gathara was deceiving minds into believing the elyr was witchcraft! What other explanation was there? He *did* need to go to Hillrun, interrogate this parcel, and find out who the mole is. But what good could be done without the elyr? He had to find Kareena. But how?

Just as he turned another street, something caught his eye. It seemed a shrub of green and yellow jutted from an alleyway. He stopped in his tracks and looked all around him. There were no shrubs anywhere else. He made his way to the alley, and when he arrived, his heart became full. The alley opened to a familiar grove, swallowing the buildings on either side.

Shywater, Ace thought. *Kareena!* He looked once again, making sure nobody was around to see him. Nobody seemed to pay any attention to him. And it also appeared as nobody in Gathara cared much for the random forest in the alley. Perfect time to move. So, he took off into the forest, following the path he remembered. The familiar needles prickled his skin and the halt of the outside city noise stirred up his excitement to see the fae. She must have seen him walking along the road and invited him to Shywater again.

"Kareena!" Ace said as he made his way to the end of the path. He brushed himself through the last bit of pine and found himself in the oasis with the unlit torches, but no fae. "Kareena?" he shouted again. She had to be there. Only an elyrian could find Shywater. He shouted her name a few more times but was only met with silence. He sat by the water. Unlike his previous visit, the sun lit up the oasis, so he could see everything clearly. The way it shone on the water revealed its true stillness. It was perfectly unmovable, silver, and reflecting every detail of his face like a freshly cleaned mirror. Anyone could have mistaken the pond for glass. He imagined being able to slide straight across with his socks.

Where is she? I can't wait forever, Rio's expecting me.

Why would she bring him to Shywater and not be there? He grunted and stood to his feet, leaning one hand on one of the torches beside the pond. He closed his eyes and remembered the night he spent with her. He pictured her breathing and swift motions. The way she glided about. He soon became uneasy at the thought of her not showing up. But, from the darkness under his eyelids, something like a flicker of light appeared. He opened his eyes and looked at the torch beside him. His heart fell, and he jumped away from it. The torch had been lit!

"I knew you were here!" Ace said as he turned in circles, facing the wall of trees.

Still no Kareena, and none of the other torches were lit.

"Come on, stop playing! Come out!"

Ace jerked his head back at the sound of leaves rustling behind him.

No one.

"Hello?" he said. Whoever was there, it wasn't Kareena. Someone else had brought him to Shywater. Some other elyrian must have lit the torch. "Where are you?" Ace stepped closer to the trees where he heard the noise. Slowly, his eyes combed every inch of the woods. He stepped closer still, now beginning to leave the pond, and further into the wooded area, where there was no path to follow. He stepped on a root.

"Ow!" said a voice.

Ace leaped back in a fright and nearly hit a tree but caught himself. "Who said that?" he said.

No response.

"Quit playing games! Show yourself!" Ace started panting. Something glistened eerily and caught his eye at the trunk of a great pine before him. He squinted and stepped closer. What were those shining balls? They were light brown and reflecting the light of the sun. He stepped closer and whatever it was lunged at him.

"Ahh!" Ace jumped back. It was the size of a child, even younger than he, now running into the forest. Some sort of goblin-like creature with tree bark for skin.

Tree . . . goblin? Ace thought. He buried his fright, as was usual when his curiosity overcame him, and took off after the goblin.

"Wait!" he said. The halfling turned his head as it kept running. Its eyes were nearly half the size of the little thing's head. The goblin leaped from side to side, dashing through the trees, and finally, with one leap into a grove of trees, it vanished. Ace stopped.

"I'm not gonna hurt you!" Ace said. "I'm looking for someone. Maybe you can help?"

The stillness of Shywater was the only response he received. Only the woods surrounded him.

"Who are you?"

No response again. Ace heard the busy bodies of Gathara strolling about the city in the distance. His head turned, and a path seemed to clear itself in the woods before him, leading straight to the city. The tree goblin had taken him to the edge of Shywater.

I need to go to Rio, he thought.

"I have to go now!" Ace shouted to the still forest. "Do you know Kareena Flare? She's a fae! Silver hair, freckles on her nose?" He waited for a response but didn't receive one. "Well, if you see her, tell her I've gone to Hillrun on an important mission! I don't know when I'll be back! But I'd really like to see her again! I need her help!" He paused once more in vain. The tree goblin was not going to reveal where he was hiding. At this, he made his way out of Shywater once more. What a strange encounter; who was the tree thing?

Ace hurried through the path lined with pine and white fir. Shortly after, he found himself stumbling on the brick path in Gathara leading to the castle. Shywater took him exactly where he needed to go, just as it had before. Hunters, young and old, went to and from the bridge over the moat. None of them seemed to notice Ace's random appearance from the mystical wood. In fact, none of them seemed to pay much attention to him at all. The boy took advantage of his luck and marched along the path leading to the castle.

Rio awaited Ace at Keele's living quarters, where they had agreed to regroup. Ace found his way up the winding staircase to Keele and Rio sitting at the table. A large duffle bag lay on the right side of the room against a wall.

"There's the kid," Rio said.

"Are you sure no one's going to suspect me coming up to your room?" Ace said. "The security loop's been fixed by now."

Keele shook her head. "I've already discussed this with the elite. They know you and Rio will be leaving for some time."

Rio stood from the table and interjected. "They're under the impression that family members of yours from Eveland are getting suspicious of you and the Peppercorns. Asking questions. And we're going to make sure they don't learn of what's going on here."

"And they believed it?" Ace said. "I mean, wouldn't we *want* more people informed about the witches and Indies?"

"Not your grandfather," Keele said. "He kept his family in the dark. Believing it was protecting them."

The stone protected them, Ace thought. *He must have known he was going to give the stone to me and put his family at risk all along.*

Ace nodded. Rio grabbed his bag, and Keele nudged Rio and Ace out the door. As the dry desert air blew against his cheeks, something burned his insides. It was the feeling of not knowing who to trust. Everyone seemed to be working against him. And what about Kareena? Did she know the tree goblin? Would she get his message? But as Rio stepped outside, following the boy, and placed his gentle hand on Ace's shoulder, the worry melted away. He looked at the drake, who smiled at him. A rare sight.

"Let's go find us a parcel," the drake said.

CHAPTER THIRTY-NINE

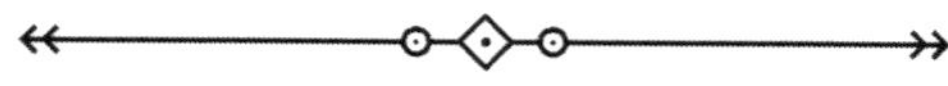

Hillrun

The ground mixed in a pale yellow and dark brown sand, with patches of green where the stubby bushes and trees sprung forth. Gathara had claimed the greenest parts of Heorg, and the most hills. Once they had left the foothills, the land was flat as a pancake. Gathara was a large city placed like a speck in the middle of nowhere, for the roads were lonely, as well as the rocky red Heorg surface. They passed signs for smaller towns nearby, but the main road lay mostly isolated from civilization. When they arrived in the airplane, it had looked like the towns were closer to Gathara than they truly were.

Ace soon shut his eyes and let the faint hum of the hovercraft engine disappear as consciousness left him. An odd mix with the anxiousness of having to interrogate a parcel soon. What if the parcel's magic was too powerful, so powerful, it broke through Ace's immunity, and he ended up cursed? Or even killed? Ace's eyes shot open again.

"Nervous?" Rio said.

"A little, I guess."

"Me too."

"Well, that's comforting."

"Hey, we told you what the risk was, kid."

Ace nodded. "I know." After the following silence proved awkward enough, Ace blurted, "Why were you going to kill Angus Kar?"

The drake turned to him and clacked his tongue, his eyebrows wrinkled with frustration. "I told you. I got mixed up with the wrong people."

"Getting mixed up with the wrong people is like robbing a convenience store. Shooting the elected President of Eveland is an entirely different thing."

"They really should've never showed you that simulation."

"Well, they did."

The drake paused before he responded. "Look, kid. I had been in Eveland, homeless, for as long as I can remember. A group of drakes found me and took me in. I didn't realize they were a gang when I joined. Eventually, my reputation started to grow. I became very good at stealing and . . ." Rio squinted an eye at him, then shifted his gaze to the road again, "other things. The point is the gang started to use me, because of my skills, for bigger and bigger jobs. Eventually they were becoming the mob. We were gaining a reputation in Eveland. I had no family. . . no one else around to talk sense into me. When Angus Kar won the election, a lot of Eveland was infuriated. . . including myself. I had done so much bad for so long; I figured I might as well do something good for Yutara. At least what I thought was something good. I was messed up in the head."

"So, you knew something was off about Angus Kar?"

Rio snickered. "You were in the simulation. You heard him talking about wanting to get rid of the Indies and everything."

"Yeah, at first, I thought he was a parcel."

Rio rattled his tongue. "At that time, I had no knowledge of the council or any witches. I just knew he was a bad man."

"Well, that's one of the things that threw me off. Kar spoke from his podium about ridding the world of the Indies, and how they would no longer bully the people of Eveland with nonsense about witchcraft and things of that nature."

Rio tipped his head as if he only half agreed. "That was his main platform. He thought the Indies were a radical religious organization. But I doubt the man was a parcel. That's something they didn't teach you before putting you in that simulation. Remember, parcels aren't always the ones who *appear* to have the most power. . ."

"They're just standing alongside the one with power. It was probably someone at Kar's table!"

The drake smiled. "Yep."

Ace remembered the slightly familiar man next to Kar. Probably someone he'd seen in history books or on TV. "But," he said, changing the subject, "I thought no one really *knew* about the Indies."

"Not anymore. Thanks to Kar's presidency, really. The man delivered on his campaign promises. He spread the anti-Indie nonsense across the nations. For the past few decades, witches and parcels flooded Yutara. Now that the peoples of Yutara believed that witchcraft wasn't even real, it gave them more power. From leadership in local and larger communities, the council ate away at the belief of witchcraft, until now, how it's nearly been diminished. Fairly soon even the faes in Breen adopted this view. Which is why many faes came to Gathara."

"So, faes were actually *for* the Indies?" Ace's mind was racing at this point. If the faes were for the Indies, why did they try to outlaw them? This must be the work of a parcel in Gathara! Someone had to be deceiving them into believing the elyr was witchcraft!

"That's a little complicated," Rio said. "We never quite knew what the faes' intentions were. Some of them claimed to serve the Indies. Others claimed to be escaping the hold that the council had on Breen but didn't believe in fighting them. And there were some who even opposed the Indies all together but came to Gathara for freedom. Faes are tricky creatures. Once we learned of their magic abilities, we became much more selective of the faes we let in."

Ace wasn't sure how to respond. He wanted to tell Rio about Kareena. Tell him the only reason anyone believes it's a bad thing is because they've been deceived by whatever sorcerer has infiltrated Gathara. But what if Rio didn't believe him? What if Rio thought he was being deceived himself?

Was he?

Was Kareena just a talented and clever witch?

No. Couldn't be. Still, it was a long shot for convincing Rio, who seemed set in his ways. Ace couldn't just *tell* the drake. He'd have to show him somehow. Show him the elyr can be used for good. Thoughts zoomed through his head like the hovercraft zoomed over the rocky red surface of the Heorg desert. He remembered the meeting where Sebastian announced himself as the Interim Halder.

"Rio," Ace said. "What's the deal with Dodger Girdleg?"

"Prime Minister of Heorg? What about him?"

"Sebastian mentioned not letting him take the Indies down. What was that all about?"

"Yeah, he's not a big fan of the Indies. He's always rattling on about how we make the jags look like a bunch of crazy people. We've never given him reason to go to war with us, but he's looked for other ways to take us down. Always watching us, waiting for us to make the wrong move. There're two reasons he hasn't just run us over with Heorg's military. One, we're not publicly causing any issues. In fact, half of Yutara doesn't even believe we exist. He openly supports those who push the idea of Gathara being a fairy tale, because it works to his advantage. If Gathara isn't real, the rest of Yutara doesn't look down on Heorg for being 'Home to the Indies.' So, if he were to overpower us, rumors of the war might spread, and it would cause economic problems he'd have to explain and so forth. Because we don't make much noise, war would cause a bigger mess than having us around. Two, I don't think he knows if he'd even win. The Heorg War did a lot of damage to the strength of Dodger's military. Anyway . . . he's looking for any opportunity he can to take us down." The drake chuckled. "Like the rest of Yutara."

Ace nodded and turned to the window. The sun had begun to drop, its color fading to dark orange. Mountain shadows of navy blue lined the horizon on either side. The road took them to a steel bridge over a wide river as purple as the ocean. On either side of the river stood palm trees with green and yellow leaves and thick clumps of the desert shrubs, much greener than those they passed by on the way there. Once they were traveling over the bridge, a small town to the right came into view, just on the river bank. The buildings were small and made of dark red clay and stone, and they only occupied the areas covered by the palms and thick shrubs lining the river.

"Welcome to Hillrun," Rio said.

CHAPTER FORTY

The Fae at the Inn

Rio landed the hovercraft just outside the town. A few jags peered from around the buildings of clay and stone.

"Remember," Rio said. "If there *is* a parcel here, he's not going to like two hunters showing up. We have to be careful about this. We want his disguise to fail. What we *don't* want is for any innocent people to get hurt or paranoid. Keep your eyes peeled and come to me if you see or hear anything suspicious. Don't make it obvious you're looking for him because it may scare him off, or he may attack you in front of a bunch of people. Although that's unlikely."

Ace nodded.

"For obvious purposes, we won't use our names. So, I'm Lun Marion: your chauffeur. And you're Logan Charm: the twelve-year-old son of Luther Charm, who's a billionaire from Eveland; and you've wanted to visit the smaller towns of Heorg for your vacation time."

"Logan Charm?" Ace said. His face looked as if he'd bitten into a rotten fruit as he spoke the name aloud.

"Got any better names?" Rio said with a smug look.

Ace scratched his chin and pondered a moment. "How about Dusty?"

"Dusty Charm?"

Ace shrugged. "Logan just sounds weird."

"And Dusty sounds better?"

"Oh!" Ace said, "Dusty Spalding!"

Rio stared blankly at the boy for a moment. "I really don't care. Pick whatever name you want. Just make sure you don't forget it!"

Ace smiled. "Got it, *Lun*!" he sassed with a chuckle.

Rio rolled his eyes and opened the doors of the hovercraft. At the push of a button, the hydraulics sounded, and the doors lifted. They grabbed their bags and made their way across the rocky red path to the entrance of the city. A small cluster of palm trees stood tall, just behind a wall of red clay. An opening in the wall offered an entrance and an arched sign above, reading *Hillrun.*

Just under the entry lay a worn path leading into the town. From it, two jags stepped forth. Their clothing was tattered cloth wrapped around their bodies in different shades of a blueish gray lighter than their skin. Their hooves clopped against the ground as they walked to Ace and Rio. One female, the other a male. Both with sharp yellow eyes. The female's clothing wrapped perfectly around her curves and trailed down her back, dragging behind her. Dust came from the ground by the edges of the cape. Her small antlers grew straight away from each other, barely curling backward at their tips. Her brunette hair flowed in thick curls all the way to her waist. The male reminded Ace much of Marg. Strong as an ox. Maybe even part ox. His chest popped through his cloth torso, and his hamstrings swallowed his knees, ankles, and hooves. Hard to believe those tiny things were holding up such a heavy creature. His antlers grew directly from the frontmost part of his forehead and curled all the way behind his head. His long black hair was pulled straight to a thick ponytail.

"Hello," the female said, a warm smile on her face.

Ace and Rio returned the greeting.

"Been a long time since Hillrun's had visitors," the male said. "'Specially a drake or Evelander. And now both come at once!" The male had a similar welcoming smile.

"What names?" the female said.

Rio went to answer, but Ace took the lead. "I'm Dusty!" He pointed at Rio. "This is my chauffeur, Pebbles!"

Rio glared sharply at Ace, a crooked smile showing his teeth gritting with rage. Ace fought to contain his laughter. The drake turned to the jags and stuck his hand out. "Pebbles," he said with a sigh. "Pleased to meet you." The jags shook hands with the drake and Ace.

"Very well. And what brings two ugs like you far as Hillrun?" the male said.

"I've always wanted to see the smaller cities in Heorg," Ace said, a beaming grin on his face. He found himself enjoying the pretending thing. "My amazing driver here is taking me through as much of the country as we can see and stopping at every town along the way."

The jags laughed together cheerfully. "Well, aren't you just cutest thing?" the female said.

Ace stopped enjoying the pretending thing.

The male jag flung his arms open. "All well with me!" he said with a cheerful look. "My name Grudge, this wife, Lag. We were beginning our Wednesday-evening-walk when saw your hovercraft. Thought we'd say hello. If need anything while here, let us know!"

"Well actually," Rio butted in, "we will need an inn to stay at."

"Ah yes!" the male said. He leaned close to Rio and pointed to the city. "Follow main road, take first left at roundabout surrounding water fountain. Follow road for few blocks, and take left at Riven Street, then first right shortly after to Cloudy Square. Few more feet on left, you will see sign says *New Nile Suites*. The owner is lady named Elly. She great friend of ours."

The female placed her hand on Rio's forearm. "Oh, she nicest fae you will ever meet."

Ace's eyes shot up. "Fae? The innkeeper is a fae?"

"Oh yes. The only fae I ever seen in Heorg. And she lovely," Lag said.

Maybe she knows about the tree goblins in Shywater, Ace thought.

"Thank you for your help," Rio said.

"Oh, welcome," the female said. "Welcome Hillrun. Hope you enjoy town."

They waved goodbye and trailed off along the path leading to the desert. Rio gave a proper bow as they left, and Ace stood waving at them with a smile.

"Why are you bowing?" Ace said.

Rio clicked his mouth. "It seemed like something a driver would do. I don't know, more proper I guess."

Ace shrugged and chuckled. "Man, those were nice people. I think I'm gonna like this town."

"Yeah," Rio said straightening himself. He turned to Ace, "don't get too close to anyone here." He leaned in and whispered, "We don't know who we're looking for yet, and everyone's a suspect."

Ace backed away and smiled. "Whatever you say, Pebbles."

"Hey, we're not here to play games, kid. What was all that 'Pebbles' nonsense?"

"I'm just having some fun," Ace said as he began walking along the path. "Lighten up. I'm only twelve, you know. A little too young to stop enjoying the little things if you ask me." Rio stood in his place for a moment, but it wasn't much longer before Ace heard the rustling of his feet catching up. But he said nothing.

Just as Grudge had told them, the main road led them under the arched entry to a fountain carved from the same red clay as the wall. Carved from the stone stood a tall statue of a jag. The statue jag stood with a puffed chest and one leg on raised on a block, swords strapped to his back and a fierce look in his eyes. Water sprung from the hooves of the statue into a pool of water with a path leading to the river. Words were carved into the outer walls of the pool reading *Chug the Traverser*.

They followed Grudge's directions and took their first left. Miniature forests of palm trees covered half the road in shadows and swallowed the clay-carved buildings. Jags trotted along the roads. Some on giyas like Ace remembered from the valley town in his simulation. Some jags took their mounts into the river to fish, and others just to enjoy the cool water on a lovely desert evening.

The boy and the drake got plenty of interesting looks from the jags, but none of them seemed frightened or threatened. Just surprised to see a human and drake walking along their tiny jag town. But still with great, welcoming smiles. Many of them waved hello. Ace enjoyed the evening air and the joyful jags merrily going about their leisurely activities.

They found their way to Riven Street, then Cloudy Square. The further into the town they traveled, the more the buildings seemed to vary. Some of white stone and others of brick and stone colored in shades of blue and gray. Cloudy Square was filled with such buildings. Either side of the road looked like a cloudy sky. And on the left side of the road hung a sign, jutting from a building of pale blue stone. *New Nile Suites.*

Once Ace and Rio arrived, they opened a wooden door painted white to a warm, cozy lobby. Ace anticipated seeing the fae, but it was only a male jag behind a counter, playing on his hologram phone. Tiny pillars, connected in arches carved from stone, held up the lobby ceiling. Two couches formed half a square, facing a hologram TV turned to a local news channel and barely audible. Just behind the TV sat a large window closed in by an energy field of a light blue tint. Candles hung from the walls, lighting the room in a dim warmth. Once they walked in, the young jag from behind the counter jolted up and set his phone down.

"Oh! Hello. Welcome to New Nile Suites," he said.

Rio checked them in. Ace kept peering at the door behind the counter, hoping a fae would walk out soon. But no luck. He had to find her. Maybe she knew how to get to Shywater. Maybe she could help him find Kareena. She would show up at some point. She had to. She owned the place.

After checking in, Rio led him up the staircase to a very narrow hall with wooden doors lined on each wall. Theirs was Room 212.

Rio rushed to his bed, threw down his bags, and pulled his blasters out. "Good thing is, it's a small town. Bad thing is. . ." Rio turned to Ace and threw him an AMHB, "it's a small town. Gives us less people to sort through, meaning we should find who we're looking for much quicker, but it also doesn't help us blend in much."

"No kidding," Ace said, "especially since we're a drake and a human marching through a tiny jag town."

Rio shrugged. "What else could we have done?"

Ace shrugged back and plopped himself on the bed across from Rio's. "So, how do we even begin to look for this guy?"

Rio stepped around his bed and sat on the side to face Ace. "We start asking questions. We want to reveal who the parcel is. But we don't want to be too obvious what we're doing here. If he finds out two hunters are searching for him, he may run."

"He won't attack us?"

"It's possible, but unlikely. Parcels usually attack when backed into a corner. Remember the simulations? I told you to start calling out things out of place they couldn't defend. Once they're put on the spot, with nowhere to turn, they eventually have no choice but to use magic to defend themselves."

"So, if a deployed hunter starts narrowing down who a parcel might be in the city they're assigned to, the parcel will just flee?"

Rio shook his head. "No. In most cases the parcel would send his witches after the hunter. Now, if a witch is sent after you, then you know you're closing in on a parcel."

"And what if a hunter captures all the witches a parcel has at his disposal?"

Rio shrugged. "Depends on the parcel's amount of power in the city. If a parcel has people of power on his side, he won't need to flee *or* attack. The *hunter* will be considered the outcast."

Ace crossed his arms. "Wow. Catching a parcel doesn't sound easy at all. I bet if a hunter does it, he's considered a hero."

Rio half grinned and chuckled uncomfortably. "It's only happened a handful of times."

"And the other times?"

Rio shook his head and lay on the bed. "Didn't end well for the hunters."

Ace felt uneasy. He paced the floor scratching his head. If parcels were this hard to catch, these warlocks could never be found by hunters. He needed to find Kareena. It was the only chance he had. He needed the faes. The elyr. It was the only way to defeat the council. Then, a thought caught his attention. He remembered what Kareena told him after he touched the light of the elyr.

The light of the elyr doesn't burn the flesh of the innocent. If he could find her and get her to somehow bring the Light to Gathara, he could use it to find out who the parcel was! He had to find the innkeeper. She must know how to find Shywater.

Ace turned to Rio. "So, what do we do now?"

"Rest," Rio said. "We've been traveling all day, and the sun has nearly set. Tomorrow we can begin introducing ourselves to the townspeople."

Ace nodded.

Ace waited patiently for the drake to fall asleep, but Rio slept quietly, and it was hard to tell. So, he waited until the late evening. Even after he was sure Rio had fallen asleep, he waited even longer. After battling his heavy eyelids for so long, he finally had a chance. He carefully removed his sheets. Rio's breathing couldn't be heard, but the timid movement of his chest assured him of the drake's peaceful slumber. He tiptoed to the side of his bed and grabbed his backpack. Best to take the Emerson Stone with him everywhere. He stepped backward to the exit door, keeping a sharp eye on the drake. Rio never reacted. He was in the clear. He turned and opened the door quietly. Lucky for him the hinges never creaked as he expected them to. He shut the door behind him quietly and made his way down the steps. Someone new was at the counter this time. An older male jag with a much broader jaw and horns thicker than the boy's arms. His round stomach sat like a squeezed plumb under his slouch as he read a magazine. He looked like a bored, gentle monster.

"Excuse me," Ace said. The jag sat up.

"How can I help you, sir?" The jag's voice was surprisingly gentle.

"I'm looking for the owner, Elly."

The jag raised one brow, as if Ace's request was impossible to meet. He looked at a clock ticking from the wall beside him.

"Uh, she not here. She never comes in middle of night unless there an emergency."

Ace huffed with disappointment. "Do you know when she *will* be here?"

The jag shrugged. "She owner. She shows up when she wants. Is there something I can help with?"

Ace shook his head. "I just—I really need to see her. It's kind of an emergency."

"You know her?"

Ace scratched his head and chuckled, "No—uh—not really. Let's just say we have a mutual acquaintance."

"Family?"

Ace groaned. "Forget it. I'll just come back and check tomorrow."

"Sorry, ug," the jag said. "I help you, but I can't call owner in middle of night. Know?"

Ace nodded. "It's cool." He turned and looked around the empty lobby. There had to be a way to find her, but he couldn't just ask in the middle of the day. Rio would want to know why he was looking for a fae and he was sure the drake would be displeased to say the least. He sighed and turned to head back up the stairs. But just before he took the first step, he paused. He recalled something different outside the window behind the TV. Something he hadn't seen when they had arrived earlier. He bolted back to the front desk and looked out the window. He had to squint, barely able to see the in the dark night from the lights inside. But it was there. He was sure of it. A small cluster of pine and fir outside the window. It hadn't been there before. Ace smiled.

Shywater.

"Something wrong?" the jag behind the counter said.

"Nope! All good, thanks!" said Ace. He darted out of the inn's front door, then turned right. Surely enough, in the alley between New Nile Suites and a building of dark brick was the familiar grove leading to Shywater. This place seemed to show up every time he needed it. Like a miracle. Like it could read his mind, almost. But there could have been a better reason this time. Maybe the tree goblin got his message and found Kareena!

The thought of seeing her again quickened his pace. He ignored the branches and needles scratching his arms as he forced his way along the path. The stillness of Shywater set in again. He knew where he was heading.

"Kareena! I'm coming!" he shouted. His backpack snagged on a tree branch for a moment. He stopped and yanked it free with all his might. The backpack pulled free and the force pushed him, so he tripped and fell on his back.

"Oof!" He gathered himself and stood to his feet. He scoped the area about him. The same unlit torches and pond were before him. Still no Kareena. Why did he keep finding Shywater but not Kareena? He needed her! He huffed with anger and threw his backpack to the ground.

"Kareena! Please, I need your help!" he yelled.

Only the still oasis responded.

Ace jerked his head at the sound of snapping twigs but saw nothing. Was it the tree goblin again?

"Hello?" Ace said. He picked his backpack up and put it on as he stepped closer to the sound. He squinted, and nothing was there. And time wasn't on his side, for he wasn't quick enough. Tree branches by the dozens flew from the forest and wrapped his legs. The branches jerked him, so he fell straight to his back. He wheezed and moaned for air, but his lungs remained empty. The branches dragged him further into the forest and he finally breathed in.

"Ow! Hey! What's going on?" He tried to grab something, but he only gathered leaves, and the tree branches wrapping his legs pulled him further still in the forest. "Help! Help!" Finally, he caught the trunk of a tree and fought against the tugging of the branches. The bark from the tree stabbed and scratched his arms as he held himself from being pulled further. He ground his teeth, groaning as he gathered all the strength he could muster. But the force of the branches proved too great, and eventually his strength left him.

"Ahh!" They yanked him away and dragged him through the forest in a flash, so the trees about him became a blur. He lifted his head to see what was pulling him. Just ahead, three tree goblins stood before one of the pine trees, manipulating the branches with their hands. The pine tree split from the middle and opened from top to bottom. Something of a red glow came from inside.

"Stop!" Ace yelled. It was too late. The branches dragged him to the red glow in the split open tree and threw him inside.

CHAPTER FORTY-ONE

Tree People

Ace's stomach rose to his throat as he fell through the abyss of red inside the tree.

Was he going to die?

He came to a halt when his back hit something soft. He lay there, flat on his back under a ceiling of dirt and mud; a red glow traced the ceiling's bumpy surface. His back didn't ache. Shouldn't such a fall have hurt him more? Instead, it felt like he was laying on a cloud.

Hearing the hum of whispers all around him, he jumped to his feet. His heart fell as he looked at the tree goblins by the hundreds circling him. They swarmed him like tiny insects protecting their nest, the tallest one reaching the height of Ace's shoulder, all their skin like different kinds of tree bark, and their eyes massive and light brown. Some goblins had narrow figures, others wide. Some had more leaves on their heads, others with none. They were dressed in tattered cloth of gray, green, and blue. But it wasn't just the goblins rendering him speechless. Where exactly was he? Trees —the largest trees the boy had ever seen—grew from the dirt ceiling downward, their branches covered in thick puffy leaves. Like clouds of green and yellow. But once the trees reached to where Ace and the goblins stood, the branches spread and wove together like a perfectly knit blanket. The puffy, cloud-like leaves wrapped around the branches. The top of the trees was the ground of this place, and the trees grew all the way to the red ceiling, hundreds of feet above him. It was like he was in an upside-down world.

The red glow covered the vast expanse of the tree world, extending for miles. It wasn't a fierce red, but more of a pinkish hue, giving the underground a sense of warmth, much like Shywater. From the ground of branches, to as high as Ace could see, some of the tree branches had wrapped themselves in such a way it made up buildings. Small homes for the tree goblins. A tiny tree village.

The sound of crackling bark followed two branches coming quickly from above and landing just before Ace. The three goblins who had brought him to this world shimmied down the branches and stood before him. One of them was the very same goblin he'd first seen in Shywater.

"Hey, look. I don't want any trouble!" Ace said, his voice shaking with his nerves. The crowds of tree people gasped, and they stood back. One of the tree goblins walked close, looking up to him, anger and worry behind his eyes. Ace stepped back. "I just wanna go back. I'm sorry if I disturbed you before. I won't return to Shywater anymore if that's what you want."

The tree goblins stared back at him wordlessly.

An idea struck him. Maybe, like Kareena, they spoke fae. He looked at the tree goblin and spoke once more. "*Thoom lonli charlock*!"

The crowd of goblins gasped so loud it shook the air. The eyes of the one before him grew heavy and he violently reached for Ace's backpack.

Ace jerked away. "Wait! I can't—"

But they didn't listen. Instead the three of them jumped on the boy and brought him to the ground. The crowd of goblins began to chant something incomprehensible. Ace tried to fight back, but they were surprisingly strong for tiny goblins. They manipulated the tree branches once again, wrapping his wrists and legs until he couldn't move, and pinned him to the ground and removed his backpack.

"Hey! Please don't! I—I need that!"

They opened the backpack, throwing his belongings from it frantically. He violently fought to shake himself free of the tree bonds to no avail.

The stone! They're looking for the Emerson Stone! They know I have it somehow. They must know I have it.

The branches tightened around his wrists and ankles until he, and all the tree goblins surrounding him, froze. For one of them had found the chest he hoped they wouldn't. The goblin with the chest walked slowly to him, displaying it in his hand.

"What? That's mine!" Ace said. The tree goblin pointed to the lock, and the others searched the backpack for the key. "The key isn't in there," Ace said. The goblin with the chest turned to him, steaming with anger. He pointed to the lock again and grunted.

"You want me to unlock it?"

The goblin pointed and grunted again.

"Then let me go!"

The goblin held the chest under his arm and signaled with his right hand. The bonds on Ace's wrists were freed from the tree, but not from his wrists. The goblins pulled them tight together, so his wrists were now bound together. The crowd of goblins closed in on him. They picked him up and carried him like a herd of ants might carry a leaf.

"Stop! Where are you taking me?" The only response he received was the roaring march of the goblins beneath. The tree people carried the boy through the underground. The path took them from hills and valleys and over rickety bridges connected between the trees, to different heights of their village. Past all the tree huts up high and down low, until at once, they brought him down one more bridge to where a cluster of huts formed a crescent shape, with one particularly large hut in the middle. Once they arrived, they threw the boy down to the ground of tree branches and leaves. They backed away, leaving him a lone human surrounded by tree people.

One goblin stepped out of the large hut in the middle. He stood the tallest of them all by far, reaching almost the same height as Ace. His hair grew in blades of grass, waving past his shoulders. In his right hand he held a long wooden staff, and a cape of rich green trailed behind him. At his approach, the tree people went silent. The caped goblin stepped close and glared at Ace with eyes of power and wonder.

"Unbelievable," the goblin whispered. His voice sounded like a calm tide gently scraping a sandy shore.

"Excuse me, Mr.—uh—Tree—sir?" Ace said. "I don't want any trouble. I promise I mean no harm to you or your village friends here."

The caped goblin laughed a gentle laugh and stood tall. "Ishvi!" he said.

The goblin with the chest under his arm came to the caped leader. "Yes, Great King?"

Oh, great, now he speaks in common tongue.

"This is the human you saw in Throon High? You're sure of it?" the King said.

The smaller goblin nodded. "Yes, my Lord." He handed the King the chest. The King took it and inspected it with curiosity. "And we found this in his belongings." Ace tried to wrestle his wrists free, but it didn't work. His nerves jittered. Whatever these goblin creatures were, they couldn't be allowed to have the stone.

"Please!" Ace said, "I didn't know I was upsetting anyone by entering Shywater. I was just looking for a friend! But if you let me go, I won't return, I promise."

"Ah, yes!" the King said. "The fae!" He waved his hand, and to Ace's surprise, Kareena stepped out of one of the tree huts.

"Kareena!" Ace yelled. The fae looked at him with the same emotionless face as she came to his side.

"Hey," she said. "So, when were you planning on telling me?"

Ace looked at her with confused eyes. "What're you talking about?"

Kareena looked at the Tree King. "King Vinan, can't we release him from his bonds? I don't think they're necessary."

"What's in this chest, human?" the Tree King said, dismissing Kareena's request. He held the chest before the boy.

Ace looked at the King and shrugged. "It was a gift from my grandpa before he passed away."

The King kneeled before him and placed his hand on the boy's shoulder. "Hiding things from me is useless here, Evelander."

Ace sneered at the Tree King. "I don't even know where *here* is! I don't have any idea who you people are or what you want with me!"

The King set the chest down, stood, and folded his arms. "How is it an elyrian doesn't know of the sixth realm?"

Ace, taken aback by this statement, tried to stand, but soon remembered his ankles were still bound. "S—sixth realm?" Ace looked at Kareena. "We're in the sixth realm?"

She nodded.

"Wait. Hold on a minute," Ace said. He turned to the Tree King. "An *elyrian?* You think I'm an elyrian?"

The goblin whom the King called Ishvi stepped forward and pointed at Ace. "I know you are! I saw you light that torch with my own two eyes!"

"What? I never lit anything!"

"He's lying, my Lord!" the goblin said, turning to the King. "He's found Throon High twice now! He speaks the language of The Light! His elyr flickered as would an elyrian's who speaks lies! We ought to hang him before he becomes a sorcerer!"

"Enough!" The King's roar made Rio's look childish.

Ace stared blankly at the Tree King. Did he light the torch? Was he an elyrian somehow? But how could it be? He was a human! Weren't only faes elyrians?

"Why were you looking for this fae?" the King said, pointing at Kareena.

Ace looked at her. "Because she showed me Shywater." He looked back at the King. "She brought me there. When I saw Shywater in Gathara, I thought she had returned, and I needed her."

"What would you need her for?" the King said.

Ace paused, unsure what he should tell an entire race of people he didn't know. "I need her . . . abilities. My realm is in danger, and the elyr may be the only thing that can save us."

"So, you do know of the elyr?"

"I know *of* it. But only because Kareena showed me. I'm not an elyrian!"

"My servant here seems to disagree. He says he saw you use The Light. Are you calling him a liar?"

Ace paused for a moment before he responded. "I—" he stammered. "I know the torch was lit. But I didn't light it."

"Then, who did?"

"I don't know! I thought it was Kareena at first. I thought she had brought Shywater to me."

The King used his staff to take a few steps toward the fae. "Why did you show this Evelander Shywater?"

Kareena lifted her head. "I had taken some time alone in the mountains to meditate on the Light when Shywater appeared to me. I went in, meditating further, when a word came to me. It wasn't audible, but I could sense it.

"'*Bring here the one who follows you,'* the word came.

"I wasn't sure what it meant until I'd finished and followed the path out of Shywater and it brought me to Gathara. Dressed in my silver robes, and having just come from Shywater, I was concerned the guards might catch me and suspect me of practicing the elyr and accuse me of sorcery. I was looking for a way out of the city and this boy here followed me. I knew, then, this is what the voice meant."

"Look," Ace said, his face long and wide with shock, "could somebody please tell me what's going on?"

The Tree King stood again and leaned close to Ace. His large eyes struck the boy with an odd mix of fear and awe. "Tell me what's in that chest, and I will give you all the answers you seek."

Ace's eyes widened. "What exactly do you mean by 'answers I seek?'"

"I guess that depends on what's in the chest, doesn't it?" the Tree King said.

Ace looked around at the goblins, anticipating his response. As he looked back into the Tree King's eyes he saw honesty. This king knew. He absolutely knew what was in the chest. Ace's heart spoke to him. He looked at Kareena and knew this Tree King could be trusted. But even if he couldn't, it seemed the boy had not much choice.

"A stone," Ace said. The crowd of goblins gasped. Not a gasp of fright, but of joy. The air hummed with their murmurs and whispers, and the Tree King smiled. Kareena jerked her head to him. Her demeanor drifted slowly from emotionless to wonder.

"A stone?" the King said. "Be a little more specific, will you?"

Ace held his bound hands forward, as if to ask to be freed. "How about I show you?" The King grinned, and with a wave of his hand, the branches loosened from his ankles and wrists and fell. The boy reached in his right pocket, where he'd kept the watch. He grabbed the chest. The boy turned the watch and placed his thumb on its glass face. The lights flickered, the tumbler thunked open, and the door swung free.

Ace's heart grew full. The stone was even more beautiful than he remembered. Viewing its beauty did stir sadness in the boy, for it reminded him of the first time he'd seen it, when Grandpa had shown it to him. He reached in the chest and pulled out the stone. Beams of radiant violet, red, and white burst from inside the stone and flooded the whole Tree World.

"The Emerson Stone," Ace said. The Tree King's eyes were even wider than Ace thought possible. The tree people stood speechless, as well as the King.

CHAPTER FORTY-TWO

King Vinan

The Tree King invited Ace and Kareena to sit with him and his servant, Ishvi. Inside the King's hut, chairs interwoven from the branches surrounded a wooden table. Draped in a lime green robe and holding a tray of wooden cups, a tree goblin entered from a separate room. He set one cup before each member at the round table. The small table had Ace pinching his elbows to his ribs to avoid being in Kareena's way, who sat just beside him. The King sat before him, and Ishvi sat to the King's left. The cups were tiny and filled with a dark liquid. Ace wasn't sure what drinks from a different realm tasted like, but his mind was too focused on other things to try it. One thought had bothered him since he'd been free: what if Rio had noticed he was gone at this point? How would he explain this to the drake? He needed to find a way to get back to Yutara.

"Thank you, Shem," the Tree King said as the servant left. He turned to the others at the table, a welcoming grin on his face.

"Shem is the finest brewer in the Tree Kingdom."

Ace smiled nervously. "Great. Look, I don't mean to be rude, and I have so many questions for you, but I'm afraid I should be getting back to my realm. People will wonder about me."

The King smiled, and his tree bark skin crackled. "Don't you worry about the time. Elyrians who enter the Tree Kingdom from another realm may return to whichever realm they came, at the very moment they left."

Ace smirked. "You're saying I could stay here for years, and when I came back it would be as if I never left?"

The King tipped his head. "Precisely. You don't know much about that stone you possess, do you?"

Ace shook his head. "I know it's been a great help to me. That's about it."

Kareena turned to Ace with frustrated eyes. "Where did you find it? I can't believe you didn't tell me you had the Emerson Stone."

"My Grandpa gave it to me and he told me to keep it secret. He said the more people that knew I had it, the more dangerous it was for me. Why does it matter to you?"

The fae went to respond, but King Vinan spoke first. "Your grandpa was wise. That stone has been sought by the council for ages. Its existence has only been known in myth and legend since its first possessor." He sipped from his wooden cup.

"You know about the council?" Ace said.

Ishvi and the King laughed. "Of course! Why do you think we live underground?"

"But you all have crazy powers! Why don't you fight them?" Ace said.

All joy drained from the King's face. "We are dangerously outnumbered, and the council have become far too powerful for us now, human. Lucky for us, our existence has become all but forgotten in Yutara. I'm not so sure the council even remembers us, otherwise they might try to come here and wipe us out."

Ace wanted to stand, but he was afraid his head might hit the roof of the King's hut. "But you can't just sit by! Yutara is about to lose the only safe city it has left. Once it's gone, the council will have all of Yutara under its control!" No one responded for a moment, but instead looked at him as if he were crazy.

"Ace," Kareena said, "what safe city are you talking about?"

"Gathara, of course!"

The King hunched over the table, fingers interlocked. "What makes you think that city is safe?"

"They're the only one that's fighting the council," Ace said.

"No, no," the King said, waving his hand and shaking his head. "They're the only ones who are *pretending* to fight the council. Gathara will be crawling with witches before long. It's only a matter of time."

"What are you talking about?" Ace said.

Kareena nudged him gently with her hand. He looked at her and she said, "The council has deceived the city into believing the Indies are working against the council. But it's a fabricated war. Some *think* they're doing good, but they've outlawed the only true power against the council."

"Yeah, but that's why I was looking for you in Shywater. If we can use the elyr to discover who the mole is, we can stop him and save Gathara."

Kareena spoke again. "Gathara was lost when they made the elyr criminal. It's a steady progression in the council's favor. The same way they've taken every city in Yutara."

"Well, what would any of you know about it?" Ace said. "You've been living underground!"

"We've been *forced* underground!" the King said. "We were once a part of Yutara, Evelander. We are no longer welcome there."

"What do you mean, you're not welcome?"

"How does the stone's keeper know so little of Yutara's past?" King Vinan asked, his gaze on Kareena. The fae shrugged.

"Ace, do you know how your grandfather found that stone?" Kareena asked.

He shook his head. "No. In fact, until a month or so ago, I didn't even know he had it. He just gave it to me and said that one day I will abolish the seventh realm with a greater . . . power." Before he'd finished his sentence, it dawned on him what Grandpa had actually meant. Greater power? He must have been talking about the elyr! Ace *was* an elyrian! But . . . how could it be? Everyone's eyes widened, and Kareena gasped faintly. The King rose from his chair. Ishvi followed.

"I knew it!" King Vinan said with a smile. "I knew it the moment I saw you and Ishvi said you were an elyrian!"

"Oh, what a wonderful day this is!" Ishvi said, leaping with the King.

The Tree King leaned close to Ace. "What's wrong with you, boy? Don't you know how great this news is?"

"King Vinan," Kareena said, "he doesn't know of the seventh realm. He doesn't seem to know much of anything about this."

The King calmly took his seat. Ishvi followed once again. "Do you know why your grandfather told you that you will abolish the seventh realm?"

Ace shrugged. "No. I've already told you everything I know. He said the map is 'within me,' or something like that. He said once I heard the map, I might not even realize it, but then the stone would be mine. I think the map was in some poem in a story he told me. But I can't for the life of me remember it." He rubbed his forehead as if it might somehow jog his memory.

The King and the fae looked at one another with wide smiles, then the King looked back at Ace. "Then, I shall educate you," Vinan said. "If it's true, what you say about your task to fight the seventh realm, then there is much you need to know."

Ishvi sighed and leaned back in his chair, sipping his beverage. "You might want to get comfortable, Evelander. This will take some time."

The King dismissed his servant's remark and began his story. He squinted and leaned his head in. He spoke with words like a sharp whisper, able to penetrate the dullest moment with grandeur. "From six realms, Yutara as we know it was formed. First, three realms of the spiritual, then three realms of the physical. The three physical are those of humans, from Earth; drakes, from Grol; and jags, from Morlog. The spiritual are those of faes, from Breen; Inglings," Vinan said as he pointed to himself with his thumb, "from the Tree Kingdom; and then there's the Realm Unknown. It is said that the Realm Unknown is what began the first realms. Something of a stirring of spiritual forces caused them into being. But in this stirring was a tension of which no one was prepared. Good and evil, light and dark, magic and the elyr . . ."

CHAPTER FORTY-THREE

Purpose

By now, Ace had forgotten any of his worries. They had been consumed by Vinan's story.

King Vinan continued, "Within the Realm Unknown the war on evil was waged. And for ages beyond our understanding, the Light overcame the dark. With each battle won, a realm sprung forth. The first was Breen. The second was the Tree Kingdom."

"And for ages to come, the three realms existed together in peace. Faes had been woken, and the Light was powerful within them, so they understood how to make use of it. From the elyr they formed their world. It was soon thereafter that the Light guided the faes into the life of their world: the trees. And by the Light they found the path to the Tree Realm. It was here they felt a source of life so powerful that they knew it must be woken. And so, they came together, and spoke to the Light, asking it to wake the life here. And so, it was, the Inglings had woken. Together, they increased in number, growing the Light to a power beyond what the darkness could bear. The more elyrians, the weaker the darkness.

"Faes and Inglings traveled through the trees between realms, guided by The Light, until one day, a realm was discovered that had not been before. Through one of the trees, an ingling stumbled from the spiritual to the physical. He gathered his fellow elyrians and brought them to this new realm. Life was felt like it had not been before. A different type of life. Of course, the faes and inglings had known only the spiritual, and had not realized what the physical was. But it was so, they came into the realm of Morlog, and saw the jags living with no knowledge of the elyr.

"And they spoke to one another, saying, 'it has been that since we have grown in number, the elyr has ruled the Realm Unknown, and suppressed the darkness. Let us ask the Light to bring the lives of this realm to know the way of the elyr, so the dark may be rid of forever.'"

Ace interjected, "So, the Realm Unknown didn't create the physical realms?"

The King shook his head. "The origin of the three physical realms is unknown to us. Their inhabitants knew once, but that history is mostly forgotten. The only thing that is certain is that the Tree Kingdom has attached them all. From the sixth realm we can enter all others, and from all others, the sixth."

"Are you saying that from this realm I can travel to any other realm I wish?" Ace said. "Even the seventh?"

The Tree King shook his head. "You must let me finish so that your questions may be answered before they are asked, Evelander."

Ace nodded apologetically, and Ishvi chuckled. "I told you this would take a while, human."

"Now," the Tree King began, "to answer your question, the short answer is yes. All *but* the seventh realm can you travel to from here. Wherever there is life, there are trees. We are the in-between, and from the trees we emerge to any realm we please. However, only one realm of physical beings remains in existence."

Ace held his tongue, knowing it might irritate the King to ask another question.

"You see, once the inglings and faes had decided to reveal the way of the Light to the jags, the darkness found an escape from its suppression in the Realm Unknown. The darkness, which had been losing the war to the Light in the Realm Unknown for ages beyond, was now desperately seeking an escape. The elyr had grown in the faes and inglings, and as the Light multiplied, the darkness dwindled. The darkness needed an exit, some way to escape its realm and spread like the elyr. Until the elyr emerged from the trees into the jag realm, the physical had been unknown. But in these creatures of the physical realms, the darkness saw a weakness. Better yet, an exit. The darkness became aware it could manifest itself in the flesh of the physical, but only at the will of a physical being. The problem was this: the elyr made known to physical beings the way of the spiritual, and thus opened the door for the darkness to deceive them.

"So, it was once these jags were taught the way of the Light, that the darkness entered them. It deceived them from within to believe the Light could be used for personal gain and power. Once these things became known to the jags, they overturned their will to evil. Darkness overcame the elyrians of the physical, they perverted the elyr to witchcraft, and the sorcerers had woken. So, with these abilities, the darkness used the jags as conduits, traveling through the in-between to find other physical realms to grow in number. It was not much longer drakes and humans were discovered and taught the dark arts of witchcraft and sorcery. Now it is here I should mention something. Not *all* physical beings overturned their will to the darkness. But the ones who saw through the deception of the darkness gave up their elyrian abilities, saying among themselves, 'It seems that this power comes from something that is incompatible with the needs of our flesh. Such a great power perverted will in return render us powerless.' Their hearts were in the right places. Unfortunately, witchcraft had become so influential in their realms that the beings of the physical were still greatly deceived by the existing sorcerers. Though they gave up their witchcraft, they were unable to discern a sorcerer from another being, and as such were deceived greatly."

Ace held his tongue again. So many questions. But they would be answered soon. He gathered himself with all the patience he could muster.

"During this time, the first sorcerers of each physical realm came together. The warlocks had woken, and the council formed. They deceived the physical beings under the noses of the elyrians. They gathered armies of sorcerers, preparing for war, while the inglings and faes believed all along that everything was perfectly fine, entirely unaware of the coming danger."

Ace couldn't help himself any longer. "You guys didn't know they were warlocks?"

The King shook his head. "Sorcerers are powerfully deceptive, human. This is something you must understand if you are to achieve the stone's purpose in you."

Ace's stomach flipped upside down. "The what?"

Ishvi sat up again. "Hey, Evelander, let King Vinan finish and your questions will be answered."

Ace sat back in his seat again, fighting his twitches. This may have been the first time he had been forced to fight back his curious urges.

"Well," King Vinan said, "as I was saying. The warlocks gathered their armies of parcels; and parcels their witch slaves, preparing for war. One by one, they caused the collapse of all the other realms through wars within. They deceived the jags against each other, the drakes against each other, and the humans against each other. And the War of the Realms had begun. But collapsing six realms was not truly their intention. They wanted to *rule* the realms.

"Now, before I continue with this, it is important to explain something. You see, human, as I have said previously, the faes and inglings were unaware of what was happening. To us, it had just seemed as the realms of the physical had simply gone mad. It wasn't until a human came to us, and revealed to us how the flesh had perverted the Light, that we became aware of witchcraft. A human with a strong perceptive eye, and an ability to see evil for what it was. An ability which had alluded the faes and inglings for so long.

"At the brink of Earth's collapse, he appeared to us. In his hand he held a red gem. The Emerson Stone. His name? Oliver Halder."

Ace's gut dropped as if a bomb had gone off inside him. Grandpa's story was true! All of it! Did they know the inscription, too? Did they know about the map?

The King went on with his story. "He came to us, stone in hand, and explained the dangers approaching. The council had grown in number, and every realm was now too full of parcels and witches. So much so that in the Realm Unknown, the darkness had grown to a greater size, and was beginning to diminish the Light. Oliver had said he knew this by a visitation from a warlock in his realm."

Jakka, Ace thought, *that was the warlock's name in Grandpa's story!*

The Tree King continued. "Seeing that the elyrians of the realms had been oblivious to this coming evil, the Light knew if it did not somehow reveal this to us, soon the warlocks would destroy us. So, it fled the Realm Unknown. No one knows how; for the Light doesn't owe its creation an explanation. He caged himself in the stone and hid away so the darkness would not know where it went. Now, hear this, human. The Light saw how the darkness had manifested itself in physical flesh to deceive the realms but could not do so with spiritual beings. And it became aware that the only way to save its creation, was the same way it lost its creation, by way of the physical. This is because of the freedom of will that physical beings have. (And I should mention that some faes have learned and adapted to this freedom of will since then, but that can be explained at a later time.)

"So, the Light watched the realms of the physical, keeping an eye out for someone worthy to contain the way of the elyr without being deceived. So far, no creature of the physical had successfully done so. That is, until Oliver. Oliver Halder had been approached by warlocks, but he saw through their deception. He saw the evil behind their motives. For this, the Light appeared to him in his stone cage. Now, when Oliver came to us, the stone in hand, he revealed to us all that had remained of the Light was there in the palm of his hand. He spoke to us of the war that would be waged soon unless we acted.

"To return to what I was saying before: the warlocks wanted to *rule* the realms, not destroy them. And so, the council saw that their armies were spread throughout all realms, but if they could be gathered together in one realm, they would become much more powerful, and ready to wage war on the Light. Once and for all. To diminish the Light forever.

"To accomplish this, they began the collapse of the other realms. The downfall instilled their inhabitants with much fear as they watched their world begin to crumble. So, the warlocks offered a safe place. And that's just how deceptive they are. From within the realms they began the collapse, then offered an escape from the very collapse they caused! They stood before each realm and told them, 'There is a safe place prepared for you. Your world crumbles, but this world will not.'"

Yutara, Ace thought.

"Yutara," the King said. "Now, Yutara, until then, had been Breen. The home of the faes. And so, disguised as elyrians still, the warlocks brought the inhabitants of the other realms through the in-between into Breen.

"As they were bringing people of other races to Breen, they told us inglings and faes that their worlds were crumbling, and they needed a safe place. Us elyrians, being deceived and not wanting any innocent persons to die, agreed to this. It was only at the collapse of Earth, when Oliver appeared to us with the stone, that we saw what they were doing. At that point it had been too late; Grol and Morlog had already collapsed, and Earth was just beginning to crumble. But we had to act on what we could. After our understanding of what the warlocks were doing, we, of course, grew in our discernment between witchcraft and the elyr. Anyone practicing witchcraft was denied access to the in-between. To the Tree Kingdom.

"The warlocks evaded this easily. In the same way the faes

called to the Light to wake the Tree Realm, the warlocks called to the darkness to wake a new realm. The Shadow Realm. Or, in other words—" the King was interrupted.

"The seventh realm," Ace said.

The King nodded.

"So, King Vinan," Ace said, "is it true that just as from the Tree Kingdom an elyrian can travel through the realms, a sorcerer can travel through the realms in the shadows?"

"Yes. From the shadows the council emerges," King Vinan said. "Now, once we saw that the warlocks had collapsed the other realms and managed to gather their armies together in Yutara, all hope had been lost. But Oliver instructed us to hold fast. He explained to us that the Light had a plan. For a time, darkness would rule, as it has been for some time already. But for the same time that darkness would rule, the council would seek to distinguish the Light, but seek in vain. For the Light would be hidden for ages to come. And though darkness will rule, it cannot wage the final war until the Light could be found. But the Light would not reveal itself until the proper time. For though the darkness has grown, the Light has the only true power. And once it does, it will do so through such a vessel, the darkness will struggle to defeat it. Until then, Oliver instructed us to remain in the in-between. The sorcerers were too numbered for us to be able to fight them. But the Light will choose its last hope, then we will be ready to fight. The final war will be waged, and the fate of the seven realms would be determined by the victory, or failure, of the chosen vessel."

Ace swallowed a bitter taste. "In other words, the stone's keeper. In other words, me?"

Silence filled the room. The King, the fae, and Ishvi exchanged glances to one another.

"No," Ace said, "there's no way! I can't do that! My grandpa chose me to run his business, not save the world."

Kareena, who had been silent until now, finally spoke. "Ace, don't you see? Your grandfather never chose you . . . The stone chose you."

The King closed his eyes, and spoke a familiar poem aloud,

"Whosoever frees the stone
Will venture not a realm alone
Seven of which will confess
Emery's chosen, Emery blessed

Come Emery, who knows Unknown
In search of no Haevyr
There is one, and one alone
Who is called a savior

Eldest, will the keeper be
'Till shadow clouds all truth
One is chosen, this day's Eve
One, all hear ye in youth

What's to come, some will believe
Despite some who deny
Stone in hand, one will deceive
And one will bear the lie

For there, in the Land of Faes
Once returned to its throne
By one, in this tamest place
The Light is set in stone

No race of faes
Nor jags, nor drakes
Nor shadow or tree
Says from Unknown
Should bear, the stone
For this fate of Eve's

Burdened will the chosen be
But should he seek his soul free

Stone and man shall trade their fate
Then, of him, come Emery"

Ishvi chimed in next. "Emery is what the Light calls himself. It's why Oliver named this gem the Emerson Stone. The prophecy is clear, Evelander. The stone revealed itself to Oliver, seeing a powerful potential in him. But the Light knew Oliver wasn't quite ready for the task he needed him for. Emery waited patiently, protecting the bloodline of Oliver until one of his descendants proved worthy of the great task."

King Vinan spoke again. "The stone had been passed down through your family in secret. At Oliver's old age, when his passing grew near, he passed the stone to his oldest living son. For the stone only protects its possessor and descendants of its possessor. And for ages beyond, this occurred. Each of the oldest of sons was given the stone and instructed to keep it secret. But soon the stone would choose its own possessor, and the prophecy would begin."

Ishvi spoke once more. "Your grandfather did a lot to bring about the knowledge of witchcraft in Yutara and try to stop it. He must have thought the stone had chosen him. And all of us will admit, he did a great deal to help the cause. He was the first of the lineage to use the immunity the stone gave him to bring about a revolution. Only it was when the stone chose you, he must have seen that his time on Yutara had only paved the way for the true chosen. You."

Ace buried his face in his hands. This was too much to take in. Everyone on Yutara was against him. How could he convince the entire world to trust him? How could he lead an entire army in a final war to save the seven realms? He was only twelve! He lifted his head and looked at the Tree King.

"How do you know the stone chose me?" he asked.

"Two things suggest this," the King said. "One, that your grandfather gave the stone to his youngest descendant, thwarting the protection of the rest of his family. No other Halder has done that in history. Two is the most obvious. You're an elyrian who has not been deceived by the darkness. The stone granted you this power. Emery must believe you have the potential to hold the gifts of the Light without becoming corrupted like everyone else."

Did I really light that torch? Ace thought. *I'm not truly an elyrian, am I?*

Kareena jumped into the conversation again. "The tree people have remained in the in-between, awaiting the return of the Light and its vessel. Faes who still practice the elyr have obviously been instructed not to teach the Light of the elyr to any physical creature. For they would eventually be deceived and turned to evil. When your grandfather created the Indies, we faes thought it was a sign that the Light had returned, and that he was the vessel. But once the elyr had been outlawed in Gathara, we lost all hope. We began to accept that the prophecy was simply legend and myth. But now I see it clearly. You aren't an elyrian, Ace. You're t*he* Elyrian. You are the chosen keeper. The chosen vessel. Yutara needs you."

Ace sighed, his face still buried in his hands. For a moment there was only silence. He lifted his head and said softly, "How am I supposed to destroy the seventh realm? How am I even supposed to find it?"

The King nudged his shoulder. "At that, your guess is as good as ours. All we know is what the prophecy speaks of:

"Burdened will the chosen be
But should he seek his soul free
Stone and man shall trade their fate
Then, of him, come Emery."

"It doesn't seem to say much at all about finding or destroying the seventh realm."

"Well, that's a little disappointing," Ace said as he folded his arms and leaned back.

"What do you mean?" the Tree King replied.

"When Grandpa Marty gave me the stone, he told me the reason he believed the seventh realm wasn't a myth was because of a map. Then he told me when the map was revealed to me, the stone would become mine. The next night, he told me the prophecy and the story of Oliver. I thought the poem was the map to the seventh realm."

King Vinan's eyes perked up. He waved his hand as if to dismiss the matter. "No, no, Ace, your grandfather didn't mean a map to the seventh realm. He meant a map of the future. The prophecy tells us how the power of the seventh realm will be uncovered and uprooted."

Ace squinted and scratched his head. It *did* seem to make more sense the deeper he thought of it. In fact, Grandpa told him the map was inside of him. His mind bounced back and forth.

"Besides," Ishvi chimed in once again, "elyrians have avoided such a journey. The Shadow Realm is an elyrian's greatest nightmare. The darkness is so powerful that an elyrian's light will fade into nothingness the moment they enter, and the elyrian will pass away."

Ace swallowed a lump in his throat. "Great."

"But," the King said, "it would not be that way with you. At least not once you are ready."

"Why not?" Ace said.

Kareena spoke next. "Unlike other elyrians, you are a physical being. Just as the Light lives in this world, caged by the stone and protected from the darkness, your physical body can act as a shield of the Light."

"You mean you don't . . . have a body?" Ace said, his eyes glancing up and down at her.

Kareena chuckled. "Of course, I have a body, but unlike a being of flesh, my body survives solely on the Light within it. If the Light fades, my body dies."

"And so," the King spoke again, "it would make sense that the Light would choose a being from a physical realm. For ages, inglings have done as instructed and waited in the in-between, shutting off the pathway to the realms except by my messenger Ishvi here; faes who practice the elyr are scarce now."

"Why?" Ace said.

"Because," Kareena responded, "the council has deceived Yutara, even the new Breen: the Land of Faes. To most faes in

Breen, the elyr is viewed as a way of life, but any practice of the white fire is deemed witchcraft and they are punished severely for it. In the rest of Yutara, witches have eyes everywhere. If a fae is caught practicing the elyr, a witch is bound to hear about it and cast the fae into the shadows. If the witch doesn't succeed, a parcel will find one."

"So, fight against it!" Ace said.

"We've been too outnumbered. The Light has weakened because the darkness is so powerful, and any attempt at fighting off witchcraft with the elyr has been met with a force of darkness too great for us to fight against," Kareena said.

"You see, Ace," King Vinan said, "we have been waiting for you. For too long have the elyrians of Yutara lived under the rule of the darkness, hiding in shame for their gift. We've resisted the urge to fight so many times, but Oliver gave us the Light's clear instructions, that if we wage war before the proper time, before the chosen vessel appears, we will surely lose. The darkness has overpowered us for ages beyond; our existence thrives on the Light: if we wage the war now, we will be overpowered and crushed. But if the Light can grow back to where it used to be . . . See, you are the only way to wage the final war, Ace. It all goes back to what I said about free will. The Light saw how the darkness used the free will of the flesh to pervert the elyr. By the way the Light was perverted is the only way it can be restored."

Ishvi leaned toward Ace. "You're essentially the conduit. As you grow the Light (the same way flesh once grew the darkness) Emery can use you as its new source."

"In other words," Kareena said, "you will be a source of light for the elyrians. The shadow realm will lose its power over the faes, and the final war can be waged."

Silence filled the room once again as Ace processed his thoughts. Kareena and the tree goblins sat with eager eyes, anticipating the boy's response. But he wasn't sure what to say. Some of this hurt him, and some of this brought joy. Grandpa hadn't actually chosen him, and such a thought came with a bitter taste. Maybe he hadn't bested the Peppercorns after all. And the

Peppercorns—the thought of them was also wrenching. But it surely wasn't worth the end of the world to see them turned to witches. There had to be a better way to bring them justice.

One thought caused him to raise his chin with pride. This being of Light, the source of all good in the universe, had chosen him. Must be greater than being picked by Grandpa. In fact, the Light chose him even over Grandpa! Of all the people of Yutara, of all the people of the seven realms, Ace Halder had been chosen for this great task. But could he do it? Was he truly strong enough? King Vinan did suggest he simply wasn't ready. Perhaps with the right training and enough time, he could develop the skills necessary to accomplish this. After all, the Light seemed to think he was the only one who could.

He looked at the Tree King. "What must I do?"

CHAPTER FORTY-FOUR

The Crystal Ocean

Kareena brought Ace to a strange ocean in the Tree World. The water was like a crystal, a spotless mirror all the way to the horizon. The sky remained the same dirt surface and pinkish hue, but no trees grew downward over the ocean. The tide brushed gently against Ace's bare feet. It was neither cold nor hot, but just the perfect temperature. Unlike the beaches in other worlds, there was no sand. Only the same ground surface of tree branches and fluffy leaves. But it didn't hurt him to walk across this surface barefoot, rather it felt like walking on a cloud. Even across the branches.

Kareena, keeping her eyes about the sea, spoke to Ace. "Here, I will teach you the basics of the elyr. How to understand it and utilize it. However, we cannot remain here forever. You will never master it in the in-between. It takes an elyrian years in outside realms, being tested by trials, to master the way of the Light." Though Ace thought the sea in the forest was beautiful, he found it difficult to shift his gaze from the fae.

"Are you saying I will have to practice this in Yutara?"

Kareena turned to Ace. "Yes. The Emerson Stone has caged what is left of the Light. The Realm Unknown is now only darkness. For the final war to be waged, the Light must grow strong enough to face and consume the darkness in the Realm Unknown. In Yutara, since you are the vessel, with every battle you win, the Light will grow. When it's ready, and when you are ready, it will guide you to wage the war on the seventh realm."

"But the elyr is outlawed in Yutara," Ace said.

"No one said the task will be easy. But the Light chose you. You must also keep in mind that every battle you lose, the darkness will grow, and the Light will fade."

"I thought the Light fled from the Realm Unknown, so it wouldn't fade anymore."

"Yes. But now that it's chosen you, and granted you the power of the elyr, it has become vulnerable to the darkness once again. Once you begin to grow the Light, the council will know that Emery has returned. They will come for you, Ace. They will try and stop you by any means."

"Does this mean I'm no longer immune to witchcraft?"

"I'm not sure. But it's important to remember, even if you're immune to witchcraft, you are never immune to deception. The stone protecting you will be of great value once you battle a sorcerer, but it serves no purpose in protecting you from deception. Your growth in the elyr will sharpen your discernment, but ultimately, you will have to protect yourself from deception."

Ace nodded.

"Come," Kareena said. She stepped forward on the water. The pale flame of the elyr appeared on her feet and hovered her along the surface of the water. "Follow me."

Ace stared in amazement. "But I don't know how to do that."

Kareena, with her expressionless face, waved her hands fluidly, and the elyr appeared at Ace's feet. The boy's face lit up with wonder, and he took an anxious step on the surface of the ocean; just as Kareena, he hovered above the water. Together, they traveled the crystal sea in silence, until the trees were nothing but a faint line on the horizon. It was only them, completely alone in the middle of a crystal ocean. Ace's heart was full, and his eagerness to learn the way of the Light overcame him.

"This is a good place to begin," Kareena said. "The stillness is needed to fill your mind. It is important for you to understand the source of the elyr's power, which is fundamentally different from that of a sorcerer. Fill your mind with truth and empty it of everything you think you understand about witchcraft."

Ace closed his eyes and breathed deep. "Okay," he said, "I—uh —I think I did it."

Kareena rolled her eyes. "Okay. Now hold your hands before you. Picture anything that brings you joy. Anything that makes your heart full."

This wasn't difficult for the boy. For the thing which seemed to bring him so much joy stood just before him. The fae herself.

"That was quick," the fae said. "Open your eyes."

Ace did so and looked at his cupped hands. A pale flame, faint and flickering, sat in the palms of his hand, not but the size of a pea.

"Wow!" Ace said, a wide smile on his face. "Why is it so dim?"

"Because you're new to this. Honestly, it's impressive you have any light at all so quickly. I was hoping you wouldn't be able to do it, so I could prove my point greater, but your concern with the weak nature of your light will still help my case.

"Learning the elyr takes time, dedication, and practice. This is one of the bigger differences between the elyr and sorcery. The council will offer you immediate gratification. Everything you want overnight. Fame, power, riches. Once someone has loved fame, riches, and power, the council will offer these things to them for a price much greater than their worth."

"What does it cost?"

Kareena stepped closer and placed a warm hand on Ace's chest. "Their soul," she said.

Ace tilted his head and squinted his eyes. "I don't understand."

"You probably have a false understanding of witchcraft. That it's extremely powerful and dangerous. And while it is dangerous, it's not as powerful as you'd think. It's limited. This is why sorcerers have mastered the art of deception. A witch, parcel, or warlock will only resort to magic out of desperation. In fact, many parcels send their witch slaves after people to avoid fighting themselves. Because, once they begin to use magic, they begin running out of fuel. And the fuel for their magic . . ." Kareena tipped her eyes at him, expecting a response.

"Souls?" Ace asked.

Kareena nodded. "The greatest difference between magic and the elyr is the effect on the soul. You see, magic requires the use of someone else's soul. Once that soul has been entirely absorbed, a sorcerer's magic runs out. The elyr is the opposite. The elyr requires the health of one's *own* soul to draw its power. The more you seek to become like the Light, the stronger the Light becomes in you. Thus, the prophecy speaks:

'But should he seek his soul freed.'"

Ace spoke once again. "And the more elyrians with healthy souls, the more powerful the Light becomes."

"Correct. Many faes have given up hope and forgotten Emery. If you can restore this hope, grow the Light, and recruit the faes back to their elyrian abilities, the council won't stand a chance."

Ace quieted a moment and allowed the fae's words to soak in, attempting to comprehend the way of the Light. He looked at the small light in the palm of his hand, still dim and flickering. This was Grandpa's cure. This is what Grandpa needed all along. This was Grandpa's Ace of Spades.

"Whatever your thought was," Kareena said, "it provoked you to want to do good. This caused the Light to appear."

Ace smiled inside. Kareena did make him want to do good. "Kareena, I don't understand how the elyr works, exactly. At the oasis, you told me the Light doesn't burn the flesh of the innocent. Here we are, standing on it above the water as well. Is it some kind of force? A fire that only burns witches? What is it, exactly?"

"The elyr is a person. Emery is the elyr, and the elyr is Emery." Ace's demeanor was anything but graceful. She'd confused him more than before they began. Kareena giggled at the look on his face. "The elyr can give and take away the gift from any elyrian he chooses. In the past, faes used the gift for many things. It can heal wounds, reveal sorcery, and it can also be used as a force. If you're not a sorcerer, the Light may not burn you, but that doesn't mean the Light can't work as a force against you. There are some stories of ancient faes powerful enough to move mountains with the elyr."

"Woah," Ace said softly.

"There is no limit to what the elyr can do. There are only limits to what *elyrians* can do. Now, let's move forward with training. Think of another thing. Something that stirs up strife in you," the fae said.

It didn't take much time for this either. The Peppercorns popped in his head right away. Before he even closed his eyes, the flame in his palm went off as quick as the flip of a switch.

"Oh my," Kareena said, "you have something trifling deep within you."

"That's okay," Ace said, he closed his eyes and pictured Kareena once again. He felt the light flicker in his palm, then drift away. He tried again, closing his eyes tightly, but the same thing occurred. He stopped at the warmth of Kareena's hand when she placed it on his.

"Ace," she said. The boy opened his eyes to her radiant face. "It cannot work that way. You can't suppress the conflict within you and hope to grow the Light. The reason your light is dim is because of the conflict in your heart. You have to solve it before your light will grow."

Ace felt a wrenching inside and a bitter taste on his tongue. He violently shook his head. "No. It's okay, watch. I'll make the Light grow."

"No, you won't," Kareena said. Her firm tone contested her otherwise gentle nature.

But he ignored her and squeezed his eyes shut. He couldn't shake the negative feelings.

The Peppercorns.

His mother.

Saving them.

He didn't want to save them. He couldn't save them. He wouldn't! No way he was going to forgive them. They didn't deserve it. They deserved to rot. Though he fought against them, small tears began to seep from the corners of his eyes.

"Ace," Kareena said softly. She stepped beside him and placed a gentle hand on his back. "This is very concerning." The boy opened his painfully brimming eyes to the fae before him. "If you cannot learn to heal from this, you will never learn to use the Light."

Ace protested, "There has to be a different way."

Kareena closed her eyes and softly shook her head. "What is it that's bothering you?"

Ace tensed himself and ignored her.

"Someone has hurt you," she said. "Someone has wronged you, haven't they? Someone has deeply wronged you or someone you love."

He looked at Kareena, his face scrunched with anger. "I can't forgive them, okay? And I won't save the Peppercorns!"

When he said this, his tension fled, and his body went limp. Kareena stepped back, a look of horror in her eyes.

"I'm sorry, Ace," the fae said. "If you don't forgive those who have wronged you, neither will the Light forgive you. To achieve the stone's purpose in you is impossible without the Light's forgiveness." She closed her eyes and waved her hand in the air. Ace gasped as he dropped into the water. The Light had left from his feet and he was surrounded by the crystal ocean. He held his breath and swam to the surface. His head broke through and he coughed up the water from his throat. He treaded the water, but his arms were weakened.

Kareena stepped to him and leaned close. "Is your grudge so strong that you would let yourself drown?"

Ace stared at her. Was she serious? "You won't leave me here," Ace said. "I can't swim that far."

Kareena stood tall. "Whether you stay here or return to shore is up to you. Not me. The elyrian within you is strong enough that you should be able to pull yourself to the surface and safely return to shore. But if you do not give up your unwillingness to solve this conflict, you will surely drown."

"But you just said being an elyrian takes time!"

"The Light I'm asking you to create is only the most basic."

"You can't do this!" Ace yelled. "It's not right! It's immoral!"

"It's the only way," she said. She turned away; the Light shone from her hands as a great and powerful flame, propelling her forward, so she traveled across the ocean at a blazing speed.

"Kareena! Come back!" Ace said with desperation. "I can't do this! Please!"

But the only response he received was her back turned, quickly drifting away until she slipped behind the faint line of trees ahead.

CHAPTER FORTY-FIVE

Confession

Ace shouted for help as long as he could. It seemed hours had passed, and no one came. His body ached with heaviness. Was this really happening? How could the fae do such a thing? He spit out the salty water creeping into his mouth. His licked his chapped lips, and his thirst overwhelmed him. Was this the end?

No, no. She wouldn't leave me here to die, Ace thought. *She couldn't. The elyr wouldn't let her.* He looked for some sort of escape. He spun himself around, only to quickly rediscover the only thing between him and the shore was the Crystal Ocean. He breathed heavily and fought himself from panicking.

"C'mon!" he said aloud. "You can do this!"

He closed his eyes. It was much harder to clear his mind and concentrate when he was treading water for his life. He tried to think of Kareena, but this no longer brought joy. Now, the only the thoughts adjoined with her were being abandoned in the middle of the ocean. He slapped the water with his hands. He grimaced as droplets splashed into his eye. He tried to rub it, but the salt water from his hands only made it worse.

"Okay," he said softly, "calm down. Don't panic." He breathed slowly. He used the smallest effort he could manage treading water, but it didn't prevent the feeling of a great weight resting on his arms and legs. He ignored them, attempting to look deep within himself to find the prompting of good. Something had to bring the Light forth.

The thought of Grandpa Marty crossed his mind. His constant smiling face and positivity. The thought of his fireside stories on family vacations.

"You're my Ace of Spades. When the time comes, you're gonna be the secret weapon that makes everything worthwhile." Ace's gut twisted. He was letting Grandpa down right now, not being his Ace of Spades. No joy. He dug further. There had to be something prompting within him to do good. Something not requiring him to forgive the Peppercorns. Just the thought of it enraged him all the more. He suppressed those thoughts. Getting angry wouldn't help him in this moment.

He coughed up more water; the muscles in his arms felt like fire. He was out of ideas. How would he even begin to forgive the Peppercorns? They didn't deserve it! They were rotten, spoiled little brats. They deserved nothing less than to be as witches forever. Why, if he were to forgive them, it would thwart his whole plan! Being chosen by the Light to save Yutara, he could finally be able to bring justice to them. How was justice not approved of by the Light? What kind of *good* was a Light who didn't agree with justice? What was Ace supposed to do? Just let them off the hook? They'd treated him like garbage his entire life. They constantly belittled him and lorded over him, like the way they were taught to by their parents! They . . . they . . .

"They killed my mother!" Ace yelled aloud. Something burst open inside him. A warm sensation flooded his body, and tears spilled from his eyes like tiny rivers. He tried to fight them, knowing his weeping would cause more exhaustion, but he simply couldn't. He lost all control.

"They killed my mother," he said again, this time much softer and lighter. His arms and legs weighed heavier than he could bear any longer. Exhaustion took him. From the corner of his eyes, he saw only black. Slowly, the black closed in a tunnel, until he saw only darkness.

Ace woke to the familiar sensation of being on a cloud. The fuzziness around him slowly cleared until he found himself in a tree hut. He sat straight up, his head imploding and rendering him dizzy. He looked down and found himself on a bed of tree branches, the fluffy leaves being the mattress. His clothes had been replaced with a white robe. Just ahead of him was an open doorway, and to the right of the door sat a small table with two chairs. Shem stepped inside from the doorway ahead, a wooden cup in his right hand.

"Oh!" Shem said as he stepped forward. He placed a wooden cup on the nightstand next to Ace's bed. "You're awake. Good. I'll fetch the fae."

"Wait," Ace said. Shem glanced at him. "Is she mad at me?"

Shem tilted his head. "Why would she be?"

"Because I didn't—" Ace paused as he stared at Shem's massive, glossy brown eyes. "Never mind."

"You need to rest, Ace," Shem said. He handed Ace the wooden cup. "This mixture will do you some good."

Shem walked out the door. Ace looked at the dark liquid in the cup. He swirled it around, then sniffed it. It had a rich, sweet tang of exotic fruit, but also a stinging mint. An odd mix. He took a small sip, regrettably so. The burning mint sent an unpleasant chill down his throat and burst in his chest. He leaned over the bed, hacking and coughing.

"It tastes bad, but it will make your headache go away," Kareena said, now stepping through the same door Shem had left from. Ace winced at the wretched liquid and set it on the nightstand beside him.

"Karee—" He coughed a few more times. "Kareena." He

cleared his throat. "How could you leave me in the middle of the ocean like that? I could have died."

The fae grabbed one of the chairs, stepped forward, and sat by Ace's bedside.

"You know I wouldn't have let you die," the fae said. "I didn't, obviously."

Ace pouted. "It was still cruel."

Kareena dismissed his remark. "It was necessary. What's cruel is what these Peppercorns have done to you."

Ace shot up. His headache and body aches began to fade, but no medicine could stop the tensing caused by Kareena when she spoke of the Peppercorns.

After they stared quietly at one another, Kareena spoke once again. "Is it true? What you yelled out loud in the ocean?"

He felt tricked. He never talked about what happened that day, and he never would. Not even his brother, who constantly persisted, could get Ace to talk about it. But now, he was backed into a corner. He had no choice. Or perhaps he did, but the fae's ocean eyes and radiant glow captivated him so much, the words simply spilled out without a thought.

"Yes," Ace said. "Well, half true."

The fae leaned closer, placing her warm hand on his. His heart skipped a beat.

"I'm sorry for what I did," she said, "but I could tell by the way your light vanished that you were holding conflict deep within. And when I saw your resistance to fixing it . . ." she paused, giving him the same penetrating stare. "Sometimes the only way to bring a hurting soul to confession is to shock it. The only way for you to become the elyrian you're meant to be is to grieve, and forgive the people who have hurt you. Now you've confessed aloud what has happened to you and you can move on."

Ace fought his tears back. He knew she was right. But . . . he just . . . couldn't . . . do it. It was as if someone built a brick wall between him and the Peppercorns. Maybe if he told her . . . maybe then . . . the fae would understand? But even when the thought of explaining what happened crossed his mind, it felt like sharp needles sank into his skin. He gulped and wiped his forehead. He looked at her angelic demeanor and exhaled in a way it seemed to deflate him. He had to tell her.

"I've been a disgrace since I was born," Ace said. He brought his head down, unable to look her in the eye, but her grip on his hand tightened. "Since I was as little as I can remember, Aunt Kaitlyn has told me that I take after my father. And not in a good way. My dad and aunt are fraternal twins. They've had this sibling rivalry since birth. Grandpa used to tell me he thought it was just a phase when they were little. But the older they got, the more divided they became. They always had to be better than each other. But Kaitlyn, my aunt, was always better than my dad at everything. At least, that's what my dad used to say.

"'Kaitlyn was better looking, more talented, and more qualified for anything Grandpa Marty ever needed!' he used to say. It wasn't until my dad met my mom that he stopped caring about this rivalry. Mom used to tell him that it was stupid to compete for Grandpa Marty's love because he loved them both equally. Slowly, but surely, my dad realized my mom was right all along. But my aunt didn't see it that way. After my dad married, and had my brother, he had moved on from the feud, and Grandpa noticed it. Grandpa's heart was full once my dad had set the past behind him. Kaitlyn, my aunt, wasn't happy about this. So, she found a way to 'beat him.' She did this by marrying a famous man from Eveland. Marcus Peppercorn, point guard for the Genesis Sabercats."

Kareena looked strangely at him.

"It's a basketball team," Ace said. She nodded. "He's one of the best basketball players in Yutara. They started having kids right away and raised them just to be better than my father's kids, which are me and my brother.

"Apparently, the little snots inherited all those traits Dad used to talk about from Kaitlyn, because they *were* better. They made mine and my brother's life awful. Especially mine when I was younger. Pranks and taunting, just stupid stuff. My father let it get to him and fell back into this feud with his sister. He started working me and my brother a lot. Pressuring us to become better than the Peppercorns. But we weren't. Especially me. I was the worst. I never measured up. We'd have reunions and family games, stuff that should be fun and bring us together. But the Peppercorns somehow turned it into a competition. They'd taunt us and say that no one loves losers. I always came in last place, and I was always reminded of it. By everyone except for one person . . ." Ace, for the first time since he'd begun his story, looked Kareena directly in the eye. His speech was broken through his tears, but the words were audible nonetheless. "My mother."

CHAPTER FORTY-SIX

Healing

Kareena's typical expressionless face made her true emotions powerful as her demeanor grew more empathetic.

"There's one day I will never forget," Ace said. "It was in the summer, and Grandpa took us to his cabin in Solomon Forest, east of Lake David. It's always been strange to me." Ace smiled, just barely. "Grandpa brought us together pretty often for how much my father and his sister hated each other."

Kareena said, "It sounds like your grandfather was trying to make peace."

Ace gave her a gentle nod. "He and my mother both. Unfortunately, it seemed to backfire more often than it did any good. It got to the point where Cameron and I would dread vacations. Not wanting to spend a single moment with the Peppercorns. But my mom always encouraged me that things would get better. My dad didn't. He was usually just quiet. Probably plotting how, this time, he would finally find a way to be better than his sister.

"Anyway, the day after we arrived, Grandpa Marty suggested we all go hunting. And, of course, the Peppercorns turned it into a competition. And as a result, so did my dad. We split in teams of two, and I was paired with my dad. The girls kept shouting in the forest how many great beasts they'd captured, and how they were going to 'win.'

"I could tell my dad was getting angry. That's when I saw something in the distance. At this time, I should mention, I was only nine years old. But what I saw was a caribou. It was huge, and would have been a great catch. Unfortunately, my dad saw it too. He shushed me and aimed his rifle. But just before he shot it, I—" Ace swallowed before he continued, "I pushed him down. I couldn't help it. I saw two babies come out of the bushes, and I didn't want my dad to kill it.

"My dad yelled at me. Then he ranted about how I never do what he asks and how I always come up short. He said I was the reason we're struggling to get ahead, and that if I didn't have the guts to kill a stupid beast, I shouldn't even consider myself a Halder."

Kareena's grip tightened around Ace's hand once more.

Ace continued, "Later that day, Tamara walked into the cabin with that very same caribou as her prize, dead and dangling around her neck. And Julie walked in with the two babies. They walked up to me and shoved them in my face, gloating and teasing.

"'Baby Ace is scared of a weindeer,' they said, waving the dead animals' faces in front of me. My dad marched out of the cabin and didn't return for the rest of the evening. I ran to my room and slammed the door. But it wasn't much later that my mom knocked on the door.

"'Ace? Can I come in?' she said." A tear spilled out of Ace's right eye as he spoke in his mother's voice.

"'No!' I yelled at her. She cracked the door open.

"'I think you did a wonderful thing,' Mom said. She waited a moment, then came and sat at my bed. 'The Peppercorns don't seem to understand the value in the heart of a person. Don't let them get to you. It takes a special amount of courage to care for something more than yourself.'

"'Dad hates me!' I yelled. She pulled me close.

"'No. He doesn't hate you. He's just lost his way. But I have a feeling you're going to help him find it again one day,' Mom said. 'You're Grandpa's Ace of Spades.' That was her and my grandfather's nickname for me."

Once Ace had finished telling his story, he noticed Kareena was considerably closer than before. Her silver hair smelled like a dewy morning mist. Their eyes met in silence for a moment, then Kareena's face was struck with surprise, and she scooted further from him.

She cleared her throat. "If you don't mind me asking. How and why did these Peppercorns kill your mother?"

Ace turned his head. It seemed strange to him; hearing the fae mention this horrid event didn't stir any resistance in him. As if the wall he'd felt earlier had slowly begun to crumble. He shrugged, his eyes turned from the fae. "I don't know exactly how, but Julie's pranks were the worst and bound to go south some time. She tried to pull a prank on us one day, and accidentally pulled it on my mom. At least, that's what Julie says. It was a bit of a freak thing because they weren't doing anything particularly dangerous, so it's hard to believe my mom died from it. That's why I don't believe Julie, there had to be something else going on. The Peppercorns really didn't like my mother."

"Why not?" Kareena asked.

"Because she, like Grandpa, tried to stop us from competing all the time. And if we didn't compete, the Peppercorns couldn't be better than us. Julie and Tamara couldn't live one day without being better than us. Neither could Aunt Kaitlyn for that matter.

"I don't remember much about the day my mom died. Only that we were at the Peppercorns' house and there was a loud noise and a scream downstairs. We all ran to the kitchen to find my mom lying on the floor. My dad ran to her side. Julie was standing there. She went on about how she didn't mean for it to go as far as it did. To this day, we still don't know exactly what Julie did. My dad never talks about it . . . Uncle Marcus and Aunt Kaitlyn don't talk about it . . . not even Grandpa talked about it."

Kareena spoke so softly to him, she might as well have whispered in his ear. "Do it now."

Ace looked at her. "What?"

She grabbed his wrist and held his hand before him. "The Light," she said.

Ace turned his head with uncertainty. Nothing inside him felt joyful. In fact, he felt more twisted up than he had before. But she mesmerized him, so he felt he would do anything she asked of him.

He looked at his hands, this time not closing his eyes. He focused his attention on the turmoil within him. Of course, after spilling his guts, it was hard to focus on much of anything different. A bitter rock settled in his stomach as he remembered the day his mother died. How was this supposed to work? What was the fae thinking?

A flicker of light shone on his hand. His jaw dropped, and he turned to the fae, who had not the slightest bit of shock on her face. He turned back to his hand and focused again. The pale flame shone from his palms. But this flame was anything but dim. The flame extended from his palm and consumed his hands, wrapping itself and extending from his fingers, illuminating the whole room with the elyr.

Ace lifted his hand of white fire before him, awestruck by what had just occurred. Kareena placed her hand on his, a smile on her face, and the flame wrapped around both of their hands.

"I don't understand," Ace said, turning to her. "I don't feel joyful."

As she turned to face him, the pale flame before them caused the fae's eyes to shine all the more, and the touch of her hand against his turned his heart upside down.

"The elyr doesn't always thrive on joy. Rather, the urge to do good. Sometimes. . ." She placed her other hand on his chest. "Pain can bring as much, or more, of a prompting as joy. By confessing this great deal of pain you've hidden away, you have taken a huge step."

"Ahem?" came a voice from the doorway. The light vanished, and the fae leaped from her chair in a flash. King Vinan had stepped inside, cane in hand. He shot a glance of distaste at the fae, then Ace. "I see you've been... uh... improving your elyr, human."

Ace chortled as he scratched his head. "Yeah, I guess so."

"King Vinan," Kareena said, "I think he's ready."

The King looked at her with worry. "What makes you think that?"

"He's begun healing, I've seen it within him. He has just made a great light. There is nothing more we can teach him here."

"He's been here only a couple days," the Tree King said.

Kareena nodded. "And for that, I can truly see why the Light chose him. I believe it guided him here to face a terrible pain he's hidden, and overcome it. This burden needed to be lifted before he went back to Yutara."

Ace stood from his bed, realizing all his previous pain had left him. The drink Shem gave him had worked swimmingly. "But, Kareena . . ." he said. She glanced his way. "I—well—I still haven't exactly *forgiven* the Peppercorns. I'm trying, but I still feel all twisted up inside."

Kareena inched closer. "That's exactly why you need to begin to use the Light in the real world. We have taught you all you can learn in the in-between. Your light will now grow, or fade, within you based on your real-world experiences. You will need to confront these cousins of yours to take the next step."

"He will need to do a lot more than that," the King said. "Sending him back to Yutara with the power of the elyr could be risky. Especially in Gathara. If he's caught, they will pool him in with the other sorcerers."

Kareena said, "We have to send him eventually. What would you have me do if we stay here? He cannot stay here forever."

Ace used the following silence to determine how he felt about these things. Was Kareena right? It didn't seem like he was ready. Just the day before, he was drowning in an ocean. He *did* feel eager to discover this parcel in the elite and take them down. His use of the elyr could reveal the mole. He looked at Kareena and her confident eyes.

"Well," Ace said, eyes fixed on the girl fae, "it's not like I'll be completely alone, right?"

Kareena smiled.

"Yes, actually, you will," King Vinan said. He stepped forward, leaning on his cane. "There's a reason the remaining elyrians have kept their distance for so long. We are greatly outnumbered. You can't just start taking down sorcerers with the Light right away."

"Why not?" Ace said. "That kinda sounds like a great plan actually."

King Vinan turned to Kareena. "You see. He doesn't even know what's at stake yet! No way is he ready."

Kareena spoke firmly, "So, teach him now."

King Vinan glanced at Ace with hard eyes. "Come with me."

CHAPTER FORTY-SEVEN

Chosen

King Vinan brought Ace a half an hour's walk away from the tree village to an area surrounded by a perfect circle of upside-down trees surrounding a larger, rotting tree. Its bark was black as night, yet it stood tall and proud. Five trees surrounded the large one, and all but one had been blackened from the large tree. But the last one stood in perfect bloom.

"They used to all be beautiful," King Vinan said. "Coming here was like coming to Shywater. Still, peaceful. The perfect place to hear from Emery." He reached out to touch one of the dead trees but stopped. His finger started to turn dark as it came close to the tree. He pulled away and hung his head.

"What are these?" Ace said.

King Vinan's eyes went soft. "The way to the other realms. All but the seventh." He walked closer, bent over his cane, and eyed Ace darkly. "Where there are trees, there is life, but the council has made it so the seventh has swallowed what life remained in the others . . ." He pointed at the last standing tree. "All but one."

Ace looked at the remaining tree. Its bark, like a coffee brown, twirled together and grew larger as it reached the dirt ceiling of the underground world. It radiated life. "Yutara," he said softly.

"Yutara," the King agreed. "Come." He grabbed Ace's wrist and dragged him to the center tree. Darkness bearing a foul odor crept into the air. He breathed it in, and it crawled through his insides like termites through wood. Dread welled in him. "Bring the elyr to your hand and touch the tree."

He didn't want to at first. He glanced back and forth between the dark tree and the ingling. Vinan nudged his head toward the tree impatiently. Ace smacked his teeth, giving in to Vinan's demands. He closed his eyes a moment and thought of whatever might prompt him to do good. At an exhale, the Light appeared at his palm, tepid and flickering, and after a few hesitant reaches, he placed his hand on the tree. Darkness took him and crawled through his body. It ached in his muscles, his brain, his heart, his soul. He closed his eyes, tensing and grimacing at the horror.

King Vinan paced the ground, circling the large tree. "What do you feel?"

"D—Darkness. E—Evil. Pain. Suffering. It hurts."

"This tree is the gateway to the Realm Unknown. Not even the inglings can open it. That tiny fire at your hand is the only piece of the Light it's seen since the Emerson Stone left . . ." He reached Ace and whispered in his ear, "And it *hates* you for it."

Ace pulled his hand free. The force of it sent him falling, so his back hit the ground. He panted, feeling his body to make sure he truly lay there, and he hadn't fallen into the dark pit the tree had placed in his mind.

King Vinan knelt beside him. "Do you sense the evil? Do you sense how great it is and how powerful it's become? It has gobbled up all but the last piece of the Light, which the Emerson Stone entrusted to you. Do you understand your task and how great it is? Do you understand your purpose?" Ace lay flat, wordless, and wide-eyed at the Tree King, still trying to gather himself from the dark place he'd just returned from. "This is something you must understand before you return to Yutara."

Ace gulped. He slowly helped himself to sit upright, placing a hand over his chest. "It's . . . so . . . dark," he said through his gradually slowing breaths. "But I could sense it . . . everyone . . . everyone is doomed! That's why generational curses can work without someone giving themselves to the council. All of us are corrupted by the council's deception!"

"Yes. This is what the flesh has done, Ace," the Tree King said. "Through flesh, it has perverted the Light." He placed a soft hand on Ace's knee, and tranquility passed through him. "And only by flesh can it be healed."

"What makes me so special, King Vinan? There are plenty of others out there who haven't given their souls to the council to obtain magic. Why me?"

"Emery doesn't owe you an explanation, Ace. But you *do* owe him your obedience." The boy caught eyes with the ingling for a few wordless moments. "And you're half wrong. While many people haven't freely given their souls to the council, that doesn't mean their souls aren't subject to it. When flesh perverted the Light for self-gain, flesh became cursed. Magic works on the free peoples of Yutara because they are corrupt. Witches use this curse to cast spells on people, and sometimes take control of them entirely. Witches may come from the weak spirited, who took the council's offer freely, but those who turn down the council suffer for it. Spells take their memory, and sometimes torment them day and night. You see, Ace, there really is no escape from the council . . . yet. For some reason, Emery saw something in you. He saw the chance to break this curse and redeem Yutara."

Ace stared at the large, rotting tree in front of him and sighed. "What if I can't do it? What if I'm not strong enough?"

King Vinan placed a gentle hand on Ace's chest and smiled at him. Their eyes stuck to one another. "You're not. But you don't have to be. The elyr will guide you."

Ace sat and pondered the weight of his task as the Elyrian for a long moment, and Vinan had left him to do it alone. The Tree King returned with Kareena what seemed like a couple hours later. He watched them approach, feeling a blissful trance come over him. His time alone to think had prepared him, and a new sense of understanding had come over him.

"The fae girl is right about you, Elyrian," King Vinan said. "I had to witness it myself first. I wanted to test you by having you hold the Light against the source of darkness in the seven realms. Your light never faded, not until you pulled away. You are ready to enter Yutara."

Ace stood, wiping the dirt from his jeans. "Thank you, King Vinan."

Kareena rushed to the ingling and gave him a strong embrace. "Thank you for everything, King Vinan."

The Tree King returned the favor, his eyes shut tightly. "Don't you get mixed up in anything too dangerous now. I want to see you back here in one piece. You understand?"

"Yes," she responded. They pulled from the embrace and looked into each other's eyes. The eyes of the Tree King welled. He dismissed it and turned to Ace.

"You watch after her. Many perilous journeys await you in Yutara. Keep her safe now . . . And guard that stone with your life."

Ace said, "King Vinan, how will I know when the armies will be great enough to wage the final war?"

The Tree King smiled and placed his hand of tree bark on the boy's chest, "The Light will guide you." The pale flame appeared lightly at the king's palm, and the boy's chest filled with warmth. "When it's time, you will rise up, the seventh realm will come, and we will be here, waiting on the Light to call us forth."

"Will we see you before then?" Ace said.

Vinan shrugged. "I don't know." Before the silence brought with it too much sadness, the King spoke again, "You will be greatly tested once you return to Yutara. With every step you take toward uncovering the council's evil, the Light will grow, but the enemy will also become more furious."

"Where do I begin?" Ace said.

"Gathara," Kareena said. "Ace, if you can restore the credibility of Gathara's government, and make the elyr known again, the Light will grow tremendously."

The King turned to the boy. "She's right."

Ace turned to Kareena. "But you will help me, right?"

"I will do what I can. But remember, when we return to Yutara, we will not be together. I left Yutara from the city, and you left Yutara from Hillrun. Both of us will return to the exact moment from which we came."

Ace nodded. "I'm sure Rio and I can uncover this parcel in Hillrun. Once I get him to reveal the mole, we will return to Gathara. I will find you when I get there."

Kareena smiled and nodded. "But we must still be careful," she said. "Right now, the elyr is considered witchcraft, and if we're caught together it could be trouble."

Ace nodded in agreement. Vinan stepped forth and placed a hand on each of the them.

"Well," the Tree King said, "the fate of Yutara rests on your shoulders, Evelander. Are you sure you're up for this?"

Ace smiled, feeling the surest of himself he'd been since Grandpa first gave him the stone. "I have to be," he said. "I was chosen for this."

Ace stepped from the trees to a still night in Shywater. He hurried along the path to find himself just outside the inn in Hillrun. The town was draped in darkness, still as the pond he'd come from. The underpopulated town had an eerie nighttime chill. Animals howled far away, and the crisp, cool wind brushed the dusty ground. He hurried back to the inn before Rio would notice he had left. He opened the door to find the familiar overweight jag standing behind the counter.

"Well, that was quick," the jag said.

Ace half grinned, scratching his head. "I thought I saw

someone I knew. But it—uh—was just a bush."

The jag squinted at him suspiciously, then shrugged. "Okay. Well, I let you know as soon as I know about when owner will arrive."

"Huh?"

"Elly? You asked about when you could meet her."

"Oh! Right!" Ace had forgotten he had been looking for the fae owner of the inn. After all, it had been an entire day since he'd returned to Yutara. "Uh, that's okay. I don't think I'll need her anymore."

"But you just—"

"I figured out my problem," Ace said as he rushed up the stairs, "Don't need her. Thanks!" The boy rushed upstairs as quickly as he could without being too loud. But behind him, he heard the jag whispering to himself.

"Weird human kid."

"Rise and shine!" the drake said. Ace rubbed his eyes as he woke to Rio hovering over him in the hotel bed. "C'mon. Time to get up."

Ace rolled over and sat on the edge of the bed. His smile stretched from ear to ear. Rio didn't suspect a thing.

"What's the plan for today?" Ace said after he yawned. Rio threw some clothes at him.

"Split up, start making friends, and keep our eyes open," Rio said. "You've been trained for this, kid. You know what to do."

Ace repeated the obvious response. "Look for power. Don't be too obvious."

Rio shot him a glance of approval as he made his way out the door. "Let me know if you find something suspicious. Do not go after a parcel yourself."

"Got it," Ace said.

"You're okay with splitting up, right?" Rio said.

Ace grinned. "Perfect."

CHAPTER FORTY-EIGHT

Grudge and Lag

The town had a lively piece about it, allowing Ace to become immersed in it and forget his recent days in the sixth realm. He kept his eyes peeled, but nothing suspicious appeared to him. Only families and friends running about their day with glee. There were those fishing in the river, others enjoying a family picnic, and some shopping. His mind wandered elsewhere despite his attempt to stay focused, his newly discovered ability at the front of his thoughts. He wondered how he would use the elyr to start revealing the witches and parcels in Yutara. How he could find the parcel in Gathara and take the position as the Halder. His heart raced. He was going to be a hero. And Rio. He could convince Rio the Light was good. Convince him the elyr was going to win the war! It might take some persistence, but the drake would learn to trust him; finding the parcel in Hillrun would be the first step toward earning it.

Which was why he needed to focus. He shifted his attention

back to his task. He needed to make a friend. Start asking questions. But didn't it seem a little suspicious to just start asking questions to strangers? He would have to start a conversation naturally. With someone who. . .

Grudge! Ace thought. The male jag and his wife, Lag. He remembered meeting them from his and Rio's first day in the city. There they were, fishing on the riverbank. Ace stepped from the dirt road and followed the slope of the bank toward the river.

"Hey, friends!" Ace said warmly. Grudge and Lag turned at the sound of his voice and smiled. Lag waved hello from her seat on the grass. The large male jag stood at once and walked to meet Ace halfway.

"Well, hey there! Enjoy first night in humble town?" Grudge said. The jag stuck his hand out. Ace grabbed it, but his hand was completely swallowed up by the meaty jag hand as they shook.

"I have," he said, wincing at the jag's grip.

Lag stuck her head out from behind the jag's large frame. "Where Pebbles?"

"Who?"

"Your driver. Pebbles," Grudge said.

"Oh!" Ace had forgotten their fake names as well. "Uh, well . . . we split up. Wanted to walk the town on our own."

"Ah," Grudge said. "Well, how about tour, yeah?"

Ace brushed aside the offer with a half frown and a tilt of his head. "Oh, I wouldn't want to bother you two."

"Nonsense!" Grudge said, slapping Ace on the shoulder. It may have been an attempted friendly gesture, but it felt like getting smacked with a boulder. "We nothing to do today. We seen this river hundred times. It not every day we meet friend."

Ace smiled. Maybe a tour would be exactly what he needed. Perhaps Grudge's tour could offer the boy clues. Ace accepted the offer.

Lag and Grudge took him through the city, filling the boy with tales of history and lore as they passed by the buildings and statues. A lot of stories in such a small town. Ace attempted to get information about townspeople, in search of something suspicious.

However, nothing proved out of the ordinary, and neither did he see a jag he thought might be a suspect. Eventually, they reached the familiar statue water fountain of Chug the Traverser.

"Oh, that Hillrun's founder," Lag said with glee, pointing at the statue.

"Yes, indeed," Grudge replied. "They say he only one to have traveled every inch of Yutara. Founded Hillrun centuries ago, before Gathara been founded. Last known jag to speak both common tongue and morlogen. Now no one know old jag language."

"That's pretty neat," Ace said. He groaned a moment later. Their walk had taken about an hour by then, and he still had no luck discovering who the parcel was. "Well, thank you for the tour, but I—"

"Oh, our house is around corner here. Would you join us for lunch?" Lag said.

"She makes best gizzard sandwich you ever taste," Grudge said.

No one else in Hillrun seemed to be as welcoming as Grudge and Lag. Ace remembered how the smaller Eveland towns didn't welcome other races as much as the bigger cities. He wondered if the same was true for the smaller towns in Heorg. And if so, what made these jags like him so much? The way they persisted he join them and gave up their entire day to show him around town seemed strange. Something was off. Something . . . he could call out. Something they might be lying about to do something bad. Something like an immediate truth.

"You know," Ace said, "that sounds lovely, actually."

"Oh, wonderful!" Lag said. The jags took him to the third road of the roundabout. Just a block down the path, they took a right down a narrower road. The street was nothing but houses on either side. Mostly buildings of clay and stone. One of which was Grudge and Lag's home. Their house had a round roof and a wooden door.

Grudge opened the door and let them in. The air cooled right away and sent a refreshing chill along Ace's back. The doorway led to a narrow hall, not but a few feet long. To the right it opened to a humble dining room. On the left, a staircase rose to a second floor, and the hall ended with an opening to a living room, where a couch and love seat surrounded a television mounted over a fireplace. Gas torches lit the walls.

Grudge invited him to sit on the couch while Lag prepared lunch in the kitchen. The jag turned on the television to the local news and they conversed in small talk for a while. Ace waited for the opportunity to start calling out the things he thought strange about them. Just as he'd been trained. Talk about anything out of place.

After Grudge had finished joyfully rambling on about his and Lag's wonderful life in Hillrun, he paused for a moment, and Ace made his move. "I really appreciate you inviting me for lunch and giving me a tour today. It's awfully nice of you," Ace said.

"Oh my, it no problem. We love visitors."

"Yeah, well. Others haven't been so welcoming," Ace said.

Grudge leaned in. "What you mean?"

"I don't know," Ace said, "it just seems like others don't like strangers as much as you two. It's nice to know there are some friendly people around here."

"Ah, don't worry about it," Grudge said, "the people of town will grow on you before too long."

"Did you see our hovercraft approaching?" Ace said.

"What?"

"When we arrived. You two walked out of the city just as we landed. Had you seen us flying in?"

Grudge sat back in his chair, a keen eye focused on the boy. "Well, yes. We were on our way for walk like we told. Just thought we'd say hi to new strangers. Hope we didn't bother you."

Ace waved his hands as if to push back Grudge's words. "Oh, no, no. I didn't mean anything by it. Just curious is all. You know, like I said. Others haven't seemed so friendly. It's almost like you've been going out of your way to welcome us."

"Sure we haven't been bother? I would hate it if were so."

"No, of course not!" Ace said. The jag's tone grew harsher. Maybe Ace was onto something. But if he was, he didn't want to push it too far. Especially if he was there alone. At least the boy knew when he met with Rio again he would have some suspects. He sat back and tried to change his thinking. No snooping. An awkward silence was finally broken by Lag coming to the living room with plates of gizzard sandwiches.

"Shall we take to dining room?" Lag said.

Ace and Grudge nodded and stood to follow her. But as Grudge walked by the boy, a temptation came over him he couldn't resist.

The Light of the elyr doesn't burn the flesh of the innocent. He remembered Kareena's words and It was as if his brain simply took over and made his decision for him. Ace brought a dim, pale light to the palm of his hand and touched the jag's skin lightly.

"Ow!" Grudge yelled. Following a sizzling noise, a thin line of smoke rose from the area where Ace had touched him. The boy went numb. What had he just done? Why would he test him right then and there? No backup to help him. Grudge was a parcel. And maybe Lag was a witch! He wiped the sweat from his forehead and looked at the door. Should he run? Confront them? Was this it for him?

"What wrong, ug?" Lag said as she rushed to Grudge's side.

"Oh, nothing," the jag said. He looked at one of the gas torches alongside the wall, "just not watching where I going. Must have got burned."

Ace's heart slowed, and his body calmed from its trembling. Grudge didn't know he'd just been burned by the elyr. Maybe he didn't even know what the elyr was. Ace needed to escape. Get out of there. He could attack when he had Rio's help, but it was foolish to stay there any longer knowing they were members of the council.

"Oh!" Ace yelled. "I'm so sorry, but I just remembered. I was supposed to meet Pebbles a half hour ago at our inn! He's probably worried sick. I really should get going."

"Aw," Lag said, "I'm sorry to hear that. Sure you can't stay any longer?"

Grudge looked at Ace with cold eyes. "We really insist. You

must stay for lunch."

Ace's pulse quickened once more as he backed from the other side of the couch, slowly making his way to the front door. "I wish I could, really. Thank you for your hospitality. But I should get going before the drake gets too worried."

Before the jags had time to argue, he realized he had reached the foyer. He turned, grabbed the door, and pulled it open. There was the road. The city of Hillrun before him.

Free, Ace thought.

The door slammed shut. Ace's heart dropped to his gut and sweat seeped from his skin. He kept his eyes ahead, fearful of turning behind him. He pulled the door open once more. It slammed shut again. Cold chills traced the hairs of his neck. He turned slowly to find Grudge and Lag at the other end of the hall, both of their eyes a dark yellow, black smoke coming from their bodies. They were shutting the door with magic.

"Please," Grudge said, "we insist."

CHAPTER FORTY-NINE

Ransom

Ace looked around the room for an exit. There was none. What was he to do? Could he take them both? He wished he had Kareena next to him. But was using the elyr to fight them wise? What if word got out about his abilities and the elite, including Rio, didn't trust him? What if he just ruined everything by using the Light to burn Grudge?

The jags advanced slowly to him. "Now, calm down there," Grudge said. "We won't hurt you now, we promise."

Ace said nothing. Behind his back, he made a tiny pale flame, ready to attack if needed. The Light flickered as his hands shook with his nerves, worsening with every step the jags took. What if his light wasn't strong enough?

"No, no," Lag said, a wicked smile on her face, "we won't hurt you at all." She and her husband continued to slowly move forward until they towered over the boy. "But your family. . . we're not so sure we can guarantee their safety."

The Light from Ace's hand vanished. "What do you mean, my family?"

Grudge grabbed the boy's arm. "Come." He dragged Ace from the foyer to the living room and threw him on the couch. "TV," Grudge said, "show camera twelve."

"Oh no," Ace whispered to himself as he sensed the color draining from his face. The TV showed Marg's house. His living room, exactly. On their knees, with something like a black smoke wrapped over their mouths, were Cameron, Julie, and Tamara.

"Let them go!" Ace cried.

Grudge grinned wickedly. He stepped toward the television, then turned to face the boy. Grudge's meaty fingers cracked as he waved his hand across the television screen and cringed his fingers. Cameron's body twisted and contorted in unpleasant ways. His older brother groaned in pain. The Peppercorns screamed in horror and went to help him. But Grudge's magic kept them held down.

"Stop it! Stop, please!" Ace said as he jumped from the couch. "I'll do whatever you want! Please, just stop it!"

Grudge released Cameron from the spell. Cameron fell limp and thudded to the ground. Ace struggled to keep his body from trembling.

"Very well," Grudge said, "now that we have your attention, our request very simple. Give us Emerson Stone."

Ace didn't know what to say. How did they know of the stone? How did they know he had it? And if they knew he had it, why not just take it from him? A thought came across his mind as he remembered Grandpa's story. A similar thing had happened with Jakka and Oliver.

"What makes you think I have it?" Ace said.

"Please," Lag said, now stepping beside her husband. It was then Ace could see that she had now turned completely into a witch. Her skin had gone black, emitting smoke. "Don't play dumb with us, human. We saw you enter and return from Shywater. Only an elyrian could do such a thing."

Grudge said, "Only stone could grant human such power."

Ace's nerves quaked. How did they know these things? How could they have seen Shywater? He stared at them wordlessly.

"You know," Lag said as she crept toward the boy. Her breath was like rotten meat, as well as her skin. "We were questioning ourselves when you first arrived. Whether or not you had stone. But once we told you about fae at inn. The way your eyes lit up. As if you'd found treasure. We watched you that evening. We watched you vanish from behind inn and return to existence."

"I don't have it," Ace said.

Grudge grunted and twisted his bony fingers, causing Cameron to twist and convulse horridly again.

"Stop!" Ace yelled with fury. "I mean I don't have it on me! I will have to get it for you."

Grudge stopped. Ace, seeing the Peppercorns' horrified faces on the screen, wished he could take back the mean things he'd said to them before.

"Where is it?" Grudge said. "Tell us now!"

"The inn!" Ace said. "It's at the inn!"

Grudge and Lag looked to one another curiously. Then back to the boy.

"Here's what's going to happen," Grudge said. "You're going walk us there. You're going be quiet, and not bring any attention to us. If you do, your family is good as gone. Understand?"

Ace nodded silently. As he stared at Cameron's limp body on the floor, his blood boiled.

Lag spoke before Ace was instructed to stand. "Don't think by killing us you can save family. We have members in Gathara watching over them now. Kill us, and they will find out and surely harm family."

They grabbed Ace's arm and yanked him from the couch. They slowly settled back to their jag appearance as they walked him to the front door. Ace kept silent, but his eyes were focused on the people around him. He prayed every corner they turned he would find Rio. But the drake was nowhere to be found. Where had he gone to? The town wasn't so big. He thought of every which way he could escape from this situation. Maybe they were bluffing about their friends in Gathara, but Ace wasn't about to gamble with Cameron's life. But nothing came to mind. Was Cameron okay? What had they done to him?

How could they know all these things about him? About his family in Gathara? As the possibilities traveled through his head, only one seemed the most plausible. The parcel in Gathara must know about all of this. Whoever it was must have found out about their trip to Hillrun and set this up. It was the only explanation. It didn't matter then. Getting Cameron and the Peppercorns to safety was the priority. Ace could figure out everything else later.

The jags stayed behind Ace the whole way, smiling and saying hello to their fellow townspeople. Ace simply kept a straight face and ignored everyone, hoping not to give away any possible signs he might be trying to warn people. They turned on Cloudy Street and came to New Nile Suites.

"Hello, welcome to New Nile Suites," said a fae. Her name tag read *Elly,* and Ace scoffed at the irony. She was old, bent, and fragile as glass, but her hair was still as new and silver as Kareena's. Ace and the jags returned the greeting as they made their way to his room. The boy opened the door to darkness. Before he could flip a switch, the jags shut the door behind him.

"Find it! Now!" Lag said in a shrill voice. Ace felt the wall until he found the switch and turned it on. He quickly ran to his bed and rummaged through his backpack.

Hopelessness took him.

Everything he'd worked so hard to protect had been ruined.

His eyes went dark as he frantically sorted through his backpack. For the chest, and the Emerson Stone, were gone.

CHAPTER FIFTY

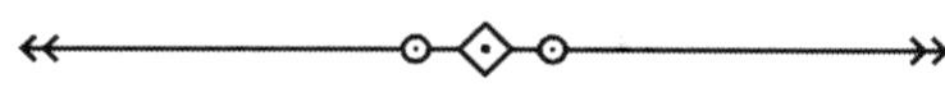

Ace Found Out

"Don't play games with me!" Grudge said, reaching to grab Ace. "Your family is—" Something whistled through the air and popped the jag in his stomach with the sound of a thump. A small yellow sun. Ace turned in the direction it came from.

Rio! Sitting up from behind the bed. Ace ducked under his bed as the drake continued to rapidly fire until he caught Lag as well, and they both fell to the ground, screeching in agony. When the shooting ceased, Ace ran to Grudge, who was becoming increasingly harder to see as the orange glow from the anti-magic cage began to swarm him.

"Please, don't hurt my family! Please! I'm sorry!" Ace yelled with desperation. Rio's hand grabbed Ace's arm and pulled him away from the parcel.

"Get back, kid!" Rio said. The witch and parcel's shrill screams slowly came to a halt as their cage wrapped them in a cocoon of magic-proof material.

"Rio! You don't understand!" Ace said as he turned to the drake. "They have Cameron and the Peppercorns! They're going to kill them!"

"Calm down, your family is fine," Rio said. "Grab your things, we need to get you back to Gathara right away."

"I can't," Ace said. "I can't leave without. . ." Ace wasn't sure whether to tell Rio or not. But what was he to say? How could he explain his situation without giving away his possession of . . .

"Your precious stone?" the drake said with disgust.

Ace stared blankly. "What are you talking ab—"

"Your stone is safe. C'mon, we need to get you to Gathara! I'll explain everything on the way." Rio picked his bags up, then threw Ace's bags at him. Ace wanted to ask more, but the moment didn't allow it. He threw his arms through the loops in his backpack and followed the drake out of the inn.

The jags of Hillrun glanced eerily at the boy and drake as they sprinted through the town.

"What about interrogating him?" Ace said.

Rio turned his head back as they continued running. "Forget him. He was planted here to distract us. The whole thing was a set up!"

They reached outside the city wall where their hovercraft awaited them. Rio threw his stuff inside and hopped in, followed by Ace. Within seconds, they had taken off and were gliding over the dirt surface.

"Rio," Ace said. "What's happening?"

"The night we arrived in Hillrun, I heard you sneaking out of the inn," the drake said. He looked at Ace with disappointment. Ace gave him a blank stare, caring more about what Rio had to say next than obtaining his approval. The drake faced the road again. "I followed you and saw you vanish on the other side of the inn. Immediately, I thought you might be a sorcerer," the drake gave him a piercing glance.

Ace's eyes widened. "Rio, you don't understand what's going on."

"I think I do," Rio said. "Just as quickly as you vanished, you reappeared, and began walking toward the inn. I found my way back to the room before you could notice. This morning, when we set out, I mentioned we should split up for a reason. When you left, I returned to the inn and went through your things. That's when I found this. . ." Rio reached in the backseat and pulled the chest which held the Emerson Stone from a pile of his things. Ace snatched it with relief.

"My chest! Why did you take it?" Ace yelled.

"I think a better question is why you had not told me what you were carrying?" Rio said.

"How much do you know about what's in the chest?" Ace said.

"Enough to know it's a witch magnet! Enough to know it's a power unreasonably great for a twelve-year-old boy!" Rio said.

Ace was taken aback by Rio's term "witch magnet." Such a phrase reminded the boy of Grandpa's advice before he disappeared.

"When you begin to uncover the map, the evils in Yutara will be awakened to your presence and possession of the stone," Grandpa had said. Now he knew he was an elyrian. Now he knew how to grow the Light . . . he was getting closer to the seventh realm . . . to uncovering the shadows. This was it. The council was becoming aware of his presence in the world.

Ace huffed and said, "Rio, you don't understand. I need this. The fate of Yutara depends on me having it." Rio glanced back to the boy a few times wordlessly. "Why did you take it?" Ace persisted.

"Because," Rio said, "once I saw that chest, I knew whatever parcel was in Hillrun would be after it. And I know enough to know how dangerous it could be if they found it . . . I knew then, sending you out on your own was a terrible mistake. Whoever the parcel was in Hillrun, they would be looking for you. That's when it hit me. If they wanted that stone from you, they wouldn't be able to just take it. Your immunity protects you from their magic. So, they would have to find another way to get to you."

"My family," Ace said. *I guess the stone still makes me immune to witchcraft.*

"Exactly. So, I hid it, and went searching for you. I called Keele right away and told her the situation. I told her to send hunters to Marg's house immediately to protect your family. But after I found you, you had already been captured by the witches. I knew I couldn't jump in and save you, for the sake of your family. So, I followed you three, waiting for the call from Keele to know when your family was safe, so I could attack. After I saw they were taking you to the inn, I got there quickly and hid before you could find me."

"So, Keele has my family then? They're okay?" Ace said.

Rio nodded.

"What about Marg?" Ace said. "is he okay?"

The drake's eyes squinted as they remained focused on the road. The drake slowly shook his head.

"Oh," Ace said, hand over his mouth. "I'm sorry, Rio."

After a brief pause, Rio began to speak again. As if to brush aside the grieving of Marg at the expense of more important matters. "The mole in Gathara knows you have the stone, and he's been trying to get it from you. He sent us on a wild goose chase in Hillrun to get you and me away from your family. The witches in Hillrun were planted there as a diversion. Once I called Keele, and she gathered a group of hunters to protect your family, it caught the attention of our enemy. That's when he realized we'd discovered his plan. He also gave away a crucial piece about himself. The sorcerer is a parcel, not a witch, because he sent witches after Keele, trying to get to your family again. Lucky for us, Gathara is full of witch hunters."

"Are you saying that witches are in Gathara right now?" Ace said.

Rio's eyes went dark as he turned to Ace. "It's worse than just that. This parcel has countless witch slaves. Including all the witches from the cellar. He's incredibly powerful. They all were under his command. Apparently, the witches we'd been capturing weren't really for capturing. But to give this parcel more power. He's released them into the city to wreak havoc . . . But I think you're missing the bigger picture, Ace."

"What's that?"

"We've narrowed down our search. Only an elite could've freed the witches from the cellar. The parcel has to be either Sebastian or George!"

Ace shot a curious glance at the drake. How could a parcel find his way into the most powerful witch hunters in the most magic proof city in Yutara? How deceptive could he be?

"Our parcel is resorting to using his slaves. He's nervous. Scared. And having been an elite for so long, there's not many more places he could run. Right now is the perfect opportunity to attack! We may have to fight our way through a million witches to get to him. But once we do, we can take this parcel down—you, me, and the other elite! And we can get the Indies back to the place where they began with your grandfather! With you as the Halder!"

Ace lit up. It was his first chance to grow the Light and start working toward his purpose. He could do it. The Light would guide him. Its power surged within him as he readied himself.

Kareena! Ace thought. Where was she in all this? Was she okay? What if she had fled the city for safety? He had to find her. Ace looked out the window. The desert was nothing but a brown and red blur as Rio kicked the hovercraft into high gear.

"Where's my family now?" Ace said.

The drake replied, eyes still focused on the road. "Right now, they're with Keele. Cameron is helping her protect your cousins, I'm sure. She's waiting for us there. Once we arrive, we will make our way to Indie Headquarters."

Ace nodded, eager to return to the city. His priority was Kareena. She could help him fend off the witches, and he needed to make sure she was safe. He felt confident in Keele and Cameron's ability to protect the family in the meantime. His heart ran as if it were in a race with the hovercraft. He looked to the red blur of the desert they sped by, eager to accomplish his mission.

"Well, King Vinan," he whispered to himself, "we'll find out soon if Emery made the right choice."

CHAPTER FIFTY-ONE

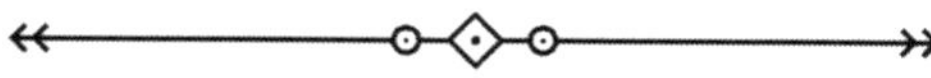

Family

Rio flew the hovercraft to the edge of the Gathara's outer wall. Masses of people fled the city, screaming and tripping over one another. Hunters guided civilians to the trains and hovercrafts. Witches flew over the crowds, casting spells, capturing civilians, throwing bombs of magic. Hunters shot them down. Some of the witches had magic like Rio had spoken of before, making things like wind and water obey their spells and sweep masses of shrieking civilians away.

Rio grabbed some weapons from the trunk and tossed a hunter's rifle to Ace. The boy had his moves planned out in his head. Save the gift of the elyr only for a life-or-death moment. No need to give away his abilities in the elyr.

He held his rifle, butt-stock to his right shoulder, finger on the trigger, left hand on the front grip, knees bent, and a slight lean forward. Rio did the same as they marched through Gathara. Witches by the thousands flew through the skies, preying on the civilians. The boy and drake ignored as many as they could, attempting to get to his family first. But there were some Ace felt compelled to jump in and save.

Rio's skill with a rifle was exceptional, but the boy's training had proved not to be in vain. He seldom missed. He kept himself focused, his emotions under control. The moment he entered the city, his mind tunneled in on the mission. He'd pull the trigger with purpose, at the exhale of his breath, and listen to their shrieks as the anti-magic brought them to the ground. One by one, they took the witches down as they fought their way to the courtyard of stone, to Marg's house.

Rio took the boy through an alley leading to the courtyard but stopped before they entered. The drake leaned out, peering around the corner of the building. He turned to Ace behind him.

"Two on the right," he whispered. "One on the left."

Ace nodded, back against the wall, now face to face with the drake. "I'll get the one on the left."

"Not ready to take on two just yet?" Rio said, half smirking.

Ace snickered. He trusted Rio's trigger speed above his own. Without a sound, the drake mouthed the countdown.

One, two, three.

They nodded.

Each of them rolled from the wall into the courtyard. The boy took his aim and fired right away. It proved to be a mistake, for the witch was not where he had anticipated. He looked around frantically. No witch. A shrill cry sounded just above him as the witch leaped into sight from the roof beside him. The shriek iced his bones. He had been tricked.

Her arms spread in a pounce above him as she sought to land on him, but he rolled on the ground away from her in the nick of time. She landed on the ground light as a feather. Her head jerked to face him, but by now he had nervously brought his weapon to aim again. His sweaty palms, as well as his racing heart, stole from his confidence. Her dark eyes and pale skin gave him goosebumps. She leaped forth once more, and Ace took his best aim but shut his eyes, anticipating his miss, and pulled the trigger. His eyes were soon opened at the sound of a thud from his anti-magic sun popping her in the shoulder. The witch fell beside him. Her limp body rolled on the brick ground as she shrieked from the anti-magic wrapping her up. Ace's heart slowed as he gathered himself for a moment.

Got her.

"Quick! C'mon!" Rio said. The boy looked at the drake, on the other side of the courtyard tree, two witches captured in their anti-magic cages behind him. Ace caught up as he and the drake ran to Marg's home, then burst down the front door.

"Ace!" said a voice which made the boy's heart fuller than he knew possible. His brother had been kneeling next to Keele, both with AMRs pointed at the door. But at the first sight of Ace, Cameron rushed to his little brother and hugged him tight. Ace squeezed back.

"I'm so glad you're okay!" Ace said.

"Same here!" Cameron said, now pulling from the embrace. "Witches came here and captured us. What did they have you do?"

"It's a long story," Ace said. "I'll have to tell you later."

Ace heard his name called again just as he saw Julie and Tamara stepping from the kitchen, behind where Cameron and Keele had barricaded themselves.

"Ace?" Julie and Tamara had said in unison. Their lips quivered, and their eyes were darkened. They were rattled.

Once the girls saw him clearly, they ran to him. Julie hugged him once more. This time, Ace felt less bothered by it, though still slightly surprised. But what really caught him by surprise is when Tamara joined in. All of them clustered together in a family embrace. Something, Ace was sure, none of them would have ever imagined possible. He couldn't remember how he used to hate them. In fact, he kind of liked them. So much so, he returned the favor in an embrace of his own.

"I guess we, like, owe our lives to you or something," Tamara said as her voice shook. Still a hint of sarcasm in her words. Even her serious words.

"Yeah, Ace," Julie said, her jaw chattering. "I was really

scared." The girl looked up at him, eyes sparkling with a strange mix of joy and sadness. "Thank you for coming back for us."

The corner of Ace's mouth curled up in a half grin. He patted Julie on the shoulder and said, "Hey, we're family." He looked at Cameron with a wide smile, then to each of the Peppercorns. "We stick together."

CHAPTER FIFTY-TWO

The Halder Returns

Ace flinched at the sound of Rio shutting the door behind him and running to Keele. "Do you know where the other elite are?" he said.

Keele nodded. "Headquarters."

"Any ideas about which one the parcel is?" Rio said.

Keele shook her head. "No. My guess is the other elite don't know either. They're all working together to stop this battle over Gathara. I'm sure the other elite still don't suspect a thing. But we know he's losing control. All we need to do is get there and call him out. If we can get him to resort to magic himself, all the elite will be there to fight him."

Cameron stepped forward, his arm around Ace's shoulder. "And a few hunters!"

Keele turned to face him and shook her head. "Absolutely not. This is far too dangerous for you. You need to get your cousins to safety right away."

"That might not be such a good idea," Rio said.

"Why not?" Keele replied.

"Splitting Ace from his family is what began all this mess in the first place. They want—" Rio turned to face the boy, then back to Keele. "—*something* from him. They can't attack his immunity, but they *can* attack his family. Right now, the witches will be hunting for them. No offense, Cameron, but you're not ready to get you and your cousins through this maze of witches on your own right now."

Keele spoke next. "So, what do you propose? It's far too dangerous to take them to Headquarters. You're more likely to run into witches there than if you left the city. And the elite will need all the help they can get to fight this parcel."

After a shaking quiet, Rio walked to Ace and pulled him aside.

"When you vanished at the inn in Hillrun, where did you go?" Rio said in a hushed tone.

"What?" Ace said. "Is this really the time to be discussing this?"

Rio's webbed ears flapped a couple times. "What I mean is, did you bring back something of value? Some knowledge or skill that can help you fight this parcel?"

Ace stared at him blankly and eerily. Did Rio know where Ace went to? Did Rio know he was an elyrian? "Yes. How did you kn—"

"Then, I'm trusting you with this. You, your brother, and Keele can offer assistance at Headquarters. I will take the Peppercorns to safety. Once you two start making your way for Headquarters, it will be a good distraction. I know the roads of this city like the back of my hand. I could sneak us out of here without the glimpse of a single witch. And even if one *did* catch us, I'm sure you trust I could take them down," Rio said.

Ace felt the urge to resist. He wanted Rio by his side for this battle. The drake was too valuable. But both his pride from Rio's faith in him, and the desire to see the Peppercorns safe forced him to agree.

"Are you sure I can do this?" Ace said.

Rio snarled and tipped his head. "I *know* you can. And so did your grandfather."

"Okay, Rio. And I'm trusting you to bring them to safety. Don't let me down."

"One more thing," Rio said softly. "Give me the stone to take with me."

Ace's eyes widened, and he stepped back. "What? Why?"

"The council is after it. That's what this whole thing is about. Dragging it through this mess of witches and going after this powerful parcel is dangerous. I'm sure you know better than I what's at stake if that stone falls into the hands of the council," Rio said.

Ace stared at the drake for a moment, pondering this decision.

"When you defeat this parcel, and restore Gathara, the stone will be waiting for you right by my side. Safe, and out of harm's way."

Ace saw the drake's point. It seemed the safest thing to do. What other options were there? The boy was aware of the stone's importance in the war and feared what may happen if it fell into the wrong hands.

"Where are you going to take them?" Ace said.

"I have some friends in the north. Deployed in Naraka, Neutrals," Rio replied. "They will offer a temporary home for us."

Ace glanced at the Peppercorns.

"Okay," he said. He and the drake shook hands. He turned to let his brother and let Keele know of the plan.

"Ace," Rio said. The boy turned to face him. "You were chosen for this for a reason. Tonight, you have a chance to prove it. Let the council know the Halder has returned."

By now, nightfall had come in pitch darkness. The witches in the city emitted black smoke, swallowing whatever light the moon and stars had to offer. Keele, Cameron, and Ace had begun their march to Headquarters to find the elite. Luckily for the boys, Keele knew her way through alleys and shrubs, so as to offer a better disguise. Every so often there would be battle still. No one could entirely evade the blanket of witches covering the city. Whoever this parcel was, he must be very powerful, for he had thousands of witches covering the city. Occasionally, they would pass by a hunter guiding civilians to safely exit the city. The city had nearly reached total vacancy.

Every moment, Ace eagerly searched for Kareena to no avail. He didn't even know where she lived. He worried she might have fled the city, or been caught using the elyr to defend herself. Difficult as it was, he shook aside his worry, knowing the priority was finding this parcel and taking him down. He reassured himself Kareena would be just fine, and when all this was over, he could find her, as the new Halder, and restore the freedom to practice the elyr in Gathara.

Squished by the narrow path between the buildings and city's outer wall, Keele led them further up the foothills. They were getting close.

"How do you know the elite are in Headquarters?" Ace asked quietly. "Wouldn't they be out fighting in this?"

Keele turned her head back. "Right now, they're sending hunters out to evacuate the city. Those who are too far between their homes and the gate are being escorted to Headquarters. That's what the elite are doing right now. Their priority is safety."

"What?" Cameron said as he stopped. The others stopped as well. "So, you're saying we're going to the castle to fight this dangerously powerful parcel, and there will be hundreds of innocent civilians camping out?"

Keele looked at Cameron with sadness and nodded. "Possibly part of his plan."

"So, what do we do?" Ace said.

"We have no choice," Keele said. "By doing nothing we're also putting them at risk."

Cameron smacked his teeth. "There has to be some other way."

"There isn't," Keele said.

Ace glanced at his older brother, then back at Keele. "The cellar!"

Cameron said, "What?"

"The cellar is covered in magic proof material, and it's empty now. If we can get the people in there, they will be much safer." Ace said.

"How are we going to do that?" Keele said. "If we randomly just start escorting the people to the cellar, the parcel will become suspicious right away."

"Even better," Ace said. "He'll reveal himself." Keele and Cameron looked at one another silently, pondering his plan. "Chances are," Ace continued, "he's going to get pretty suspicious once we arrive there if he knows we're onto him. I mean, look at what he's done to the city. He's in full on panic right now. Once we get to Headquarters, we'll need to get the citizens to safety right away."

Keele looked at Cameron. "Can you handle that?"

"What?" Cameron said. "why me?"

"This fight is Ace's," Keele said. "This is his opportunity to prove his worth as the Halder. Me and the other elite will be a necessary asset for him."

Cameron's frustration faded with a moment of silence. "Okay," he said with a soft exhale, "I'll do it."

A deep scream came from the other side of the buildings they hid behind. Not the scream of a witch, but a person. Ace moved closer to the alley where he could see the street. In a flash he saw a young hunter running away, followed by several witches.

"We have to help him!" Ace said.

"He's not the mission," Keele said. "He's a hunter, he knows what he signed up for."

Ace disregarded Keele with distaste and ran along the alley.

"Ace!" Keele yelled. "Come back. What are you doing?"

The footsteps of Cameron and Keele trailed behind him as he set his back against the stone building. He rolled slightly, peering out into the wide street. The endangered hunter fired at the witches as he ran for his life, but they were beginning to overwhelm him.

There were three.

Four.

Five.

They flooded in from every corner of the street. The dark smoke began to engulf him.

Keele and Cameron caught up to Ace.

"Ace," Keele said, "there's no hope for him."

"Not if we don't help there isn't," Ace said. The boy glared at Keele with determined eyes, and rolled out of the alley, rapidly firing at the witches.

"Ace!" Keele yelled.

The witches shrieked and screamed at Ace's firing. Each one of his anti-magic bullets landing perfectly as he desired. He even caught the witches swarming in from the alleys surrounding the road. With every shot he felt the power of the Light surge through his veins. Ace and the young hunter were outnumbered, but the witches were outmatched.

"Let the council know the Halder's returned." Ace remembered the drake's parting words to him. Each word deepened in meaning with every landing shot.

The witches shrieked and fled Ace's firing. But they didn't run away. The young hunter had become a vessel for them. All the witches Ace hadn't already shot fell on the hunter's body and began to take control of him. The hunter fell to the ground, rolling and grunting as the witches cast a spell to control his body. Ace stopped shooting. What could he do? He couldn't harm the hunter.

The hunter's body calmed, he rolled over, and slowly stood to his feet. Ace's chest caved with fear. He recognized the hunter then. The fae with no tattoos. The very one he'd sat next to at the recall. The fae looked at him with dark eyes. It looked like black spider webs crawled from his eyes and wrapped around his face. His wicked smile turned black.

"Harm us, Halder," the witches spoke in unison through the fae's mouth, "and harm your friend."

The fae lunged at him, running at an unnatural speed. Ace's instincts took him, and time seemed to slow. Keele and Cameron had begun to run from the alley to help. But Ace knew there was nothing they could do. Only one thing could help the fae then. The Light.

The fae lunged. Ace exhaled calmly, and all the power he'd felt from the elyr flowed from his heart to the tips of his fingers. He held the pale flame before him. The white fire shot from his fingers in such a quantity, it wrapped the fae in a jacket of pale light. The shrieks of the witches were evil and wretched as they had never been before.

He pinned the fae to the cobblestone ground. Smoke rose from the fae's body, and the witches shrieked more as the Light burned them. Ace leaped on the fae, holding him down with the white flames. He stared fiercely into his dark eyes, full of panic.

"You know this Light. You know this power," Ace said. The witches gave him a shrill cry. "Leave the fae at once or it will continue to torment you."

The darkness drained from the fae's face. The witches fled his body like a swarm of flies and scattered about the air above them. Ace took his weapon and shot them down without breaking a sweat. Perfect aim.

Cameron and Keele stood in the street, staring at Ace with their jaws on the ground. Ace looked at the fae, who's face had been relieved of darkness and replaced with astonishment, and helped him to his feet.

"What was that?" the male fae said. "Who are you?"

"I'm the Elyrian," Ace said, "and I'm here to save Yutara."

CHAPTER FIFTY-THREE

The City Watch Room

Keele, Ace, and Cameron brought the fae along with them. Another hunter could always be helpful. They decided the fae would help Cameron escort the civilians to the cellar. Keele and Ace led the way, rifles in hand, now approaching the castle.

"You want to explain what that was?" Keele said quietly.

"Not really," Ace answered.

"Listen, kid. I'm letting it slide for now, seeing as there are much more important things to worry about, but don't think you're getting off the hook. You just used magic to save that fae, and when this is all over, you're number one on my suspect list."

"Think about it, Keele," Ace said. "Do you think I would use magic like that in front of you?"

"What's going on?" Cameron said from behind them.

Ace pointed at Keele. "She thinks I'm a parcel because of what I did to help the fae. This is why there's a parcel in the elite right now, because the Indies have been deceived."

The scarred fae stepped forward quietly. "Lady Keele," he said, "I'm not sure what it was he used to save me, but I do not believe it was witchcraft. Having just been controlled by magic, and then saved by him . . ." The fae paused as he gave Ace a look of joy. "He's on our side. I can promise you."

Keele didn't look convinced. "Let's just find out who this parcel is and save Gathara. We'll talk about this later." She stomped away along the road.

The others fell in behind her, but Ace slowly caught up to lead with her again. The walk only lasted a few more minutes before the castle was in sight. The few witches by the castle were fended off by a line of hunters at the end of the bridge, helping escort civilians to safety. Ace and his crew slipped into the small crowd being led to the castle.

Once they reached the Great Hall, they stopped and gathered themselves together. The crowds were luckily minimal in Headquarters, but slowly growing. The priority was bringing the panic to a halt and getting the civilians to safety.

"Cameron," Ace said, "you and the fae start telling the hunters to get these people to the cellar. Tell them a parcel is in the castle, and it's the only safe place they have."

Cameron and the fae nodded. "Got it." Ace and Keele continued along the Great Hall.

"Any idea where the elite are?" Ace said.

"Watch room," Keele said with a slight nod.

"Why would they be watching students train right now?"

"No, kid. Not the Trainee Hall watch rooms, the City Watch Room."

Ace looked at Keele blankly.

"Follow me," she said. The woman turned right to a smaller hall. One which led to the inner courtyard of the castle. A place of rich grass and brick sidewalks. The night sky was black smoke covering the vast city.

At the other end of the courtyard stood a wall with an arched opening, which led to a large tower surrounded by many smaller towers. They jogged along the path and Ace stared at the tower ahead, wondering what their plan was.

"Keele, how do we go about doing this?" he said. "Do you have an idea if it's George or Sebastian?"

"No idea. We're just gonna have to do our best to catch them in a lie. The elite will pick up on it. They're trained." They reached a wooden door entering the tower and she stopped. "Start thinking about anything you can call them out on, but be careful. We don't know how many there are."

Ace tilted his head. "Well, it's a parcel, right?"

Keele nodded. "Has to be. Hard to imagine a witch having control over all the witches in the cellar."

"Well, then, it can't be more than one," Ace said.

Keele shrugged. "Right. You know what I mean. Get to thinking." She opened the door and began walking up the winding staircase. Ace trailed behind her as a thought crossed his mind.

"We don't know how many there are?" Why would she say such a thing? He remembered Keele telling him parcels and witches usually stay away from each other, so there wouldn't be more than one. But . . .

Grudge and Lag. And if the parcel were here, all these witches of his would be close to him.

He slowly crept up the stairs, falling behind. Thoughts wisped through his mind faster than he could control . . . The simulation room . . .

"Keele, wait," Ace said.

She stopped and looked down at him.

He caught up to her. "During my training, you ran all my simulations, didn't you?"

She squinted at him. "What? We don't have time for this, kid." She turned to walk up the stairs and stopped still like a statue. Ace knew why, for it caused him to stop as well. It all came to him at once. He was right. Keele was the one running his simulations. *She* was the one trying to turn him against Rio! He caught his breath and stepped back, for black dust had fallen from Keele's clothes and spilled on the floor. Fear exploded in his heart. He looked at her, preparing to bring the Light to his hands . . . but . . . he . . . . couldn't.

His body went rigid. All his muscles tensed, and Keele eyed him darkly.

Ugh. Keele. What . . . how could you?

He thought he was actually speaking, but soon realized it was only in his head. A force invisibly squeezed him until his squirming stiffened like stone.

Keele! What's going on? Kee—

Keele stepped forward, her arm extended toward him, and a wicked smile telling of victory. What was happening? How could she hurt him? The stone protected him, didn't it? He couldn't react to any of it, for the paralysis had taken every bit of his self-control. He fought it.

Groaning.

Moaning.

Clenching.

Twisting.

Turning.

The only thing he noticed was Keele's wicked smile. He and the witch conversed in thought.

You're a sorcerer! he said.

Keele scoffed with dark eyes. *No, Ace. You are.*

She pulled a hunter's hand blaster from a pouch in her vest, aimed it at him, and pulled the trigger.

CHAPTER FIFTY-FOUR

Rio's Secret

The anti-magic sun fled Keele's barrel and hit Ace like a truck. The force smashed his back against the wall and he fell the ground. The orange light enveloped him like a fire able to burn but not kill. It ate at his energy, so he fell limp as a noodle, rolling around and crying out as, he horridly realized, a caught witch would do. His skin went pale. His mouth dried. Dark tunnels swallowed his vision. He lay flat on his back, staring at the flickering torchlight against the ceiling.

Keele leaned over, now blocking the ceiling from his line of sight, and laughed mockingly.

"Keele . . ." Ace's speech was soft and frail. "How could you?"

Keele pouted at him and leaned close. "It was pretty easy once you gave us the stone, actually."

Us? Ace thought.

She reached her hand down and grabbed him by his shirt collar. She carried him further up the stairs and through a set of double doors, dragging him behind her. She dragged him through a dark hall, then up a few more stairs which led to a trapdoor. She burst the trapdoor open to the City Watch Room and threw Ace over. He smacked down on the hardwood floor, unable to protect his fall as the anti-magic straight jacket pinned his arms to his side.

The room was a cylinder of glass, overlooking the Gathara skyline covered in a dark smoke. George and Ihana sat in hover chairs, fidgeting with holograms projecting from the large glass window. Sebastian stood behind them, running the operation, and turned when he heard the thump of Ace landing on the ground, then went to help Keele up from the trapdoor.

"I found our mole," Keele said as Sebastian pulled her to the surface.

Ace tried to speak, but the anti-magic weakened his voice to a whisper. "She's lying. It's her. She's a witch!"

"Good job, Keele!" Sebastian said. "I was worried we wouldn't be able to find him."

Ace noticed a horrifying thing on the hologram windows. A webcam. The kind of webcam the elite used when they needed to communicate to each other in the field. Behind this webcam were Julie and Tamara Peppercorn tied up in an anti-magic cocoon just like Ace, weakened and pale. But even worse. Just in front of them stood the filthy drake himself.

"Great work, Keele!" Rio said from behind the screen. "Sebastian, I can't express how sorry I am that I doubted you. I fell for the parcel's deception. I failed you."

"We've got him now," Sebastian said. "That's all that matters."

"What of the brother?" George said as he turned to face Sebastian and Keele.

"He's on his way to the cellar as we speak," Keele said.

Cameron! Ace thought. *No!*

Sebastian turned to face Ace on the ground, his eyes dark and telling. The Interim Halder stepped slowly toward the boy, then leaned to face him eye to eye. Ace shivered.

"I have to admit, you nearly had me fooled," Sebastian said. "Marty's letter . . . your 'immunity' with the witches." He used finger quotes. "Your so-called skill in the simulations. And, being twelve?" Sebastian chuckled lightly and buried his face in his hands in a self-loathing manner. He lifted his head again to face the boy. "It was brilliant. *You* are brilliant. Using the witches in the cellar as your slaves to make them not attack you. Make you seem like you had Marty's gift. And you almost did it. You almost infiltrated the government Marty Halder established. You almost made the first step toward bringing down the last stand against the council. But you failed. And the council failed."

Ace tried to refute, but dizziness took him. The tunnels closed further in. He could hardly tell dream from reality. All he could utter were the faint and desperate whispers. "Keele's the witch. Rio's the parcel. You have the wrong guy. Save my family, please! Save my family!"

Sebastian leaned an ear to Ace, then stood. "He's mumbling gibberish. Better get him to the cellar before the anti-magic swallows him whole."

"But, sir," Keele interjected, "isn't he a bit dangerous to be kept alive?"

"Take him to the cellar for now," Sebastian said as he turned to face Ace. "I've got a special punishment for this parcel."

The rest of their conversation drifted to mumbling and babbling as Ace's consciousness began to slip from him. But one thought passed through his mind before the tunnels closed. A thought which likely triggered his passing to darkness. For the truth of it weighed on him as hopelessness and failure. All was lost.

Rio is the parcel. And I gave him the Emerson Stone.

BOOK ONE END

Did you enjoy this book?

If you could leave a review on amazon, apple books, kobo, barnes & noble, or wherever your preferred online book retailer is, it would be a tremendous help!

Thanks for reading, and rock on,
D.P. Rowell

Also By D.P. Rowell

The Queen of the Milds

A Vranon Lore Novel

Her first love is her people. A dark magic will destroy them all.

Angel, princess of the greatest kingdom in Vranon, has only ever wanted the best for her people. But to be the good princess her mother desires, she must smile, wave, and refrain from meddling in duties unfit for a princess.

One evening, the gifted royal sage relays a message he read from the heavens. The felled, a malicious race wielding an unstoppable magic and a special hatred for mankind, have broken free from the abyss to claim the land for themselves. They won't rest until every man and woman is enslaved or killed.

Without the powerful guardians known as the milds, all hope seems lost. Until Angel uncovers secrets from her past.

Magic runs in her blood—magic that could summon the milds. If she can learn to wield it, her people have a fighting chance. If not, she'll forever be the princess who failed her kingdom.

With the wisdom and guidance of the gifted sage, Angel escapes her mother's clutches and ventures on a perilous quest to find the milds. She must race against the felled hunting her down, trust a thief who swears he's an ally, and stand toe-to-toe with fearsome giants before facing her greatest challenge: becoming who she was born to be.

The fate of Vranon rests upon her shoulders. Will Angel lose hope or endure? Find out today! Dive into an adventure of magic, self-discovery, and the makings of a legend.

About the Author

I've always been fascinated by the power of stories. Stories can unite us to pull for the hero, prompt us to take a stance on objective moral truths, encourage us to keep pushing when all seems lost, and shape our hearts around what we're willing to fight for.

There's really no limit to what a great story can do.

There's a reason we spend our childhoods daydreaming of being Luke Skywalker, Cinderalla, Spiderman, or Wonder Woman; because we identify with the hero. There's something unique about human nature that urges us to believe we're part of something bigger than ourselves. It tells us there's greatness somewhere deep down, and the stories we allow into our hearts help define that part of us.

If I can play any part in revealing that greatness in you, I'd consider it a great honor, so thanks for letting me be a part of your world!

States & Stories: I traveled all over the states by train, car, and flight, for over 4 years, and I was writing the Emerson Chronicles the entire time. It was an awesome experience because my characters got to experience new places at the same time I was, and what they experienced in the different cities was highly influenced by what I experienced. If you'd like to see a photo gallery from my trip, head over to my website (dprowell.com) and click the blog. I included brief descriptions of how each city specifically influenced the cities and landscape in different parts of Yutara.

Printed in Great Britain
by Amazon

72865416R00201